Dear reader,

Your first book always has a very special place in your heart. It is often a result of years of writing, re-writing, tears, glasses of wine, hopes and fears and a dream that sometimes seems impossible. At the turn of the century, as we slipped into the new millennium, I finally finished *Honeycote*, and sent it out into the world. A few weeks later, I had my first book deal.

I wanted to write a book about a large, slightly glamorous and sometimes dysfunctional family who live in a large rambling house in the Cotswolds. The inspiration for their business came when I was still working as a script editor in television and was researching locations for a new drama. I fell across a tiny brewery, steeped in tradition, that had been in the same family for generations. It was the perfect backdrop for my story, ripe for power struggles, feuds and takeovers, as well as complicated affairs of the heart, betrayal and good old-fashioned greed and envy.

And so the Liddiards of Honeycote Ales were born. Little did I know when I first started thinking about them that their antics would sustain me over three novels. But they endlessly provided me with material: the relationships between parents and children, husbands and wives, siblings, friends, lovers . . . And, of course, the brewery itself is a big part of village life. Many of the locals have been working there for generations, and the pubs belonging to the brewery are a rich source of story material, with their roaring log fires and cheeky barmaids.

From a_____hen

at Honeycote House, to hapless, feckless Mickey, who can't get by on charm alone for much longer, the Liddiards and their friends and neighbours are loveable, high-spirited and endlessly fascinating. At the root of their escapades is the importance of family, friendship – and, of course, food.

The books were first published as *Honeycote*, *Making Hay* and *Just A Family Affair*. We have re-titled them and given them a gorgeous new look so they can all be devoured in one greedy sitting. They are filled with passion and scandal – and are just a little bit naughtier than my later books. Perhaps it's all that country air?

I still long to live somewhere like Honeycote. Whenever I re-read these books I feel as if I belong there. I want to go for Sunday lunch at the Honeycote Arms, whizz around the tiny lanes in a battered old sports car, be asked to the Liddiards' for Christmas drinks . . . For Honeycote seems idyllic whatever the season, whether the hedges are white with blossom or snow.

So curl up on the sofa and come there with me. Fill up your glass of wine or your mug of cocoa and see what the Liddiards are up to. I know you will love them, for all their faults and impossible behaviour. You will laugh, cry, blush and fall in love, just as I did all those years ago.

And I suspect their story is not over yet . . .

With love,
Veronica Henry

Veronica Henry has worked as a scriptwriter for *The Archers*, *Heartbeat* and *Holby City* amongst many others, before turning to fiction. She won the 2014 RNA Novel of the Year award for *A Night on the Orient Express*. Veronica lives with her family in a village in north Devon.

Find out more at www.veronicahenry.co.uk, sign up to her Facebook page f/veronicahenryauthor or follow her on Twitter @veronica_henry and Instagram @veronicahenryauthor

Also by Veronica Henry

Wild Oats
An Eligible Bachelor
Love on the Rocks
Marriage and Other Games
The Beach Hut
The Birthday Party
The Long Weekend
A Night on the Orient Express
The Beach Hut Next Door
High Tide
How to Find Love in a Book Shop
The Forever House

THE HONEYCOTE NOVELS
A Country Christmas (*previously published as* Honeycote)
A Country Life (*previously published as* Making Hay)
A Country Wedding (*previously published as*
Just a Family Affair)

A COUNTRY CHRISTMAS

Veronica Henry

First published in Great Britain in 2002
by Penguin Books Ltd
This paperback edition published in 2017
by Orion Books,
an imprint of The Orion Publishing Group Ltd
Carmelite House, 50 Victoria Embankment
London EC4Y 0DZ

An Hachette UK Company

1 3 5 7 9 10 8 6 4 2

A CIP catalogue record for this book is
available from the British Library.

ISBN 978 1 4091 7528 5

Typeset by Input Data Services Ltd, Somerset

Printed and bound in Great Britain
by Clays Ltd, St Ives plc

www.orionbooks.co.uk

A COUNTRY CHRISTMAS

I

A single bell tolled out with authoritative finality. Eye-watering winter sunshine drenched the little churchyard at Honeycote, highlighting the dewy cobwebs that stretched from grave to grave. A mound of earth indicated the most recent, the latest in a line of Liddiards that stretched back hundreds of years.

He craned his neck to assess the turnout. They were all there. Patrick, seemingly unperturbed, the only betrayal of any emotion being the speed at which he smoked his cigarette before tossing the nub end into the freshly dug hole. Sophie and Georgina stood behind him, unnaturally pale in their black school coats, lending an air of Victorian melodrama to the tableau. He thought this was probably their first funeral, if you didn't count the elaborate arrangements they'd made for various guinea pigs and goldfish over the years. Kay was chic in rigidly tailored black, a huge hat and impossibly high heels – he knew she'd be wearing stockings. Lawrence was at her side, etiquette requiring them to be united. Even Cowley was there from the bank, in a shapeless suit, his Christmas Biro clipped into the top pocket, no doubt luxuriating in a morning away from his desk: this was about as much fun as Cowley ever had.

And Lucy. She'd rejected widow's weeds in favour of palest grey, her only concession to mourning a black velvet ribbon that held back her curls. She was wearing a pearl necklace he'd given her the Christmas before, an over-generous gesture he hadn't been able to afford. As ever.

As she arrived at the graveside to stand beside his brother James, there was just time for him to notice her slipping her hand into his before the vicar started intoning the familiar words.

As the first clod of earth began to hit the coffin, Mickey Liddiard summoned up every last drop of energy from his bones and pushed. But the lid of the coffin was stout, hewn from a mighty oak, and wouldn't give . . .

'Mickey! Mickey!'

Lucy anxiously shook her husband awake. She could feel his heart hammering as he thrashed beside her. He sat bolt upright, drenched in sweat, and looked at her in alarm.

'You've had one of your dreams again.'

Mickey slumped back on the pillows, relief that it was all over flooding through him. But Lucy could still sense anxiety.

'What on earth were you dreaming about? You were tossing and turning—'

'I don't know.' Mickey feigned puzzlement. He could remember only too well. 'You know what dreams are like. You wake up and they're gone.'

It was the third time this week he'd had the dream, or one like it. He'd wondered about having it analysed, but thought perhaps the meaning wasn't all that hidden and that quite simply he had a fear of dying and nobody giving a toss. He screwed up his eyes to look at the clock. 'What's the time?'

Lucy stretched out her arm and turned the miniature carriage clock to face her. 'Nearly six.' She frowned as Mickey threw back the blankets. 'You don't need to get up yet, surely?'

'I need a shower.'

She watched his shadowy outline pad across the room and pull back the heavy, interlined curtains, letting the very first fingers of early morning light in. She could see him clearly now. He was tall, broad-shouldered, and with still no sign of a middle-age spread despite having celebrated his forty-third birthday six months before. He had just enough gravitas in his features to stop him looking boyish, but he had a bloom of youth that he didn't deserve and that his contemporaries resented given his lifestyle and no thinning hair as yet, not even a sprinkling of grey in his thick brown hair.

He was definitely a handsome man in anyone's books, but as he gazed out of the window there was a frown marring his features that Lucy didn't like. She suddenly felt a need to reassure both him and herself. This wasn't the first time she'd woken him from a nightmare lately. She patted the empty space in the bed beside her.

'Come back to bed.'

Mickey shook his head. He was wide awake now, the adrenalin from the dream still pumping through his body, and his head was already whirling with the problems the day held in store for him. He reflected grimly that he had no respite these days, only a brief half-hour after the first few glasses of wine, in that mellow period between being relaxed and becoming totally plastered. Why could he never stop at that point? Why did he insist on getting completely out of it, so he became melancholy, his fears waxed rather than waned and his sleep was troubled?

He turned to look at his wife. She was wearing the necklace she'd had on in the dream, and didn't look a day older than the day he'd married her. But then why should she? She had nothing to worry about. She knew nothing of his problems, that was for sure.

'What are you doing today?' he asked her.

'The girls are breaking up for Christmas tomorrow, I've got to hit the supermarket and do a big shop.'

Big shop. Big bill.

'Why? Sophie's always on a diet and Georgie only eats treacle sandwiches—'

Lucy grinned. 'Well, I've run out of treacle. And I need to start stocking up for Christmas. I'm not going to get caught out again this year.' As soon as she said it, she had a vision of herself at the end of a huge queue in Sainsbury's. It was her annual ritual, resolving to be organized and failing. But there were always better things to do than make lists and fill the freezer.

Mickey walked over and dropped a kiss on her forehead. She caught a whiff of the sweat that had now dried on him. It smelled of panic, not exertion, and she suddenly felt glad he'd chosen not to come back to bed. Lucy wasn't fastidious, but the smell was unfamiliar on him. It unsettled her.

Moments later, as the warm water washed away the remnants of his dream, Mickey considered the day ahead. He resolved to be positive and confront his problems for a change, instead of seeking out one of the displacement activities he was so fond of, the ones that helped him avoid the real world. He'd get to the brewery early, try to get on top of the mountain of paperwork he knew was waiting for him. It was unlikely to have disappeared. It had been there for months.

As it was still so early, he decided to walk. He usually drove, which was pretty inexcusable as the brewery was scarcely three-quarters of a mile from the house, but today he thought the exercise would do him good; it might clear his head a bit. He could always get Lucy to pick him up later if he couldn't face the walk home.

It was a brewing day, which meant scruffy clothes rather than a jacket and tie, so he pulled on jeans and one of the dark green polo shirts he'd recently had made up with the brewery logo on the left breast. They'd been an attempt to establish some sort of corporate identity at Honeycote Ales; make it look as if he had his finger on the pulse and was in control. It was funny how something so simple managed to paper over the cracks. Everyone had been very impressed.

Lucy had fallen back to sleep, so he slipped out of the bedroom carrying his boots and went down into the kitchen. It was unusually quiet, this room that was so very much the heart of the house. He knew that in an hour or so's time it would be full of life. Sophie would be filling the liquidizer with fruit and yoghurt, making one of her revolting smoothies, bemoaning their lack of a juicer. Georgina would be toasting thick-sliced white bread on the Aga, while Patrick, always the last up, would be drinking thick black coffee, unable to communicate until he'd had his fix of caffeine. Mickey didn't relish the unnatural silence – he found it disconcerting rather than relaxing

– so he grabbed a banana from the fruit bowl, picked up his waxed coat from the back of the chair where he'd left it the night before and slipped out of the door. Thrusting his hands deep into his pockets, he walked down the drive and out of the gates of Honeycote House, turned right and carried on at a brisk pace until he reached the village.

There were a surprising amount of inhabitants abroad even at this early hour. A suited executive drove past in his BMW, en route to Eldenbury two miles away; the little market town boasted a much-coveted station on the main line to Paddington, which brought London within a commutable ninety minutes for those who wanted to retreat to the Cotswolds each night. A brace of young workmen in a battered van set off for a building site just outside Evesham six miles the other way. There they were employed on yet another estate of the characterless homes that seemed to be springing up everywhere. The postman was hurrying through his round so he could get to his second job, tending the gardens of the wealthier inhabitants of the village. He found he could charge what he liked for keeping the lawns and hedges manicured, because he was reliable and knowledgeable and wasn't too ruthless with his pruning.

Honeycote had gone the way of many other villages in the area. The school and the police house had each closed down and been converted into picturesque homes. The post office remained valiantly open and stayed so only by means of constant diversification. But despite these casualties, other businesses had emerged in their place. A young mother had started a mail order children's clothing company, providing outwork for many other women in the village who were handy with a sewing machine. An old chapel was stuffed to the gills with reclaimed furniture and artefacts of the kind people moving to the country felt their houses should be furnished with, and did very well. There was certainly a style of entrepreneurialism thriving in Honeycote, but it was a sad fact that many of the locals who had been born and bred here could no longer afford to buy the higgledy-piggledy, gingerbread cottages that lined its streets.

At the far end of the village, Mickey passed the Honeycote Arms, the very first of the brewery's tied houses to have been purchased by his great-grandfather when he'd first hit on the idea of changing from farming to brewing. The pub was looking tired and ramshackle, in need of love and attention, though not even the peeling paintwork could detract from the loveliness of the mellow stone from which it was built. Nevertheless, it was hardly a good advert, and Mickey averted his gaze as he walked past. Apart from anything, he didn't want to get into conversation with Ted, the landlord. He didn't feel like exchanging niceties.

A little further up the road a sturdy set of pillars were topped by a wrought-iron arch proclaiming the words Honeycote Ales. The driveway continued for a hundred or so yards before dropping steeply down into a bowl in which the brewery nestled.

Had it not been contained within this bowl, the tower of the brewery would have dominated the village, hanging over it as if to remind the inhabitants of its importance. As it was, the steeply pitched lead roof with its trademark weather vane could only just be seen from the main street, if one knew where to look. At the bottom of the drive there was a cobbled courtyard, surrounded on three sides by the brewery buildings. The heart of the operation was the tower in the centre, four storeys high, with the malthouse to the left and the offices to the right, behind which were further outbuildings, garages and stables, mostly now defunct. A pair of lorries painted with the green and gold Honeycote livery were parked up in front of the entrance to the cellar, awaiting barrels of beer to be taken to the brewery's ten tied houses. They were mostly small country pubs, all within a five-mile radius of Honeycote, scattered along the nearby border between Gloucestershire and Worcestershire. They probably consumed less beer in a week between them than one town centre theme pub on a Saturday night.

It was in this rare moment of calm that Mickey was able to survey his legacy. In a couple of hours' time the place would be a hive of activity, as the giant steam engine that powered everything burst into life and another day's brew would begin. Soon the air would be filled with a rich, malty fug that could be smelled as far as the village – an enticing vapour that encapsulated years of tradition and know-how. It was all very well, he thought, being handed a business like this on a plate, but he hadn't inherited his great-grandfather's pioneering spirit, nor his grandfather's long-sightedness and careful planning, nor his father's efficiency and capacity for hard work. Which was why he was in such a mess now.

He stopped and looked into the room that served as a common room-cum-canteen for the twenty or so staff he employed – nothing grand, but somewhere warm they could boil a kettle for a cup of tea or chew on their sandwiches. He noticed a couple of balloons stuck on the wall and a banner proclaiming 'It's a girl!', and remembered that one of the young lads who drove for them had had a baby the week before. Mickey was reminded all too clearly of his responsibilities. Another mouth to feed, albeit indirectly.

As he approached the entrance to the offices, he looked at the brass plaque commemorating the brewery's centenary forty-nine years before. There had been a huge village party to celebrate – free beer for everyone (of course), a pig roast, music, dancing, fireworks – all paid for by Mickey's grandfather. Each Honeycote pub had built a huge beacon, and there was a point, high on Poacher's Hill just outside the village, where each fire could be seen twinkling.

Mickey calculated that if they could limp through another eighteen months, they could celebrate a hundred and fifty years purveying ale, but he strongly doubted there would be any cause for celebration. If there were to be any fireworks, it would be the outrage caused by mass redundancies – for he wasn't the only one whose family had been dominated by the brewery for generations. He had a couple of young lads working for him whose grandfathers had worked for his own grandfather. In some ways, Honeycote Ales was a big extended family in itself. Brothers and sisters, fathers and sons, husbands and wives had all trooped up the lane from the village to take their place shifting barrels, cleaning pipes, answering phones.

He heard someone whistling and realized he wasn't alone. It was Eric Giles, the engineer, whose front teeth had been knocked out in a village hockey match and never replaced, but who, according to local legend, had the body of a god under his boiler suit. Eric had learned to tend the steam engine in the boiler room from his own

9

father, and could turn his hand to mending anything. He loved his work, adored the engine, and Mickey knew he could bank on Eric's loyalty well past his retirement. He was in there now, checking the engine over, polishing her up, happy as anything. It made Mickey envious, and for a moment he fantasized about swapping jobs. Until it occurred to him that he wouldn't have a bloody clue how to go about Eric's work, and that Eric would probably make a far better job of running the brewery than he was.

It was with a heavy heart that he climbed the stone steps to his office and slid the key into the lock, for his problems at the brewery were only the tip of a rather large iceberg . . .

2

Miss Cowper laid down her biography of Nelson and sighed. Until now, she had found the intimate minutiae of the tactician's life utterly compelling, but she had read the same page three times and all that was going through her mind was the contents of the e-mail she had received earlier that afternoon.

In all her days as headmistress of Redfields, she had never encountered such *froideur*. She could, just about, have accepted receiving the news in a letter: the matter was indeed delicate and personal and she could appreciate Mr Sherwyn not wishing to discuss his private life over the telephone. But an e-mail that had obviously been typed by his secretary? She imagined the scenario: 'Irene – book me a table for lunch at Eduardo's. And confirm tomorrow's flight: make sure I've got a window seat. Oh, and e-mail Mandy's headmistress – tell her Mrs Sherwyn and I have split up . . .'

And now it was up to Miss Cowper to tell Mandy. Initially, she had felt inclined to refuse Mr Sherwyn's request to break the news to his daughter, but as he had indicated that he would be out of the country for the next few days, she was left with little alternative. Half the girls at the school were boarders, so, being in *loco parentis*, Miss

Cowper often found she had unpleasant news to dish out, but it was usual in the event of a divorce or separation for the parents concerned to take their daughter home for the weekend while they told her themselves, and a special, kindly eye would be kept on that pupil when she returned. Mr Sherwyn's request was a first, and Miss Cowper reflected that it might be harder to explain to Mandy why her parents had chosen not to tell her in person than to tell her they had separated. A few white lies would be necessary; she certainly wasn't going to present the facts to Mandy in the bald, ugly manner they had been presented to her.

Miss Cowper was proud of Redfields. She'd managed to transform what had been a less than mediocre girls' school into a huge success story. She'd turned it round in the past five years, doubling the number of boarders and also attracting an impressive quota of day-girls in a catchment area of up to thirty miles. And although it would never have the kudos of Cheltenham or Malvern, Redfields boasted a happy, healthy environment that turned out happy, healthy girls with the confidence to achieve their ambitions, even if they weren't heading for rocket science. But she sometimes wished the parents would leave everything up to her. She'd make a perfectly good job of bringing their daughters up if only they wouldn't interfere.

She ran her eye down the list of Mandy's classmates. One of them would have to be told in advance, to give the poor girl a shoulder to cry on. Sophie Liddiard. She was sensible; unlikely to gossip to the other girls before Mandy chose to tell them herself. She lifted the phone that connected her to the school secretary and debated a tot of Dutch courage from the handsome decanter that housed the sherry she dished out to visiting parents. Afterwards, she promised herself. She needed all the wits, tact and diplomacy she could muster for the task in hand.

Later that afternoon, when everyone else had been dispatched off for compulsory games (Miss Cowper was a stickler for fresh air and exercise, even for the sixth-formers), Mandy Sherwyn and Sophie Liddiard sat on the huge stone sill of the mullioned window that dominated Mandy's study bedroom. A half-demolished box of Maltesers lay between them.

Sophie sighed as she reached for another chocolate and looked down at the tops of her legs. If black opaque tights were supposed to be slimming, why did her thighs look so enormous? She looked enviously at Mandy's colt-like limbs strewn carelessly in front of her, and carried on listening in round-eyed sympathy to the details of her meeting with Miss Cowper.

'Apparently mum's gone to Puerto Banus to recuperate. Fornicate, more likely. There's a slimy bloke at her health club who's got an apartment there.' Mandy shuddered at the memory of the man, leathery and drenched in after-shave, endeavouring to put his hand up her skirt on more than one occasion. She'd solved that problem by wearing snow-white, skin-tight shorts that gave the creep even more idea of what he was missing but nothing to hide his hairy hand under.

'That's awful. Aren't you upset?' Sophie, who always found it very hard to hide what she was feeling, was intrigued by Mandy's matter-of-fact manner. If Miss

Cowper had just told her that her parents had split up, she'd be hysterical, she knew she would. She could feel tears welling up just imagining it. But Mandy merely shrugged and bit a Malteser in half neatly, surveying its honeycomb interior. She looked up at Sophie gravely with her baby-blue eyes. Sophie wondered if she dyed her eyelashes – they couldn't be natural, surely.

'With any luck she'll bring me back some shoes. They've got great shoe shops over there.'

Sophie thought, with a seventeen-year-old's grasp of psychology, that Mandy was studying the Malteser too intently to be convincing and was probably devastated deep down. She decided not to probe too deeply. After all, she didn't really know her well enough to go delving into her innermost feelings: Mandy had only joined Redfields in the sixth form and even after eighteen months this was probably the first time they'd had a one-to-one conversation, privacy being a rare commodity at Redfields. If she wanted to pretend everything was fine, then Sophie wasn't going to push it: she'd just make sure Mandy knew there was a sympathetic ear if she needed one.

Mandy, however, wasn't pretending. She'd let a few tears trickle out in front of Miss Cowper, primarily because she knew it was expected and it didn't do to let your headmistress think you were in any way odd. Also, something deep down inside told her that it was a tiny bit sad that she wasn't able to care, and the crocodile tears had relieved that feeling. At least the emotional display would make Miss Cowper feel she'd done her job properly. She'd shown such genuine concern that Mandy had been touched. If it had been her own mother making a perfunctory attempt to comfort her, Mandy knew she'd have been suffocated by the fumes of Poison dabbed on her perpetually racing pulse points.

She and her parents lived what Miss Cowper, being a historian, would have dubbed a *laissez-faire* existence. Mandy knew she got in the way of her mother's pursuit of sport (both vertical and horizontal) and her father's moneymaking, but didn't want to spend time with them any more than they wanted to spend time with her. She threw herself into the whirlwind regime that her mother organized to keep her out of the way during the weekends and holidays – tennis, ballet, riding, photography, gymnastics, even, one half-term when her mother was particularly desperate to dispose of her, dried flower arranging – thus becoming an accomplished and self-sufficient child. She was as overjoyed as her parents were when they hit upon the idea of sending her away to board for her A levels. As her father had driven out of the school drive, waving his hand with its bejewelled pinkie out of the car window, she had felt an overwhelming sense of relief. Perhaps now she'd have the chance to settle down and make some friends. Her peripatetic lifestyle had made her adept at making acquaintances but not at forging deep friendships.

She'd been an object of envy amongst the other girls when they'd learned of her curiously independent and sophisticated lifestyle. They'd all have died for their own self-contained suite with satellite TV, a TopShop charge card and an account with a cab firm that would take her anywhere she wanted. But they didn't understand it was all a meaningless pay-off, or why she was almost deliriously happy at Redfields. At least here she was somebody. The recognition she'd received after winning the inter-house tennis match still made Mandy glow with warmth inside. No hollow parental praise, no empty reward in the form of a crisp twenty-pound note from her father, but genuine back-thumping congratulations and glee. She was beginning to realize what it meant to have her own identity, and that it was up to her to make what she would of her life.

'What about your dad? Won't he be upset?'

Mandy shook her head, a rueful smile playing on her lips. 'He'll be too busy flogging bathrooms to notice, I expect. Anyway, they've never really liked each other, my parents.'

Sophie was inwardly appalled. Only a minute ago, she'd have given anything to be as thin as Mandy. But not now. That was too high a price, to have parents that thought so little of each other. Her own parents adored each other – you only had to look at them. She was excited at the prospect of breaking up for the Christmas holidays the next day, and spending nearly four long weeks at home. She and her younger sister Georgina were day-girls, but their home was nearly twenty miles away and the travelling was a drag. She sometimes wished they boarded, but she knew her parents wouldn't be able to find the extra money for the fees. She suspected they were struggling as it was, and if it hadn't been for Georgina's hefty sports scholarship they might have found themselves at the local comprehensive.

The two girls sat in companionable silence for a moment reflecting on their respective predicaments. Sophie let her mind wander ahead to the next Saturday night. Her brother Patrick was organizing a charity dance – he was on the committee for some reason. And so was Ned, so he was sure to be there. Sophie toyed with asking Mandy for some advice about Ned – she was bound to be an expert on blokes and how to handle them – but decided it would be selfish, so she offered her another Malteser instead. Chocolate, in her experience, was very comforting.

Kay Oakley slipped into the car and out of her black suede court shoes. Three-inch heels were no good for driving, but they'd been a necessity today. While it usually suited her to accentuate her diminutive frame, she liked to look people in the eye when she was doing a deal. That way they got the full benefit of her mesmerizing, some said almost alien, green eyes. Before she drove off she checked her hair in the vanity mirror – she'd only just had it done and she wasn't sure how the new style would hold up to the rigours of the working day. But her hairdresser was an artist – it was razored and sliced to perfection, and highlighted to suit, giving her an artfully tousled style that belied the amount of time it took to perfect each morning. She dusted herself with some bronzing powder to take away the pallor induced by a day under artificial lighting, slicked on some lipstick and spritzed a squirt of Allure on to each wrist and down her cleavage.

She pulled out of her parking space, then tutted with annoyance as she saw the long line of cars edging painfully slowly towards the exit. She should have left the Exhibition Centre earlier; but the best business was often done at the end of the day, when people were tired and capitulated more easily. She'd negotiated an excellent price on a range of rustic kitchenware: the garden centre had already opened an extensive delicatessen, so this seemed a logical diversification to Kay. Whether it would to her husband Lawrence was another matter; but at least he'd be mollified by the knock-down price she'd got.

The queue edged forward another three feet. Kay's patience left her. She pulled sharply out of the line and accelerated to the front, where the next escapee was about to insert his ticket into the machine that activated the exit barrier. Kay could feel forty pairs of angry eyes boring into her back as she lowered the electric passenger window and adopted a suitably distressed expression. She indicated the mobile on the seat next to her.

'I'm awfully sorry. I've had a phone call . . . It's an emergency. Would you mind?'

Kay never tempted fate by lying. She was merely economical with the truth. She *had* had a phone call earlier: from Lawrence, to find out what time she'd be back. ('Not before midnight, darling. More like one. I've got to do dinner with some of the suppliers – keep them sweet.') And it was an emergency: if she didn't see Mickey tonight, she'd die. It had been almost four days and she needed her fix.

Of course the driver let her out, and she flashed him a smile of such triumphant brilliance that he instantly realized he'd been duped. But by then she'd reached the freedom of the open road, and put her foot down hard. As she gained the motorway, she glanced at the digital clock. Just over an hour, traffic willing. The thought sent a pulse racing between her legs, and she put an experimental hand down to feel it. God, it was as strong as a heartbeat. Anticipation made her push the speedo up past ninety. The little Boxster managed it effortlessly. It was her ally, and the result of one of the few battles she'd won with Lawrence; if he'd got his way she'd still be lumbering along the feeder road in a Range Rover. OK, so you couldn't get much in it, but speed was more important to Kay than capacity. To her mind, its only slight drawback was lack of anonymity. A Range Rover went unremarked in most of the places she frequented; a high-powered electric blue sports car did not, which was sometimes inconvenient. But Kay was expert at weighing up pros and cons, and right now her choice was saving her precious time.

Austin Healeys really weren't meant for screwing. But Patrick Liddiard was damned if he was going to sacrifice his pride and joy for the luxury of getting his leg over in comfort. Besides, Kelly was obliging and supple and didn't seem to mind having her head jammed up against the window, judging by the appreciative noises she was making. He knew her appreciation was genuine, for he'd long concluded that the only thing that wasn't fake about Kelly were her orgasms. From the roots of her candyfloss hair to the tips of her false nails (he'd had a terrible shock once, when he'd found one of them in his Calvin Klein boxers), she was a walking temple of artifice. Patrick could only be sure that her heart-stopping breasts were her own because a publican's daughter studying beauty therapy at the local college couldn't possibly afford implants.

Ten minutes later, as Kelly retrieved her G-string from the glove compartment, Patrick stared out of the window. He never watched her get dressed; it inevitably depressed him and made him wonder, as she struggled into her cheap, gaudy, too-tight clothes, what on earth he was doing with her.

He knew the answer, of course. Because even if Kelly's conversation was limited to the regurgitated contents of

Hello! magazine, at least she took his mind off things with her effervescent babble. She was uncomplicated and great in bed. What more could you ask for? The last thing Patrick needed at the moment was a girl who made endless demands and played mind games. He'd gone down that road before – it was exhausting. And at the moment he needed all his mental energy.

As Kelly prinked in the vanity mirror, he pondered his predicament. He hadn't really expected things to turn out like this. His father had always insisted, from a young age, that Patrick should feel no obligation to step into his shoes at the brewery. For Mickey himself had been groomed to take over from his father before him, and he felt strongly that his children should be given the chance to choose their own path in life without being unduly influenced by the spectre of Honeycote Ales.

But it hadn't been that easy to escape the legacy. Patrick had never been a great academic, and had scraped through his GCSEs with just enough marks to get into the sixth form to do A levels. They, however, had proved a spectacular failure. Mickey had been furious, not with Patrick, but with the school for allowing him to suffer all those years of struggling before admitting academic defeat. He'd taken him off to a crammer in Oxford, where within half an hour they'd pronounced Patrick borderline dyslexic. Had it been diagnosed at an earlier age, they said, he would have been spared the humiliation of always coming bottom of the class, being branded a 'thicko'. Patrick was somewhat relieved. In his head, he'd never felt intellectually below his peers. It was just that he hadn't been able to express himself on paper, and now he felt vindicated.

Mickey had been beside himself with guilt, and had totally over-compensated for what had not been entirely his fault. But he blamed himself for choosing the wrong school for Patrick, for trusting them to take charge of his education when clearly they were incompetent. He knew Patrick's confidence had taken a severe knocking over the past few years, and he wanted to atone for what must have been a total nightmare for the boy. As compensation he gave his son a salary from the brewery, without actually giving him any responsibility with which to earn it. So Patrick became what was really a glorified temp, standing in whenever anyone was ill, whether it was driving the delivery lorry, humping sacks of hops or supervising the stringent tests they had to undertake several times a day. Although as a result Patrick was more familiar than anyone with the workings of the brewery, albeit on a junior level, Mickey was insistent that he spend the rest of his time working out what he really wanted to do with his life.

And now, at just twenty-three, Patrick realized that he'd reached something of a dead end. He didn't have good enough qualifications to get a job of the sort of calibre he felt he deserved – sending endless CVs to estate agents and wine merchants had proved that. He couldn't face another envelope landing on the mat with a rejection letter politely refusing him so much as an interview. He'd toyed with the idea of art college – if he excelled at anything, it was drawing – but the establishments he'd visited had appalled rather than inspired him. The students seemed pretentious, intent on shocking rather than the pursuit of the aesthetic. So that idea had gone out of the window. Of course, what he'd really like to do would be to race his Healey, but as that involved spending money rather than earning it, it wasn't really an option. He had to content himself with its restoration, a slow but rewarding process that helped him take his mind off things from time to time.

Meanwhile, being around the brewery had aroused his interests, despite Mickey's constant reminders that he was a free agent, that he should become a hot air balloonist or a lion tamer before taking up an official position at Honeycote Ales. But Patrick was gradually coming to the conclusion that this was where his future lay. After all, he loved Honeycote – the house they lived in, the countryside, the people, the way of life. And he knew he was lucky. A lot of people spent their entire lives trying to get away from where they'd been born. So he'd come to a decision – he was going to ask his father for a proper managerial position. He was going to stop messing around and do some hard work, earn his salary. He knew he was going to meet considerable resistance from his father, who seemed to be under a lot of pressure at the moment. In fact, deep down Patrick suspected that Mickey was keeping him at arm's length deliberately, and it irked him. He wanted to be able to help. But it was going to be a question of timing, finding the right moment to ask. He sighed a deep sigh.

Kelly, happy now with her handiwork, turned to him and cooed:

'You're ever so quiet, baby. What's the matter?'

'I was just asking myself if, really and truly, there was any point to all of this.'

Panic-stricken, Kelly clutched the arm of his jacket. 'What – you mean you and me?'

Patrick felt his teeth go slightly on edge at her touch.

Funny, when only a few moments ago he'd been all over her. He realized that he was going to have to let her go. Kelly's parents, Ted and Eileen, ran the Honeycote Arms. And in this supposedly classless society, he knew that class had never mattered more. If he was going to be management, he couldn't be seen sleeping with the hired help. He wondered whether this might be the opportune moment to give her the boot, but he was too tired for histrionics.

'No, no – I mean life in general. What is there to look forward to?'

Kelly's lips, shimmering with Rimini Razzle, formed a perfect circle as she pouted and looked at Patrick reproachfully from under her fringe.

'It's my twenty-first in a couple of months.'

Oh God. How could he have forgotten? Cold vol-au-vents, the Birdie Song and a ghastly cake with a huge silver key. Patrick smiled, as if this reminder had lifted the weight of the world from his shoulders. 'Oh yes.' He switched on the ignition. 'Shall I drop you home?'

'You'd better. I've got to do a bikini wax tomorrow in front of the whole class. I'm really nervous.'

Patrick felt ill-equipped to offer reassurance, so he simply reversed out of the gateway and headed along the road that would take him back into Honeycote. As the little car roared through the outskirts of the village, Patrick looked down the wooded slope into the deep bowl that housed the brewery. In the moonlight, he could just make out the ghostly shape of the old shire-horse who used to pull the dray. The dray was long out of commission, but they'd kept Toby out of sentimentality. He was over thirty; if they hadn't he'd have gone for dog meat, so he lived happily in retirement in the small paddock behind the malthouse.

Something suddenly caught Patrick's eye and he frowned, slammed on the brakes and peered down into the darkness. Damn! He'd thought so: there was a light on in the brewery office. He'd heard they'd appointed a new Excise chap at Gloucester – an eager beaver by all accounts, keen as mustard – but surely the days of midnight swoops on breweries were gone? You'd have to be crazy to attempt an illicit brew these days. Crazy or desperate: there was too much to lose, too little to gain.

Patrick sighed. He'd better go and introduce himself; make sure this new chap understood that Honeycote Ales didn't appreciate people breathing down their necks. Cursing softly under his breath and ignoring Kelly's squeaks of bewildered protest, he swung the car round and set off back down the hill.

The Fox and Goose, the Honeycote Arms or the Red Lion? Mickey had narrowed the field down to three, but couldn't bring himself to pinpoint a final choice. One of them had to go, that was definite. And of the ten tied houses that made up Honeycote Ales, these were the ones making least money and needing most investment. Which meant they would fetch less, but at this stage of the game any amount would help. Mickey ran his hand through his thick dark brown hair and sighed. There was going to be uproar whichever he chose. How the hell was he going to explain to the world at large that after nearly a hundred and fifty years of paternalism, Honeycote Ales was going to sell a pub from under one of their loyal and faithful tenants?

Mickey knew he only had himself to blame for the situation. The sad fact was, he might have inherited a family business but he wasn't a businessman, no matter which way you looked at it. It was a miracle they'd made it into the twenty-first century – it was certainly more by luck than good judgement. He just wasn't ruthless enough. He couldn't take the bull by the horns, basically because he was terrified of change. He found it so much easier to keep things as they were, than have to take the blame for implementing some radical change that hadn't worked. But he knew he was reaching crisis point. All the pubs owned by the brewery needed massive refurbishments, just to bring them up to scratch and to keep the Health and Safety people placated. Not only that, but the machinery at the brewery was out of the ark: several key pieces of equipment needed repairing. It was only a matter of time before something integral to the whole shooting match gave up the ghost.

What was needed was a substantial cash injection. He was going to have to sell one of the pubs. Which was ironic, because he knew that he should actually be looking to increase his stable in order to justify keeping the operation going. The prospect broke his heart, but one of them had to be sacrificed in order to save the rest.

He drained his glass, stood and paced across the ancient wooden floorboards of the brewery office, coming to rest in front of the yellowing map produced for their centenary celebrations all those years ago. It outlined the brewery's catchment area, with Honeycote and the heart of the operation in the centre, surrounded by a pen and ink drawing of each pub. The artist had added a decorative border depicting their various signs – the Fox and

Goose, the Roebuck, the Peacock . . . Mickey had always found the map whimsical and sickly, but as Honeycote Ales's image was that of a slice of quintessential English country life, he supposed it was appropriate.

In moments of contemplation he always came to rest in front of this map and amused himself identifying the animal illustrations with their human counterparts. He, of course, was the handsome, wily fox forever seeking refuge from relentless pursuit. Lucy was the deer, a dainty, wide-eyed innocent unaware of the dangers lurking and who must be protected at all costs. The peacock in the bottom corner crept unwelcomed into his line of vision. It was not an indigenous creature, but an imported trophy that brought glamour and status to its owner. And, apparently, trouble.

Kay. For the umpteenth time Mickey cursed whatever genetic defect had blessed him with such a surfeit of impulsiveness when it came to her; it was as powerful as a drug. But gradually the stakes had climbed higher and higher, and now he was seeing with a frightening clarity just what he had to lose.

How the hell had he got himself into such a mess? Wherever he turned, he faced the consequences of either his ineffectuality or his self-indulgence. The thought was sobering, so he went to pour himself another Scotch and was surprised to find the decanter empty. Reassuring himself that there had only been an inch in the bottom when he arrived, he reached into the waxed jacket he'd hung on the back of the door. Relief flooded him as he felt the familiar cold pewter of his hip-flask. As the sweet, fiery sloe gin spread through his gullet the security of its warmth relaxed him, so much so that when he turned to find Patrick in the doorway he was momentarily off his guard and waved the flask cheerily at his son.

'What on earth are you doing here, Dad? It's nearly midnight.'

Mickey's eyes slid over to his paper-strewn desk. Was there anything incriminating? Probably not, but Patrick had a shrewd mind and could put two and two together astoundingly quickly for one who'd failed his Maths GCSE three times. He walked carefully back across the office and began gathering up the documents.

'Just looking over the last quarter's figures. Not brilliant.'

'I know that, Dad. We all know that.'

Mickey forced himself to meet Patrick's eye. He knew that look from old. The dark eyebrow slightly raised, the sardonic twist of the mouth: exaggerated patience tinged with accusation – it was pure Carola. A selective memory had enabled Mickey to banish the image of his ex-wife from his mind. Most of the time. Now he was all too clearly reminded of the horrible turn events had taken when he'd brought her back to Honeycote all those years ago.

They'd met at university. Mickey had eschewed Oxford in favour of King's College, London, on the basis that one could only take so much punting and a metropolitan existence was likely to be far more enriching. And indeed it was, for he'd never have met Carola in that city of dreaming spires, with her loathing of anything that smacked of elitism. It was her hair that had attracted him – a wild mass of black, tangled curls that hung down her back. That and the warm, spicy animal scent Mickey felt sure only he could smell, and that now, after years of experience, he could readily identify as desire. They'd done it everywhere, even on the Tube late one night between Tottenham Court Road and Goodge Street, and Carola had talked passionately about her beliefs and her plans to change the world. She was, apparently, an anarchist, forever going on marches and attending rock concerts in support of some oppressed minority or other. Mickey had always listened politely to her rantings but reserved judgement, knowing that he and his family represented much of what she was against. She'd taken his silence for agreement, his two Clash albums for commitment to her cause, and he'd been naive enough to think she wouldn't hold his duplicity against him.

When she announced she was pregnant and an abortion was out of the question, Mickey, still intoxicated by the feral creature he'd ensnared, marched her off to the nearest Register Office. Carola, who thrived on being unpredictable, had been so enchanted by the perversity of flouting her lack of convention that she agreed to a wedding. She'd worn a Victorian nightdress so tight across her rapidly expanding breasts that it was a contest as to whether they or the Registrar's eyes were going to pop out first.

Before he'd had a chance to tell his parents of his latest folly, they'd been tragically killed in a sailing accident off Salcombe. The plan had been for him to finish his degree, then do a pupillage at a Scottish brewery owned by a friend of his father's, in order for him to learn the ropes objectively before becoming second in command. That was now out of the question. Mickey had no choice but to take over as managing director straight away.

Carola had been totally bemused to find the contents of their little bedsit ensconced in Mickey's school trunk and a black taxi ticking outside the door. Still alarmingly ignorant of her husband's legacy, she'd demanded what was to become of their education. Mickey had tersely reminded her that as their baby was due in four months, neither of them were likely to be getting a lot of work done. She could finish her degree another time. And he wouldn't be needing one now.

More than twenty years later, here he was facing that accusing stare in its next incarnation. He didn't like to think about what had happened in between: he had too many regrets. Not that he'd ever regretted Patrick – he thought the world of his son – but he was keenly aware that he was no longer a boy, easily fobbed off, and not, despite his lack of academic prowess, a fool either. Mickey raised his flask in an attempt to play for time.

'Drink?'

'No, thanks. I'm driving. As, I presume by your car outside, are you.'

The remark was pointedly sarcastic. He shouldn't have to take that. Mickey raised the flask to his lips in a gesture of defiance, then realized it was empty.

The journey had been trouble free, and Kay smiled as she sped up the familiar narrow road, lined with drystone walls and overhung by ancient oaks. It was enveloped in a soft velvet blackness that a stranger would have found disconcerting but she found alluring, leading as it did to her haven. At last she reached the gates, where the words Honeycote Ales re-affirmed her destination in black, curling wrought iron. The noise of her tyres on the gravel jumped up as she swung into the drive and she wondered if he could hear it too. The luminous green of her digital clock flipped to midnight: perfect timing. They always had perfect timing.

She turned the last corner of the sinuous drive and smiled as she saw his car and the welcoming light in the brewery. Then she slammed on the brakes. There was another car. She only needed a split second to take in its identity before spinning round and accelerating back the way she came. Now her heart really was racing, and it wasn't with anticipation. Her mouth was dry with fear. It was the first time she'd come so close, and even now she couldn't be sure she hadn't been seen.

Kelly had been sitting as patiently as she could in Patrick's car. Although it was bathed in a pool of light from the office window, she couldn't help feeling nervous, and she was getting cold. She touched the icy tip of her nose and pulled down the vanity mirror to see if it was going red. As she did so a sudden flash glanced off the glass. She turned, and caught the tail lights of a car disappearing up the hill. She could just make out the number plate mounted on an electric blue bumper. She frowned. There was only one person with an electric blue car that she knew of.

She felt glad at least that it had provided her with an excuse. She wouldn't have liked to interrupt Patrick otherwise. He was strangely unpredictable, all over her one minute and distant the next, and she couldn't understand why. She scrambled out of the car, smoothed her dress down over her hips and headed into the brewery.

As she walked into the office, Patrick scowled but Mr Liddiard smiled. He seemed genuinely pleased to see her, but then he was always nice.

'Sorry, but someone came down the drive.' There was an ominous silence. 'I was scared; it's spooky—'

Mr Liddiard came over and put a comforting hand on her shoulder. His breath smelled of booze; not all stale and beery like some of her father's customers, but he'd definitely been drinking.

'I'm sorry, Kelly. I didn't realize Patrick had left you out there all on your own.' He turned to his son. 'Why don't you take Kelly home and I'll finish up here. There's nothing we can resolve at this late hour anyhow.'

Kelly thought Patrick looked rather cross, and she didn't look forward to the drive home. Nerves, as usual, made her babble.

'I think it was Mrs Oakley's car. You know, that gorgeous Boxster her husband bought her. Lucky thing . . .'

By now, Patrick was looking crosser than ever, and Kelly decided she'd better shut up.

3

Mandy Sherwyn sat glumly on her suitcase, hugging her coat round her as protection against the spiteful breeze that was buffeting a new batch of leaves across the drive. The caretaker, had he not already set off for Christmas at his sister's, would have been exasperated as he'd painstakingly swept the full length of the drive that morning in anticipation of the parents' arrival.

A car turned in through the gates and Mandy rose to her feet, but she soon sat down again. No taxi firm her father used would dream of sending an ancient, mud-spattered Volvo to pick her up. She watched with interest as the car rattled to a halt, the passenger door opened and an ebullient Irish wolfhound, looking more like an animated loo brush, ejected itself at top speed. It streaked across the lawn, barking urgently, and proceeded to dig up Miss Cowper's prize rose bed. A young woman emerged from the driver's side, oblivious to the dog's trail of destruction, and ran anxiously up the steps leading from the car park to the wide path that bordered the front of the school.

As she approached, Mandy could see that she was, in fact, older than she appeared from a distance. Late thirties, she guessed, but still enchantingly pretty. Her chestnut hair fell loose and wavy to her shoulders, while her eyes perfectly matched the voluminous toffee-coloured jumper that was obviously cashmere, but was made totally understated by ancient, faded 501s and a pair of suede loafers that were irretrievably scuffed but undeniably expensive.

Mandy wondered whose mother she could be. She'd thought she was the last to be collected, as taxi drivers had no sense of family loyalty to ensure they were on time. She was surprised, therefore, to see the arched doorway of the side entrance open, and Sophie Liddiard burst out, followed in hot pursuit by her younger sister Georgina, who was for some reason sporting a pair of reindeer antlers.

'Darlings!' The woman gave each girl a quick hug. 'I'm sorry I'm so late. I had to wait ages for the farrier. You know he's always late . . .' The three of them chattered and laughed as they loaded up the end-of-term paraphernalia. They looked more like sisters than a mother and her two daughters. Mandy bit her lip and turned to watch a subdued saloon making its way up the drive. This looked more like it. She picked up her case and walked down the steps. As she passed the Liddiards' car, Sophie smiled at her sympathetically.

'Is this your dad?'

Mandy shook her head. 'He's sent a taxi. He's away on business till Sunday.'

Sophie looked aghast. 'You mean you're going to be on your own till then?'

Mandy did her best to make it sound no big deal. 'It's OK – the housekeeper's going to sleep in. And she'll do my meals and stuff . . .' She couldn't make herself sound convincing. Who in their right mind would want to spend three days rattling about in a huge, sterile house with a half-deaf housekeeper for company?

Sophie turned to her mother. 'Can Mandy come back with us?'

Lucy smiled without a second thought. 'Of course. If you're sure your parents won't mind?'

Mandy hesitated. She wasn't used to lowering her guard, and she was embarrassed that she'd made the Liddiards feel pity for her. Perhaps they felt obliged to invite her. She looked at them: Sophie was surveying her with genuine anxiety and her mother's smile was warm and inviting, not that of someone who'd been cornered. As the taxi driver climbed out of his car and approached her, she suddenly found herself knocked flying by the loo brush, who'd finished her perusal of the flower beds and was now greeting her with a warm, joyous lick.

'Pokey!' Sophie pulled at the dog's collar to no avail.

'Miss Sherwyn?' The driver's nasal voice betrayed his Birmingham origins.

In the midst of the chaos Mandy's mind was suddenly crystal clear. She smiled at Sophie's mother. 'I'd love to come. My parents won't mind a bit.'

She didn't add that they probably wouldn't even notice and, minutes later, found herself sitting in the front seat, having pushed aside a mound of Fox's Glacier Mints, riding gloves and loose change. She'd phone dad's secretary Irene later, tell her what she was doing.

'There's a box of eclairs in the back somewhere,' said Lucy. 'I knew you couldn't wait till supper.'

A hurried search produced an empty box. A sated Pokey stuck her head over the back seat. There were howls of protest from Sophie and Georgina.

'Never mind,' said Lucy. 'Nearly home.'

There was much arguing over what music to put on.

Lucy overruled them all and chose Nina Simone. They all started singing along: 'My Baby Just Cares for Me' . . .

Half an hour later, Lucy slid the car through a huge stone gateway that no longer bore any gates, and up a pot-holed drive that sprouted grass at regular intervals. In front of them lay a house that looked as if it had nestled in this spot since the dawn of time, and had actually laid down roots. It was a substantial size, but so mossy, mellow and crumbling that it didn't seem at all grand. It didn't stand to attention, or seem worried about the odd missing roof tile or cracked window. Like a truly beautiful woman, it stood unselfconscious and with no need of cosmetic artifice. It took Mandy's breath away.

'How long have you lived here?'

Sophie wrinkled her brow trying to calculate.

'I don't know. For ever. We were all born here. And Dad, I think.'

Lucy intervened. 'It used to belong to the local squire. He was a dreadful gambler – lost every penny, so my husband's grandfather bought the house off him.' She smiled ruefully. 'Brewing was the business to be in then. There were lots of thirsty farmers around, who weren't worried about drinking and driving. Not like now.'

'It's beautiful.'

'You might not be so enamoured once you've spent the night here. It's freezing – bed socks and hot water bottles, I'm afraid.'

'And there's never any hot water for a shower. Sophie and I have to shower at school.' Georgina sounded outraged.

Mandy grinned, sure they didn't mean it. She stepped

35

reverently into the flagstoned hallway of Honeycote House, and as she was ushered into the biggest kitchen she'd ever seen, she was overcome by a wave of desire. For there, in front of her, was everything she'd ever wanted.

It wasn't the size. Her parents' ostentation had taught her that big certainly did not mean beautiful. No – what was truly overwhelming was the feeling that this was a room where people had fun, where people wanted to be and, more importantly, wanted to be with each other. Its charisma was tangible, seductive, and Mandy was instantly under its spell.

The focal point was the table, which sat twelve comfortably and was ranged on both sides by wooden church pews. When you looked closely, you could see there were sets of initials carved at random all over it. Sophie explained that whoever sat there had to leave their mark. Mandy thought of her mother's dining table, protected first by a heat-proof undercloth, then mats at each place setting, then a starched cloth over the top. And always napkins in a bishop's mitre. She knew there'd be no such fripperies here. Her eyes moved to a large pine dresser. There was no carefully arranged display of cut glass and bone china, just a hotchpotch collection of mementoes haphazardly arranged, which clearly hadn't seen a duster for weeks. Photos of family antics were stuck on to the walls with browning Sellotape, a faded sofa sporting a ham-bone and a coating of hairs indicated Pokey's territory and a row of empty champagne bottles were inscribed in black marker with the events they had celebrated (Sophie's GCSEs, Pokey's puppies, Georgina making the county netball team). There were hardly any gadgets apparent: a coffee machine and a toaster but certainly no dishwasher, merely a huge stone sink piled shamelessly high with washing-up.

Mandy was given tea in a chipped Bart Simpson mug. And, when Mr Liddiard got home, champagne in an ancient and heavy crystal glass to celebrate the end of term. They had shepherd's pie for supper: not a microwaved supermarket offering, but ground steak flavoured with herbs and garlic and mushrooms and, strange yet deliciously appropriate, baked beans. Then ice cream, not presented in prissy little glass bowls with fan-shaped wafers, but served from the tub at the table and smothered in Mars Bars that Georgina melted on the Aga. And all the way through the meal the Liddiards laughed, chattered, laughed again and, most of all, listened to each other.

Suddenly, everything fell into place and Mandy knew she'd found the way forward. This was the answer. A house where you had what you wanted, not what you thought you ought to have, and where nothing was done for effect, but for a good reason, or maybe for no reason at all other than you just felt like it. And where everyone was made welcome. Somehow, effortlessly, the Liddiards had made her feel one of the family, which made Mandy realize she'd never been made to feel one of her own. Silently, she vowed that she'd recreate all this for herself, someday, somewhere, somehow. She was just toasting herself with the last drop of champagne in her glass – it wasn't every night you found the meaning of life – when the door opened and in strolled a tall, languid-looking young man with satanically dark eyebrows. Laughing, he gave each of his sisters a high five, kissed Lucy and nodded to Mickey. Sophie drew Mandy forward.

'Patrick, this is Mandy, from school. Her parents are away so—'

'Great. The more the merrier. Have you told her about Saturday?'

'Not yet—'

Patrick sauntered round the table, his rangy, Levi-clad legs covering the distance effortlessly, and he held out his hand to Mandy. She took it: it was warm, dry and confident. Somehow, she didn't want to let go, but she did, and watched as he reached out for the bottle of red wine his father had opened and casually filled himself a glass. His hair was sleek, blue-black, cleverly cut to look as if it needed cutting, with an untameable lock that fell forwards on to his eyes. He pushed it back and smiled at Mandy, and she felt her insides turn to syrup.

'We're having a charity fund-raising bash at the local hotel. I'm on the committee, for my sins, so I'll wangle you a ticket.'

Mandy realized that his eyebrows looked so dark because his eyes were icy-blue. She smiled back.

'Thanks. But I haven't brought anything to wear.'

'I'm sure Sophie can lend you something.'

Sophie squawked with indignation. 'Me? I haven't got anything for myself – only that old maroon velvet. Georgie can wear that.'

It was Georgie's turn to be outraged. 'I don't want your disgusting cast-offs—'

'Now, girls. Don't panic. We'll go through everything tomorrow and see what we can rustle up.' Lucy was anxious to avert the sartorial panic that an impending social occasion always brought.

'But there isn't anything!'

Mickey, mellowed by the wine and further softened by the knowledge that he had his whole family around him and therefore couldn't be cornered by Patrick, came to the rescue.

'I'll take you shopping in Cheltenham tomorrow.' The squeals of joy gratified him. Patrick grinned at Mandy.

'It doesn't take much to make some people happy.'

That, thought Mandy, was what made them so lucky. She could have any frock she wanted, and it had never made her happy. She had an idea what would, though, and it really was frighteningly simple. She gave herself a mental pat on the back: not only had she found the way forward tonight, but now she had the key.

After the excitement had died down, Patrick produced a penknife from his pocket and Mandy went through the ritual of carving her initials on the table, although it was difficult to find a space. As she carefully scraped an M, followed by an S, she promised herself that one day she would rub out the last letter and replace it triumphantly with an L for Liddiard.

Next morning, Mickey felt as if his head was in a vice and some particularly nasty rodent had crawled into his mouth and died. As he walked into the kitchen, the smell of percolating coffee made his stomach churn. What he saw at the table, however, made him forget his hangover. Mandy was sitting in one of his old shirts with the sleeves rolled up and precious little else. She was smiling at him; saying something – what was it? Mickey could hardly hear through the pounding of the blood that had rushed to his head.

'I'm sorry, Mr Liddiard. I spilt hot chocolate all down my front last night and I didn't have a spare nightie. I found this in the ironing basket. I hope you don't mind?'

'It's only fit for the bin.' Lucy was doing battle with the percolator, which hissed malevolently at her. To Mickey it sounded like a mighty roar. 'I've been trying to make him get rid of that shirt for ages. It's gone completely at the collar.'

'Oh, you should never get rid of your favourite clothes. I always think they're like old friends, don't you?' Mandy was fiddling absent-mindedly with the third button down. Mickey couldn't look at her. She couldn't possibly know the effect she was having, with her long legs, semi-clad at the breakfast table. Could she?

He looked at Sophie instead.

'God, I'd throw all my old clothes away tomorrow, if I could,' she was saying fervently. 'By the way, Dad, you haven't forgotten you're taking us to Cheltenham? We need some serious retail therapy.'

Why had he ever opened his mouth? He was supposed to be meeting Kay at two, to make up for that debacle the night before last. She'd arranged it specifically; she was twitchy about whether they'd been seen. He'd told her that she needed to toughen up a bit – she always found the danger of being caught a thrill, until it became a possibility. Never run away from the scene of the crime, he'd said, and if you get caught never admit to anything. A plausible excuse can always be found. She replied, rather tartly, that she wasn't a seasoned adulterer like him. He'd have to go and placate her. He wouldn't mention that Kelly had seen her. He didn't know what Patrick had made of it – he didn't have the mental energy to go down that path.

'Are you all right, darling? You look ghastly.' Lucy had managed to wheedle a cup of coffee from the machine and was handing it to him.

'No, no – I'm fine. I've just got a heavy day ahead of me.'

That was an understatement. A nightmare of a day. A meeting with Cowley at the bank: Mickey knew exactly what he was going to say, but he would have to sit there and listen to him say it because you had to play by the rules of people you were horribly in debt to. And now he was going to have to cancel Kay and go shopping with the girls in Cheltenham. He dimly remembered promising to buy them party outfits. Christ, how was he supposed to pay for those? He'd have to tell them no. Better three disappointed schoolgirls than one wrathful Kay. He tried to judge their reaction. Georgie was happily mashing a banana, her faith in her father implicit. Would she mind? She wasn't as obsessed with her looks and her clothes as Sophie seemed to be, though he suspected it was only a matter of time. She was fifteen, bordering on that dangerous age when girls seemed to turn into sirens almost overnight, exposing flesh and slathering themselves in make-up in a determined effort to torture every male for miles around. Thankfully, trophies and cups seemed to be more important to Georgie than Wonderbras and lipstick, and Mickey hoped it would stay that way. Lacrosse matches he could cope with; hormones he couldn't.

Sophie, however, was a different matter. She was already looking at him anxiously, a hint of panic in her eyes.

'You haven't forgotten, have you, Daddy?'

He couldn't do it; he couldn't let her down. She'd lost half a stone this term and she was so proud. The layers of podge that Lucy had spent years reassuring her were just puppy fat really were finally melting away. Exquisite bone structure was emerging from her previously plump cheeks. His little duckling was becoming a swan, and she deserved the fine feathers to go with it.

Kay would bloody well have to lump it.

'Of course not. I'll meet you here at half eleven.'

Sophie whooped and hit the table in an American gesture of triumph that made the coffee cups rattle and Mickey wince. He couldn't go back on his word now. He was always putty in the hands of his daughters. He looked at Sophie again, her eyes shining with excitement, and realized with sadness that at best he probably only had a couple more years of her to enjoy. She was only a few years younger than Lucy had been when he'd met her. He allowed himself to wonder who she'd meet and marry; how he'd feel about any of her suitors. He hoped darkly that none of them would turn out like him. A feckless, duplicitous wastrel. His daughter deserved better than that. Mind you, so did his wife.

Mickey wished he could crawl back into bed and sleep off his indulgence, but it wasn't an option. He'd better go and put a suit on. That way the bank would think he was taking them seriously.

It was a credit to Graham Cowley and his loyal customers that his bank, or rather the bank of which he was manager, was the only one in Eldenbury to stay open five days a week. The little town couldn't really sustain any more. It was situated on the Oxford to Evesham road, and was essentially split into two. The Oxford end was rather smart and served the tourists, being filled with antique shops and art galleries that required a bell to be rung before entry. The Evesham end was more utilitarian and served the locals, with its Budgens and Chinese takeaway. The

Horse and Groom sat firmly in the middle, with a foot in both camps, and Cowley could see it from his office window, the Honeycote Ales sign swaying gently in the breeze.

Honeycote Ales's greatest strength, he reflected as he flicked through their file, and probably its saving grace, was the fact it made bloody good beer. A rich, deep gold, with a curious sweetness that matched its name, the brew was acclaimed both locally and nationwide. Real ale fanatics, notoriously purist and difficult to impress, lauded Honeycote Ale as one of Britain's finest, and recommended all the pubs in their guide as being unspoilt and traditionally welcoming, all sharing an uncontrived charm. Largely of local Cotswold stone, they were rickety, quaint and warm. Their decor was conventional olde worlde – original, not faked by a design company – with the usual smattering of horse brasses, farming implements, hunting prints and fading, tattered chintzes, the patterns barely discernible. Open fires, beams, flagstone floors: traditional country hostelries where locals, from landowners to farmhands, could rub shoulders to moan about the latest dictates from Brussels, and could, if they wished, choose a warming soup or a hearty casserole from the menu. There was nothing adventurous in the culinary stakes – no polenta or rocket – but good, wholesome, home cooking that the landladies had learned at their own mothers' feet.

Thus packs of ramblers planned their routes along the Cotswold Way via Honeycote pubs, knowing that they could slake their thirst with a well-deserved pint of the local nectar and confident that they would not be greeted with snotty requests to remove their muddy boots, but with platters of doorstep sandwiches filled with thickly cut beef and eye-watering horseradish. Most of the locals had been weaned on the stuff, and experienced their first kiss giddy on its hidden strength. Londoners with weekend cottages brought their chums in for a 'proper' pint, not the gaseous excuses for beer served in the pseudo-Victorian hostelries they frequented in the City. But none of these were enough to sustain the monstrous overheads the brewery now faced.

Good beer and loyalty – customer loyalty, staff loyalty and family loyalty – that's what had kept Honeycote Ales afloat and seen it through many a rough patch. But even that magical recipe could fail in the wrong hands. And charm wasn't enough any more. Of course, you had to have a Unique Selling Point (Cowley despised all these new marketing terms, with their over-important capital letters and acronyms), but it was what you did with your USP afterwards that mattered and the truth was Mickey Liddiard did nothing but the bare minimum.

Cowley wasn't looking forward to his meeting with Mickey that morning. Their meetings were usually kept on an informal level, with Mickey taking him on a guided tour then standing him a good roast lunch at the Horse and Groom. Being a bank manager in a small market town didn't allow for much fun and Cowley had always enjoyed these little outings. He appreciated good beer and found the somewhat antiquated machinations of the brewery fascinating. Honeycote Ales was small enough to allow itself the luxury of traditional methods and high standards. The mounds of golden Herefordshire hops and malt barley, the ancient wooden tuns and vats, the pure clear water that was drawn up from underground wells and the mighty engine that drove all the pumps and machinery: the purity and simplicity of the operation showed itself in the perfection of its brew. It was a dream formula for the millennium, with its harking back to all things bucolic and nostalgic; the sort of venture that over-driven high-flyers dreamed of escaping to when they felt the first naggings of an ulcer.

Yes, Honeycote Ales was a very viable proposition indeed. Put it on the open market and it would be snapped up, if not by one of the predatory larger breweries whose hungry jaws it had done well to avoid thus far, then by a moneyed entrepreneur who fancied playing at having his own pubs. No doubt that would result in some of its less charming rough edges being smoothed off – several of the pubs, for example, still only had outside toilets – but there would be a concomitant rise in profit.

It was Cowley's job today to point this out to Mickey Liddiard as diplomatically as possible. He'd therefore felt the need to put their meeting on a more formal level than usual, and had asked Mickey to come into the bank. He wanted to feel confident and have the upper hand, and he knew that meeting at the brewery held too many distractions; that he would be too easily seduced by his surroundings and the notorious Liddiard charm.

Of course, unauthorized overdrafts were not uncom-mon in these days of sticky cash flow. The bank generally sent out a letter advising the culprit of their overdrawn amount and the charge that would be added to their ac-count on a daily basis until the debt was cleared. This was usually enough for the culprits either to clear the amount or come in to arrange an official loan. He'd sent Mickey five reminding letters to date.

Cowley knew there was trouble by the nonchalant way

Mickey kept assuring him there wasn't. His confident smile, the airy wave of the hand, his pseudo-exasperated references to late-payers all pointed to what Cowley thought of as the reverse ostrich syndrome – trying to stick his head in the sand. But anyone who thought they could fool Cowley had got him all wrong. His slow, deliberate manner and seemingly cautious way of thinking did not mean he could not spot trouble on the horizon. What he needed to establish today was whether Mickey's own head was in the sand, too – whether he knew the extent of his problems or if they were going to run away with him. Cowley was very good at shutting the barn door before the horse bolted.

Getting Mickey to come clean on their first meeting would be well nigh impossible, but at least Cowley would be able to start putting the pressure on gently by reassuring him that the bank would be there for Honeycote Ales as long as he played by their rules. Any funny business these days and the rug was pulled out, no questions asked. Meanwhile, he'd worked out two solutions to the brewery's problems, neither of which Mickey would like.

He broached the first and less controversial over a mediocre cup of coffee, which he was interested to see Mickey did not touch. Was it really that disgusting, or was the hangover from which he was obviously suffering so bad that liquid intake was not yet possible? Cowley felt in a stronger position immediately and plunged straight in.

'Why don't you sell off one of your tied houses? It would give you a cash injection, which you obviously badly need, and a bit left over for general improvements. Some considered investment . . .'

Mickey looked at him as if he had suggested selling one of his own children. 'This is just a temporary cash flow problem—'

Cowley smiled, and Mickey was startled to notice a wintry chill in his eyes. The placebo was having no effect.

'I think you should consider it.'

He wasn't to know Mickey had been agonizing over this very possibility for weeks, and had finally concluded it was out of the question. He couldn't bring himself to do it.

'And in the meantime, can I assume you won't be drawing any more cheques on your account until we see something paid in?'

What about the wages? And the next consignment of barley? It suddenly occurred to Mickey that the colour-less, docile chap he'd dragged round the brewery so many times and stuffed to the gills in the Horse and Groom was a wolf in sheep's clothing. Bile rose in his throat, but he swallowed it and smiled.

'I'm expecting something in the next couple of days.'

Cowley smiled. His lips were thin and liver-coloured, too dark for his pale, papery skin. Mickey badly wanted to escape. And have a proper drink. Not coffee that smelled like gravy browning. But Cowley was shuffling through his file in a manner that didn't seem conclusive. He spread his hands out carefully on the table and hit Mickey with his second proposition.

'I think you should also consider appointing a proper sales manager. Beef up your off-sales instead of relying on your tied trade.'

Mickey knew there was sense in the suggestion.

'Maybe Patrick—'

Cowley thought he'd nip that suggestion in the bud while he could.

'Patrick's too young and green – he could do more harm than good. Someone with experience could improve things dramatically. Leave Patrick to do whatever it is he's best at.' Cowley made this sound as if he didn't think that was a fat lot. 'You need to get a real salesman in – someone hungry and aggressive.'

Someone who didn't spend half their time poncing about in a sports car chatting up women. Cowley had seen Patrick speeding through Eldenbury on several occasions with a girl in the front seat, clearly not on brewery business even though he was drawing a salary.

'A shark, you mean?' Mickey's reaction was just what Cowley expected.

'That's the way it needs to be these days.'

Mickey looked at Cowley and thought he looked a little shark-like himself: cold eyes, sharp teeth.

'We've never employed aggressive sales tactics.'

'Then perhaps you should.'

The tone was mild but it was a statement rather than a question. Mickey shifted uncomfortably. A tot from his hip-flask wouldn't really be appropriate at this point, tempting though the thought was.

'I don't know that we can support another salary.'

'Then perhaps you should look at how you're staffed.'

There was a deadly silence. Cowley's training meant that Mickey broke it first.

'You're saying get rid of Patrick.'

'It's all very well keeping things in the family, but you should ask yourself how useful Patrick really is to you. Is it worth the whole company going down the drain just to keep him in beer money – if you'll forgive the play on words. I mean, what does he actually do for his twenty grand a year? Not a lot, as far as I can see.' Cowley allowed himself another little smile. Mickey was starting to find them unnerving. Was Cowley merely chuffed by his little attempt at wit, or was he enjoying the situation? He rather suspected the latter. 'Believe me, there'll be plenty of people waiting in the wings if you don't pull your finger out.'

If Mickey hadn't been on the end of this ruthless appraisal he would have been speechless with admiration. For years Cowley had struck him as someone who wouldn't say boo to a goose. Now here he was, sharpening the knife and preparing to stick it in as far as it would go. Mickey didn't mind betting he'd got a buyer up his sleeve already. He wondered if he was in for a cut as well, but figured Cowley was probably relying on his imminent pension too much to risk insider dealing. He decided to call his bluff.

'Really? Have you got a particular buyer in mind?' He was pleased to see Cowley look startled. He thought he'd make him squirm a bit more. 'I mean, I know we're over our limit a bit at the moment, but the brewery's not actually yours to sell yet, is it?'

Mickey knew he was pulling rank as one of the bank's oldest and most valued customers, but he hadn't appreciated this meeting one bit. Cowley's tone had verged on blackmail. He expected an immediate and profuse apology, and was perturbed to see Cowley looking at him with puzzlement and pity.

'Mr Liddiard' – he'd never called him that before – 'are you actually aware of the extent of your debt to the bank at the moment?'

Later, Cowley felt sorry that Mickey had seemed to take everything so personally. It was his job on the line, after all. And at the moment Honeycote Ales had the biggest unauthorized overdraft in the county.

By midday, Mickey and the girls had reached the middle of Cheltenham, parked satisfactorily and reached the haven of the town's biggest department store. He'd raided the petty cash tin and given Sophie and Georgina fifty pounds each to buy an outfit for the party. He felt guilty, as he knew this wasn't really enough, and there was nothing he'd have loved more than to have given them carte blanche, but he couldn't. He'd also felt embarrassed handing them cash in front of Mandy, feeling it beyond the bounds of hospitality to fork out for her, but she'd mollified him by flashing a credit card. He agreed to meet them an hour later in a nearby pizza parlour. As soon as they were out of sight he bolted for the basement where the payphones were secreted. What with the bank manager, and Lucy, unusually for her, being at home all morning, he hadn't had a chance to call Kay. At times Mickey wished he had succumbed to a mobile like everyone else in the world, but the inconvenience of being permanently contactable outweighed his occasional desperation for telecommunication. He scrabbled in his pocket for change, dialled Kay's number and leaned against the wall for moral support. There was no reply.

Mickey threw the phone back on to the receiver in disgust. Why did people have mobile phones if they didn't bother to answer them? He walked back to the lift, gloomily wondering how the hell he was going to pay for lunch. Cowley had been pretty explicit about what would happen if he wrote another cheque. In the lift was a sign for the imminent arrival of Santa in his grotto. How simple it would be if he could send a note up the chimney asking for a hundred thousand pounds. He debated taking the lift to the top floor and ending it all, but instead he got out on the third floor and headed for Ladies Lingerie. Guilt always made him generous. That was one of his better faults.

In the office at Barton Court garden centre, Kay had ignored her phone. The number that flashed up was one she didn't recognize. Her husband Lawrence frowned.

'Aren't you going to answer it?'

'It's bound to be one of the reps from the exhibition. They're obsessed with follow-up calls. Let them wait.'

Lawrence smiled. That was one of the things he loved best about his wife. She was a tough cookie.

'How about lunch somewhere?'

It had been one of the busiest weeks of the year for the garden centre, and Lawrence had been working practically round the clock. Although he was good at delegating, he was also a control freak. As he rarely relaxed himself, he didn't see why anyone else should, so he always kept his staff on their toes, never let them become complacent. But today he fancied taking Kay somewhere to celebrate. He'd printed out the figures for the past two weeks that morning and their turnover was up by an astonishing percentage. If he and Kay couldn't take time out to congratulate themselves, then what was the point?

'We could go into Cheltenham. Stop off at Sampson's.'

Sampson's was their favourite jeweller. Lawrence always liked Kay to choose her own Christmas present – he'd never seen the point in expensive surprises that might need to be changed. He believed in getting things right first time.

Kay looked at him, surprised. Lawrence wasn't given to spontaneous gestures. She wondered how to extricate herself without rousing his suspicions or offending him.

'It's a lovely idea. But I've got to go and supervise the tree decorations at Elmhurst Grange. I had to send over two girls who haven't got much of a clue . . .'

'No, you're right. Don't want to muck that one up.'

Lawrence had been delighted with his wife's ability to sweet talk Lord Elmhurst into thinking he needed a twenty-foot bespoke Christmas tree in his baronial entrance hall. And he knew Kay would oversee it with good taste. She always seemed to know what was right. And with any luck, Lord Elmhurst would be impressed. Lawrence hoped he might get a day's shooting out of it one day. He had a secret desire to hobnob with the local gentry.

Kay came over and ran a teasing finger down the inside of his lapel.

'Maybe tomorrow?'

She dropped a kiss on his cheek and picked up her bag.

'I've got to run, or I'll be late.'

She hurried out to her car. She should just have time to nip to Elmhurst Grange and check that the tree was being dressed to her liking before meeting Mickey. She'd call in again on the way home to approve the final work of art, then do Lawrence his favourite supper. She'd seen a fleeting look of disappointment on his face when she'd turned down his invitation, and for the first time she felt a stab of guilt as she drove off to meet her lover.

In the Young Designer section, Sophie was feeling rising panic. The thought of the dance the next night filled her with a mixture of excitement and dread that made her stomach churn, exacerbated by her present dilemma: what to wear?

This crisis had not been helped by the speed at which Georgina had homed in on a long-sleeved green dress with a net skirt. As soon as her sister had made this choice, Sophie became agonizingly convinced that the green dress was the one item in the entire shop that might have remotely suited her. Now she felt tears of desperation well up in her eyes as she searched frantically through the racks. Her hand was hovering over the hanger of a long, crinkly black skirt and top with beading round the neck. It would certainly hide a multitude of sins. She was just holding it up to herself to check the length when a very definite voice sounded in her ear.

'Not unless you want people to think you're telling fortunes. You'll look like a pregnant gypsy. Besides, ethnic is so out.'

It was Mandy, holding a carrier bag that indicated she'd also made her choice. Sophie burst into tears.

'I'm too fat for anything else!'

'Rubbish. You've got a fantastic figure.'

Sophie stopped in mid howl, astonished. She'd always felt so self-conscious next to Mandy, who was as stream-lined as a greyhound.

'Me? What about you – you can wear anything you want.'

Mandy shook her head. 'I'm as flat as a pancake, I've got knobbly knees and arms like coat-hangers. Whereas you—'

'I'm a big fat lump.'

'You've got curves! You go in and out in all the right places. You should make the most of it, instead of trying to hide behind those baggy clothes all the time.'

This was true. Sophie felt envious of all her friends, who strutted round in the dinkiest, tightest outfits possible, while she hid behind capacious sweatshirts. She just wasn't a crop top sort of a person. But here was Mandy, who could get away with something cunningly fashioned out of a man's handkerchief, telling her otherwise.

'If you've got it, flaunt it. OK, so maybe hot pants and a halter neck aren't quite the thing, but if you got a really glamorous outfit, a Hollywood starlet dress . . . No one goes for the half-starved look any more.' Mandy darted off and started ransacking the rails. Sophie followed, unsure, as the feverish search ensued. Floor-length, thigh-length, knee-length, mid calf, silk, Lycra, sequins, chiffon, sleeveless, backless, strapless: all were rejected before Mandy finally came to rest in front of a red velvet creation with a boned bodice. Sophie looked horrified. It would cling to all her lumps and bumps.

'Not with the right undies,' Mandy assured her. She held the dress up against Sophie and nodded in satisfaction. 'Pull-you-in knickers and a push-you-up bra. And we'll get some fake tan.' Sophie gulped, and felt a surge of excitement. Mandy grinned.

'Let me make you over. It'll be cool. You won't recognize yourself.'

Sophie looked at the dress again, wanting to feel as sure

as Mandy. Just as she felt nearly convinced, she flipped over the price tag and her heart sank. It was more than double what her father had given her.

'I can't afford it,' she said flatly.

Mandy tossed the dress over her arm and marched to the nearest cash desk. 'I'll pay for it. As a thank you for having me. You'll need your dad's money for accessories. And make-up.' She peered at Sophie. 'Have you got any make-up?'

'I've got some mascara. And some spot cover.'

Mandy passed her credit card over to the sales assistant and turned decisively back to Sophie.

'Make-up first. Then accessories. Then lingerie.'

Mickey had remembered that this particular shop didn't bother to check on your credit card limit if you spent under a certain amount, and so came out of lingerie with a pair of cream satin pyjamas for Lucy. To have bought anything more suggestive would have been crass and, moreover, suspicious. Besides, Lucy wasn't an expensive underwear sort of person. She looked utterly sexy in whatever she wore, whether it was her own Marks & Sparks briefs, Sophie's old gym knickers or, when she was behind with the washing, Patrick's beloved Calvin Klein boxer shorts. It wasn't that she didn't like clothes, but she reasoned that if it didn't show it didn't matter, and would rather spend the money on vet bills or shoeing the horses.

Satin pyjamas were indulgent but sufficiently utilitarian to please her. On Sundays, the one day that she didn't get up at dawn to exercise one or another horse (a couple of girls from the village were more than happy to do it), Lucy loved pottering about for hours without getting dressed, especially after one of their infamous parties. They always had chilli con carne and lemon meringue pie followed by dancing on the flagstones in the huge entrance hall, where it didn't matter if the gallons of red wine being drunk got spilled. Lucy had an admirable quality that eluded many women: she was able to leave the clearing-up for a time when she felt equipped to cope with it. No two a.m. skirmishes with the Marigolds, no manic dawn raid with half a gallon of Fairy Liquid and a J-cloth. She was quite happy leaving the detritus festering in the kitchen while she sat curled up in the window seat rehydrating with orange juice and watching snowdrops or daffodils or honeysuckle, depending on the season, nod in the breeze. And Mickey thought cream satin pyjamas would be just the thing to do that in.

Not for the first time, and not for the last, he asked himself why it was he was treating Lucy so appallingly. Not that she knew. Or, if she did, she hid it beautifully, adding yet another qualification to her status as the perfect wife. Why the hell was he jeopardizing their marriage? Any man would jump at the chance of a lifetime with Lucy. She was pretty, sexy, funny, good-natured, self-motivated, a brilliant mother, could whip up a feast for fourteen at short notice without complaining and didn't whine if something needed fixing – she either fixed it herself, got someone in to do it or put up with it. Even the aspects of her personality that could, at a stretch, be considered faults were the quirks and eccentricities that made her human. She was untidy, but never sluttish, and her untidiness merely added to the chaotic charm she left in her wake. She was scatty, forgetful and often late, working on a different set of priorities to most people, but she never forgot anything really important. And she was hopeless with money. Not extravagant, but just completely unaware of how much things cost and how much she'd spent. Mickey was grateful for this particular failing. Whilst he was only too aware of the state of their bank balance, he could be sure Lucy would be in blissful ignorance. And just to make sure, their statements always went to the brewery. Shit – he'd better make sure they were well hidden. Patrick was definitely suspicious. What of, he couldn't be sure, but he'd better not leave any evidence lying around.

Mickey sighed. He was guilty of too much. And he was tired: tired of trying to hide all the time and tired of trying to justify his actions to himself.

His favourite platitude – used by men to excuse themselves and by women to console themselves – was that what he was doing with his dick had nothing to do with what he felt in his heart or in his head. He loved Lucy, undividedly and unashamedly. And he certainly didn't love Kay – sometimes he thought he didn't even like her. But when she lay there, the insides of her thighs milky white, parted like her crimson lips, desperate in her need for him—

Perhaps that was it. Perhaps that was why he felt driven to behave this way: he needed to be needed. For Lucy, adored, respected and protected by everyone around her, didn't really need him . . .

At once, Mickey felt cheered that he might have found himself an excuse. He cemented it by remembering the two previous times he'd been unfaithful to Lucy. When she'd fallen pregnant with Sophie, she'd been so dreadfully ill, not just for the first three months but all the way through, violently retching if she'd taken so much as a sip of water or eaten so much as a crumb. Eventually she'd been hospitalized and put on a drip. Mickey had been frantic, had hardly left her side, convinced that this skeletal figure with its obscenely swollen belly could not survive. The doctor, misjudging his concern, constantly reassured him that the baby was not suffering, that it was living off Lucy's reserves, but Mickey didn't care about the baby. He spent hours at her bedside, holding her hand: her bones showed through as white and brittle as spillikins. Horrified by what he had done to her, and charged by her need for his constant reassurance, all thoughts of sexual activity had left him.

When Sophie had finally been born he had been amazed that such a bonny creature could emerge from Lucy's etiolated frame. He'd been staggered, too, that Lucy could take so lovingly and warmly to the parasite that had caused her such suffering. She'd even insisted on feeding the baby herself. Mickey had tried to put his foot down, but as Lucy pointed out, now she was no longer pregnant she could keep food down, was putting on weight already, and she wanted to give her baby the best start in life. So intense was the bond between mother and baby that Mickey had suddenly felt an outsider. They didn't need him; he'd done his bit.

A few weeks later, he'd bumped into a nurse from the hospital – he remembered her bringing him cups of coffee and packets of biscuits throughout his bedside vigil. Now he was no longer preoccupied, he realized how pretty she was. The consequences were sadly predictable.

When Lucy fell pregnant with Georgina less than a year later, they'd had one of their very few rows. Mickey had been aghast at the thought of Lucy being pregnant again – there was no real need; they had Patrick and Sophie. But Lucy had insisted that no two pregnancies were the same, and it wouldn't be like before.

It was the same; possibly even worse. Mickey had been all things to all people throughout the nine months: mother, father, husband, cook, nursemaid, nanny and housekeeper. Never before had so many been so dependent on him. But once Georgina was born, it was all over. He felt dismissed. When Patrick had politely refused the offer of a bedtime story from Mickey – Lucy did the voices so much better – he had slunk off to the Honeycote Arms and found solace in whisky and the barmaid.

Eventually, of course, he'd come to his senses, and he and Lucy settled into family life. For the next ten or so years they'd lived in contented happiness, bringing up the three children in Lucy's special brand of organized chaos. Until Georgina's formidable talents on the lacrosse pitch and netball court had awarded her a scholarship to Redfields. It seemed only fair that Sophie should go too, and Mickey was relieved to have found them both a place at a decent day school – he shuddered to think of boarding fees.

Nowadays, though, with prep and after-school activities, the girls were rarely home before seven and had to go to school on Saturday mornings, which meant the house was quiet most of the week. And with Patrick hardly a child and seemingly nocturnal, and Lucy totally absorbed in her horses, Mickey felt somewhat superfluous to requirements. It was no wonder he'd found himself at a dangerously loose end.

Chuffed with himself for pinpointing the explanation,

Mickey made his way out of the store into the streets of Cheltenham and mulled over the implications. His pleasure was short-lived. By the time he had found the pizza parlour, he was in the depths of despair. It was no good. It wasn't Lucy's perfection that made him behave like a total shit and take up with someone like Kay, who was probably the world's worst wife, would undoubtedly be the world's worst mother if she ever made the sacrifice to become one and was certainly in the running as the world's worst mistress, with her constant demands for flattery, attention and, very tiringly, sex. Sadly, he had to conclude that much as he might try to twist Lucy's blameless existence into some Freudian explanation for his shocking behaviour, it was basically down to his own spineless, weak-willed, lily-livered (and he certainly would be lily-livered if he carried on drinking the way he was) and utterly unforgivable selfishness. Excusing himself on the grounds that he had to feel needed was monstrously egotistical: no jury would sympathize with that defence. He was as guilty as sin.

Mickey was tired of all the thoughts whirling round his head and the tarnished images of himself that his mind tauntingly conjured up. There was only one way to stop his conscience pricking. He ordered a carafe of house red. If it was real gut-rot, perhaps he might not drink too much of it.

Wishful thinking. By the time the girls arrived, in a flurry of carrier bags, he'd ordered another half-carafe, making sure the waitress took away the empty one. At least a half looked better. He wasn't sure how aware teenage girls were of parental drinking habits, but he preferred them to think he'd only just started.

'Successful shopping?'

'Brilliant.'

'What did you get, Dad?'

Before he could stop her, Georgina was inside the bag.

'Wowee, sexy. Satin jimjams.' She held them up against her. 'Who for?'

'Your mother, of course.' Did he sound defensive? 'And don't go poking around in shopping bags just before Christmas.'

Not that he could afford to buy them anything else. The dresses would have to be their main present. He'd run that one past them later. In the meantime, he had a more pressing problem. Kay. She'd be furious he hadn't gone to meet her. Perhaps he could give her the pyjamas as a peace-offering? No. A gift would only be misconstrued as an admission of guilt and Mickey needed all the weapons he could get at this stage of the game.

Game? Could it really be called that? Games were fun, harmless, inconsequential, forgettable. He supposed that was how it had started . . .

From an early age, Kay had known that the one thing she wanted out of life was a wealthy husband. She was unashamedly materialistic and saw nothing wrong with wanting nice things. Of course, the message being preached these days was that a girl could get whatever she wanted for herself. And Kay was bright: her careers adviser was pushing her towards university. Yet she had not a shred of personal ambition in her body. She'd read about fifteen-hour working days, seven-day working weeks, office politics, sexual harassment – all the things that successful women seemed to suffer in order to get on.

But Kay couldn't see the point of slogging your guts out to get what you wanted when you could marry and have it on a plate in return for having supper on the table. Surely that was one of the benefits of being a female? Why did the magazines waste ink persuading you otherwise?

Initially, however, she would have to work whether she liked it or not. She needed money and contacts to put her plan into action, as a suitable husband was unlikely to find himself wandering up the dull, tree-lined street on the outskirts of Slough where she lived with her parents. Her father had his own business, successful enough to have moved his family from the flat over the shop into a nice three-bedroomed semi, and he was proud of his pretty daughter, even her over-sharp tongue, which he put down to her cleverness. Kay had always had him wrapped around her finger, and at sixteen she wangled fees out of him for a smart London secretarial college and left school, ignoring her teachers' wails of protest. Her mother once dared to point out mildly that they did office skills at the local tech; Kay didn't think that even merited a response.

She got up at half past five every morning to get a complicated timetable of buses into Kensington. By careful observation of the other students, she had soon assumed an utterly convincing county mantle. She pushed her shoulder-length blonde hair back into an Alice band, bought the best imitation pearls she could find and trawled charity shops for navy cashmere. When all twinges of Slough had been eradicated from her accent, the transformation was complete. By studious application, she also emerged with breathtaking shorthand and typing speeds and so it was not surprising when she very quickly landed herself a job as a receptionist at an upmarket estate agent in Windsor.

Her skill at assessing clients' needs was soon apparent, and before six months were up she was made a junior negotiator. Kay was delighted – not to find herself up a rung on the career ladder, but because there could be no better way to trap a wealthy husband than to show him around desirable residences, of which they had many on their books.

Now she had a salary, albeit a fairly basic one, Kay was able to embellish her image as the potentially perfect wife. Aided and abetted by the several pounds of glossy magazines that landed on her doormat each month, she assessed the right amount of highlights (just enough blonde to look natural, rigorously maintained every four weeks to avoid any hint of root), learned the power of artfully combining a few basic designer items with classic M&S and signed up for lessons in cookery, riding and driving, at which she was diabolical, fearless and lethal respectively. After passing her test first time, she bought herself a little convertible Golf GTI. She would have preferred a BMW, but the Golf provided maximum effect for minimum expenditure. It was classic and classy, and – if the James Bond movies were to be believed – there was no greater turn-on for a man than a leather-gloved blonde expertly handling a sports car. She perfected turning up at appointments just in the nick of time, screeching to a halt and sending fountains of gravel flying, then coolly emerging, one hand outstretched, the other clutching her second most expensive investment, a Mulberry briefcase.

She had several false starts in the great husband hunt. One already married candidate strung her along for nearly a year, assuring her divorce was imminent, until she laid down an ultimatum, upon which he promptly disappeared. Another time she came dangerously close, having even been for a wedding dress fitting in Beauchamp Place, when she discovered her intended was verging on bankruptcy and was marrying her in the misguided hope she'd get him out of it. Kay emerged unscathed, unmarried and secretly delighted that her disguise as a well-bred young county gel with a rich daddy was so convincing. Yet another turned out to be nastily violent when drunk and the risk of a fractured jaw or a broken nose soon outweighed the lure of the drunkard's bank balance.

At thirty, horror of horrors, Kay had found herself a senior negotiator with her own secretary. She had a naturally shrewd and businesslike mind which made her drive a ruthless bargain, resulting in a sheaf of successful sales as the property market began to recover once again. Thus she found herself in the very position she had always eschewed: successful career girl – no, woman – whose working life threatened to take over, with no hint of a husband in sight.

Then one day a curt male voice on the telephone demanded to be shown round a particular Thameside property immediately. Intrigued by his assertiveness – Kay admired people who knew how to get their own way – she agreed to meet him in ten minutes. The house was one she coveted herself: newly built on an old site, it was equipped with every modern luxury but retained the charms of a mature garden, an old boathouse and magnificent terraces leading down to the river, where she could fondly imagine herself entertaining.

As she drove in through the electronically operated

gates, and saw Lawrence Oakley standing proprietorially by the balustrades of the patio, looking across the gardens to the Thames glinting in the distance, she knew instinctively that this was her man, that he was neither married, bankrupt, drunken or violent, and that he would be unable to resist her charms. Once she'd decided to unleash them. His premier impression was to be that of a successful businesswoman. If she was to marry and be kept by him, it was important that he should always know what she was capable of; that she was perfectly able to look after herself; that she wasn't some brainless Home Counties airhead.

She shook him coolly by the hand, then led him round the property in a matter-of-fact manner, no gushing hyperbole, no unctuous grovelling, as she knew this was a man who could make up his own mind. When, at the end of the tour, Lawrence offered fifty grand less than the asking price, cash, yes or no by this time tomorrow, Kay gulped inwardly, knowing the vendors would jump at the offer, then smiled and said asking price or nothing and he could contact her at the office if he wanted to up his offer.

Later that afternoon, against his better judgement but intrigued, Lawrence went in and upped his offer by thirty thousand. Split the difference, said Kay, and you can have the keys next week.

Lawrence took her out for a drink to celebrate the deal and offered her a job on the spot. She took it.

He was a builder, or property developer, as he preferred to be called, and she was to negotiate the sales of twenty-five executive homes in a labyrinth of cul-de-sacs. In six weeks, she'd sold eighteen of them and had a pretty good idea of the sort of profit that was sitting in Lawrence's pocket. A lot. She'd also ascertained, via snippets of gossip from his secretary, that he had a selection of pretty, inter-changeable girlfriends whom he took to social functions and otherwise ignored. Things were boding well.

Lawrence wasn't altogether attractive. Kay guessed he was thirty-five, but he looked forty. He had tight red-dishblond curls that were starting to thin, a pale, freckled complexion that flushed suddenly red when he was ex-erted, exalted or angry. He was short but with stick-thin legs and narrow shoulders that no amount of expensive tailoring could make imposing. Yet what he lacked in looks and stature he made up for in force of personality. Lawrence was driven and driving, motivated and moti-vating, energetic and energizing. One meeting with him and even the strong-minded Kay found herself wanting to sell the world on his behalf, despite knowing her cut would be minimal, for he had the knack of making people want to do things for him. It wasn't charm, for he was singularly lacking in that. But he could paint a picture of an irresistible future that one instinctively wanted to be a part of.

When Kay sold the very last house, he took her out to dinner. Until now, she'd kept him very much at arm's length. She knew he was impressed by her businesslike demeanour, her cool professionalism, but she'd performed as something of an automaton, never giving him a glimpse of the woman underneath the designer suits she could now afford to wear. But after three months of intensive research, Kay was entirely satisfied that he was the man for her. It was time for the armour to come off.

She chose her outfit carefully, for he was to witness a

theatrical unveiling, and her costume would be instrumental to the effect. Over the softest, satin underwear and sheer stockings, she drew a black silk-jersey dress. From the front, it looked perfectly demure: straight-sleeved, slash-necked, it clung softly to just above the knee. But the back was breathtaking, plunging in a spectacular V to the base of her spine, from where a row of tiny covered buttons marched in a straight line down to the hem. It was a dress few people could wear, as only the smallest, tautest, pertest buttocks could do it justice, but Kay knew, from rigorous dieting, that there was not an ounce of spare flesh on her. Over it, to divert suspicion and just in case she bottled out, she wore a black velvet jacket. Her only concession to colour was a shocking pink chiffon scarf wound carelessly round her neck.

Lawrence had chosen a popular waterside restaurant on the Thames, and though it was only early May it was warm enough for them to drink champagne on the terrace. Kay kept her jacket on, suddenly and uncharacteristically nervous, while Lawrence ordered dinner from the waiter without referring to her once. That didn't bother her; she trusted Lawrence's choice. His money would have taught him what were the finer things in life. She didn't mind that either. After all, she'd had to learn herself.

The meal was perfect. They had fresh, young spears of asparagus, the first of the season, which Lawrence wolfed, eating all the accompanying brown bread, and Kay savoured appreciatively. Then pretty pink noisettes of lamb with tiny new potatoes, after which Lawrence pushed aside his plate, filled up both their glasses and professed he wanted to talk business. The waiter whisked away their plates and anxiously proffered a dessert menu beautifully handwritten on cream parchment. Lawrence waved it away.

'Raspberries and cream for the lady. And two glasses of Beaumes de Venise. And we'll have coffee by the fire.' He turned to look at Kay. 'I've got a proposition for you.'

Kay raised an eyebrow playfully and smiled, raising her glass to her lips. It was a tauntingly suggestive move, and she could see it had taken Lawrence slightly by surprise. He outlined his proposal nevertheless.

'I've got five other projects on the go. Two holiday complexes, a school I've converted into flats, a small shopping arcade and an estate of luxury starter homes. They're all due for completion over the next year. I've got sales negotiators lined up for each of them, of course. But they're scattered all over the country and, frankly, I want to spend my time moving on to future projects, not messing about dotting i's and crossing t's. I need someone to oversee all the sales, make sure prices and targets are being met . . .'

He trailed off and looked at Kay, who nodded her interest and took another sip of wine.

'You would be my eyes and ears. I'd still be making the decisions – you're not experienced enough to take full responsibility. But you've definitely got what it takes to frighten the underlings into proving themselves. That's what I haven't got time to do.'

Kay's raspberries arrived and she spooned them up singly and carefully, listening politely to Lawrence. The sweet, sticky Muscat oozed down her throat and gave her the courage for what she was about to do. When she'd finished, Lawrence guided her into the hotel lounge, where she sank into a glorious tapestry-covered sofa by the warmth of a roaring fire. The heat allowed her to slip out of her jacket, and she leaned back on to the velvet cushions, the inky-black silk of her dress slithering and draping itself to great effect over her limbs. She toyed carelessly with the ends of her scarf, winding them round her fingers, allowing herself to seem sensuously preoccupied.

She saw Lawrence's eyes flicker over her, and again the surprise registered in his eyes. His voice thickened slightly, whether from the drink or desire she could not tell, but he placed his arm very casually along the back of the sofa. He met her gaze and smiled a wolfish grin.

'You're being very quiet. I know what you want to know. How much?' He leaned in towards her. 'You tell me. And I'll throw in a BMW.' He waved a finger. 'But remember. Don't show yourself up by being greedy. You tell me what you think's fair.'

Kay paused. This was the moment she needed maximum effect. She leaned forward to the low, carved oak coffee table and poured a little splash of cream into her coffee, allowing Lawrence the sight of her smooth golden back. She stirred the spoon round twice in her coffee, then sank back into the cushions and smiled across at him.

'I'm not interested.'

Lawrence had barely recovered from what was one of the most erotic sights he'd seen in his life and he thought he'd misheard.

'What?'

Kay said it again and Lawrence felt the blood rush to his face. He was floored, unusually for him, and he hoped she wasn't going to try to make a fool of him.

'Look, there's no point in playing hard to get. I've said name your price; there's plenty of others I could call—'

'I'm not interested. I'm getting married.'

69

Lawrence was puzzled. He couldn't remember seeing Kay with a man, or mentioning one, or any gossip from the rest of the staff. He smiled. 'Congratulations. Anyone I know?'

Her green eyes glittered in the firelight as she leaned towards him and whispered one word in his ear: 'You.'

Thus Lawrence found himself outmanoeuvred for the first time in his life. On this occasion, however, he didn't mind. He understood the terms of the deal perfectly. And he regained the upper hand by taking Kay to bed that very evening, where she had been pleasingly ingenious with the silk scarf she had been wearing.

Then he spent five minutes – as much thought as he ever gave to anything – debating the wisdom of what he was about to do. He knew it was time to get married and he wanted an equal, albeit one he could control. And he wanted someone who would take an interest in his next project – his most ambitious yet. Kay met all the criteria. Not only that, he felt sure her genes would dominate and she would give him beautiful children. There was no point to any of it if he had no one to hand it on to, and time was marching on. He fell asleep with his mind made up.

Next morning Kay came into the office to find someone else at her desk. The secretary handed her a Mulberry document wallet that exactly matched her briefcase. Inside, also matching, were a chequebook cover filled with temporary cheques and a keyring that held, presumably, the keys to Lawrence's house: the one she'd sold him less than a year before. There was also a neatly typed list. This outlined the date of their wedding, the church, the reception, the menu, the wine list, the guest list, the top table seating plan and the honeymoon destination. Kay could see to the minor details. Hymns, flowers, bridesmaids. The things that didn't interest Lawrence. Kay knew he was making it clear that by marrying him she would have to play by his rules. It struck her as an excellent arrangement.

And so their partnership began. It wasn't long before Lawrence embarked upon his master plan. He'd bought the crumbling Barton Court estate, on the outskirts of the village of Honeycote, some years before, paying only a quarter of a million cash because nobody in their right minds could afford to take on such a white elephant in the depths of a recession. Everyone thought he was mad, but Lawrence was happy to bide his time. A firm believer in what goes down must go up again, he could afford to sit on it until inspiration struck. And in the meantime, he watched. The locals laid bets amongst themselves as to what he would do with it. The smart money was on yet another country house hotel with golf course and helicopter launch pad for the enjoyment of wealthy Americans and Japanese. What eventually emerged, however, was beyond anybody's wildest dreams – except Lawrence's. For he had an unnerving instinct that verged on the clairvoyant, and before long he'd concluded that when times were hard people stayed at home. In the garden. And if they were to spend so much time there, they wouldn't mind spending a little bit of money making it look nice. And by the tail-end of the nineties, he'd spotted a trend emerging – a rash of gardening programmes and green-fingered celebrities – which gave him a vision.

The vision was of a gardening theme park: a commercial venture on such a scale that visitors would make day trips from as far afield as Oxford and Birmingham to indulge their horticultural fantasies. Lawrence did not have innate good taste or the ability to transform things, but he knew when a thing needed doing properly and how to get people to do it. Plundering the ranks of local National Trust properties, he poached a bright young girl to mastermind the research and development, and a head gardener to oversee the landscaping.

First the old greenhouses were repaired, acres of glittering glass winking in the sunlight, and rows and rows of seedlings were pricked out to flourish in the atmospherically controlled environment. Lawrence had made sure that, while the buildings retained their Victorian splendour, they were fitted out with the most technologically advanced propagation equipment available. Then the ancient walled garden was restored to its former glory, many of the original plants having survived and the layout still faintly discernible underneath the prolific growth.

Lawrence had never been a man of the earth, but he found himself strangely excited as his project took shape. The mellow, faded brick of the old buildings, the soft, verdant glory of the surrounding landscape and the flourishing of the long-neglected floribunda all provided a seductive patina that disguised what was to be a clock-work marketing machine. This was the way to do business. Lawrence smiled as he looked ahead to a future of discreet pickpocketing: people were lulled into a false sense of security as they enjoyed the aesthetic tranquillity of their surroundings, then found themselves spending money in the subconscious hope of recreating it at home.

It would not just be a question of popping out for a packet of seeds: at Barton Court, every style of garden was laid out in resplendent perfection and every magical ingredient was available for purchase. As well as the more traditional cottage and herbaceous layouts, there was a stark Japanese arrangement, with decorative pebbles and bonsai; the Monet lily garden, where you could even buy your own Giverny bridge to take home; parterre herb gardens (these proved very popular, being simple but effective and easily maintained – Lawrence was particularly pleased because the mark-up on herbs was massive); a children's garden, complete with Wendy house and wishing-well. There was a half-acre plot of the most exotic garden statuary, where anything from a tiny terracotta vole to a life-sized unicorn (the horn could be gilded at extra cost) could be purchased to enhance your creation. And if you didn't want anything for the garden, there were plenty of alternatives: a Country Pursuits section, for decoy ducks and personalized wellies, a bookshop, a deli, a florist's . . . There were two places to eat: a tearoom in the elegant Orangery, where apple-cheeked ladies in mob caps served up shortbread and Darjeeling; and the self-explanatory Stables Restaurant, which served delicious meals, the recipes of which were, of course, available in the *Barton Court Recipe Book*. The restaurant was always full to bursting at Sunday lunch as entire families descended on Barton Court for the day. Parents could browse safe in the knowledge that their children were being looked after by two harassed nannies in Mr McGregor's Potting Shed, which had its own little shop full of sweets and rubbers and pencils and models, for Lawrence was keenly aware that most children these days had a disposable income as soon as they could speak.

The highlight of the operation had been the draining and re-landscaping of the ornamental lake with its magnificent fountain. This had as its focus a statue of Flora, goddess of spring, a graceful figure holding aloft a cornucopia filled with flowers. Lawrence was entranced by her exquisite detail and adopted her likeness as the garden centre's logo.

The day Barton Court opened to the public, Lawrence held a ceremony to celebrate the first playing of the fountains for more than seventy years. It was his personal celebration; a present to himself. As thousands of gallons of water roared through the underground pipe system, he felt the surge of triumph running through his veins. Water exploded into the air, millions of droplets cascading over Flora's youthful curves, and Lawrence smiled. He'd had the power to recreate this spectacle. He'd timed the opening to perfection: the whole nation was gardening-mad. People who didn't know one end of a trowel from the other were suddenly keen to get their hands dirty. He doubted whether any other man in England could have pulled it off. And judging by the roar and applause of the crowd that had gathered to watch, Barton Court was a guaranteed success. Lawrence looked forward to profiting from his prescience.

There was a mixed reaction locally. The garden centre certainly provided a lot of employment, right down to the gangs of young boys with walkie-talkies who organized the parking with military precision. And no one could deny that, despite the overt commercialism of the venture, the house and grounds had been sympathetically restored and landscaped. The entire operation was screened from the road by battalions of ancient oaks, so it could not be damned as a blot on the landscape. An elaborate system of entrance and exit routes to the north, south and east ensured that surrounding traffic was only a headache at the absolute height of the season.

So Lawrence and Kay took their thrones as king and queen at Barton Court. Yet it was not an entirely happy alliance . . .

Sex for Kay turned out to be as much of a chore as loading the dishwasher or sorting the socks, but with an added inconvenience: it was one task she couldn't really offload on to any of the staff. And, unfortunately, Lawrence had a pretty insatiable libido. She didn't really want to offend him, or alienate him, and she knew that he was quite likely to pass her over for a more enthusiastic model if she didn't hack it in the bedroom stakes, so she'd learned very quickly to do what he liked and pretend to enjoy it. Kay had always assumed she was frigid, and accepted it on the basis that sexual and financial gratification didn't go hand in hand. After all, she had always had an ulterior motive in all her relationships up to and including Lawrence. They were all premeditated, not launched into on account of some mutual chemical attraction, and Kay had learned how to go through the motions for her own ends.

So meeting Mickey Liddiard at a dinner party and feeling uncontrollable desire had been a revelation to Kay. Sex for its own sake. The novelty of that was a turn-on in itself. It wasn't hard to contrive a meeting; he'd been easy to seduce. And quickly she became an addict, experimenting with different highs and not caring how she got it.

The ensuing affair had initially been thrilling and torrid.

Up until now, anyway.

Kay had been feeling an increasing sense of detachment from Mickey lately. She was pretty certain there was no competition on the horizon, but he definitely had his mind on other things.

Sitting there now, in the car park of their usual rendezvous, nails tapping impatiently on her leather steering wheel, she realized things were coming to a head. He wasn't going to turn up. It was twenty minutes past their agreed meeting time. She switched on the engine and roared out of the car park. Kay didn't hang around for anyone.

Mickey gestured discreetly to the waitress to bring him another glass of red as she came to take their food order. He suppressed the nagging voice that told him by now he was well over the limit: the pizza should soak most of it up. But as he sat there contemplating his predicament, surrounded by his two trusting and beautiful daughters and their friend comparing lip-gloss shades on the backs of their hands, Mickey caught sight of his drink-flushed reflection in a mirror and shuddered. He was drowning in a morass of self-gratification, and yet again concluded he only had himself to blame.

Mandy got up to go to the loo. Sophie was showing him a peep of her dress.

'You've got to wait till I've been made over before you see it properly. But it's ace.'

As she tucked it back into the bag, Mickey caught sight of the price tag and frowned. He was sure he'd only given her fifty quid. Sophie reassured him.

'It's OK. Mandy paid for it. Her dad's totally loaded. And Patrick told us not to pester you for money. I know it's a bit tough at the brewery.'

Her sympathy could not have made Mickey feel

more humiliated. Just as he had during his meeting with Cowley, he felt bile rise in his throat. He hoped it wasn't his bloody liver packing in already. He'd got a lot to do, and dying wasn't going to help. Mickey drained his glass as he ran through his resolutions.

Step One. Give Kay the boot. Tricky.

Step Two. Get the brewery back on its feet. Trickier.

Step Three. Give up the booze. Trickiest. And he couldn't possibly do it until he'd resolved Steps One and Two.

But he was going to do it. He didn't owe it to himself, worthless scumbag that he was. But he owed it to Lucy. And Patrick. And Sophie and Georgina.

4

James Liddiard had struggled to open his eyes that morning, and when he did he was presented with a pair of creamy freckled breasts. He knew there was little point in resisting because it was deadline day at the paper, and his girlfriend Caroline needed the adrenalin of sex so she could, as she put it, go and kick ass in the classified ad section that she ran. So he dragged himself out of his stupor and joined in with as much enthusiasm as he could muster at that hour in the morning.

Afterwards, he lay with the morning sun dappled across his face and watched Caroline get dressed as if she was going into battle. She had a selection of power suits with nipped-in waists that accentuated her femininity. Her wild red curls were scraped back into a severe plait and the disguise was finished off with a pair of Dolce e Gabbana heavy-framed glasses. Formidable.

They'd met just over a year ago, when he'd just refurbished the art gallery he ran in Eldenbury and had gone to place a discreet advertisement announcing the relaunch. Within minutes, she'd sweet-talked him into an advertisement feature. It was very hard to say no to Caroline and he'd ended up with a double-page spread and the night of his life.

They'd been an item ever since, to the astonishment of their mutual friends. He was the archetypal English gentleman, *Brideshead Revisited*, an aesthete. She was feisty, ballsy, upfront. They had little in common but their need for space. James thought of the girl he'd given the boot eighteen months ago. A pretty enough little thing, blonde and well bred; on the surface she was far more his cup of tea. But she'd been hideously clingy, always looking for reassurance and dragging him past jewellers' windows. And she'd run his diary like a sergeant major, had tantrums if he didn't feel inclined to turn up to some social function or another that she thought they should be seen at. James had heaved a sigh of relief when she'd finally got the hint. Caroline never gave a toss if he expressed reluctance to go anywhere, and for that he was grateful.

She stood before him now, at the end of the bed, ready for action.

'Tea?'

'I'll do it.'

He swung his legs out of bed. He wanted proper tea, made with loose leaves in a pot that had been warmed. He didn't want the string of the tea bag still dangling over the edge of his cup, which he knew was what Caroline would give him.

'What are you doing today?'

'VAT returns.' He mimed a yawn. 'And there's a viewing in Tetbury. I might go over there this afternoon.' He wasn't actually lying. Only by omission. Though he wasn't sure why – surely there was nothing incriminating about going for a hack with your own sister-in-law? It was all perfectly above board.

*

79

Later on, VAT returns completed with indecent haste, James's boots rang out on the cobbles of the stable yard at Honeycote House. There was a whicker of anticipation as several curious horses peered over their doors in the vain hope that this unexpected visitor might be bringing them a late-morning snack. An irate whinny indicated the stable he was looking for. He stopped outside for a moment and watched as Lucy placated a huge iron-grey gelding, fondling his ears and nuzzling his neck. Lucky old horse, thought James, as he slid back the bolt. Lucy looked up and smiled with pleasure.

'James – hi.' She caressed the horse proudly. 'What do you think? This is Phoenix. Isn't he beautiful?'

James reached out to pat the brute's muscle-bound shoulder. As he leaned over, he thought he caught a faint trace of Diorissimo through the rich smell of dung dropped by the agitated horse.

'What's the story?'

'He keeps bucking. Dumping his owner. But we're going to sort you out, aren't we, boy?'

Phoenix didn't look sure; just looked at James sideways and put his ears back.

'He seems quite highly strung.'

Lucy wasn't perturbed.

'He just needs someone who's not frightened of him. And I think he's got back problems. I'm going to get the physio out – if he's in pain every time someone sits on him, no wonder he's bucking.'

James smiled. He loved the way Lucy was so confident, so fearless. She'd gained a reputation locally for being something of a miracle-worker with problem horses. You could bring the most unmanageable, ill-tempered animal to her, and within weeks she could turn it into a well-mannered obliging ride that you could, as she put it, sit your granny on. People always told her she could make a fortune from her talent, but she hated charging properly for doing something she loved, and inevitably ended up out of pocket. To her it was enough reward to see a happy horse. But that was Lucy all over, thought James, as he watched her tighten up the buckle on Phoenix's girth.

It was wonderful to see someone who worked with horses for the sheer pleasure of it, not for profit or gain or the need to win. James thought of Caroline, who competed at local events as if her life depended on it, asking a hundred and ten per cent of her horse and never, in James's opinion, giving as much back.

Caroline kept her horse in livery on the outskirts of Evesham, where she lived and worked. It had occurred to James on more than one occasion that it would make sense for her to stable Demelza at Honeycote House. Sophie or Georgina could muck her out for pocket money, and it would mean they could see more of each other at weekends. But the thought of Caroline and Lucy spending more time in close proximity than was necessary deterred him from making this suggestion. It would only complicate things in the long run, he felt sure. God forbid that the two women might actually become friends. They had little else in common, but the horsy bond could be a strong one, he had found over the years. The most unlikely companions could gel given an equestrian interest.

James himself had been somewhat put off riding by his mother. She'd always kept a stableful at Honeycote, had ridden side-saddle with the local hunt for years and had forced both James and his brother Mickey to compete with the local pony club from an early age. She'd been a rabid pot-hunter, bellowing at them from the sidelines. James had loathed it and been terrified; Mickey, of course, had bagged every cup going but didn't give a toss. Thus James had given up riding as soon as he'd gathered enough nerve to stand up to his mother, and hadn't had anything to do with horses for years. But he'd recently taken to hacking out with Lucy when she had an extra horse that needed exercise – which was more often than not – and he found that when the sport wasn't forced upon you, it was quite pleasurable. And he needed the exercise; he was hurtling towards forty, after all. Besides which, it gave him a bona fide reason to spend time with Lucy . . .

Satisfied that Phoenix was safely tacked up, Lucy gave the horse a final pat before opening the stable door and leading him out. James's mount was already tacked and waiting in the adjoining stable.

They set off at a brisk trot down the drive. Phoenix was skittish, prancing sideways and tossing his mane, but Lucy gave him his head and refused to rise to his antagonistic behaviour, so the horse soon settled down and fell into step. Lucy smiled in satisfaction.

'You see? The girl that's been riding him lets him wind her up. I bet she's been pulling his mouth to pieces. He just needs a free rein. Look.'

She held up the horse's reins with her little finger, demonstrating just how little resistance she was showing him. James thought it was interesting that Lucy dealt with animals just as she dealt with humans, using the line of least resistance. By the end of the ride, Phoenix was calm and co-operative.

It was only when they were back at the yard, and the

horses had been untacked, that it became clear something was troubling her. As they were walking back up to the house, she turned to him suddenly and asked:

'Has Mickey mentioned anything to you lately, James?'

He forced himself to hold Lucy's gaze, but he found all the questions in her treacle-brown eyes unnerving. He deliberately misunderstood her query.

'He hasn't mentioned him, no. But you're obviously doing a great job—'

'I'm not talking about the bloody horse!' The uncharacteristic sharpness in her tone made James wince. 'I don't know what's the matter with him these days. I mean, you don't stick brandy in your morning coffee unless there's something seriously wrong, do you?'

Oh God, thought James. What was it that made him such a coward when it came to Lucy? Why couldn't he just come out with it, that he thought – no, knew – that her husband was a drunken, spineless waste of space, and then just take her in his arms, lay her down in the hay and kiss her, tell her it was all going to be all right?

He remembered the first time he'd met her. He and Mickey had had the run of Honeycote House following their parents' death. After Mickey's first wife, Carola, had moved out, James had moved in for a short time. He'd just spent eighteen months in a lowly paid position in a London auction house, where he'd learned everything he needed to know about the antiques and paintings he loved, and he was hoping to set up in business locally. The two of them lived in abandoned bachelordom with a long-suffering 'woman that did' who adored them both, and they soon became the toast of the county – a pair of handsome, well-heeled young bucks whose tastes for wine, women and song were well documented, though it was generally agreed that James was a gentleman while Mickey was an unscrupulous bastard. This didn't necessarily make one more attractive than the other – it depended entirely on your tastes.

One spring afternoon James had been faced with the unpleasant task of having their mother's Jack Russell, Raffles, put down. The little dog had been an integral part of the household for nearly twenty years and somehow his demise signalled the end of an era even more than their parents' death. Mickey had steadfastly refused to have anything to do with Raffles' disposal, as he hated responsibility, so it was left to James to call out the local vet. Richard Soames had done his job discreetly and humanely in the scullery, covering the little dog's body with the tartan blanket that had lined his basket for as long as anyone could remember, while James slugged back Scotch in the kitchen. Lucy had come with her father on his rounds – at eighteen she had just left school, but was undecided as to her future, so her father gave her pocket money to help him out while she made up her mind.

When the deed had been done, Lucy had come into the kitchen while her father washed his hands. A look of concern had crossed her face when she'd seen James's angst. She'd put a timid little hand on his arm and reassured him gently: 'You did the right thing. You couldn't have let him go on suffering.' An arrow had pierced his heart, injecting him with sweet agony as he fell head over heels in love. But he'd thought she was far younger than she was – fifteen or sixteen – so he kept his distance. He cursed himself many a time after, for he'd left the door wide open for his brother, who had no such scruples and besides had bothered to do his homework and discovered that Lucy was older than she looked. Strangely, the horses at Honeycote suddenly seemed to need more veterinary attention than ever before and Richard Soames and his daughter became regular visitors.

And so, one fine summer's evening less than a year later, James had suffered indescribable torture when Mickey carried Lucy, shrieking with laughter, into the Honeycote Arms and announced he was going to marry her. James had wanted to warn her then, take her to one side, tell her she was one of many, that Mickey was sleeping with most of the girls in the county – all the good-looking ones, anyway, and some of the ones that weren't. And tell her the salutary tale of the first Mrs Liddiard, the true story, not the watered-down version that Mickey would have given her, the one that depicted him in a good light.

No one had been surprised when Carola had fled Honeycote House not long after Patrick was born. It was obvious to everyone that Mickey wasn't going to tolerate her, especially when she started whinging about further education, a career and a life of her own. Aghast at the prospect of a *Guardian*-toting and hirsute wife (he'd once revealed to James in a shocked tone that Carola never shaved under her arms), Mickey had given her a quick divorce and a handsome settlement, enough to put a deposit on a small flat and finish the degree she felt had been so unfairly snatched from her. He'd put Carola and the solemn, round-eyed Patrick on the train to Paddington, waved them goodbye and, apart from getting horribly drunk in the pub that night (which was hardly out of the ordinary), seemed unaffected by their departure.

James had been shocked by the callousness of this

behaviour, and although he'd never said anything had felt rather ashamed of his brother. He certainly couldn't bear the thought of Lucy, a fragile little creature perched by the fire where the flames leaped joyfully in the hearth, suffering the same fate when inevitably Mickey tired of her in the course of time. But of course he'd said nothing, just given Lucy a congratulatory kiss on the cheek and accepted Mickey's invitation to be best man. He supposed it was fraternal loyalty: a dull trait that boring old farts like him felt strongly about and shits like Mickey didn't know existed.

And now it was nearly twenty years later, and Lucy hadn't been duped and cuckolded and made a fool of, as he'd feared. Her skill with horses obviously worked on humans, for she seemed to have tamed the incorrigible Mickey, much to the disappointment of legions of women in the county who'd come to look upon him as fair game. Of late, though, James had been suspicious of his brother's behaviour. He knew the signs only too well; knew how susceptible Mickey was to flattery; knew that when he was under pressure he capitulated easily. And he'd seen the way Kay Oakley looked at him.

But he still couldn't bring himself to say anything to Lucy, because deep down he had a terrible fear that if he did she would never forgive him for shattering her illusions, and might even come to despise him for being the bearer of bad tidings. Thus James heard himself adopting a falsely hearty tone, and hated himself for doing it.

'I expect it's business. Everyone's up against it these days. I'm sure trade'll pick up now it's Christmas.'

He smiled reassuringly. Standing there in the gloom of the stable, fiddling with Phoenix's lead rope, Lucy looked ridiculously young, like some refugee from Pony Club camp in her jodhpurs and polo neck, strands of chestnut hair escaping from her plait. James knew she was far from convinced, but she smiled back at him with a slightly helpless shrug.

'Oh well, come and have some lunch.'

In the kitchen, over bacon sandwiches and a bottle of chilled Pinot Grigio, James suddenly felt grateful for his streak of cowardice. He knew he could never live up to his brother. He'd always known that. That was why, from the very beginning, he hadn't wanted anything to do with the brewery. It was Mickey who'd been moulded and groomed to take over from their father. Of course, had James wanted a position, there would have been one, but he'd always shied away from anything that allowed him and Mickey to be compared.

The irony of it was, of course, that James would have made a far better managing director than Mickey. He was shrewd, quietly cunning and had an unerring gut instinct for the right time to do things. Just after Mickey had taken over at the helm, James swapped the majority of his shares in the brewery for the freehold of one of the pubs in Eldenbury high street. It had seemed like a fair swap at the time: the pub was surplus to requirements as most of the brewery's trade was done from the Horse and Groom, and there seemed no point in Honeycote Ales competing with itself at such close proximity. James had converted half the pub into an art gallery, which proved to be a roaring success with the wealthy tourists that flocked to Eldenbury both winter and summer. The other half he'd converted into a house for himself, a painstaking period renovation of a gentleman's residence that doubled as a showroom for the antiques he was also trading in. Soon he'd acquired enough of a reputation to focus on exporting container-loads of antiques to the States, where he had dealers practically queuing up on the docks to wait for his wares. And now he was wealthy enough to be able to please himself and delegate the running of the gallery, so there was nothing really taking up his time.

But despite his success, despite the wealth that he was waiting to share with someone and despite his elegant town house that was decorated with the ultimate in good taste, he suspected Lucy could never really want him. She belonged here, in the chaotic warmth that was special to Honeycote House, and with Mickey: reckless, dissipated, randy but nevertheless sexy and exciting Mickey, who was all the things that safe, reliable, predictable, good old James wasn't.

Later, when Mickey came back with Sophie and Georgina and an extraordinary creature with endless legs and a Birmingham accent, James said his hellos and then his goodbyes. He slipped away quietly and made himself a cup of tea in the solitude of his Smallbone kitchen, which never rang with laughter or tears or arguments or debate. He barely ever ate there. Mrs Titcombe, his cleaning lady, scrubbed his state-of-the-art oven once a month even though it was probably never even turned on, in direct contrast to the Aga at Honeycote, which had years of Sunday roasts encrusted upon it. Perhaps he should start cooking for Caroline? Perhaps he could discover a new passion to patch up the empty hole in his life?

Mickey told him time and time again that what he needed was the love of a good woman, but in James's view Mickey had pinched the only one worth having and he couldn't summon up any strength of feeling for any other. He considered his relationship with Caroline. She was twenty-nine, flame-haired (Mickey said ginger), feisty (Mickey said aggressive) and striking (Mickey said tarty). It was ironic that Mickey was so staunchly anti-Caroline, that he incessantly asked why James bothered with him. James privately thought that Mickey was scared of Caroline, who was pretty assertive and, James was certain, enjoyed torturing Mickey by refusing to flirt with him.

Anyway, he didn't need his brother's approval. It wasn't as if he and Caroline were heading for the altar: if he couldn't have Lucy he didn't want to marry anyone.

James flicked the remains of his tea into the sink and carefully rinsed out his cup, reflecting for the hundred millionth time in his life on what might have been.

Then, as he wiped the cup on the crisp linen tea towel left out by Mrs Titcombe, he allowed himself for one luxurious moment to dwell on what might yet be. Mickey had looked the worst he'd ever seen him and he'd guzzled down the remains of the Pinot Grigio before you could say knife.

Stealing wives might not be part of James's moral code. But rescuing them wasn't out of the question. Even if it meant standing by and watching his own brother hang himself.

It was bloody freezing and Patrick shivered under the battered flying jacket he always wore for driving the Austin Healey in winter. By the time the car had warmed up he was turning into Barton Court and had to slow down to manoeuvre the speed bumps.

He could never be sure why it was he felt so responsible

for his father's behaviour, and felt such a need to rectify his faults. He found it strange that he could both worship and despise Mickey; look up to him and yet at the same time look down. It was almost as if the roles were reversed, with Patrick an indulgent father and Mickey some recidivist toddler whose sins were repeatedly forgiven on account of his charm. Largely, of course, what Mickey got up to was none of Patrick's business and didn't affect him in the least. But his misdemeanours of late were becoming an increasing threat on many counts.

Patrick knew the brewery was in big trouble. He knew, because he couldn't find them, that the bank statements wouldn't hold good tidings. Bitter remarks from the men who worked round the clock about late payment of wages didn't go over his head, nor did worried queries from the tenants. And he felt ashamed that he couldn't meet their eyes and give them reassurance, even though he felt responsible for their welfare, for he had no power and no knowledge. But he was keenly aware that his own father held these people's futures in the palm of his hand.

Confrontation with Mickey was pointless. The phrase 'in denial' could have been coined especially for him. Patrick didn't know what he could do to halt the decline. He could hardly overrule his father, as he was no great businessman himself and only had a couple of years' experience at the brewery. Running to the bank was out of the question, as he couldn't risk drawing Cowley's attention to the situation. For the moment, therefore, Patrick had set himself the task of trying to discover the extent of the damage through espionage, and then perhaps going to James for advice. James had never shown any great interest in how things were run at the brewery, but he was still a shareholder, albeit a minor one. And he was his godfather, so Patrick knew he could trust him, that anything he said would be treated in confidence. Furthermore, James bore the Liddiard name, the name that was in danger of being besmirched. He would help him uphold the family honour.

What Patrick wanted more than anything was re-assurance that there was some way out of this mess that wouldn't bring disgrace on the family. He'd seen too many documentaries about bankruptcy, erstwhile millionaires having to sell their last possessions and falling on the mercy of friends and relatives. When he let his mind wander far enough, he saw himself back on his mother's doorstep, and her mocking smile. She'd love it if Mickey failed. She'd feel it was poetic justice for his greedy, capitalist ways. Not to mention revenge for snatching Patrick away all those years ago, trumping her with his cash when she'd fallen on hard times. Patrick couldn't actually remember the events all that clearly, but he'd been told the story often enough and now it had become legend.

After Patrick and his mother had left Honeycote House, visits to his father had been rare, but one day Mickey had turned up in Ladbroke Grove to take his son back home while Carola went on some hippy-dippy trail of self-discovery. Mickey had been appalled by the flat they were living in, whereas Carola had been proud. It was student accommodation she and her mates had got on the cheap – sub-standard council housing because the bath was in the kitchen. Too fucking right it's sub-standard, Mickey had thundered, and had grabbed the bewildered Patrick.

The drive down the motorway had been terrifying, as Patrick could only ever remember being in a bus, not a car driven at ninety miles an hour. Mickey had got Patrick back to Honeycote that night, and managed to find him some cornflakes, before tucking him into a huge bed piled high with blankets in a room with its own fire. Patrick had gone to sleep warm for the first time in months. He awoke, curious but wary. His father clearly thought the world of him, but didn't have a clue what to do with a small boy.

Mickey had been living alone in the house. After Patrick and Carola had left, James had only stayed at Honeycote for six months before moving to Eldenbury to renovate the pub. He seemed to be continually coated in brick dust and plaster. Mickey, meanwhile, was barely capable of looking after himself, let alone his son. Luckily, the daily help made them porridge for breakfast that first morning, which Patrick and Mickey both wolfed. Then Mickey had taken him to see the horses. He'd put Patrick on his favourite chestnut and the little tot had felt on top of the world. It was a turning point for both of them. Patrick whooped with excitement, letting his feelings show for the first time in front of his father, and Mickey was proud. His son was born for the saddle. From that moment on, he was determined he should be brought up at Honeycote.

He'd phoned James and dragged him away from restoring his cornices to celebrate his decision at the Honeycote Arms. Lucy Soames had come into the pub for a warming bowl of soup after a hard morning helping her father and had found the two of them, rather perplexed, trying to force-feed Patrick steak and kidney pie. Unbeknownst to

James, Mickey had got to know Lucy quite well, having called out her father on several pretexts to look at malingering horses.

'He won't eat it.' Mickey had forgotten that Carola was a vegetarian and that Patrick had probably never been given meat. Lucy had come to his rescue.

'Of course he won't. He probably hasn't even got all his teeth yet. Steak, Mickey, for God's sake.'

'I don't know, do I?'

'Use your common sense.'

She'd taken charge immediately, sending out to the kitchen for mashed potato, then painstakingly mixing it with gravy and feeding it to Patrick with a spoon, not minding the mess in the least. Mickey had offered her a job as live-in 'father's help' on the spot, and thrown in a stable for her horse as a sop. Lucy had accepted the post eagerly.

Thus Patrick found his little world turned upside down, rather for the better, as Lucy took him on long conker-strewn walks and spread acres of paper out on the kitchen table for finger-painting and made him jelly and ginger-bread men and boiled eggs with soldiers. Meanwhile, a rather ugly custody battle began between his parents, but it was no contest – an inner-London slum versus a Cotswold mansion? Carola hadn't helped her cause by throwing a yoga handbook at Mickey in her fury, which had cut him over the eyebrow. Mickey won.

As Patrick settled into Honeycote, he began to pray that things wouldn't change, that his mother wouldn't demand him back and that Lucy wouldn't find a job looking after a nicer little boy somewhere. So when he found his father and Lucy kissing in the hallway one day, he knew his prayers had been answered, and he'd trotted up the aisle five months later in a smart navy overcoat with brass buttons, relieved. Patrick had adored Lucy unreservedly from that day on, and hadn't felt in the least betrayed a few years later when she'd given birth to first Sophie, then Georgina. On the contrary, he felt honour bound to protect all three of them – hence today's mission.

He found Kay arranging a display of handpainted serving plates and bowls on a baker's shelf. He watched for a moment and admired her talent as she created a tableau of rustic living, mixing the tableware with jars of Christmas chutneys and preserves and filling the bowls with surprisingly realistic plastic fruit. As she stood back to admire her own handiwork, Patrick moved forward to stand beside her.

'I'm sure they'll walk off the shelves.'

'I guarantee there won't be any left after the weekend. Do you want me to save one of those bowls for Lucy? I'm sure she'd like one for Christmas.'

'I'm sure what she'd really like is for you to stop screwing her husband.'

Kay remembered what Mickey had told her: deny, deny, deny. She looked Patrick straight in the eye.

'I don't know what you're talking about.'

'Yes you do.'

He held her gaze unremittingly. She broke away. She'd never been good at confrontation.

'Have you told Lucy?'

'Of course not. What would be the point?'

'So you're just warning me?'

'I'm telling you.'

Kay sighed. 'I wouldn't expect you to understand, Patrick. It's very complicated.'

'No, it's not. I mean, you don't love him, do you? You're not going to jack everything in just to be with him. It's just an affair; a bit of self-gratification for the two of you—'

'Don't be so patronizing.'

'At the end of the day, it's just sex. At least, I'm sure it is for Dad.'

Kay took in a deep breath. She wasn't at all sure how to deal with Patrick. Despite his youth, he was surprisingly authoritative, with an underlying menace that she found unsettling. She had to be careful. There was too much at stake to risk him calling her bluff and telling Lucy. Or worse, Lawrence. What she needed was time.

'We can't talk here.'

'I know. Meet me in half an hour at the Fox and Goose.'

'Won't people talk?'

Kay couldn't resist taunting Patrick, even though she knew it might be dangerous. He just smiled.

'Not at all. I want to discuss you supplying hanging baskets and floral arrangements at all our pubs. Bring some quotes.'

With that, he walked off. Kay watched his retreating figure in bemused amazement, not knowing what to think. What perturbed her more than anything as she went to find her car keys was the realization that rather than dreading their confrontation, she was looking forward to it.

The Fox and Goose had what it rather grandly termed 'Private Conference Facilities', which was in fact a charming upstairs room with a sloping wooden floor which could, at a push, seat twenty round a table. People often hired it for eighteenths or twenty-firsts or fortieths or any other occasion when they couldn't face catering for large numbers in their own homes. Patrick had phoned ahead to make sure it was free, and ordered smoked salmon sandwiches and champagne to be sent up for his working lunch with Mrs Oakley. On his arrival he stressed that they shouldn't be disturbed. He took the lunch tray up himself, deposited it on the table, noted approvingly that it had been set very prettily with proper cutlery and glasses and a huge vase of fresh flowers, then set off to check down the corridor. The Fox and Goose also did B&B, and Patrick had flipped through the reservation book while the waitress was finding an ice bucket, ascertaining that three of the four rooms were free. Avoiding room two, he peeped into the others to decide which was the most suitable and settled on number one. It was the largest, with a high, brass bed and its own en suite bathroom. It was unlikely that anyone would go in there, as the chambermaid had seen to every detail, and unless someone arrived unexpectedly to check in within the next hour the coast would be clear.

It wasn't that Patrick was too tight to pay for a room. He'd probably have got it free anyway, one of the perks of the job. But it made it all the more exciting to keep the encounter clandestine. It heightened his mood and gave him a feeling of power.

When Kay arrived, demure with her briefcase, he went through the motions of asking her prices, enjoying her obvious inability to weigh up what was going to happen next. He nailed her down on the supply of hanging baskets and bedding plants for their pubs, with the assurance that she would oversee the job herself, then emptied the last of the champagne bottle.

'Drink up.'

She looked at him over the rim over her glass and drank obediently. As soon as she'd finished, he reached out and took her by the hand, leading her down the crooked corridor that smelled of beeswax, before opening the door of room one and ushering her inside. She crossed her arms.

'You're very presumptuous.'

He put his finger to her lips to silence her.

'Ok. Here's the deal. You stop seeing dad and you can have me instead.'

Kay gasped. She didn't know whether to laugh or slap him.

'Don't be ridiculous.'

'I'm not. I'm assuming you haven't got any real emotional attachment to him, so it's basically just sex. In which case, I can assure you, you'll be better off with me.'

Just over an hour later, Patrick drove away satisfied that his mission had been accomplished. He was quietly confident that nothing his father could do would match his own performance. He had Mayday Perkins to thank for that, the barmaid from the Horse and Groom in Eldenbury. Mayday was wild, famed for driving round Eldenbury one night on the back of someone's motorbike wearing nothing but a pair of fishnets and a safety helmet. When he was sixteen, Mayday had taught Patrick everything she knew about what girls liked, how far you could go and how to surprise them. He'd certainly done that, judging by Kay's response. She was hooked, he was certain. Now he just needed to make sure that she kept her side of the bargain.

Kay lay back on the bed in the Fox and Goose, naked and exhausted. She felt no desire to get dressed and leave, though she supposed she must. Even though Patrick had satisfied her once, twice – maybe three times, she couldn't be sure – she was still on fire. She'd made up her mind about two things. One – she had to have the arrogant little bastard again. And two – she wasn't going to keep her side of the bargain. No way was she going to let Patrick Liddiard dictate his terms to her.

As she crawled off the bed, she couldn't believe how turned on she still felt: as if someone was driving a molten corkscrew of pleasure through her. The boy was something else, that was for sure. She wondered how she had ever got through the first thirty-five years of her life thinking sex didn't matter.

5

It was the afternoon of the dance, and Lucy and the girls were all booked in at the hairdressers in Eldenbury. Sophie and Georgina both needed a trim, and Lucy wanted her hair put up. Mandy thought she might like a hot oil treatment as her ends were feeling quite dry, and although Lucy was doubtful that the Clip Joint would do hot oil treatments, she went along for the ride anyway.

The salon was at the top end of the high street, the rougher end, next to an ironmonger's, which had an extraordinary assortment of inexplicable articles hung outside the door that must have taken an hour each end of the day to assemble and disassemble: metal buckets, washing lines and pegs, bird-feeders, dustbins. Mandy couldn't imagine giving any of the items house room, but something caught Lucy's eye and she dashed inside.

'Rat poison. There are tell-tale signs in the tack room.'

Mandy followed Sophie and Georgina after their mother, and felt as if she'd stepped back fifty years. Inside it was dark and dank, with splintered wooden floorboards and shelves piled treacherously high with mysterious objects. Two men in brown overalls hovered in the shadows, flicking ash carelessly from the ends of their cigarettes with no regard to health or fire hazard. Immediately they saw Lucy one was at her side in attendance, and no sooner had she made her request than he pulled out a stepladder, clambered to the top and triumphantly produced a box with a gaily coloured picture of a rat, teeth bared. The price was handwritten on a green dot sticker; Mandy wouldn't have been surprised if it was in shillings.

'Mind you keep the other animals away, now.' The man wrapped the box up carefully in brown paper. 'One of our customers had a Yorkie ate some of this last month and died.' He Sellotaped the edges down neatly and handed the box to Lucy, grinning. 'Mind you, they look like rats. That's four pounds eighty-nine.'

'Can I put it on account?'

The man got out a large ledger and scratched his head. He shut the book rather hastily and looked at Lucy, slightly worried.

'Do you mind paying cash? Only it's just past the middle of the month – we haven't done out the new account sheets yet.'

'Sure. No problem.' Lucy happily drew out a tenner and the transaction was completed.

Mandy followed the others out, humbled, in a strange way, by this experience. She had no idea that places like this existed. How far more efficient it was than the massive DIY superstores she was used to, which, despite their bar-codes and computerized stock-taking, still never had what you wanted. And how lovely that they let you have an account.

If the ironmonger's was a revelation, the hairdresser's was even more of a shock. The window was half covered by a sagging grimy net curtain and three crooked black and white photos of rather dated bouffant hairdos gave away the trade behind the door. Inside, the decor was pink and grey. The floor was covered in a mottled peeling lino that, thankfully, camouflaged a morning's worth of split ends that had fallen to their fate. The reception desk was formica-topped with a fake pine veneer front and would have looked more in place in a Chinese takeaway. On the wall behind the desk someone had cut out a collage of hairstyles circa 1978 and covered it in stickyback plastic. Three cracked grey vinyl chairs perched in front of plastic shelf units displaying an array of combs, hair-clogged brushes, rollers and hairspray. A lumpen assistant with drooping bosoms, legs like tree trunks and a drunken centre parting was rinsing out a perm at a shrimp-coloured sink, dabbing ineffectually at the client's neck with a towel, grey not to match the colour scheme but because it had once been white.

Mandy thought she'd rather have her head boiled in oil than risk anything in here. Before she could think of an excuse and beat a hasty retreat, however, the proprietor, Wendy, came bustling out from the back room, hurling aside the curtain of multi-coloured plastic strips that screened the kitchenette.

'Sorry, just having a fag. Stressful, this job. You have to listen to everyone's problems.' Wendy grinned, showing a mouthful of nicotine-stained teeth, which coincidentally matched her hair. She wore a faux denim shirt, studded with pearl appliqué and knotted at the waist over snagged black ski pants. Her feet were thrust into ancient flipflops. The paint on her toes matched that on her fingers only because they were both horribly chipped. 'I hope you haven't got any problems?'

'We just want a few miracles worked, that's all. We've got

a party tonight.' Lucy drew Mandy forward, who didn't like to protest. 'Mandy wanted a hot oil treatment—'

'No worries.' Wendy spent all her time between clients watching Australian soaps in the kitchenette. She pulled a fiver out of the drawer and waved it at her assistant. 'Nip over to the chemists, would you, Trish?'

Impressed by the service, Mandy resigned herself to the fact that a conditioning pack with blow-dry couldn't really do her any damage, and she could always wash it again before tonight if the worst came to the worst.

Half an hour later, she realized she'd completely underestimated Wendy's talents. Lucy's hair was coaxed, teased and backcombed into a sophisticated and elegant chignon, with not a pin showing. Sophie's unmanageable waves were tonged and waxed and pinned on top of her head into a riot of tumbling curls that gave her that just-fallen-out-of-bed look. Georgina's girlish bob was snipped into chic precision that sent her into gales of delighted laughter as it added two years to her. And once Mandy's treatment had been rinsed off by the stolid Trish, Wendy painstakingly dried it segment by segment until it hung dead straight and shining like a gleaming mahogany table top.

The real shock came when it was time to pay: it was less than a tenner each. Mandy thought of the salon her mother dragged her to in Solihull, all white marble and potted plants and expensive lighting. The trendy proprietor, with his goatee beard and pierced eyebrow, wouldn't pick up a pair of scissors for less than fifty quid.

The life she'd been leading up till now was clearly just one big rip-off. And if she hadn't been to the Liddiards', she could have gone through the rest of her life thinking you had to pay through the nose to get what you wanted.

*

On the way home, Lucy opened her window to adjust the wing mirror – there was a wire loose; it kept going wonky – and everyone shrieked. They'd all been sitting still as statues.

'Shut the window, Mum!' screeched Georgina.

'Sorry!' Lucy grinned and turned round to look. 'You're all right: not a hair out of place. I've just got to stop for petrol.'

Even the garage was antiquated; OK, it was self-service, but the pumps were ancient and you could hear the numbers clunk as the clock went round.

'Get some chocolate!' shouted Georgina as Lucy went into pay, but she didn't hear.

'I'll go,' offered Mandy, and scrambled out of the car.

Inside, Lucy was waiting by the counter while the cashier flicked through the tray of accounts to find the Liddiard file. She drew it out, then looked a little embarrassed.

'I'm ever so sorry, Mrs Liddiard. You'll have to pay cash . . .'

She held up their account. A yellow Post-It had been stuck firmly and defiantly on the front, and emblazoned in red writing was 'Cash until further notice'. Lucy peered rather puzzled at the note, then smiled reassuringly at the mortified assistant.

'Oh God. Sorry, Linda. Mickey must have forgotten to drop the cheque in. Honestly . . .'

Linda, unconvinced but wanting to be, smiled. She'd doubted Lucy would make a fuss, but somehow that made it worse. Linda hated anything to do with money. Now she was just relieved that this wasn't going to be an issue. Lucy picked up her handbag to find the cash.

'Linda, I'm so sorry – I've only got three quid but I've put fifteen in.' Lucy looked up, stricken. 'Shall I leave you my wedding ring? Isn't that what people do at petrol stations?'

Obviously this was meant as a joke. But privately Linda thought of saying no, she'd better not leave it, because the boss would have no hesitation in selling it to cover what the Liddiards owed. Mickey was fast becoming the county's most notorious bad payer. She did her best to smile again, inwardly panicking. She wasn't sure what to do. If she called the boss down, she knew he'd tell Mrs Liddiard straight out that they had sent no less than four final demands to the brewery. Linda knew Lucy didn't have an inkling and would be horrified if she knew the truth. And she wanted to protect her. People always did.

Suddenly a clear voice rang out.

'Here. Have this. Dad sent me tons of cash for the holidays. You can give it me back when we get to Honeycote.'

Lucy turned to see Mandy holding out a twenty-pound note. Thankful that she was to save Linda any embarrassment, she fell upon it. She had no qualms about borrowing money for what would in effect be scarcely half an hour.

'Mandy – you're an angel.'

She handed Linda the note, who hastily scrabbled for change and handed it over, relieved to have avoided any sort of confrontation. Lucy smiled at Mandy, who was choosing chocolate bars.

'Don't let me forget I owe you. I've got a head like a sieve.'

'I won't.'

Mandy handed over another fiver for the sweets she

had decided upon. As she waited for her change, her eyes fell on the Liddiard account. Unlike Lucy, she scrutinized the figures. And the dates. They hadn't paid a penny for three months. And they owed the garage close to a thousand pounds. Mandy frowned to herself. Twice in one day. Lucy seemed oblivious, but to Mandy's sharp little mind, something was up.

Sophie sat in the car and prayed to God for the willpower not to eat any chocolate. She'd been good all day – just a banana for breakfast and a piece of toast and Marmite for lunch – and lying flat on the bed this morning, her hip bones had definitely felt sharper. She was determined not to eat anything before the dance, except maybe a glass of milk to line her stomach, otherwise she'd never be able to pour herself into her dress.

The dress. The very thought of it filled her tummy with butterflies. Even now she wasn't sure she would have the nerve to wear it. But there was no alternative; she had absolutely nothing else remotely suitable to wear and, besides, no way was Mandy going to let her chicken out. She knew she looked stunning in it: her reflection, strange and unfamiliar, had told her she did when she'd tried it on. Mandy, who was not one to pay false compliments, had been genuinely thrilled by her transformation; and Georgina's jaw had dropped open in scandalized admiration as Sophie stood, shy and self-conscious, in the middle of the changing room. But after years of hiding behind loose shirts and baggy sweaters it was going to take a mountain of self-confidence to go through with this change of image. What would everyone think? Most important, what would Ned Walsh think?

For he was definitely going to be there. She'd double-checked nonchalantly with Patrick earlier. And he was going to be sitting at their table. She hadn't dared ask Patrick to sit her next to Ned. Not that Patrick would have teased her, for he thought the world of Sophie and took her very seriously, unlike most older brothers. But once she had expressed a public interest, however slight, she could no longer deny her feelings to herself.

Really, it was quite weird the way things were turning out. She and Ned had grown up together, as the outer reaches of his father's farm lay snugly alongside the boundary of Honeycote House. He was an only child, and with both parents busy on the farm he'd been saved from a solitary existence when the Liddiards had informally adopted him as an honorary brother. None of them ever had to ask plaintively if Ned could stay for tea, as Lucy unquestioningly fed him if he was there. And if at the end of a long day's intensive playing Ned had still not been collected by one or other of his parents, he would be thrown with the rest of the Liddiards into the huge roll-top bath with its claw feet and then into Patrick's top bunk. He and Sophie had been led out on chubby ponies, wrestled in piles of dried leaves in their anoraks and mittens, purloined peanuts at their parents' respective cocktail parties and giggled at the back of midnight mass together, warmed by the potency of the punch they'd been allowed.

Sophie could put her finger on the moment when her feelings for Ned had changed. It was at the last point-to-point of the season, which had been unexpectedly cold. She had been wearing her full-length waxed coat, standing with some friends outside the beer tent, when

Ned, heartily under-dressed in a tattersall shirt and yellow cords, had bounded up to her and insinuated his way into her coat in a mock attempt to shelter from the bitter wind. It was a light-hearted gesture: even Ned's girlfriend at the time was quite unthreatened by it, as everyone knew Ned and Sophie were if not quite like brother and sister, then at least cousins.

But there was a moment when Ned's arms clasped themselves around her waist and she felt his broad chest against hers, and Sophie found herself suffused with a hot, sweet heat from top to toe. Fleetingly their eyes had met, then suddenly Ned had released her, scuttling back to his girlfriend's side, and she'd felt cold, empty and rather desolate.

They'd hardly seen each other at all that summer, but just before she went back for the autumn term, he and his family had come over for Sunday lunch. Whereas once they might have slipped off together for a ride, or a walk, or to watch the *EastEnders* omnibus, Ned seemed reluctant to leave the table, preferring to sit with his father and Mickey and Patrick, drinking red wine, talking and laughing in very loud voices. Sophie had wandered round the house in a burning torment, not knowing why she was so miserable or what she wanted, and bewildered by the image she had in her head: of Ned sitting on the squashy sofa in the snug with her on his lap, dropping warm, affectionate kisses on her neck. She had ended up falling asleep on that very sofa, then woken scarlet with shame and embarrassment at the turn these thoughts had taken in her dreams. Since then she'd tried to convince herself that it was just her age and that Ned was obviously the object of her fantasies as he was the only male she really knew. Gradually, as the days of term slipped into weeks, she'd managed to suppress the memory and reincarnate the image of Ned as a boisterous and brotherly figure.

But as the dance tonight loomed, Sophie couldn't pretend to herself that Ned's reaction was not the single most important one. Even if every other guest jumped up and burst into spontaneous and admiring applause on her entrance, if Ned was left untouched it would all be for nothing. Every now and then her mind would whir like a camera on automatic drive and a succession of shots would torment her: Ned's face, normally merry and smiling, frozen in horror, disgust, ridicule or disbelief.

The thought made her feel quite sick; sick enough to banish any desire for chocolate. Which solved the immediate problem at least. When Mandy emerged from the garage with two Flakes, a KitKat and a bar of Fruit and Nut, she couldn't face a single bite.

Ned Walsh was Patrick's lifeline; the only other male close to his own age in a thirty-mile radius who still lived at home, or so it seemed. He had even less academic prowess than Patrick, but lived safe in the knowledge that he was going to inherit a substantial slice of the county. Ned sometimes wondered if this was a curse rather than a blessing as it left him little choice as to his future. Lacking the qualifications to get on to even the most mediocre of agricultural courses, Ned was now learning how to preserve his inheritance hands-on.

The physical demands of labouring on a thousand-acre mixed farm were Ned's saving grace, for were he not involved in strenuous toil from dawn till dusk, his five foot seven frame would have given him more than a passing resemblance to Humpty Dumpty. Instead, his shoulders were magnificently broad and his stomach, despite gargantuan fry-ups, was hard. A thatch of strawberry blond hair topped a perpetually ruddy face, his twinkling eyes were fringed with ridiculously long lashes and a trio of dimples lurked one either side of a continuous smile and one in the midst of a very pronounced chin. Happy-go-lucky and good-natured, Ned had worked out a simple equation in life: to work incredibly hard, then to go out and have a proportionate amount of fun, which basically meant drinking as much beer as possible, maybe getting lucky with a girl and definitely being sick at the end of the night. This formula looked set to continue until such time as he chose a particular girl to share his inheritance and cook his breakfasts, whereupon the beer drinking would continue, getting lucky with girls would stop and he would be sick less frequently and more surreptitiously.

Ned was particularly looking forward to the bash this evening. He and Patrick had been press-ganged on to the committee by the good ladies of the parish in order to liven up the proceedings. Tonight they had got to the Gainsborough Hotel early, to help set out the room and do the seating plan.

He and Patrick had just finished putting jet-propelled balloons at each place setting. Designed to whizz around the room until finally deflated, they were the committee's attempt to deflect their notoriously high-spirited guests from starting a food fight. Whether the balloons would provide a suitable alternative was yet to be seen. Ned thought not: there was nothing more satisfying than catching someone's lapel with a stodgy serving of duchesse potato.

The Gainsborough had put up with this rumbustious behaviour for years. Its function room was huge, tattered and fading. The food was mediocre but cheap and the dance floor was big and sported a huge glitter ball. And as the whole affair was not about gastronomy, but bopping till you dropped (as the cheesy resident DJ liked to put it), it was the ideal venue.

Patrick was standing in front of the table the Liddiards had reserved. It seated twelve and Patrick frowned as he shuffled a batch of handwritten place cards. It was going to be a nightmare, working out who to put where, especially as there were more women than men. And tempting though it was, he didn't dare sit himself near Kay: he wasn't yet sure how she was going to react. He was pretty confident he had hooked her, but until he'd worked out the next move it was best to keep her at arm's length. With both his father and Lawrence at the table, he needed to play safe.

Ned sauntered over as Patrick started experimenting with the cards on the table.

'Can't everyone just sit where they want?'

Patrick shook his head. 'Dangerous.'

'Why?'

Patrick didn't answer, and put Ned's name down decisively. Ned craned his neck to see who he'd been put next to.

'Kay Oakley? She terrifies me. She might mistake me for the starter . . .'

'Just keep telling her how gorgeous she looks and she'll be eating out of your hand. Do you mind Georgina on the other side? She'll need someone her own mental age to talk to—'

Ned thumped his friend on the arm in good-natured assent and watched as the rest of the cards were laid out. James on Kay's other side, then Lucy. Then Lawrence. Then—

'Who's Mandy?'

'A friend of Sophie's from school.'

'She must be a babe.'

'I hadn't noticed.'

'Crap, Patrick. Else what's she doing next to you?'

Patrick just smiled. Mandy's placing was very strategic. She would protect him from Kay's advances and any suspicion Lawrence might have. And as she was the Liddiards' house guest it was only right that Patrick should sit next to her. She was the perfect cover. In the back of his mind, Patrick had to also admit that yes, she was good-looking, but he really hadn't given her that much thought. He already had his hands full, what with—

'Shit! Kelly!' He turned to Ned, horror-struck. 'I promised her she could come. Shit!'

'What's the problem? There's room. She can sit between me and Kay.' Ned starting shuffling name cards, quick to arrange protection for himself.

'I don't think so—'

Ned was startled by the panic in the normally cool Patrick, who was thinking as quickly as he could. Kelly could go in between his father and Lawrence. They could both gawp down her cleavage, as she was bound to wear something spectacularly revealing that would keep them both in thrall all night. James's girlfriend Caroline could sit on Lawrence's other side – she'd keep him busy – with Lucy on her other side. Further round he'd have to put Sophie next to Georgina, because there weren't enough men. It was, after all, the Liddiard table, so they should be the ones to make the sacrifice for the sake of politeness.

Patrick stood back and assessed the controversy potential of the table. As minimal as it could be. Now his biggest worry was whether Kelly would mention spotting Kay at the brewery the other night. He hoped not; her memory was not remarkable for its retentiveness. But sod's law said she would come out with it. He toyed with asking her not to mention it, but shuddered at the questions that would follow and decided it wasn't worth reminding her. He'd have to take the risk.

Kay sat at her dressing table in a white velour robe and switched on the light that illuminated the large mirror in front of her. It was harsh and dazzling. Good. If she could smooth out all her imperfections under this glare she would look flaw-free in more subdued lighting. And she had to look her best tonight. She was going to make Patrick want her and realize he couldn't call the shots.

She turned her head to one side to check her jawline: still not slack. The cosmetics salesgirls really knew their stuff these days. Now her moisturizer had soaked in, she began with a painstakingly careful application of foundation that smoothed away all the tired lines and gave her skin an almost peach-like sheen. To her eyes she applied a dark, smudgy charcoal, giving them a dramatic intensity that pleased her. Blusher accentuated her bone structure and the entire mask was fixed on with a fine dusting of powder before the final berry-red was applied to her lips. Kay gazed at her handiwork and practised a smouldering gaze across a crowded room, an icy turn of the head and finally a playful little come-hither smile.

'That's not for my benefit, I don't suppose.'

She leaped out of her skin and saw Lawrence in the mirror, holding out his cuffs for her to fit in the cufflinks.

'Facial exercises. My beautician says it's important—'

'Rubbish. You're just vain. Always have been. You look great.'

Kay smiled her thanks weakly. She knew what was coming next. Lawrence slid the lapels of her dressing gown down over her shoulders and slithered his fingers over the silk of her bra, then reached his hand down to loosen her belt. Unwillingly, she slipped the dressing gown off. Refusal would put Lawrence on his guard immediately. She looked at him in the mirror and saw him smiling behind her, his erection poking out from under his dress shirt.

'You know you love looking at yourself.'

Kay gritted her teeth and did her best to relax. It would all be over more quickly if she did.

At six o'clock, the phone rang, breaking James's reverie. It was Caroline, saying she was going to be late; she'd been schooling Demelza and had forgotten the time. She'd see him at the hotel.

Caroline's terrible time-keeping was one of the things about her that could have irritated James if he'd let it. She was a total flake, while James was a stickler for punctuality. They were poles apart.

In fact, as he put on his perfectly starched dress shirt, he wondered how on earth it was they'd lasted so long. But in a strange way he enjoyed the fact that Caroline had a career, was independent, and that they were two individuals who sometimes enjoyed each other's company, as and when it suited them. Caroline didn't demand any emotional investment from him. She seemed almost self-sufficient. And James appreciated that; it gave him room in his head to fantasize without feeling guilty.

If he was honest with himself, he wanted a partner who was disposable; someone he could get rid of quickly and easily in case the day ever arrived when Lucy needed him. He felt in his bones that perhaps that time was getting nearer. She'd let her guard down the other day; he could see that she was worried and needed reassurance. And Mickey was getting more and more reckless. James knew the brewery was in trouble – not that Mickey had confided in him, but because anyone with an ounce of business sense could see that an operation like that could only survive with considerable investment and confident management. Neither of which Mickey could provide.

His conscience pricked at him. If he had any loyalty to his brother he would take him to one side, perhaps offer him some of the spare cash he had idling in return for a bigger share of Honeycote Ales. But James was sick and tired of being a gentleman and doing the right thing. Had it ever got him what he wanted? No, much better to wait for the crisis to come to a head and be seen as a white knight.

After all, here he was, nearly forty and still on his own, with half of Eldenbury putting him down as in the closet because he hadn't got a wife and bought fresh flowers every week. It was bloody well time to suit his own ends. And it wasn't as if he'd put Mickey's head in the noose. He'd stuck it in himself.

Payback time, thought James. Time for all that patience I've shown over the years to get me what I really want. And if I have to sacrifice my brother in the process, so what? It had always been one-way traffic. He couldn't remember Mickey ever doing him any favours. Not that he'd ever asked.

Bugger it – he was going to stand by and watch while the whole operation was brought crashing to its knees. No marriage could survive that – not the way Mickey was drinking. And if his infidelities came out into the open at the opportune moment . . .

He felt slightly ill having made this decision. It went against the grain. But he consoled himself with the thought that Lucy didn't deserve the treatment she'd been getting over the years. She deserved adoration, to be put on a pedestal and worshipped.

He toasted himself with half an inch of fine malt whisky, which took the edge off the conscience that was needling him, slung a white silk scarf round his neck and went out to his Aston Martin.

Lucy had ten minutes to get ready. She had to have a bath – she reeked of horse-muck.

'Can I have your water, Mickey?'

Mickey was shaving and looked at the layer of scummy foam floating on the surface.

'I wouldn't.'

It would have to be a quick blast under the shower, trying to keep her hair dry. She couldn't undo all Wendy's hard work. She flipped quickly through her wardrobe for an outfit, and decided on black crêpe trousers with her highest strappy Russell and Bromleys, a black boned camisole and a silver see-through organza shirt knotted at the waist. A dress was out of the question: she knew she didn't have any decent tights and she hadn't shaved her legs for three days. She ripped off her jumper and jodhpurs and poked them to one side with her foot, then rummaged in her drawer for some decent underwear.

As she tipped out her handbag to fill her evening bag, Lucy remembered what had happened at the garage that afternoon.

'Hey – I filled up the car this afternoon. They made me pay cash. Said the account hadn't been paid.'

'I must have forgotten to send off the cheque.' Mickey's reply was neither too fast nor too slow. Lucy stood still for a moment. She could probe him further. In the back of her mind, she'd thought Linda's expression had implied more than just a late cheque. She wondered if it was connected to the disquiet Mickey seemed to be feeling at the moment. It was a can of worms. To open or not to open, that was the question . . .

Mickey was holding his breath when Lucy darted naked into the bathroom, grinning. 'Hurry up, you bath hog. I want a shower.'

Hugely relieved, Mickey picked up the shower attachment and aimed it playfully at her.

In the end, she had minus five minutes to get ready, while Sophie, Georgina and Mandy waited impatiently in the car.

6

Kay was feeling unsettled. Clasping a glass of what the waitress had called champagne, but was really fizzy white wine, she prowled the room for something to take her mind off the fact that none of the Liddiards had arrived yet and that, inwardly, she was starting to panic. This must be how junkies felt when they went cold turkey: the thought of a whole evening without Mickey or Patrick was sheer torture and she really didn't think she'd be able to bear it. All day she had been looking forward to the perverse pleasure of both of them at the table.

She'd considered Patrick's ultimatum of the day before and dismissed it. The sex had been mind-blowing; she'd had to admit that. And his cold, calm self-control had frightened her a little, made her feel that he might be capable of anything. But afterwards, when he'd gone, she reasoned with herself. He was a boy, for God's sake, only twenty-three. And by his own admission, he couldn't blow the whistle on her and Mickey. She was going to play him along, play them both along. Father and son. She'd never felt so alive.

The only thing that slightly marred the prospect was the thought of Lucy. Kay liked Lucy – everyone did – and despite herself couldn't help feeling the tiniest bit guilty.

But, she reminded herself, Lucy must be doing something wrong, else why was Mickey always so hot for it?

She buried the thought at the back of her mind and amused herself in the meantime by embarking on her own little fashion award ceremony, something she always did when bored at social functions. She circled the room, giving marks out of ten, with penalties for slovenly lack of attention to detail (tights under peep-toes, visible bra straps). She prided herself on being able to identify the origin of most of the outfits. She herself shopped religiously at an upmarket boutique in Cheltenham, who knew her exact requirements and phoned her up whenever they had something in they thought she would like, but she was always keenly aware of what was available elsewhere. It was immensely useful for summing people up, knowing where they shopped. Not that there was much in the way of high fashion out here in the sticks: you'd think you couldn't get *Vogue* in the village post office. Her eyes were drawn to the chairwoman of the committee, a nightmare in bubblegum pink ruffles with an enormous bow attached to her arse. Surely someone could have said something – didn't she have friends? Kay thought she looked rather like one of those coy dolls with net skirts people bought to stick over their spare loo rolls, and earmarked her for the special prize of Worst Outfit of the Evening. She awarded a nine to an elegant black satin dress cut on the bias (someone's friend from London, probably) and eight to a bronze sequinned tunic. She was just about to give another eight to a pair of crêpe palazzo pants topped with silver organza when she realized it was Lucy.

Immediately her stomach lurched and her heart leaped

into her mouth. To stop herself looking too anxiously behind Lucy for either her husband or her stepson, she took a sip of wine – now warm and flat – and allowed her eyes to slide imperceptibly towards the doorway.

The cold turkey was over. Her fix was here. Just as a junkie revels in the sweet narcotics pumping into his bloodstream, so Kay revelled in the warm tingle that began between her legs and travelled through the network of her veins to the tips of her fingers. There was Mickey, his bow tie artfully askew, proving that he had tied it himself and would never, like many of the guests here tonight, resort to a made-up one. And Patrick, divine in his grandfather's dinner jacket, charming the Loo-Roll Cover, carelessly accepting a glass from the hovering waitress, waving at friends and not, Kay noted, scanning the room for her.

Behind Patrick, she frowned to see what were disconcertingly two definite tens. A young brunette, hair parted in the middle and falling past her shoulders in a shining sheet, was clad in a cream satin sheath that fell to the floor, but was cleverly slit at both sides to reveal long, golden, firm-thighed legs when she moved. It was adorned only with a huge silver heart hung on a black silk cord that fell to just above the girl's pubic bone. The subtle simplicity of the outfit showed a maturity that belied the wearer's years.

Next to her was a vision far from subtle, in fact totally overt, whose effect was so breathtaking that every male would soon be slavering with longing and every female green with envy. Luscious breasts surged out of a brocade bodice, from where swathes of deep red, luxuriant velvet clung to her generous curves. High-heeled satin mules peeped out from under the frock and a tiny little beaded drawstring bag hung from the girl's wrist. Head piled high with a mound of tumbling, tortoiseshell-coloured curls, she bore the air of a recently ravished courtesan. She was Moll Flanders, Nell Gwynn, the Wicked Lady, all in one. Kay silently approved: here was a girl who really knew how to dress for effect, who was proud of her body and wanted to rejoice in its ripe splendour, not emulate some wasted stick insect. Kay mentally awarded her Best Dressed Female, ten out of ten plus, then froze. Bile rose in her throat as she saw Patrick take the girl's arm and lead her into the room.

It was only when Georgina, looking sweet but definitely her age, appeared at the girl's other side that Kay realized the vision was Sophie. Her astonishment was huge, but not as huge as her relief that at least this gorgeous creature would be no competition for the two men in her life. She knocked back the last of her drink, plonked it on the tray of a passing waiter and glided across the room to greet her lovers.

Two hours later, Patrick was not in good humour. He'd been thrown off-course from the start by the shock of seeing Sophie. He hadn't recognized her in her finery. She looked stunning, but she shouldn't. She was Sophie, for God's sake – and what right had that little Brummie strumpet to turn her into a sex object? For he recognized Mandy's handiwork – no way would Sophie think up that outlandish garb for herself. Someone had spent hours smothering her in fake tan, painting her toenails bright red, even putting on false fingernails. Patrick couldn't bear to watch the gaze of every male in the room following his sister with wolfish intent. Not that Sophie was aware – she only had eyes for Ned. Who'd backed off at a rate of knots in abject terror when he, too, had realized her true identity. Instead, Ned was playing court jester to Mandy, relaxed because he knew he could never presume to win the affections of a girl like her and free to be his natural, boisterous, fun-loving self. Mandy was loving it. She thought he was hilarious, which of course he was. And Sophie, poor, darling, trussed-up Sophie, was trying so hard to pretend she didn't mind.

What incensed him further was that Kay seemed to be flouting his authority. Occasionally, she would waft past him, squeezing his elbow or touching the back of his neck with a teasing hand, and once at dinner, when she could be almost but not totally sure that no one was looking, giving him a wink. And she was patently all over Mickey. They were dancing together now, and although to anyone else it wouldn't have seemed out of the ordinary – everyone was fair game at one of these dos – it was obvious to Patrick that she hadn't called anything off, and didn't have any intention of doing so.

He was going to have to regain the upper hand quickly. He cut into the dance, claiming Kay nonchalantly off his father, and pulled her close to him, moving in time with the music. He pressed his mouth to her ear and she shuddered at the warmth.

'You haven't kept your side of the bargain.'

'How do you know?'

'I told you, I haven't got a problem with blowing the whistle on you and Dad. I just thought it would be nicer for everyone concerned if we resolved it my way.'

'Perhaps I need reminding once more just what the deal is, exactly.'

'Very well.'

He guided her by the elbow out on to the terrace, down the steps and across the lawn, then through a little copse of trees to a stone-built gazebo. Kay leaned against one of the smooth, round pillars, wishing she smoked or had something to do, for she suddenly felt unsure of the next move. Patrick was so calm and controlled, so sure of himself. It was unnerving in one so young. She smiled at him in the dark.

'Thank you for lunch yesterday. I enjoyed it.'

'So much that you seem to have forgotten what we agreed.'

'I haven't. It's just that there's a time and a place for everything.'

'Excuses, excuses.' Patrick's lips curved upwards in a mocking smile. Kay shuddered as she remembered where else they'd been, as he pulled her away from the pillar, slid the straps of the dress off her shoulders and slowly undid the zip that ran the full length of her spine. The dress fell in a pool of copper-coloured silk at her feet. She stepped out of it, clad only in lace-topped hold-up stockings – no underwear, as the fabric was too unforgiving. Patrick knelt in front of her. He was unwrapping a little packet that Mayday had given him last time they met.

'What is it?'

'Just a little bit of fairy dust.'

He insinuated a hand between her thighs, indicating that she should part them. She did so, fascinated, and watched as he licked his middle finger, dipped it in the powder then gently, very gently, applied it to her clitoris. Kay could scarcely breathe. His touch was gentle, like butterfly wings. But all too soon, he withdrew his hand, rubbing the remains of the cocaine on to his gums.

Patrick wasn't much of a user, but he didn't like waste. He looked at Kay, who was wide-eyed with anticipation. The coke wouldn't hit her bloodstream quite yet, she'd still be feeling numb, but within half an hour she'd be an inferno of unrequited lust. There was no way she wasn't going to come running to him for gratification. Patrick knew his sexual prowess was pretty unbeatable – Mayday had graduated him with honours – but just to ensure that her mind was totally blown, he'd put a little bit of icing on the cake.

'Is that it?'

'Just you wait.'

'How long?'

'Get rid of Dad. Then come and find me. Turn round.'

She did so, obediently, and he solemnly zipped her back into her dress. She felt a sudden electrode shooting through her as he pressed his thumbs into the flesh at the back of her neck, massaging her.

'In the meantime, just relax and enjoy it.'

Kay swallowed hard. It was all she could do not to throw caution to the wind and rip off her dress again. She wanted him to slam her up against the pillar and fuck her brains out. But from what she'd experienced of Patrick already, she knew she'd have to play it his way.

'I'll go and find your father.'

'Good girl.'

He strode off across the lawns back to the terrace, leaving Kay smiling in disbelief. Good girl, indeed. The cheek of the boy was breathtaking. She gathered her skirts up to follow him and found her legs would barely hold her. She felt as if two Alka-Seltzer had been dropped into her bloodstream, as a sweet, fizzing sensation stemming from the place he'd touched between her legs started coursing its way through her veins.

At ten o'clock, Caroline finally turned up in a fuchsia frock, fuck-me shoes and a feather boa. She'd been for a drink, or what looked like several, with some bloke from the livery yard where she kept Demelza. He'd some cheap tack for sale, no doubt off the back of a lorry, but Caroline loved a bargain. James felt vindicated, because it disproved Mickey's theory that she was only after him for his money. In actual fact, Caroline never asked him for anything, except when she was pissed, when she demanded either champagne or sex. James was already at the bar procuring the former when she swayed up to him and hooked him round the neck with her boa. She didn't apologize for her late arrival, just kissed him full on the lips and grabbed the bottle off him. She didn't bother with niceties like glasses when she'd had a few.

'I supposed I've missed the food. Never mind – it's always foul at these dos. I'm going to go and dance.'

She took a slug of champagne, spilling half of it down her impressive cleavage, handed back the bottle and sash-ayed off to join the throng on the dance floor. He knew from experience that it was only a few more glasses to go before she was on the table. He'd have to keep careful count from then on, so he could extricate her before she started a striptease.

As he carried the bottle and several glasses back to their table, he caught Lucy in his eyeline. She was sitting on the edge of her seat, deep in conversation with someone. She looked animated, vivacious; her eyes were sparkling as she tipped back her head to laugh. James felt a hideous ache at the very core of his soul. He loved her so much it hurt.

Sophie, having drunk no more than half a cider or the odd glass of wine in the past, had discovered this evening why it was that people drank. It really did make you feel good; more confident. It had been a funny evening. She'd had so many compliments and admiring glances heaped upon her, but wasn't sure how to behave. She might look like a glamour-puss, but she was still plain old Sophie Liddiard underneath, with no sparkling cocktail conversation and no witty little rejoinders to bandy around. More disconcerting was Patrick's behaviour. He had treated Sophie with icy courtesy on arrival, and Mandy with not even that – he'd completely ignored her. So when, after a couple of glasses of sparkling wine, she'd found that the edges of her reality were blurring and that she was able to chat happily to people without feeling self-conscious, Sophie had helped herself to more than half a dozen glasses from the trays that were circulating. It had also helped her to cope with the fact that Ned had kept his distance. Somehow, she'd prepared herself for that eventuality for so long that it didn't matter. He was bound to find Mandy more exciting, more interesting, more attractive. Now she was teaching him the dance routine to 'Tragedy', with much hilarity as Ned had no sense of rhythm whatsoever. Sophie allowed herself a smile and consoled herself with yet another glass of wine.

Suddenly, however, she found herself feeling most peculiar. She was talking to Jonty Hobday, the local farrier, and he courteously replenished her glass yet again with some cool white wine. It was hot and she was thirsty so she drank it down – she was getting used to the taste. She put her glass down on the table and turned to smile at what Jonty was saying, then found she had to put her hand on his arm to steady herself as a wave of giddiness came over her. He didn't seem to mind, just smiled and carried on talking to her. The only trouble was she didn't seem to be able to hear what he was saying. There was a whooshing, whirring sound in her head, relentlessly pounding like the blades of a helicopter. And just as her head seemed to be spinning one way, her stomach was spinning the other. She felt hot and panicky. She needed fresh air, and to sit down. She clutched at Jonty's sleeve and tried to speak, but all that came out was a jumble of syllables. Desperately hoping he didn't think her odd, or rude, she left his side in search of the exit. She found herself remarkably unsteady on her feet, but managed to make her way through the crowds, tottering and swaying, occasionally holding on to people for momentary support, muttering 'Shmeee' for 'Excuse me'.

As she emerged on the other side of the dance floor, the helicopter in her head whirring louder than ever, she saw with relief an exit and a corridor, and a white door that she was sure must be the ladies. At least there she could sit down for a moment, splash some cold water on her face and wait for the effects of the alcohol to wear off. It shouldn't take long – after all, she'd felt fine five minutes ago.

Reaching the sanctuary of the corridor, she suddenly felt horribly, horribly sick. It must have been the salmon terrine: as bile rose in her throat, that was all she could taste. The white door was ahead of her. She couldn't see the sign that indicated whether it was ladies or gents, but by now she didn't care. She lurched for the door, pushed it open, staggered inside and knew she didn't have time to make it to a cubicle. In front of her she saw a gleaming wall of white tiles and a sink over which a sign mysteriously read 'hand wash only'. She grabbed the sink's cool ceramic edge and leaned over just in time.

Relieved, she lifted up her head and looked into the furious face of a man wearing a funny white hat. In the dim recesses of what was left of her brain, she realized that she had just thrown up in the hotel kitchen, before passing out cold at the chef's feet.

Kay, almost insensible with lust, panicked when she saw Mickey approach. He took her by the elbow – like father, like son – and whispered that he needed to talk to her. She'd been plucking up the courage to accost him herself, but didn't yet feel in control. She looked around for Patrick, but couldn't see him. She turned to Mickey, eyes glittering.

'Let's go to the gazebo.'

Mickey reckoned that was as good a place as any to give someone the boot, and followed her out of the French windows. Five minutes later, he was wrong-footed as Kay clung to the silk-moire lapels of his dinner jacket and murmured that they couldn't carry on, that it wasn't right, that it was tearing her apart knowing she could never really have him and that they had to stop before someone was hurt. It must be his lucky day, thought Mickey, who'd tanked himself up with at least a bottle of Chablis and several whiskies in preparation for his first resolution. He supposed nearly being caught at the brewery the other night had unnerved her. He nodded in agreement and patted Kay reassuringly on the shoulder.

'I've been thinking the same myself, but I didn't want to say anything. You're quite right – better to quit while we're ahead.'

She nodded her assent and Mickey breathed an inward sigh of relief. He wasn't going to get away that easily, though. Just as he thought he was out of the woods, Kay hooked her finger into his waistband and pulled her to him.

'Let's make this the last time.'

Mickey could see her nipples clearly through the sheen of her dress and wasn't sure whether it was the cold or desire. He decided on the latter, judging by the way her eyes were wide, her breath shallow. He thought he'd better not decline – he'd got away pretty lightly, after all, and once more was hardly going to make any difference.

In the event, however, nature took its toll. Whether it was nerves, the drink, the cold or the fact that Kay seemed particularly and terrifyingly voracious, he couldn't be sure, but for the first time in his life, Mickey couldn't manage it.

On the dance floor, the DJ had gone into smooch mode. As Eric Clapton struck up, everyone under thirty abandoned the floor with groans, while everyone else clutched indiscriminately at the nearest member of the opposite sex. James melted when Lucy insinuated herself into his clasp.

'I haven't a clue where Mickey is,' she said dreamily. Drink made her languid, unbearably sexy. James pulled her to him and moved to the music as Eric said it for him: she looked wonderful tonight.

Behind them, Caroline had hooked another unsuspecting victim with her feather boa. James prayed she'd last to the end of the song before she got any bright ideas about an impromptu lap dance . . .

Kelly was in a strop. She couldn't find Patrick anywhere. He hadn't paid her any attention all evening and now he'd disappeared. Someone mentioned that they'd seen him heading for the gazebo earlier, and she picked her way over the lawn like a fastidious flamingo, her diamanteé stilettos sinking two inches with every step. There was somebody in the gazebo all right. She peered into the darkness. It wasn't Patrick, though. Pink with embarrassment when she realized who it was – and what they were doing – she tottered her way back up to the terrace.

7

Write and tight-lipped, Patrick had got Sophie out of the hotel as quickly and discreetly as he could after she'd been sick. His dad, he knew, would get a cab later – he could take Lucy, Mandy and Georgina. They were all still happily bopping away and wouldn't want to go. He carried her out to his car. She soon came round when the cold air hit her and he struggled to get her into the front seat. Twice on the way home he had to stop and let her be sick again, but he didn't once reproach her as she sat in the front seat quietly sobbing. By the time they got back to Honeycote House she was looking more like her old self. Dreadful, but her old self. Her make-up had worn off, her hair had collapsed and she was wearing Patrick's dinner jacket draped round her. They hadn't had time to stop and look for her coat.

He took her into the kitchen and appraised the damage. She was still drunk, but he thought she'd probably got rid of every last trace of alcohol in her stomach, if the dry retching on the last stop was anything to go by. Patrick debated whether to let her go straight to bed and thereby ensure the worst possible hangover, which would hopefully prevent her ever getting into such a state again. But he thought she'd probably suffered enough punishment already for something he didn't consider to be her fault, so he forced her to drink four large glasses of water and wash down a brace of paracetamol before helping her up the stairs to her bedroom.

She was incapable of getting herself undressed, so he decided that the best thing was to shove her under the duvet fully clothed. If the dress got ruined, so what? He certainly didn't care if he never saw her in it again.

He tucked her in gently and looked down at her. She'd fallen asleep straight away and he sympathized in advance for the way she'd feel in about eight hours' time when she came to. He tucked a strand of hair behind her ear and bent down to plant a kiss on her cheek. A caring and very brotherly kiss.

As he looked round the room he noticed with distaste the female detritus cluttering Sophie's dressing table. Tubes of fake tan and Immac and glue for sticking on eyelashes and fingernails, bottles of perfume and dozens of lipsticks, hairspray, dirty cotton wool balls and tissues. To him it looked like a stripper's dressing room, and he felt an urge to sweep it all into the bin. Then he realized he was being ridiculous, positively Victorian. But he still couldn't help feeling a surge of anger. He could never look at Sophie in the same light again.

As he settled into the chair beside her bed, he wondered briefly about Kay and whether it had been safe to leave her at the ball in her condition. But he felt quite confident that she would keep her side of the bargain. He smiled at the possibility that Lawrence would probably be in for the shag of his life when they got home. Anyway, he couldn't go back to the hotel now. He had to keep a vigil at Sophie's bedside. He was pretty sure she wouldn't be sick again, but he didn't want to risk it.

James slid the Aston Martin through his black wooden gates and hopped out to shut them. Time and again he'd wondered about remote control, but it went against the grain. They were paranoid and unspeakably naff, and what was two minutes, even if it was freezing. Caroline was practically unconscious in the front seat, drunk and dishevelled. He'd seen her feather boa go out of the door round someone else's husband.

He shook her awake gently, praying the cold night air wouldn't bring her round too much, that she'd just want to crawl into bed and sleep it off. He couldn't bear the thought of her demanding sex. The trace of Lucy's Diorissimo still clung to his dress shirt, reminding him that less than an hour before he'd held her in his arms. She'd put her head on his shoulder, held him close, as if taking comfort.

James knew he was romanticizing. Lucy had probably clung on to him because she'd had too much champagne. And he'd seen her get into the taxi with Mickey not half an hour before. They'd looked very much a couple – Mickey had draped his dinner jacket round her because she hadn't brought a coat.

But screwing Caroline now would desecrate the memory; he'd somehow feel as if he was being unfaithful. He managed to slide her into his bed and pulled the blankets up under her chin, tucking her in firmly before she got any ideas.

Patrick was woken by the sound of the taxi dropping everyone off. He could hear Mickey and Lucy talking and laughing down the corridor, swapping notes on the events of the evening. He could bet his father was leaving one particular section out.

Patrick barged into the bathroom where Mandy was cleaning her teeth and glared at her across the black and white tiled floor.

'You'll have to keep an eye open for Sophie during the night. She's been as sick as a dog – no thanks to you.'

Startled, Mandy put down her toothbrush.

'Me?'

'What the hell did you do to her tonight?'

'What do you mean?'

'You made her look like a slag.'

'She looked brilliant.' Patrick was glad of her choice of adjective, for it highlighted the Birmingham twinge in her accent and took the edge off her attraction. 'Everyone thought so.'

'And how could you flirt with Ned like that?'

'I wasn't. We were just having a laugh. I don't fancy him or anything.'

'So you just did it to wind Sophie up?'

'What do you mean?'

'You know what I mean. Sophie's mad about him. No wonder she went and got blind drunk.'

'Shit.' Mandy look at him in anguish, and he was surprised that she sounded so genuine. 'I didn't know. Honestly. Why didn't she tell me?'

Patrick wasn't going to be taken in. He knew what women were like. Bloody good actresses when they wanted to be. He wasn't going to let her get away with it.

For a few moments they stared each other out. Then Patrick let his eyes travel down Mandy's nightshirt, down her long, lightly tanned legs and up again. Her nipples stood out like shirt buttons under the soft cotton, and as their eyes locked again he reached out and caressed one lightly with his thumb. She took in a sharp little breath, but didn't move, and he knew that if he could feel her heart it would be pitter-pattering like a rabbit in a trap.

He took another step forward, until he was so close that he could feel her breath on his face. She looked up at him, wide-eyed and expectant, as he put his hands behind her head and pulled her forward to meet his lips. His first kiss was gentle, almost imperceptible, and she shut her eyes for a moment, savouring the taste and feel of him as an expert would a new wine.

Then in a second she was on him, drinking hungrily at his mouth. Patrick was surprised by the depth of his own response. He wound his fingers roughly in her long, dark, silky hair, so unlike Kelly's, which was bleached, back-combed, gelled and sprayed until it felt like Shredded Wheat. Kay's, too, was brittle through years of expensive and subtle highlighting. Mandy's skin was baby-soft and Patrick had no fear of streaky orange foundation being left on his white dress shirt. He breathed in her scent, a faint, lingering trace of lemons, not a cloying assault on the senses; both Kelly and Kay were devoted to expensive, over-powering perfumes that lingered wherever they went. She was delicate, natural, beautiful, and suddenly Patrick wanted her very, very badly.

He tilted her head back for a moment to look into her eyes. Her pupils were huge with desire and he could feel her small breasts rise and fall against his chest in time with her quickening breath. He smiled, and she smiled back at him, rather unsure. He touched the pretty dimple that appeared at the side of her mouth with his finger, then delicately traced the outline of her mouth. Her eyes were half closed, like a cat in the ecstasy of attention.

Suddenly a picture of her face as she flirted with Ned sprang into his mind. Mandy need only have snapped her fingers and Ned would have been hers, slavering in adoration, while Sophie sat by watching in abject misery, her chicken marengo untouched as the adolescent pangs of unrequited love gnawed at her insides. Patrick thought Mandy had probably got exactly what she wanted all of her life. And now she thought she'd got him. He'd been seduced by her pretty packaging; the hard little heart wrapped in layers of pink tissue, tied with a ribbon and labelled 'Take Me'. It was, admittedly, difficult to resist. But, unfortunately for Mandy, Patrick's heart was harder than his penis. Just.

8

On the flight from Nice to Birmingham, Keith Sherwyn stuck his legs out into the space allowed him by travelling Club and sipped on a restorative brandy and ginger ale. He avoided the seasonal mince pie that reminded him Christmas was only just over a week away: all that French food, much as he'd enjoyed it, had left him with a slightly unsettled stomach. Derek Legge, the fellow in charge of refurbishing the Sheikh's yacht, had insisted on taking him on a gastronomic tour of the south of France. The Sheikh was prone to sacking people overnight on a whim, so Derek was making the most of his expense account while he still had it and Keith had benefited from his profligacy.

It had taken considerable time to persuade Legge that black granite in all the bathrooms would slow the vessel down considerably. The Sheikh had his heart set on it and Derek suspected that being the bearer of bad tidings would be a sacking offence. Keith couldn't help feeling that Derek blamed him in some way, but he couldn't change the fact that granite was bloody heavy. Finally, under a Picasso and over foie gras at the Colombe d'Or in St Paul de Vence (Keith felt that the painting and the pâté were both overrated, but didn't say so), he'd talked

Derek into a resin substitute that wouldn't sink the boat. He didn't tell him that his profit margin would be substantially higher as there would be less labour involved in installation. The Sheikh had, miraculously, agreed – speed, it seemed, was more important than surroundings – and after that it had just been a question of pinning down the accessories: taps, towel rails, toothbrush holders, et cetera.

For the past four days Keith had allowed himself to think of nothing but business. This had been a lucrative contract that needed attention to detail, so he'd been able to force himself to give it his undivided attention. Now, however, as the plane sped back over the Channel towards Solihull, which he knew would seem so soulless after the chic, bustling glamour of the south of France, Keith was left with little choice but to contemplate his disastrous personal life.

He stared out of the window at the white wisps of cloud scudding beneath them, and finally allowed himself to feel. He waited for the pain of abandonment to twist at his gut, the agony of desertion to tear at his heartstrings – but there was nothing. Not even a little stab of self-pity. He wondered if perhaps the brandy had numbed his feelings, but that was ridiculous – the shot he'd been given wouldn't have made a toddler tipsy. He leaned further back into the padded headrest and tried to focus on his predicament. A glossy air hostess passed by him and smiled.

'Looking forward to going home, sir?'

Disconcerted, Keith roused himself up and realized with amazement that he'd been smiling to himself, and that the only feeling filtering through was a secretive, schoolboy sense of glee at having escaped some sort of eternal detention. He raised his glass to the hostess.

'I certainly am.'

He could go home and put on his favourite holey jumper, stick his still-shod feet up on the coffee table, drink beer out of the bottle and not worry about the rings it left, have the TV on as loud as he liked and completely ignore the telephone. Instead of being forced into his designer tracksuit and 'house' shoes, having to pour his beer into his shiny monogrammed tankard with matching silver coaster, having the TV drowned out by Barry Manilow or Garth Brooks and leaping up to answer the phone in case it was an invitation to the social function of the year. Even though they had an answerphone. Because, Sandra had explained to him severely and incessantly, some people didn't leave messages if they thought you were out, especially if it was a last-minute thing.

He was glad! He was bloody glad she'd left him!

Admittedly, he'd been taken aback when Sandra had stood in the hallway last Wednesday, surrounded by her fifteen pieces of matching Samsonite and clutching the ridiculous vanity bag that held most of her face, and announced she was leaving. Two minutes later a cream Mercedes with tinted windows had drawn up and Keith, shell-shocked, had automatically helped her out with her cases. He'd stared in disbelief at the puny, callow youth that had leaped out to open the boot – she couldn't be leaving him for this, surely? – then realized with a sinking heart that of course this was not her lover, but his driver.

Keith could read no expression in Sandra's eyes, hidden behind her sunglasses. The only information she volunteered was 'He's taking me on holiday' and Keith knew from the accusation in her tone that herein lay the only explanation he was going to get.

Neglect. He hadn't paid her enough attention. Keith was aggrieved. Bathrooms didn't sell themselves, especially not bathrooms with onyx sinks and gold taps and Jacuzzis big enough for an entire rugby team. Obviously this was another one of life's little equations: you couldn't make millions and your wife happy.

He mentally wished whoever Sandra had run off with good luck and, as the plane started circling around the familiar Legoland below, Keith contemplated his immediate future with something bordering on relish.

Mandy slid her arms around his neck and breathed in his warm, musky scent. She could feel his iron-hard muscles ripple under her embrace as she nuzzled up against him, and rubbed her cheek against his. But the recipient of her affection was not impressed. He wanted his oats. Literally.

As Phoenix gave a snort and stamped his foot impatiently, Mandy tangled her fingers in his mane and patted his nose with the other hand.

'I'm sorry, boy. I don't know what to give you. You'll have to wait.'

She hugged him again, but he wasn't consoled. She was, just a little bit. Phoenix was like a giant teddy bear and that, in her confused and bewildered state, was what she needed. She'd lain awake all night, her emotions raging from fury to despair to cringing embarrassment back to tooth-grinding rage, while Sophie slept the blissful sleep of the innocent in the next bed.

Even worse than her state of mind was the state of her body. Again and again she ran over the events. Patrick's hot, sweet kisses on her neck, his warm lips caressing her nipples, his wicked tongue tracing its journey over her stomach, dipping into her navel and finally coming to rest at its destination, where she'd been brought to the brink of—

What? Something, that was certain. Patrick had clearly known what he was doing as, leaning against the wall for support, she'd writhed and clawed at her body with the thrill of the new sensations sweeping through her. When he'd slipped a finger inside her she'd cried out with the shock, unable to help herself, and she felt herself tighten with pleasure around it as he continued his exploration until she could barely stand.

Then, suddenly, he had stopped. She'd sunk to the floor, breathless and gasping, and looked up at him in bewilderment. He'd looked down at her, given a little matter-of-fact shrug made even more infuriating by the belittling smile that accompanied it, and walked out, leaving Mandy in a humiliated heap.

Mandy had never had an orgasm, but she knew that, despite the delicious waves that flooded through her, something even better had been about to happen. And Patrick had known, had judged her responses so expertly that he'd left her in this agonizing limbo – and he'd done it quite deliberately.

At dawn, hot and restless, eyes burning through lack of sleep and the scalding tears that had slid out, despite herself, when the frustration of the evening's events became too clear in her mind, Mandy had left the gloomy shadows of the bedroom and slipped through the house, heavy with the deep sleep of revellers, and out into the stable yard.

The air was cold and crisp and held promise of a beautiful day ahead. The early mists would soon be banished by dazzling sunshine and the air would carry glorious wafts of decaying leaves and wood smoke. Mandy, her senses already heightened, had breathed in her surroundings and felt strangely exhilarated.

Phoenix hadn't been a good listener, absorbed as he was by his own troubles, but telling him her problems had helped Mandy sort things out in her mind. She wanted Patrick, unquestionably. She wanted what he'd been about to give her, desperately. But more than either of those, more than anything she'd ever wanted in her life, more even than the Sindy gymkhana set when she was eleven, she wanted revenge.

How neat it would be if she could think of a way of getting all three.

Twenty minutes later, Mickey, who'd come out for a blast of fresh air to get rid of his hangover, found her curled up in the corner of the stable fast asleep. He shook her gently awake.

'You could have been trampled to death.'

'Phoenix wouldn't do that.'

'He wouldn't mean to. Horses' brains are only the size of walnuts.' Funny, that's just what his brain felt like this morning – small and brown and wrinkled. The two pints of orange juice he'd already drunk had done nothing to plump it up. Still, the fresh air would either kill or cure it.

He held out his hand to Mandy and pulled her to her feet. 'What are you doing out here, anyway?'

'I couldn't sleep.' Mandy's little sigh told Mickey this

was nothing to do with the facilities at Honeycote House, and her troubled face told him not to probe any further.

'Can you ride?'

Thanks to her mother's regime of extra-curricular activities, there wasn't much Mandy couldn't do. 'I haven't been for a while. But I know one end from the other.'

'Come on, then. No one else will be up for ages, and I could do with blowing the cobwebs away.'

Mickey found her a beautiful bright chestnut cob called Monkey – because of his big, round, brown eyes, not his behaviour, Mickey assured her – and Mandy swiftly tacked him up, running her hands reassuringly down his soft nose and blowing into his nostrils so they could make their acquaintance quickly. She borrowed someone's hat and a discarded Puffa from the tack room and swung up on to Monkey's back: the little horse stood politely as she did so.

Mickey, meanwhile, led out a magnificent, towering bay whose hooves scuttered alarmingly over the cobbles as she span round in little half circles, leaving Mickey swearing on the ground below. Mandy reached down and caught the mare's bridle, holding her firmly under the chin so Mickey could leap on.

Soon they were clattering out of the yard and on to the soft grass of the track that led into the nearby woods, leaving the sleeping inhabitants of Honeycote House behind. Mandy had always been a confident rider, if a little inexperienced, and she soon forgot her initial nerves and became absorbed in her surroundings. A squirrel surveyed them quizzically from high above, then bounded away. The horses, snorting with eagerness in the early morning freshness, blew plumes of frozen air from their nostrils, and Monkey's legs did two strides for every one of the bigger horse.

Eventually, the grassy track dwindled down to a narrow path winding its way through tangled woodland. Now the leaves had fallen it was possible to see the way through, but Mandy imagined that in the height of summer it would be like fighting your way through a green sea. Even now she had to duck overhanging branches and twist out of the way as brambles whipped at her clothes. Mickey, two hands higher, had even more to contend with, and bent down low over his horse's neck all the way through, until eventually the dense trees cleared and they came out into the bright, early morning sunlight on to a narrow road, hugged on both sides by low, drystone walls, that formed a narrow ridge along the back of a hill.

'This way,' said Mickey. He seemed anxious to get somewhere, and urged his horse into a trot along the road, which was so ancient, so little used, that grass grew in a thin spine along the centre of the tarmac. Mandy squeezed Monkey forward, his little legs twinkling in an effort to keep up, and she felt uplifted by the exercise. They finally came to a halt.

'This is Poacher's Hill,' said Mickey. 'It's the highest point for miles.'

Villages were clustered like little golden nuggets, spires and turrets giving away the existence of the most secluded. Mandy drank in the glory of the view and tried hard not to think of Patrick, his black hair contrasted against the crisp white cotton of his pillow, his lean limbs wrapped up in his duvet. She was sure he hadn't spent a night in mental and physical torment. No, he would have slept easily without a care, without a second thought for her.

Next to her, Mickey drank in the vista also. It was as familiar to him as the back of his hand, almost his birthright. What had happened to that bloke in the Bible who had sold his birthright? Nothing good, he was sure. And now he was on the brink of doing it himself. Not the whole kit and caboodle, of course. But it still felt like a betrayal.

'You can see all of our pubs from here,' he told Mandy. 'Or at least, the villages they're in. You'd probably need a telescope to spot the actual buildings.'

He pointed out a couple of the ones that were visible to the naked eye. Then he showed her the farmland that had originally belonged to his great-grandfather, who had grown tired of being constantly at the mercy of the elements for his welfare and so had turned to brewing in the middle of the last century.

'The Walshes own what was his farm now. You met Ned last night.'

Mandy felt a stab of guilt, though she knew she had nothing to feel guilty about. Patrick had made it quite clear that he thought she'd been after Ned. Poor Sophie – she'd have to make sure she hadn't got the wrong end of the stick. She didn't want to lose her friendship, and she knew girls fell out over far less.

Beside her, Mickey sighed. Mandy looked at him, concerned, and he smiled ruefully.

'Have you ever made a resolution, Mandy?'

'I make them all the time. To drink eight glasses of water a day. And to take all my make-up off before I go to bed, that sort of thing. But I always break them.' She frowned. 'Is something the matter?'

'Nothing that a couple of hundred grand wouldn't sort out. Don't suppose you could lend it to me?'

'Sorry.'

They laughed together. Mandy was curious. What Mickey was hinting at tied in with what she had witnessed the day before, and she wanted to know more.

'Are you in big trouble, then?'

Mickey cursed his indiscretion. He must still be pissed.

'No – not really. It's just cash flow. Boring, boring. Come on, I'll race you to the end of this track. You can have a head start.'

Rising to the challenge, Mandy wheeled Monkey round and dug her heels into his side, giving the little horse his head. Mickey gave her fifty yards and followed at a steady pace, allowing her to win by half a length. She was flushed with triumph and exhilaration, and he hoped all traces of their conversation had gone out of her head. After all, cash flow was hardly of interest to an eighteen-year-old, was it?

Then he wondered why he was worrying. Everyone was going to find out soon enough, once the word got out. For he'd made a decision, and it wasn't a happy one.

As soon as he got off the plane at Birmingham airport, Keith became a driven man. He located his Landcruiser where he'd left it in the long-term car park, then called his secretary at home on his mobile. She was paid generously, so he didn't feel guilty about disturbing her on a Sunday. First, he cancelled all appointments for the next three days. Irene was respectfully and silently shocked. He hadn't cancelled so much as a meeting since he'd had shingles four years ago, but she didn't demur. Instead, she filled him in on Mandy's whereabouts. Apparently she was staying with the Liddiards of Honeycote House, somewhere in the Cotswolds. Irene had checked them out with Miss Cowper at Redfields, who'd assured her they were a very nice family – they ran a brewery, apparently. Keith was very fond of the Cotswolds. He'd taken American clients there in the past, and it inevitably took their breath away and persuaded them to order container-loads of traditional roll-top baths and toilets with overhanging cisterns so they could recreate a little bit of England for their impressionable customers back home.

It was still only eight o'clock, but Keith decided that instead of going home to his mockingly empty mock mansion, he'd take a drive down to Honeycote and collect Mandy. It would be nice to take the four-wheel drive somewhere it might actually get dirty – he wasn't sure he'd ever even put it into four-wheel drive – and he'd take the Liddiards out to lunch to say thank you for having her.

Little more than half an hour later he was bowling merrily along the picturesque 'B' road that his AA map reliably informed him would lead to Honeycote. He felt a silent wonder as he passed through storybook villages, sleepily complacent in their charm, perfect plumes of smoke curling from their chimneys. Their perfection lay in their irregularity: zigzagged roof-lines encrusted with silver-green lichen, mullioned windows with leaded panes that never saw a drop of Windolene, assorted chimney pots, grand next to humble, all hewn out of buttery stone and laid out along little lanes that twisted and curved and rose and dipped so that you turned a corner and were suddenly surprised by a steep grassy bank, the welcoming frontage of a pub or the strangely restful prospect of a churchyard, gravestones leaning at all angles. Keith marvelled that real people lived in these fairytale settings, then supposed that in fact it was not all roses. The downside would be the coachloads of tourists that inevitably trawled through their midst each summer, the lack of anywhere to park, the pubs filled with screaming day trippers – and an economy dependent on these locusts.

Nevertheless, Keith could feel himself relaxing in these surroundings. He slid Mozart into the CD player and hummed happily to himself as he negotiated the rest of the journey. He pondered on how he had once or twice suggested to Sandra that they move out of stifling, sub-urban Solihull to somewhere more tranquil and restful, but she had been mystified by the idea and refused to give it even a second's consideration. What about their Social Life and the Golf Club? And (the reason that had convinced Keith that of course he was being whimsical) Mandy's Education. Keith realized now that Sandra hadn't given a fig about Mandy's education, or indeed Mandy at all, but had been afraid of being forgotten in the countryside and losing her place on the rung of the social ladder. And presumably the attentions of her lover, though whether this was the first or the fortieth, Keith had no idea.

Maintaining his business meant he'd lost touch. He didn't know his wife, or his daughter, but had found himself on the treadmill of making money to keep them happy and had forgotten the magical, free ingredient: attention.

And, he realized further, he'd forgotten himself. Sure, he had his little luxuries and indulgences, but coming out here had made him aware that he had long stifled a more sensitive side of himself. Although he was a pedlar of monstrous bathroom fittings, he had a surprising sense of the aesthetic that had been somewhat suppressed in recent years.

Keith found himself reversing up the road and tucking his Landcruiser into a makeshift lay-by that had emerged out of necessity in order to let oncoming vehicles through. He felt that as an outsider it was his duty to reverse: living here one must get sick of giving way day after day. Moreover, as he delved deeper into the countryside he found his usual aggressive and thrusting nature evaporating. As he entered the little town of Eldenbury he glanced at his watch and, seeing that it was only just ten o'clock and far too early to bowl up to someone's house unannounced on a Sunday, he decided to get out, stretch his legs and absorb his surroundings.

He walked down the little high street, wishing he felt less of an outsider in his suit and tie. He felt as if he had 'townie' tattooed across his forehead. Eventually he came across a small shop that sold 'Country Clothing for the Discerning Gentleman'. He patted his inside pocket to make sure of his wallet and went in. Time for a transformation.

He selected a tattersall check shirt, a cravat, a pair of moleskin trousers and a greeny-blue chunky wool sweater. Five minutes later, he emerged from the changing room – really the cupboard under the stairs hung across with a gingham curtain – fully dressed in his new guise, and asked the surprised assistant to fold up his suit and put it into a carrier bag. He then perused the shop for accessories: a tweed cap, a fine pair of brogues and a waxed jacket. Soon he had run up a bill that amounted to more than the shop usually sold in a week.

As he went to pay, handing over his credit card to the

delighted assistant, he realized with a pang of self-loathing that this was the way he and Sandra had always done everything. When they'd taken up golf, they'd gone and bought all the clothes, all the equipment, all the accessories, before even setting foot on the green. It had been the same with tennis. And skiing. Keith thought now what prats they had probably looked on the beginners' slopes at Val d'Isère, standing out like beacons in their gleaming outfits and falling over instantly.

Now here he was, doing it again. Trying to buy his way in. Trying to tog himself up like a country gent when to really belong here, he knew, it needed to be second nature, uncontrived. But even the oldest, most distressed waxed jacket had started off as new once, he reasoned. Short of pinching someone else's, he had to wear it in.

It wasn't a day to feel defeated, decided Keith. In fact, it was probably something of a new beginning. From now on, he could be anyone he liked. He didn't have to take his wife into consideration, worry about what she thought or wanted. He remembered all the ambitions he'd suppressed over the years, places he'd toyed with visiting that Sandra had turned her nose up at.

So, even if he was behaving like Mr Toad with a new passion, he'd waited long enough to be allowed to indulge himself. Reassured, Keith happily chose a Swiss Army knife from the display cabinet. It boasted nearly fifty cunning attachments, and Keith felt sure it was going to come in very useful.

He sauntered out on to the street and immediately felt at home, part of the scenery. Up ahead, he saw a pub, the Horse and Groom. A sandwich-board boasted that it was open all day for tea, coffee and good food. Keith thought a cup of coffee was just what he needed before he phoned the Liddiards to announce his arrival.

The creature behind the bar was like no one Keith had ever seen. Long, thick, back-combed black hair, eyes barely visible beneath layers of kohl, combat trousers and a T-shirt that proclaimed Fantastic Cleavage Under Kit, she wasn't quite what he expected behind the bar of a Cotswold coaching inn. Her accent made her sound as if she should be out in the fields picking peas, a country burr that seemed both naive and knowing.

'What can I get you, sir?'

'Just a coffee, please.'

He looked along the bar, then noticed the pumps bore the logo of Honeycote Ales. He remembered his conversation with Irene.

'Is this a Honeycote pub? Owned by the Liddiards?'

'At the moment it is, yes, sir.'

'At the moment?'

The girl leaned forward confidentially. Keith could see that her T-shirt told the truth.

'Word is they're going to the wall. Everyone reckons they'll go bust any minute.'

'Really?'

'Why do you want to know?'

'Just curious. My daughter's staying with them at the moment.'

The girl put a hand to her mouth, as if alarmed she'd been indiscreet, but her eyes were laughing. Her bitten nails were painted a deep blood red.

'Oh dear. Perhaps I shouldn't have said anything.'

'It won't go any further.'

'If you see him, tell the young master Mayday sends

her love.' She flashed a set of Hollywood white teeth at him. Keith promised he would and walked away to drink his coffee, feeling rather as if he'd walked into a film. And he had to admit he was eager to cut to the chase – what she'd told him had aroused his interest. He couldn't wait to meet the Liddiards of Honeycote and find out more about their business.

Two miles away, in a poky little bedroom over the lounge bar at the Honeycote Arms, Kelly had hardly slept all night. At nine, she'd begun the repairs to her party-ravaged face by applying a fifteen-minute clay mask. That would draw out all the toxins. She'd drunk far too much wine, even though it was dry and she didn't like dry, but Patrick had refused to buy her a bottle of her favourite German wine all to herself. That had been the first sign: normally he was all too happy to ply her with alcohol so he could get into her knickers. Not that she needed to be drunk to get them off for Patrick. Oh no. Contrary to what her appearance might suggest, Kelly hadn't had many lovers, but of those only Patrick had ever made her feel like that.

Off with the mask and on with the revitalizing moisturizer. Let it soak in for five minutes. Patrick had been horrible last night, and Kelly couldn't understand why. He'd hardly spoken to her and when he had he'd snapped. And then he'd disappeared.

Under-eye concealer – got to get rid of those black rings. Eyeliner. Lipliner. Eyebrow pencil. It had been a pretty strange evening altogether. She'd spent most of it talking to Lawrence Oakley. He'd been very interested in her beauty therapy. Even hinted that he might set her up in her own salon when she'd passed her exams. Mascara. Lipstick. Done.

Satisfied that she now looked presentable to the outside world, Kelly decided she would slip downstairs and share a pot of tea with her mum. Eileen would be dying to hear about the dance the night before – what everyone was wearing, who was drunk, who disgraced themselves – and Kelly loved nothing better than a good gossip to an appreciative audience. She slipped her feet into a pair of fluffy bunny rabbits masquerading as slippers and made her way down the back stairs that led from their private accommodation to the heart of the pub. She was puzzled to hear voices coming from the bar, as she was pretty certain they'd had no B&B guests the night before. She peeped through the glass porthole and frowned. Mickey Liddiard and her dad were sitting at a table, deep in conversation. She pushed the door open slightly and was surprised to hear her father's tone. She was sure she'd never heard him talk to Mickey that way before. The two men got on well and often shared an amiable beer. But this conversation was far from amiable. Kelly strained her ears.

'Eileen and I wouldn't last two minutes at the Blue Boar. It's not our cup of tea at all – you know that.'

'The thing is, Ted, I've got no choice.'

Ted stared at Mickey long and hard. Mickey squirmed under the contemptuous gaze.

'Eileen said you'd do this. I said you wouldn't.'

'This is the last thing I wanted to happen. You're my two most loyal tenants—'

'Well, you've got a funny way of repaying our loyalty.'

'If there's anything else I can do—'

'Give us a decent reference. We're going to need it.'

Ted walked stiffly from the table and Mickey dropped his head into his hands. Ted's quiet, wounded dignity had been worse than a stand-up row. He went behind the bar and pumped three shots of Scotch into an empty glass.

'I hope you're going to pay for that.'

He whirled round to find Kelly staring at him accusingly, fully made-up and dressed in a pink towelling dressing gown and rabbit slippers. He fumbled in his pocket for change, but before he could proffer the few coins he had, she had spun on her heel and walked out.

Skipper fixed a malevolent eye on the mound of grated carrot that was rising tantalizingly in front of him, let out a squawk and viciously eviscerated a grape. He was keenly conscious that his keeper's mind was elsewhere, and was frustrated that it was not in his interests to put up too vocal a protestation. He knew from experience that it would result in his swift removal to the back room for a diet of daytime television chained to his perch. He loved it in the kitchen, for there were rich pickings for a parrot, but in order to avoid detection by the Environmental Health the deal was he had to keep quiet.

The grape duly demolished, he cocked his head to one side and surveyed Eileen shrewdly. Although he had been a present from the regulars for Ted's fiftieth birthday, it was Eileen who fed, watered and cleaned him, and he was fond of her. He could see this morning that she was distracted. Her hand flew up and down the sides of the grater with its usual satisfying rhythm, leaving mounds of yellow and orange that would soon be transformed into a vat of lunchtime coleslaw. Skipper hoped for a share of the raisins that Eileen always sprinkled in after the mayonnaise, but she seemed in a world of her own and to have forgotten he was there. He weighed up whether an affectionate nip on the ear would work in his favour, and decided not. There was a deep crease between Eileen's brows that he had come to recognize as bad news.

Eileen was indeed intensely preoccupied and it was only when her knuckles scraped violently on the side of the grater, causing a few droplets of blood to fall on to the carrot, that she realized how deep her reverie was. For half an hour now she had played out a dozen different scenarios in her mind, and she hadn't been enamoured with any of them. No matter how hard she tried, she couldn't find any pleasing explanation for Mickey Liddiard's arrival here at half past eight on a Sunday morning. He was a lazy bugger, in her opinion; not a natural for a breakfast meeting.

Her passive acceptance of her role as the landlord's wife, rather than landlady, meant Eileen had not insisted on accompanying the men into the bar when Mickey had asked Ted for a word. Baps didn't fill themselves, after all, and Eileen hadn't run the kitchen at the Honeycote Arms for twenty years without knowing that a half-hour slip in the schedule would mean chaos later on. She stuck a blue catering plaster on to her grazed finger before scooping up the mounds of carrot, cabbage and onion into a mixing bowl, then slopped in glistening spoonfuls of mayonnaise. As she stirred, she strained her ears to see if she could pick up the tone, if not the content, of the conversation that lay so tantalizingly close behind the swing door.

She knew this was the moment she had been dreading for the past three years. Ted had often scoffed at her, but Eileen was neither an optimist nor a sentimental fool. It was her sharp business sense, her eye for detail, her meticulous book-keeping that had kept the pub ticking over for the past few years. Not to mention the hours of drudgery and graft that she put in behind the scenes. And she had picked up enough snippets of information from her customers to know that a business needed to be streamlined these days to be successful, to run without an ounce of fat. And streamlined Honeycote Ales was not. Furthermore, she'd gleaned from knowing comments made the other side of the bar that the Honeycote Arms was a potential gold mine. It was large, yet not unmanageable, secluded but not isolated – in other words, ripe for development. Eileen knew in her waters that they were living on borrowed time. When the swing door finally opened and Ted appeared, she felt a surge of pity for him. He always trusted people and thought she was a cynic. It must be awful to have to learn the hard way.

Ted put a hand on her shoulder that felt as heavy as her heart.

'Sit down, love.'

'I already know. He's selling the pub over our heads, isn't he?'

'He's given us first refusal.'

Eileen snorted.

'The building's worth three hundred thousand. Before you even take the turnover into consideration.'

'We could borrow. The interest rate's low—'

'Ted. We're both over fifty. I don't want to go into that kind of debt at my time of life!'

'Mickey reckons we could get an investor. A sleeping partner.'

'He'd know all about that, of course.' Eileen's lips

were pursed. 'Anyway, would you go to him for business advice? He's killing the goose that lays the golden eggs. You mark my words, the whole shooting match is going to go down the pan. Anyway, he can't sell the pub over our heads without offering us an alternative.'

'He has. The Blue Boar.'

Eileen looked at Ted in disbelief.

'He can't be serious.'

The Blue Boar was the one Honeycote establishment that stuck out like a sore thumb. A purpose-built pub on a housing estate to the east of Eldenbury, it had been a tactical investment by Mickey's father in the early seventies. It boasted satellite TV and karaoke nights. Vast quantities were consumed therein, ensuring regular visits from the local constabulary. It was profitable, but at what cost?

'You realize that if he offers us that and we turn it down, he's under no obligation to find us an alternative.'

Eileen sat down heavily and looked at the walls around her.

'Twenty years in February.'

'I know.'

Eileen's eyes filled with tears.

'I don't understand. We've done no wrong. We've worked all the hours God gives and more, poured our heart and souls into this place. While he's been drinking and wenching and gambling—'

'You don't know that.'

'Don't I just. I could smell whisky on his breath for a start. Dutch courage, no doubt.'

She spat the words out vehemently. Ted was surprised. Eileen was normally so tolerant, non-judgemental, ready to see both sides of the story. He was usually the one who overreacted and had to be calmed. The truth was, though, he was still in shock and the news hadn't really sunk in, while Eileen had just had her worst fears confirmed. He patted her awkwardly on the shoulder and was wondering whether to get her a medicinal brandy, when the door swung open and Kelly walked in, now immaculate in a pair of black trousers and a polo neck.

'What is it, Mum?'

Eileen was dabbing at her eyes with the tea towel she'd slung over her shoulder earlier. It stank of onion and accelerated rather than staunched the flow of her tears. She looked up at her daughter.

'Never work for anyone else, love. Always be your own boss.'

Kelly looked at her dad for confirmation of what she already feared. He'd aged about ten years in as many minutes.

'Liddiards are selling the pub out from under us.'

'They can't!'

'Of course they can.'

'But why?'

'He's in trouble, isn't he? You've heard the gossip.'

Kelly digested the enormity of what she'd just heard. Her first thought was that the news would explain Patrick's behaviour the night before. Why he'd been so distant, so anxious to keep her at arm's length. She went to give her mum a reassuring hug.

'I'm sorry, Mum, but I've got to go out for a bit. I've promised someone a manicure. Will you be OK?

Eileen took in a deep breath, nodded and smiled. 'Of course. There's no point mithering. Things might change.

And even if they don't, we're still here and I've got lunch to make.'

'I'll be back at tea.'

Kelly dropped a kiss on her mum's forehead and smiled at her dad. Ted managed a wan smile back. Bless her, he thought. She doesn't realize the implications of what's happening. Even if they got a generous payoff from Honeycote Ales, which they weren't entitled to if they turned down the Blue Boar, there was no way they were going to be able to afford a house that resembled the accommodation they enjoyed at the Honeycote Arms. They'd be lucky to be able to afford a three-bedroomed box on the sprawling estate that the Blue Boar customers inhabited. Every week in the paper there was another horror story of drug addiction, violence, robbery, car theft . . . even though it was nestled in the very heart of the picturesque Cotswolds that most people assumed was immune from the grim realities of the underworld. Ted shut his eyes to close out the picture. He'd always wanted the best for his family. Another ten years and they'd have made it. Kelly and her brother Rick would have been settled in their own lives and he and Eileen could have retired to the B&B on the North Devon coast that they'd always dreamed of. He supposed that dreams were there to be broken, even if you kept your copybook unblotted. Ironic really, that Mickey, who must have the most blotted copybook for miles around, was going to walk out of this unscathed while they paid for his misdemeanours.

Kelly, contrary to her father's belief, was very much in the picture. She jumped into her car and drove very fast away from the pub, not entirely sure where she was going. She'd felt red-hot rage before, but only very occasionally, for she was a good-natured creature in general. This time, as she drove, the anger she felt was white hot and molten, and out of its ashes emerged a very clear resolution.

Anyone who passed Kelly off as naive was mistaken. Patrick in particular had always underestimated her and assumed her to be unobservant. But in fact Kelly missed very little. And now she had been alerted to a hidden agenda, she started to look back over the events of the past few days and read a great deal into them indeed. Her image as a bimbo beauty therapist was very useful, for it meant people weren't as careful as they might be in covering their tracks. Usually it wouldn't matter, for she wasn't vindictive or spiteful – people could carry on as they liked as far as she was concerned. Until someone she loved was harmed.

More than anything, Kelly was fiercely protective of her parents. Despite their hardworking and hectic lifestyle, they had always managed to put their children first, sacrificing hard-earned time off which could have been spent on themselves and spending it with Kelly and Rick. Selfless support and encouragement meant Kelly and Rick had been able to pursue the paths they had wanted, knowing they always had a warm and loving home to come back to, and spare cash had gone into paying tuition fees, financing courses and equipment that the children had needed. Dependent as they were on their trade, both Eileen and Ted realized the value of independence and wanted their children to do well for themselves.

Kelly had a few snippets of information in her mind that, until now, she had chosen not to piece together, as she had always been fond of Mickey and had given him the benefit of the doubt. But now she was putting together a collage that made a very interesting picture. The other night at the brewery, for instance. That had definitely been Kay's car. She must have known Mickey was there. And she wouldn't have expected Patrick to be there. So why disappear up the hill as if the hounds of hell were after her unless she had a guilty conscience? And last night's little tryst in the gazebo merely confirmed Kelly's suspicions.

So, if Kay and Mickey were having secret little meetings, Kelly was all for putting a spanner in the works. She'd sat next to Lawrence Oakley at dinner last night long enough to get the measure of him. He wouldn't take kindly to being cuckolded. He was the deadly, manipulative type. And also, Kelly knew by the way he had put his warm hand on her thigh, just high enough to feel the top of her stockings through her dress, he was the type that was putty in the hands of fluffy young blondes. He'd joked about being a guinea pig for her massage exam; told her to give him a ring if she needed practice. She'd got his card in her pocket. As soon as she was far enough away from her parents not to arouse suspicion, she pulled over, got out her mobile phone and began to dial.

He answered after three rings.

'Lawrence Oakley.'

'Mr Oakley . . . ?' She affected a little tremor in her voice, to heighten the drama.

'Who is this?'

'It's Kelly. From last night?' She allowed the tremor to break. In her experience, turning the taps on full worked every time. 'Oh, Mr Oakley, it's awful. I just didn't know whether to tell you or not. I hope I'm doing the right thing . . .'

Lawrence frowned, swivelling round in his leather chair, wondering what on earth the girl was on about. He remembered her from last night. Pretty little thing.

'What is it?'

'It's your wife. And Mickey Liddiard.' Kelly gulped. It wasn't in her nature to drop people in it, but it was the only way she could think of to punish Mickey. She couldn't backtrack now.

'What do you mean?' Lawrence had a horrible feeling he knew exactly what Kelly was going to say.

'They're having an affair . . .'

Lawrence managed to keep his voice under control as he thanked Kelly politely for letting him know and hung up. He was surprised that he wasn't overcome by anger, as he would have expected, but a terrible cold dread right in the centre of his heart.

Keith arrived at Honeycote just after midday. Lucy greeted him warmly and made him his fourth coffee of the day.

'I'm sorry about you and your wife. If there's anything we can do – Mandy's welcome here any time . . .'

Keith was a little taken aback by her confronting the issue so boldly and for a moment wasn't quite sure what she was talking about. Then he remembered: he'd been deserted and left holding the baby, albeit a comely eighteen-year-old baby quite capable of looking after herself.

Lucy was smiling at him kindly, and he wasn't sure whether he should assume a mantle of self-pity, self-defence or self-righteousness. Instead, he merely shrugged. 'All bad things must come to an end.' He thought that made him sound bitter, so he grinned and flipped a digestive out of the packet Lucy handed to him. 'Actually, coming here has made me quite forget. Is it something in the air?'

'Maybe.' Lucy smiled. 'You'd better stay for lunch, in that case. It might keep you in oblivion a little longer.'

'Absolutely not.' Keith's assertion emerged with a vengeance. 'I'm taking you all out for lunch. To say thank you for having Mandy—'

'Too late,' countered Lucy. 'I've already put a joint in. I'll just have to do a few extra spuds.'

When Mandy came down with Sophie and Georgina, she gave her father an uncertain smile, part embarrassed, part sympathetic. He was overcome by the urge to hug her fiercely but as they had until now been a singularly undemonstrative family he felt it was not the time to start behaving like an over-emotional Sicilian at his only daughter's wedding. He thought how wonderful she looked, dressed in jeans and a borrowed sweater, her hair windswept and her skin only coloured by the fresh air.

Mandy had, in the back of her mind, worried that her father would be an embarrassment to her and would shatter the haven she had found at Honeycote. But he wasn't at all: far from it. From the moment he walked through the door he seemed unusually relaxed and determined to enjoy his surroundings. There was no blustering, no boasting, no cringing references to how much things cost or how much they must be worth. He didn't, as she'd been convinced he would, play his usual party trick of valuing the property. He was proud of being able to price any house in the West Midlands to the nearest five hundred pounds. But Honeycote House seemed to have worked its charm on him and somehow he knew that this house had no price, that its true worth was in the fact that the bathrooms hadn't been refurbished for fifty years, and not once did he open his mouth to say, 'I can do you all this in wipe-clean repro with whirlpool bath, power shower and matching bidet – discount for cash.'

Mickey, who seemed to have come back from his early morning ride with a great weight taken off his shoulders, had been delighted to welcome an extra guest to lunch. Everyone tucked in to roast beef and Yorkshire pudding to bolster up their hangovers. Mickey and Keith hit it off immediately, and Mickey chatted with pride about Honeycote Ales. Keith seemed fascinated by the whole operation and Mandy was relieved. They hadn't had a moment alone yet to talk about her mother, but her father didn't seem unduly distressed. She was also grateful for the fact that Patrick had disappeared off somewhere and didn't join them for lunch. She wanted to escape from Honeycote without seeing him. She wanted to go away and lick her wounds, not have salt rubbed into them. And the next time she saw him, she swore to herself, he'd want her as much as she wanted him.

After lunch, Mickey offered to show Keith round the brewery. As soon as he stepped over the threshold, Keith felt as if he'd gone back a hundred years. He climbed the rickety stairs that led up to the top of the tower, surveyed the gallons of liquor cooling in their copper-lined vat, breathed in the yeasty, hoppy vapour and felt a stab of envy.

He plied Mickey with questions, not because he was nosy but because he was intrigued. He was interested to see that Mickey was very bullish about their position: there was no hint of the troubles the extraordinary girl in the Horse and Groom had warned him of. The little minx must have been winding him up.

Mickey finished the tour by giving him a sample of their best bitter. Keith had never been a real ale man, but found he savoured the beer's depth, its toasty, nutty top notes and the underlying sweetness that made its name so appropriate. When Mickey offered to invite him back on a brewing day, he leaped at the chance. He hadn't enjoyed himself so much for ages.

Later, when Keith and Mandy had parted with many thanks and promises to meet again soon, Mickey sat in the quiet of the brewery office, heaved a sigh of relief and congratulated himself on the past twenty-four hours' work. This time the day before yesterday he'd been sitting in a pizza parlour in Cheltenham in the depths of despair, and now, here he was, almost back on the straight and narrow. Why on earth hadn't he taken stock of his life sooner? Kay had been surprisingly compliant the night before. And Eileen and Ted – well, of course they weren't thrilled, but he'd find some way of making it up to them.

He looked down at the glass of whisky in his hand and considered his resolutions.

Two down, and only one to go.

Maybe this was going to be easier than he thought.

9

After Honeycote House, The Cedars seemed even less welcoming than usual. As Mandy and Keith crossed its threshold, the cocktail of cleaning agents conscientiously applied by the housekeeper assaulted their senses: harsh chemicals barely disguised by the cloying scent of pine or citrus. Honeycote smelled of coffee, dogs, toast, ashtrays and fresh flowers. It smelled of life, whereas Keith found coming home rather like stepping into a morgue, with any sign of life immediately embalmed.

Father and daughter looked at each other self-consciously, both wishing they were somewhere else. Rather than being liberating, Sandra's absence was inhibiting. She'd left a vacuum that neither of them was sure how to fill. Mandy was exhausted, from lack of sleep the night before and the emotional turmoil Patrick had left her in, while Keith felt suddenly and inexplicably deflated. Buoyed up by his pint of Honeycote Ale and a glass of rich, thick claret, he had been full of resolve on the drive home, daydreaming, as Mandy dozed in the seat next to him, about the new world he could create for himself now he had a clean slate. But once back on his own territory it all seemed like an impossible dream. His world was too far removed from the Liddiards' for him to be able to glide effortlessly from his into something resembling theirs. His was a domain of remote-control garage doors, underfloor heating and self-cleaning ovens, without a speck of spontaneity. Everything was regulated, programmed, timetabled . . . how could he break the habits of a lifetime?

Depressed, he walked into the spotless kitchen and looked around the sterile environment, where every appliance was discreetly hidden behind a bespoke, hand-built cabinet, as if it was shameful to admit that your dishes needed washing or your food needed chilling. He took a little bottle of French beer out of the refrigerator and reached into a cupboard for a glass. With distaste, he noticed a trace of Sandra's frosted cappuccino lipstick on the rim. Somehow, this jerked him out of his depression, and he marched over to the bin (also cunningly disguised) and dropped the glass in, listening with satisfaction as it smashed against the stainless steel at the bottom. Then he flipped the cap of the bottle, raised it to his lips and drank defiantly.

Mandy appeared in the doorway. She looked upset, almost on the verge of tears.

'What is it, love?'

'Look what she left in my bedroom.'

She thrust an envelope at him, covered in Sandra's scrawl: 'I hope you'll understand one day, darling. In the meantime, buy yourself something nice for Christmas.' Inside was a cheque for five hundred pounds.

'What, exactly, am I supposed to get? To make up for the fact my mother's gone off with someone half her age?'

Mandy's tone was uncharacteristically vicious, and Keith was perturbed to see her blinking back tears.

'I'm sorry, love.'

'I don't care that she's gone. I just care that she doesn't care.'

'I know.'

Keith was surprised to find that comforting a sobbing eighteen-year-old wasn't as disconcerting as he thought it might be. Sandra's desertion had created an unspoken bond between them. They were united. But they had decisions to make. Choices.

'I'm thinking of selling the business.'

The words popped out before he'd even realized that was what he'd been thinking. Mandy stopped mid-wail and looked at him in surprise.

'Since when?'

'Since two seconds ago. I don't need to put myself through it any more, now your mother's gone.' He paused briefly. 'Why should I carry on doing something I hate?'

'I didn't know you hated it.' To Mandy, his words sounded almost sacrilegious. Her father had always seemed devoted to his work, spending evenings and weekends tying up deals, unable to tear himself away in order to spend time with his family.

'Once you've got on to the treadmill, it's very hard to get off. And I had to keep your mother in the style she thought she was accustomed to. All this doesn't come cheap, you know.' He waved a hand round the room, but the gesture was further-reaching. 'It was all totally pointless, wasn't it? Slogging my guts out to make her happy.'

'So if you're going to sell up – then what?'

'I don't know. Something that makes *me* happy.'

Keith knew that his tone was bitter and cynical, and that Mandy shouldn't have to cope with her father's problems on top of her mother's departure. He stroked her hair and he was gratified that she nuzzled into him. For the first time in years he felt a flicker of warmth from human contact. He felt a surge of anger, too, that he had missed out on so much; that he didn't really know his daughter, nor she him. He was going to explain everything to her, as best he understood it.

Together they made a pot of tea and a pile of cheese on toast – they were both surprisingly hungry, even after their huge lunch – and took it into what Sandra had always called the snug, although that was a grave misnomer. The room positively stood to attention. Clutter, that was what the room needed, decided Keith, and resolved to leave the Sunday papers lying around for the next week in a gesture of defiance.

When they'd eaten, Keith began to talk, trying to paint as unbiased a picture of what had brought the Sherwyns to this point as he could. And Mandy listened in wonder, sitting on the floor with her arms hugging her knees, round-eyed, as her father, the man she'd always considered remote and disinterested, emerged as sensitive and grossly misunderstood.

He supposed that most people ended up in circumstances far removed from their own burning ambition. It had been his father who had pushed him into plumbing, had insisted he get a trade when he failed to get into grammar school and had got him an apprenticeship. It was a good choice on his father's part, for Keith was meticulously neat and tidy in his work, which made him popular with clients. And it didn't take him long to work out that he was a natural salesman; that he could talk someone into having something ten times more elaborate than they had originally conceived when he went to price up a job. Not that he ever tried to rip them off. He was just so enthusiastic about what he had to offer, painting a vision of the bathroom that would change lives, that people invariably forked out for that little bit extra, the appliance that was going to turn a necessity into a luxury. Only trouble was, he was making the money for his boss, not himself. He was never going to make himself a million on the flat weekly wage he was paid. He gave himself two years to learn as much as he could on the job at someone else's expense, while saving up enough cash to give him the courage to go out on his own.

His boss was furious when he left two years to the day he'd been taken on, and swore Keith would never work in that town again. But Keith had gained himself such a reputation that customers swapped allegiance in droves. Soon he had more work than he could manage alone and had to recruit his own team, training them up himself and ensuring they maintained his own exacting standards and targets. He did deals with local building firms to fit bathrooms in all the estates that were springing up around Solihull, and as the en suite was the new must-have it proved more than lucrative. He was ahead of the game with every fashion: Jacuzzis, whirlpool baths, bidets, power showers, saunas. It seemed there was no end to what his customers could be seduced into buying.

The day his accountant told him that unless he went out and bought himself a new car, he was going to be in for a hefty tax bill, Keith realized he was on his way to becoming a successful businessman. He'd never even contemplated a new car. His parents had a deal with a friend of theirs who worked at Longbridge, who bought a new Rover every two years with his staff discount. Keith's parents always bought his old one from him, selling their old one on to Keith. Which meant he had a four-year-old Rover every two years, a deal he was quite happy with as it always had full service history and low mileage.

Now he felt it was time to be reckless. He spent a week perusing all the garages in the area, inspecting what was on offer and seeing what sort of a deal he could get, before settling on the most frivolous vehicle he'd seen: a white Scimitar SS1 sports car that was hugely impractical but brought a smile to his face the minute he put his foot down. And it seemed that it came with an added bonus. The salesman had jokingly referred to it as a tart's trap, and it certainly did attract the attention of women. No sooner was the ink dry on the paperwork than the young, immaculately dressed receptionist handed him his keys, wistfully mentioning that she'd have loved a go in it, and now would never have the chance. Keith fell for her hook, line and sinker. It was a beautiful spring day and he was desperate to take his new acquisition for a spin. He offered to pick her up after work and take her for a drink. The girl blushed, accepted his offer and introduced herself as Sandra. Her father owned the dealership: she was working there to get some experience, as her father felt it was important for a woman to be able to stand on her own two feet these days.

Nine months later they married, and Keith felt the first twinges of unease as Sandra lorded it over his relations at the wedding, which they held at one of the larger hotels in Solihull. He was most uncomfortable with the airs and graces she bestowed upon herself in front of them; her father's success had obviously gone to her head. Keith tried to compensate for her rudeness, but it was obvious to him that Sandra felt she had somehow married beneath her, even though her father had only made his fortune in the past twenty years. He banished it to the back of his mind. She was certainly nice enough to him. She was supportive, encouraging, always looking for ways he could improve his business. She was a shrewd little cookie – she'd picked up quite a few tips from her father on how to do deals, attract new customers and get repeat business. Not that Keith needed teaching – he was a natural – but it was nice to have someone to chew over ideas with at the end of the day.

But as he became more and more successful, so Sandra became less attentive and more demanding, not just wanting to keep up with the Joneses, but the Smiths, the Browns – the entire telephone directory. As fast as he made it, she spent it, and at first he had felt proud that he could provide in this way. In the space of seven years, they moved from a modest three-bedroomed box to a grand, five-bedroomed luxury home built to their own specification. Or rather, Sandra's. He replaced her Mini Metro with a black Mercedes with personalized number plates. She had become unrecognizable from the seemingly artless, carefree creature he'd whizzed off in his car that spring evening. She spent her time driving between the gym, the hairdresser and the beautician, being sun-bedded, frosted and manicured, burning up his cash.

And it was a one-way deal. It seemed the more he showered upon her, the more Sandra withdrew from him and withheld any sort of affection. It was amazing that Mandy was conceived at all. And Sandra made it quite clear that being pregnant and giving birth had utterly revolted her, so Keith could forget trying for the son he secretly so desperately wanted. Just like Midas, everything Keith touched had turned to gold, but he was far from happy. To compensate for Sandra's perpetual tight-lipped frostiness, he buried himself in his work, where at least he commanded respect, if not affection. And in the back of his mind he always wondered how Sandra would treat him if the money stopped coming in. It was all she'd ever wanted him for, he now realized. But it didn't bear too much reflection.

He didn't know when the affairs had started, but he knew they existed and felt it best to ignore them. He'd tried his very best to please Sandra in bed, even sneakily ordering *The Joy of Sex* from his book club to see if it would give him any clues. But she was obviously looking for something he couldn't give her. The affairs never lasted long – it was as if once she had conquered someone she lost interest – and so Keith didn't really find them a threat. In fact, he found them something of a relief, for while she was embarking upon an encounter she was remarkably good-natured at home. They gave her something to think about, stopped her from dwelling on what was wrong with her life and what material possession she might want Keith to strive for next.

So here they were. She'd left him, despite all his efforts and his total tolerance. He'd spent half a lifetime working his fingers to the bone for someone who had little or no regard for him. What a waste. He wondered what would have happened if his father hadn't marched him into the plumbers' merchants thirty years ago. His dream until then had been to draw cartoons for comics, to create his own superhero. Admittedly that ambition had long since faded. But he knew he'd be quite happy if he never saw a tap or a washer or a plughole again.

Keith outlined all of this to his daughter, missing out the little details he considered too sordid to share, though why he should feel any loyalty to Sandra he didn't know. And what was most gratifying was that Mandy had come and given him a huge hug at the end of his story, a gesture of love and reassurance that almost made his heart burst.

He surveyed Mandy, and wondered what she wanted to do with her life. How well equipped was he to set her on the path she wanted to travel? Was it responsible parenting to encourage your children in whatever they wanted to do, however unfeasible it seemed? Or, just as his own father had done, was it better to take matters into your own hands and steer them down the path you felt was most suitable?

After all, perhaps his father had been right. Keith had been incredibly successful in the career that had been chosen for him. The fact he was miserable was down to his marriage. Perhaps if he had chosen a different woman to share in his success . . .

Either way, Keith had no idea what Mandy wanted to do, whether she wanted to be a weather girl or an archaeologist. She'd hinted at a career in interior design, which Keith approved of, as everyone seemed to be into it these days – thanks to all those programmes where people came and painted your kitchen bright pink and suggested you keep your fruit and veg in galvanized buckets. Perhaps they could set up their own company together – he could buy a little shop somewhere in the Cotswolds, somewhere fashionably wealthy. There was no way it wouldn't be a success, what with his business acumen—

Hang on a minute! He was doing just what his father had done. Projecting his own ideas and ambitions on to Mandy. And no young girl in her right mind would want to go into business with her father. He made up his mind to get to know her over the next few days, find out what made her tick, what she wanted to do.

In the meantime, he had a more pressing question.

'What do you want for Christmas?'

Mandy grinned. 'A horse?' Mandy had asked for a horse every Christmas since she was three. It was the nearest the Sherwyns had ever got to a family joke.

Keith rolled his eyes tolerantly. 'Not that old chestnut again. We've got nowhere to keep it.'

'Loads of places round here do livery. And if we get one that lives out, it wouldn't cost too much.'

'But you're away at school most of the time.'

'Maybe I could weekly board? I could come home every weekend. Then you wouldn't get lonely.'

Keith had to get up and walk over to the drinks cabinet, so that Mandy couldn't see the tears threatening to spring up in his eyes. He was more touched than he'd ever been. And increasingly furious with himself that he'd given his daughter so little time.

'We'll see.'

These were the only two words the lump in his throat would allow him to say. But Keith was interested to see that Mandy didn't persist, unlike her mother. Sandra would have taken his refusal as a challenge, nagged and nagged until he was worn down. Then two weeks later she'd have lost interest and he'd be left with a horse to get rid of. Mandy just shrugged and asked for driving lessons instead.

Keith had never felt so full of resolve. He'd phone Lucy Liddiard in the morning, get her advice. See if she knew of any horses for sale. He might even ask her to look out for one for himself. He'd never ridden before in his life, but it was never too late to start.

He just hoped it wasn't too late to start with Mandy. Get to know her. Give her a bit of the life she deserved before she set off on the rocky road on her own. He looked around the house, as soulless and impersonal and luxurious and efficient as any first-class departure lounge. It had to go. Everything had to go.

IO

Three days before Christmas, Kay was digging around in her handbag, looking for the list she'd made for the last of her shopping. It was the garden centre staff party that evening and she was supposed to be buying their presents. She tipped out the contents of her bag on to the breakfast bar and a couple of tampons rolled out, ringing a tiny alarm bell in the back of her mind. She didn't seem to have used any for weeks. She flipped through her diary, trying to remember the last time she'd had a period. As she was horribly irregular and never wrote it down, she couldn't work it out.

Should she panic? She thought not. She was often late – weeks, sometimes. Anyway, she was ninety per cent certain she was infertile. All the same, it had been a long time. Perhaps she'd get a test on the way home. It would stop her brooding. Kay always liked to know how she stood one way or the other. She shoved everything back into her bag and forgot her dilemma, concentrating instead on the job in hand.

She battled her way through Cheltenham with half of Gloucestershire, doing all her duty shopping in the first hour and saving the fun till last. She wanted something special for Patrick. After much agonizing, she settled on a beautifully soft sage green cashmere scarf that she knew would look divine tucked into the collar of his flying jacket. She wouldn't wrap it; she'd just coil it round his neck the next time she saw him. She shuddered deliciously at the prospect, thinking about the warmth of his skin on her fingertips. She made her way hurriedly back to the car park, slowing to a halt outside the chemist. It was teeming with people buying unimaginative gifts of bubble bath and perfume and aftershave for their nearest and dearest; she really didn't think she could be bothered to fight her way through the throngs to the pharmacist's counter. However, now the doubt was in her mind she knew she wouldn't be able to relax until she found out one way or the other. She went in and perused the pregnancy testing kits, wondering which one would give her the answer she wanted. Not that she knew herself. At length she grabbed the most expensive. It was bound to be the right choice.

She drove home with the stereo on full volume, the bass vibrating through her, making her long for Patrick. He'd met her again three days before to make up, so he said, for abandoning her at the Gainsborough. Kay savoured the memory of what he had done to her, and looked forward to being able to give him the scarf. Too soon, though, she remembered she had something to resolve before she could think about their next union.

She got back to Barton Court, dumped all her packages on the kitchen floor, then went upstairs to the bathroom with the tester. She picked at the cellophane in frustration with her red-tipped nails, until finally the package was free and she was able to withdraw the unfamiliar apparatus from its box. She stared at the white plastic for a moment, peering through the minute clear window that would soon hold her destiny. She tried to analyse what she felt, but she was riding on a tide of uncertainty. Whatever the result, it would pull her into focus, and until that moment she was in an agonizing limbo. She read the instructions carefully, feeling slightly ridiculous as she held the stick in the stream of pee she'd saved up, then set it carefully down on the windowsill to wait.

The second hand on her Rolex moved round painfully slowly. Kay hadn't known until now that it took thirty-seven seconds to walk the entire top corridor of Barton Court and wondered if that could be included on the estate agent's particulars if they ever decided to sell. She went back to the windowsill after the requisite three minutes and picked up the stick. There were two blue lines in the window. Confused, she picked up the instructions again to double-check what this meant.

As if her body wanted to confirm the result, Kay was overcome by a wave of nausea. Rushing to the loo, she leaned over the blue and white china bowl and retched and retched until she was empty. Shakily, she washed her teeth and face, then took a deep breath before looking at herself in the mirror. She looked different, even from this morning. It was not just that she was pale and drained; there was something that hadn't been there before. Knowledge. Knowledge of the little being inside her; a little cluster of cells. But whose? Only one thing was certain. That half of them were hers.

Suddenly her waistband felt uncomfortably tight. She'd noticed that her waist had been a little thicker lately, but she'd put it down to her age, her metabolism slowing down, and had promised herself membership of a gym in the New Year. Now the reason was obvious. Kay made herself a cup of tea, threw it up and prepared to face her husband.

Lawrence strode proprietorially through the garden centre, noting with pleasure that all the Christmas trees had nearly gone and that the decorations were seriously depleted – selling trees as a loss leader, at a rock-bottom fifty pence a foot, had been a stroke of genius. The kindly-looking pensioner he'd hired as Father Christmas was dandling toddlers on his knee outside his grotto while their parents, Lawrence hoped, flashed the cash. He looked at his watch and decided to stroll over to the house for some lunch. Kay should be back from her alleged shopping trip by now. He wondered if she'd taken the opportunity of an illicit liaison with Liddiard.

Kelly's revelation hadn't entirely surprised him, though he was annoyed that he hadn't worked it out for himself. If Kelly had cottoned on, so might other people, and Lawrence didn't do humiliation. But before he took action, he needed proof – he didn't want to go steaming in and making accusations without solid evidence. After all, he only had the word of a brainless little bit of fluff who for all he knew bore a grudge against Mickey and might be stirring things out of malice.

He was going to bide his time.

'Darling, I've got some wonderful news.'

Kay shook her head in frustration. For the past hour she'd been experimenting with how to break the news to Lawrence. In the end she needn't have worried. Lawrence came into the kitchen, took one look at her and asked what was wrong.

'I'm pregnant.'

The words were bald, but she knew with Lawrence there was no beating around the bush. You had to come straight to the point. She didn't quite know what reaction she was expecting, but when he stared at her and his eyes went dark, as black as ink, and he turned on his heel and left the room, she knew she'd blown it.

They'd talked about starting a family not long after they got married. Kay had been unsure at first, being only just over thirty, but Lawrence was keen not to be too aged a parent. They weren't scientific in their attempts to procreate, but certainly did it often enough to be in with a fighting chance. When nothing had happened after eighteen months, Kay had casually broached the subject of fertility treatment and had been somewhat relieved when Lawrence had dismissed it out of hand. If it wasn't meant to be, he'd said, then who were they to interfere with nature? Kay had read enough articles about IVF to know that she didn't really want to be first in the queue, and had been happy to leave it at that. So she couldn't have kids. So what? If the snotty, whinging specimens she'd come into contact with were anything to go by, she wasn't missing much. Then Lawrence had become absorbed in Barton Court and the subject seemed to be forgotten, to Kay's relief.

Deep down, however, Lawrence was tormented by what he considered to be their failure. He needed more information. After making exhaustive inquiries as to the best consultant, he found himself in a small cubicle doing something unspeakable into a test tube, only to be told by a grave-faced Frenchman that his sperm were weak, feeble and intent on swimming the wrong way, and that without scientific intervention they would never reach the goal they were destined for. He was, to all intents and purposes, sterile. He found it, as well as incredibly painful, somewhat ironic that the purveyor of seed to half of Gloucestershire and Oxfordshire would never sow his own.

He hadn't told Kay. It was a painful secret he kept locked away; something that he need never humiliate himself by revealing as she seemed quite happy to remain childless, at least for the time being. She blamed herself, of course, and he never thought to disabuse her of the fact, but then neither did he rebuke her. They just had a tacit agreement that Oakley offspring were not to be.

And now she had told him she was pregnant. He cursed her for not being more prescient, not guessing at the truth, but why should she? She'd never heard the consultant's doom-laden words – 'It would take a miracle.' And he knew bloody well there hadn't been a miracle. He knew that in the split second it had taken Kay to meet his eye.

So now their partnership was over. There was no way he could allow it to continue. It wasn't a tragedy, more of an inconvenience. They'd worked well together.

As he drew his chequebook out of the right-hand drawer of his desk and pulled the lid off his fountain pen, he was perturbed to find tears stinging his lids. He brushed them away angrily, debated the sum he was going to write in the oblong, signed his name with a flourish, then went to unlock his filing cabinet.

He walked back into the kitchen where Kay was sitting at the breakfast bar, cradling her head in her arms. She looked up at him as he wordlessly held out the letter from the consultant. Her stomach churning, she read through the diagnosis, then looked up at Lawrence.

'Why didn't you tell me?' she croaked. 'You let me think it was my fault . . .'

He gave a dismissive shrug.

'And you were going to let me think that brat in your belly was mine?' His tone was flat. Emotionless. 'Hard to say which is worse, isn't it?'

He handed her an envelope containing the cheque he'd just written.

'You can keep your car as well. You've got half an hour to pack.'

'Lawrence—'

'There's no discussion, Kay. There's nothing to say. You've got no defence.'

Half an hour later, Kay sat in her car, shell-shocked, suppressing a strange desire to laugh uncontrollably at the absurd turn her life had taken. Only two hours ago, she'd been quite oblivious, happily doing her Christmas shopping. Now, here she was, banished from her own home, estranged from her husband, pregnant, with a cheque for a quarter of a million pounds in her pocket.

She knew there was no point in trying to worm her way back into Lawrence's life. She knew when he made a decision it was final. And she considered she'd got away quite lightly. When she'd taken the cheque, she'd accepted the deal. She was out of his life. End of story. She'd packed her clothes, some toiletries, dug out a few private papers she might need and marvelled at how her life had fitted into the boot of her car.

She hadn't really had a chance to take in the implications

of what he'd told her, or feel aggrieved that he'd never chosen to tell her before. All she felt was relief that their confrontation hadn't been uglier.

So where now? What now? It was three days before Christmas – what the hell was she supposed to do? She certainly wasn't going to go back to her parents. Her scenario was daunting enough without bringing Slough into the equation. Kay rarely left anything to chance, but she was finding it hard to be rational, so she pulled out the AA map she found in the pocket on the back of the driver's seat. She'd open it and drive to the very first place that caught her eye.

Frome. Somerset.

It took her just over an hour and a half to get there.

Somehow the further one got from the Cotswolds and the nearer one got to Bath, the local stone lost its warmth and became rather forbidding. Kay wondered if that really was the case, or if it was her state of mind. As she drove down the steep hill into Frome, she looked anxiously round her, for Kay was a great believer in first impressions. It was quite a plain little town, more down to earth than Elden-bury, but clearly lively, as the high street was lined with a bustling street market. Signs for the public library and municipal buildings were more prominent than those for local tourist attractions, indicating that real people actually lived here. But Kay was also pleased to note a decent butcher and a delicatessen, and amongst the 'turnips' were quite a few well-dressed women, as well as some decidedly alternative types – to which Kay had no objection. At least the local community wouldn't be narrow-minded, which was pretty important in her condition. Furthermore, Bath was only twenty minutes by car, from where London was less than two hours by train. She thought she might be able to survive here.

She sought out a local independent estate agent and perused the properties for sale. Prices were way down on the Cotswolds, despite Frome's proximity to Bath. But that was a definite advantage. She'd need some change from what Lawrence had given her to live on. However, the selection of houses for sale was disappointing: a large majority were on modern estates, of which there were clearly several in the locality, or dreary little poky terraces, or apartments in converted buildings of the type Lawrence used to specialize in and which Kay knew were always grossly overpriced. The estate agent explained that there was an area of Frome that was particularly sought after, with attractive period properties, but these were usually snapped up even before they were advertised, and because of the time of year they had nothing of interest on their books at the moment.

Despondent, she turned away, but not before a sign in the window caught her eye: experienced sales negotiator wanted.

She mulled the prospect over in her mind. She could talk her way into the job, she knew she could. And she'd be good at it. And once her foot was in the door, she'd get advance notification of the best properties coming up on the market. She wasn't sure what sort of salary a senior sales negotiator commanded these days, but it was certainly more than the big fat nothing she was earning at the moment.

She was in the middle of outlining her experience to the office manager when the door opened and a tall young girl with a cloud of red hair whirled in and interrupted the proceedings. She'd had her house valued by them earlier in the week, and wanted to put it on the market straight away, although the agent protested that less than a week before Christmas was hardly ideal. The girl was insistent, however. She'd been offered a job designing kitchens in London and needed to move the first week of the New Year. She'd be heartbroken leaving the Coach House, she said, but it was a career opportunity she couldn't turn down.

Kay's ears pricked up at the mention of the Coach House, and she lingered and eavesdropped as the agent persuaded the girl that there would be no one available to type up particulars or, indeed, to show prospective purchasers round for the next two weeks at least, but they would be delighted to take the instruction on in the first week of the New Year. Kay was appalled by the agent's apathy and lack of professionalism – she herself would have had a signature on the dotted line and a board up before you could say knife – but she had a feeling that this was probably par for the course in Frome. Besides, their slack approach was going to work in her favour. She slipped out of the office and waited round the corner for three minutes before the girl appeared.

'Listen, I couldn't help overhearing you in there. Your house sounds just like what I'm looking for. Could I have a look at it?'

The girl looked at her slightly warily.

'I'm a cash buyer. If I like it, I'll give you what the agent valued it at, and you'll save yourself the fees.' She smiled winningly. 'A couple of grand wouldn't go amiss, surely? Especially if you're moving to London.'

The girl's eyes lit up at the thought.

'Where are you parked? You can follow me.'

She had difficulty keeping up with the girl, who whizzed through the warren of Frome's backstreets, littered with junk shops masquerading as antique shops that might, nevertheless, contain treasures if you looked hard enough. Finally the girl led her up Maddox Street, which was tiny and narrow with barely any room for parking. Kay bumped the passenger-side wheels of her car up on to the pavement outside the stout red door of the Coach House with its heavy wrought-iron knocker.

For once, the term 'deceptively spacious' applied, for what seemed like a modest terrace on the outside hid a home of generous proportions. As its name suggested, it had been the coach house for its more substantial neighbour, and had retained all the architectural charms, being a magical mixture of stone walls, flagged floors, deep, warm pine doors, black beams and wrought iron. The huge living room stretched up for two storeys, heated by a wood-burning stove, and a glorious set of French windows led out on to a tiny walled garden. The rest of the house was cunningly built on several different levels, with steps leading up and down to a snug but efficient bathroom, or a light-filled studio area, or a pretty but useless little balcony. The kitchen positively oozed warmth, fuelled by a dark green oil-fired range and fitted out with a simple but hand-built kitchen of reclaimed oak. All the walls were painted a crisp, bright white. Fixtures and fittings were understated but tasteful. It needed nothing doing to it.

Half an hour later, against her better judgement and all the negotiating skills she'd ever learned, she found herself offering the asking price, cash, for a quick completion.

She wanted to be in as soon as possible after the New Year. The girl hugged her, and hoped she'd be as happy in the Coach House as she had been. Kay hoped so too.

By five o'clock, Kay was exhausted. Trying to find a hotel so soon before Christmas had been a struggle, and she wasn't unaware of the irony of the timing and her condition. She had eventually hit upon a charming inn four miles outside Frome that had just had a cancellation. Wearily, she made her way up to her bedroom and congratulated herself on finding a perfect haven, with its oak floors, tapestries and a huge stone fireplace with crackling logs. She sank on to the four-poster bed and drank thirstily from the bottle of sparkling mineral water on the bedside table. Feeling a little more refreshed, she assessed her predicament.

She'd found herself a home – hopefully, subject to all the usual hoops home-buyers had to jump through. And she had an interview just after Christmas for the negotiator's job – the manager from the estate agent had phoned up on her mobile to confirm it. If she got the job she'd bloody well shake that office up – little did they know they'd lost a sale through their apathy.

There was just one more thing to organize, but Kay felt too shattered to face that particular hurdle. She got as far as picking up the local phone directory, but her eyes became heavier and heavier as she ran through the list of names and she finally fell into a deep, much-needed slumber.

Next morning, she awoke feeling refreshed. She treated herself to bacon and eggs, as she'd missed supper the night before, and a long, hot bath. Then she steeled herself and picked up the phone book again. There was one more thing to arrange before she could relax. She looked up the local doctor's surgery, registered herself as a temporary patient and made an urgent appointment. The GP she saw was grave, young and as sympathetic as could be expected as she explained her plight: she was pregnant, it was unwanted and she needed to arrange a termination as quickly as possible.

The doctor explained he'd have to give her a routine examination before proceeding with the formalities. He'd waited for her to get dressed again before asking her to sit down. Somehow, Kay knew from the expression on his face that all the plans she had so successfully made in the last twenty-four hours were out the window.

'I'm afraid a termination is out of the question.' She started to protest.

'I'm quite happy to pay. I don't care how much it costs—'

'It's not a question—'

'Look, I'm on my own. I haven't got a job. How can I possibly—'

The doctor had cut her off.

'Mrs Oakley, you're five months' pregnant. Well past the cut-off date for an abortion. I'm sorry.'

II

Patrick was keenly aware that he had been neglecting Kelly. Not only during but since the night of the dance, and he felt about as guilty as Patrick ever felt about anything, so he got in his car and drove down to the Honeycote Arms.

The welcome he got was as unexpected as a slap in the face. He was lucky he didn't get one of those as well. Kelly marched out with her hands on her hips before he'd even got out of the car.

'I don't know how you can show your face here.'

'Look – Kells. I'm sorry about the dance. Sophie was as sick as a dog and I had to take her home. There was no time to tell you—'

'And no time to phone me since?'

'It's been hectic at the brewery.'

'Yeah. I suppose you've been planning what to do with the profit from this place.'

Patrick frowned.

'Or hasn't your father told you his plans?'

'What?'

'He's selling the Honeycote Arms. You can imagine what sort of Christmas we're going to have, while you all sit up there drinking yourselves stupid and feeling pleased with yourselves—'

'Kelly, Kelly – hold on. Who told you this?'

'Your dad told my dad.'

'I didn't know – I promise.'

'Would you have done anything about it if you had?'

'Of course!'

'Crap. There's nothing you can do, Patrick. Honeycote Ales is going bust. Everyone knows it. I expect we're just the first in a long line of loyal and faithful tenants you're going to evict—'

'Evict?'

Patrick looked wildly round for evidence that this was some kind of a joke. But in his gut he knew it wasn't. He tried to put a reassuring hand on Kelly's arm.

'Let's go somewhere for lunch. We can talk about it. I'm sure things aren't quite what they seem. I'm sure you've got it all wrong somewhere.'

'No, Patrick. I haven't. What I got wrong was thinking there could ever be anything between you and me.'

Kelly looked at Patrick with contempt and turned on her heel, slamming the door to the pub with a finality he knew not to challenge. He felt chilled to the bone. And deeply ashamed. Ashamed that he could be so ignorant of what was going on at Honeycote Ales. This was serious. This was people's lives that were being fucked around, not just the mere tightening of the belt his father had hinted at once or twice. Patrick had been worried that he might have to swap his car for something less glamorous. How shallow did that make him?

Patrick sank despairingly back into the driver's seat and felt totally powerless. If only he'd paid more attention to the way things were run at the brewery, maybe he'd be able to see a way out. Instead, he had next to no idea of the damage that had been done. He knew they had massive overheads. He knew they weren't turning over a huge amount. He knew they faced competition from all the other pubs and restaurants in the area. But all those things had been the case for nearly as long as the brewery had been running. They'd always survived before.

He needed to look at the paperwork. He needed to know exactly what was going on and what could be done about it. He didn't trust his father to be doing the right thing, necessarily. If Patrick was guilty of pratting about when there was hard work to be done, then so was Mickey, in spades. Kay was evidence enough of that. And he knew Mickey would go for the easy option, because he always did.

Patrick rammed the car into first, and sped off down the road towards the brewery.

Kelly watched out of the window a little sadly. She'd never kidded herself that she and Patrick had any great future together, but it had been good fun while it lasted. She shrugged and turned away. Never mind – there were plenty more fish in the sea. Someone else would turn up and whisk her off. In the meantime, her parents needed her support, which meant she could hardly go sleeping with the enemy.

Ned had spent all morning selling mistletoe at the farmers' market in Eldenbury. It was Friday, and Christmas Day was on Sunday, so the world and his panic-stricken wife had come out in force to buy their free-range turkeys and organic vegetables. Luckily most of them had been quite taken by the idea of a sprig of mistletoe to hang in the hallway, so by midday he'd sold out completely and had a satisfying pocket of cash. It was one of the few perks his father allowed him – every year he drove the tractor round the farm gathering every sprig he could lay his hands on, which he then sold for a pound a go. He didn't bother keeping any for himself. There was only one girl he wanted to kiss and he knew it was going to take more than a paltry piece of mistletoe to win her over.

He'd felt sick to his stomach for the past few days. Ever since the night of the dance. So much so that he, Ned Walsh, who could wolf down half a dozen rashers of bacon, several eggs and the best part of a loaf of bread for breakfast alone, had barely eaten. For he'd been hit by a thunderbolt: he was totally, utterly and hopelessly in love. He didn't like it, and he didn't know what to do about it. He'd never realized that feelings could knock you off your feet like this, even a proverbial brick shit-house like him.

Sure, he'd had girlfriends. Several. And he supposed he'd loved a couple of them, in that he'd have been extremely upset if they'd been squashed under a tractor. But when their dalliances had come to a mutual, natural end, he hadn't spent much time grieving. On to the next, that was his motto. But this time it was different. He couldn't get the vision of this particular girl out of his head. And he couldn't bring himself to talk to anyone about it. He was embarrassed that he felt so vulnerable. He'd managed to hide his feelings the night of the ball with his usual high jinks and shenanigans. He didn't think anyone had guessed how he really felt. Especially not Patrick. He thought Patrick would probably deck him if he knew the thoughts he'd been harbouring about his sister. Well, half-sister.

Ned had been gobsmacked when he'd seen her. He'd known she was coming and he'd been looking forward to having a laugh with his old mate. He'd expected her to turn up in her usual maroon velvet, slightly podgy, slightly flushed. 'Sofa', he'd always called her, and she hated it, thinking he meant that she was the size of one. When she'd appeared, Ned had barely been able to stutter out a few words of greeting and had fled to the bar to recover from the shock of this new Sophie.

He'd wanted to talk to her, desperately. But he didn't know how. He was terrified. He couldn't believe that he'd once snuggled up with her in makeshift tents, totally un-selfconscious, giggling, sharing midnight snacks. Now she was this unapproachable goddess. He'd watched in agony as she'd circulated the room, men flocking to her side like bees to a honeypot. She'd had an air of confidence he'd never seen before. She always used to hang back at social gatherings, squirming with shyness if anyone spoke to her and had always been grateful for Ned's company, as he'd shielded her from any unwelcome attention. The night of the ball she'd barely spoken two words to him. Then, like Cinderella, she'd disappeared. The only thing he could be grateful for was that she'd gone with Patrick. She'd been taken ill, apparently. He hadn't seen her since. Normally in the holidays she phoned him up straight away, to go for a ride, or to the flicks, or just to go to Honeycote for spag bol and Budweiser. But he hadn't heard a word. Obviously, he didn't fit into the lifestyle of the new, streamlined Sophie. Gloomily, he made his way out of the market and over to the Horse and Groom. He felt like getting totally trolleyed.

Mayday saw Ned sitting at the bar, drinking a pint of Honeycote Ale as if it was going out of fashion. He looked pretty glum for Ned, who could always be relied on to be smiling. She sneaked up behind him and tickled the back of his neck. He knew from the vanilla-scented waft of Angel who it was. She hoicked herself up on to the neighbouring bar stool, giving him a glimpse of creamy thigh through the slit in her leather skirt and a double helping of equally creamy breast trapped in a tightly laced black top.

'What's the matter with my favourite farmhand?'

She always called him this, despite the inheritance that was waiting for him around the corner. Ned let out a heavy sigh in reply, draining his pint.

'Girly trouble, is it?'

She put her head on one side and looked at him knowingly from under the heavy curtain of black hair that fell over her kohl-ringed eyes. She strongly favoured the seventies rock chick look, mixed in with anything else she fancied from other eras. She was big on tattoos and piercings, beaded plaits, biker boots, chunky silver jewellery, love beads and leather thongs. Not necessarily what you'd expect from a barmaid in a market town, but the customers loved her cheeky backchat and open smile.

Ned just grimaced into his pint in reply to her query. But she persisted. Mayday loved other people's problems, as she never seemed to have any of her own.

'Come on, tell Aunty Mayday. I'm well versed in affairs of the heart, as you know. Perhaps I can give you some advice.'

'I'm miserable, Mayday. Unrequited love. It's a terrible thing.'

She dropped her voice and leaned into him. Ned had a tantalizing view of her cleavage.

'Well, lucky for you, I've just finished my shift. Why don't you come upstairs and I'll do your cards? See what the future holds.'

Mayday liked to project herself as some sort of mystic. It was all total bollocks, of course – she didn't have a clue how to read cards. But people liked to believe what she said, as she always told them what they wanted to hear. She liked to steer them on the right course in affairs of the heart. She was a true romantic where other people were concerned. She loved a happy ending. She could see what Ned needed was a prod in the right direction.

Knowing full well he shouldn't, Ned followed Mayday up to the attic room she inhabited at the top of the inn. She'd painted the walls dark purple, which gave it the air of some latter-day opium den. The lingering wafts of a half-smoked joint on her dressing table added to the illusion. Mayday picked up the joint, relit it, then leaned over and breathed the hot, sweet smoke into Ned's mouth. He felt himself relax; felt all his cares and worries melt away. She patted the pile of batik-covered cushions covering the mattress that served as her bed, and he fell on to it. Mayday put Jimi Hendrix into her cassette player, flopped down beside him and they finished the joint, staring up at the golden stars she'd painted on the ceiling, transported by the swirling melodies.

Mayday squashed the roach out in a plant pot, then rolled on to Ned, giggling. He protested feebly as her hands started to explore.

'I thought you were supposed to be reading my cards.'

'Later.'

Mayday rolled off the mattress, sauntered over to the window, threw it open and leaned her elbows on the sill. She stuck her rump out, covered in its shiny leather shell. Somehow Ned knew she wouldn't be wearing any knickers.

'Go on. Do your worst. I'm going to stand here and watch the world go by.'

Afterwards, Ned felt slightly ashamed. He reasoned that you couldn't be unfaithful to someone if you weren't actually going out with them. Didn't have a cat in hell's chance of getting anywhere near them, in fact. But he wouldn't have wanted Sophie to know that Mayday's screams of pleasure had made heads turn to look up at the window to see what the commotion was, wondering if someone was being murdered. Mortified, he'd pulled her back into the room, and she'd borne down on him, flushed and giggling.

'Your turn now.'

'No—'

Ned had put up a half-hearted fight, trying to pull up his jeans. Once he could excuse, while twice to him indicated some sort of commitment. But Mayday was still feeling aroused from her exhibitionism and skunk always made her horny as hell.

Afterwards, she read him his cards. She assured him that he'd secure the object of his affections before the twelve days of Christmas were past.

'I don't think I'm good enough for her, Mayday.'

'Rubbish. Any girl on the planet would be lucky to have you. You're a true gentleman. And kind. And a good laugh. And not a bad shag, for a farmer.'

Ned tried to look convinced. Mayday gave him a nudge of encouragement.

'What you need to do is get her a present. That'll give you an excuse to talk to her.'

'She won't want a present off me.'

Mayday gave a tut of impatience.

'You can argue with me all you like. But you can't argue with the cards. It's meant to be. So come on. Let's go shopping.'

She slipped into several yards of swirling purple crushed velvet and her biker boots as Ned struggled back into his jeans, somewhat dazed. Then he stumbled in Mayday's wake out of the Horse and Groom into the melee of shoppers and tried to forget the fact that his father would be expecting him home for milking any minute.

Earlier that morning, Keith had scrambled into the attic and brought down the Christmas tree that had adorned The Cedars' lounge for the past four years. It stood eight foot high and had multi-coloured lights that flashed in sequence. He didn't have to plug it in to realize that it was the height of bad taste, even if it had cost him the best part of two hundred quid. They'd get a real one. And they'd put it in the snug, which was starting to feel a bit more welcoming now he'd left two empty coffee cups and his slippers in there. He looked at the box of frosted stalactite icicles and baubles encrusted with fake snow, and tipped them straight in the bin.

He sent Mandy off into town with a list of presents he needed for his various staff, trusting her taste. He made it a longer list than was really necessary, because he'd got a lot to do before she got back. As soon as she was out of the door he hit the phone.

He made three phone calls. The first to a friend of his who did something inexplicable to do with venture capital in Birmingham.

'Ray? Keith. I've made a resolution. About a week too early, you might think, but why wait? I want shot of the business. Ask around, will you? See if anyone's interested. I'm open to any reasonable offer. And there's a drink in it for you.'

There'd been a stunned silence, and then agreement from Ray, who indicated to Keith that he thought they'd be probably be queuing up.

Keith then dialled the local estate agent to get them to come and value The Cedars. He wanted it on the market first week of the New Year. Then he called Honeycote House. The phone rang for a long time before Mickey finally answered. Keith felt a bit of a fool, explaining what he wanted.

'Mandy's been after a horse since she was three. I think I'm finally going to give in. The trouble is, I haven't a clue where to get one. Or what to look for. Or even how much they cost.'

Fantastic, thought Mickey. He might not be able to run a brewery, but he knew a cash opportunity when he saw one.

'That's no problem. I'm sure we'd be able to help you. You've got to know what you're doing when you buy horses. Even quite respectable people will sell you nags only fit for the knacker and you've got no real come-back.'

'That's great. I'd give you commission, if you found the right one.'

Mickey laughed his smoothest, most charming laugh.

'I wouldn't hear of it. How much did you want to spend?'

There was an embarrassed silence.

'I don't really know. How much is a horse?'

'How long is a piece of string? Like anything, you get what you pay for.'

'I suppose I want something safe. That looks nice.'

'She wants something half decent. She's quite a good rider.'

Mickey thought back to Mandy racing him on Monkey. She'd given it her best shot; what she lacked in style, she made up for in guts. As he pondered the memory, a thought suddenly came to him.

'Something's just occurred to me. I think we might have the very horse here.'

Five minutes later, the deal was done. They agreed to meet early that evening for Keith to hand over the cash – he had insisted. And, of course, Mickey hadn't put up a great deal of resistance. Three grand in fifty-pound notes was going to save him from seven sorts of shit. The only fly in the ointment was what Patrick was going to say when he found out.

Lawrence had patrolled the garden centre in tight-lipped white fury for the rest of the afternoon. The staff cowered in fear, not daring to ask why the Christmas party had been so suddenly cancelled. And no one ventured to ask where Kay had got to, as this was obviously the source of his rage.

When Kelly had revealed the truth about Mickey and Kay, Lawrence had been devastated, more so than he liked to admit even to himself. He knew their marriage wasn't the conventional match made in heaven, that they didn't exactly bill and coo at each other, but in some ways he felt it worked better than a lot of superficially successful marriages. So to find out that he'd been utterly mistaken, that what he'd thought was a united front was a total sham, had shaken him. And a tiny little bit of him still hoped that what Kelly had told him wasn't true. Not that he'd thought Kelly had been lying, for she didn't strike him as malicious. But she might have been mistaken. Now he knew she hadn't been.

Lawrence tortured himself wondering what Liddiard was able to provide his wife with that he couldn't.

And now he knew that Mickey had spawned the child in her belly, he was gutted. The bastard had given her what Lawrence so desperately wanted, though it was only now that he knew how much. Men weren't supposed to be broody, were they? He was finding that he had to hurry past the grotto in the garden centre, in case he found himself mawkishly gazing into a pram or ruffling the hair of some toddler waiting for Father Christmas. He'd never taken any notice of children before – only to wonder how they could contribute to his profit margins. Perhaps it was because when you were told you couldn't have something, you suddenly wanted it. Especially when somebody else had it.

He'd had no choice but to banish Kay. He couldn't have borne the questions, let alone the answers. Lawrence wasn't one for talking things over. He'd be every counsellor's nightmare. But now, suddenly, his life was empty; a total vacuum with no hope of being filled. He didn't kid himself that they'd had the perfect marriage. It was based on rather cynical, unwritten rules. But it had worked. At least, he'd thought it had. Obviously not for her.

He heard the tills ringing merrily, filling up with cash, and the noise seemed to mock him as he wondered what the point was. What was he going to spend it all on? What the bloody hell could he buy to fill the hole in his life? Or at least patch it up temporarily.

Sex. Maybe that was what he needed. A physical focus; total pleasure; something that would obliterate the bitter thoughts that whirled round his head.

He picked up the phone and got through to Kelly at the pub.

'Kelly?'

'Yes?'

'It's Lawrence Oakley.'

There was a small silence and Lawrence could imagine her mascara-laden lashes blinking in surprise before she replied, slightly wary.

'Hello.'

'I know it's short notice, but I've got some shopping to do in London. I need some help choosing things – I thought you'd be just the person. If you're not doing anything.'

Lawrence wanted Kelly to be quite happy, in the first instance, that there was an above board reason for their trip. So that she could justify it to other people as well as herself. He could tell by the upset in her voice when she'd spilled the beans about Kay and Mickey that she had a strict moral code that her dress sense belied.

He could almost hear Kelly turning the proposition over in her mind, wondering what the catch was, and if it was a trap of some sort. He laid some more bait.

'And we could have dinner somewhere.'

He was surprised but pleased when she agreed.

'OK.'

'Can you be ready in half an hour? I'll pick you up.'

There was a slight hesitation.

'Can you pick me up from the bus shelter in the village?'

Sweet. She didn't want her parents to see her picked up by an older man. She knew what they'd think.

'No problem.'

He drove her up to town in his Jag. She was impressed with his car but not, it seemed, with his CD collection, and quickly retuned the radio to something which churned out endless power ballads. She was surprisingly relaxed and chirruped away to him in the car. He supposed it went with the job – being a beautician must be a bit like being a hairdresser, and you probably needed to be able to talk at length on inane subjects. Neither of them mentioned Kay. Somehow, both of them knew that was a chapter in his life that was now closed. Time to move on.

He took Kelly on a whistle-stop tour of London that left her awestruck. They went to all the shops she read about in the magazines she lived for. She drooled over their clothes, then bought cheap imitations in the chain stores along Knightsbridge that she was young enough and thin enough to get away with. She didn't yet need the cut and the quality of designer clothes. Later, she helped Lawrence choose presents for his right-hand staff – he usually left this task to Kay, but he needed to see through his excuse. Anyway, both his PA and the centre manager had worked doubly hard over the past couple of days and hadn't asked him any questions, for which he was grateful. He wouldn't dream of thanking them verbally, but an extra-generous gift would say it all. They'd understand. They knew how he worked. That's why they'd stayed in their jobs for so long.

Not once did he offer to buy Kelly anything, as this would have altered the dynamics of the day's arrangements and Lawrence didn't want to move too quickly, or for Kelly to feel compromised. Besides, the last thing he wanted was to look like some sort of sugar daddy.

Dinner, however, had been part of the original deal. Lawrence ordered Bellinis for Kelly, which he knew were delicious but deceptive. He himself drank Bollinger, which he let her sip from his glass. Her nose wrinkled – she liked the bubbles but it wasn't sweet enough for her.

He'd chosen the restaurant carefully and watched, amused, as she lapped up her surroundings, overawed by the glamorous clientele who Lawrence knew were people just like her only with a bit more money who'd come out dressed to the nines to impress each other, but who she thought were all minor celebrities. When she actually did spot a bit-part soap actress dining with her boyfriend, she was ecstatic. Lawrence knew it was time to move in for the kill.

'You know, we could stay.'

Kelly had looked at him with saucer eyes.

'It seems a shame to drive back now when you're having so much fun. We could check into a hotel, then go on somewhere else for a drink.'

He named a couple of celebrity haunts nearby and she took the bait.

'I'll see if I can get us a couple of rooms. I very much doubt it, this near Christmas, but you don't know if you don't try.'

He disappeared to make a discreet phone call. She wasn't to know he'd booked a room months ago – he always came up to town just before Christmas with Kay to do their shopping and take in a show. He came back, beaming.

'I managed to pull a few strings. They had one suite left. I can have the sofa . . .'

Kelly looked at him knowingly but grinned. She was going to play along.

Two hours, several cocktails and a couple of hundred quid later, Kelly led Lawrence by the hand down the corridor and into their suite.

'Now it's my turn to treat you,' she said. 'You can have a complimentary massage.'

She darted into the magnificent bathroom and came out with a pile of white, fluffy towels. Quickly and efficiently, she laid two on the bed and told him to strip, proffering another towel for him to cover himself, then disappeared back into the bathroom while he took off his clothes.

Lawrence had to admit to himself that he hadn't expected her to be so assertive, but he didn't mind. He folded his clothes neatly, wrapped the towel around his waist and lay face down on the bed in expectation. Kelly came out of the bathroom in the ubiquitous white hotel robe, bearing a basket full of freebie lotions and potions. She picked through them until she found a bottle of oil. She sniffed it appreciatively and poured some into her hands, letting the warmth of her skin heat it up slightly before she began her work.

Lawrence groaned, half in agony, half in ecstasy, as Kelly massaged his back with expert fingers. She took her thumbs and ran them one either side of his spine until they reached the hard knots at the back of his neck, then worked her way down. It was expertly done. He could tell as his muscles started to relax and the tension of the last few days began to slip away that he was in the hands of a professional. It was almost better than sex. He was just starting to feel himself drift away, the first few waves of sleep starting to wash over him, when she patted his bottom decisively and ordered him to turn over.

He came back to full consciousness with a start and rolled over obediently, glad that he'd been too busy relaxing to embarrass himself with an erection. He made sure he covered himself discreetly with the towel, as he still wasn't sure what the rules were, whether this was the preamble to a sexual encounter or whether this was it. He met Kelly's eyes to see if he could take his lead from her. She smiled at him coquettishly as she undid the knot at her waist. He gulped as the white towelling robe fell to the floor. Underneath she was wearing a hot pink satin corset, her waist squeezed into ridiculously tiny handspan proportions. Lawrence didn't know why he was surprised. It was obvious to anyone that this was the sort of underwear Kelly favoured. He supposed it was because he hadn't necessarily expected to see it.

She held up the bottle of oil and lasciviously tipped it up, allowing a steady stream to drip between her legs. She started to massage herself, and Lawrence watched in wonder as her hands worked their way up and down her tanned, toned thighs, each time coming nearer and nearer to her—

'Take off that towel.'

Lawrence had never allowed any other woman to take control in his life, but didn't need telling twice. He flipped the towel away obediently.

He reached out with eager hands, desperate to touch her, but she wagged a finger in reproach.

'Hands by your sides, please. Until I've finished. Ladies first.'

Later, when Kelly was curled up under the feather duvet, fast asleep, Lawrence felt a sudden rush of insecurity. What if the sex had just been thanks for the money he'd lavished on her, and she hadn't wanted to sleep with him at all? What if she'd just felt obliged and the whole encounter had been professionally stage-managed: mind-blowing, but meaningless? What if he'd just been used?

Suddenly, Lawrence felt panic clawing at his guts. What the hell was he doing with this girl? He must be mad! When Kay had dropped her bombshell, his reaction had been a knee-jerk. He'd been so ruthlessly single-minded that he hadn't actually given himself a chance to think over what had happened; he certainly hadn't given Kay a chance to explain. Should he have given her the opportunity? There was a little voice inside his head that told him there were always two sides to every story. And he knew that after the consultant's revelation, a little bit of him had died. Could he have shut Kay out without meaning to . . . ?

Lawrence told himself to snap out of it. Nothing Kay could have said would have made any difference. She had humiliated him, and more than anything else he was a proud man. Which was why he wouldn't admit, even to himself, that his heart and soul had been ripped out that afternoon. He might never have vocalized it, but in his own way he had loved Kay deeply. He couldn't imagine anyone else fitting into his life so well. They'd been a partnership. A team. It was a pity events had conspired to destroy them. But he wasn't going to wallow in self-pity and regret. It was time to move on.

He brushed his teeth vigorously, showered and put on the robe that matched the one Kelly had been wearing earlier. Then he went and sat on the bed, and watched her sleeping. She was going to help him forget, and for that he was grateful. But he resolved never to let himself become vulnerable again. He'd thought he was tough, invincible, ruthless. He'd learned the hard way that he wasn't.

He reached out his hand to stroke Kelly's hair, running his fingers through her tousled blonde tresses. She stirred and her eyes opened blearily. She managed a little suggestive smile.

'Wasn't that enough?'

Did she feel she owed him? All those cocktails, dinner, an expensive hotel – he supposed he could have demanded more attention.

'No. You go back to sleep.'

He pulled the duvet back over her and she snuggled down. He thought he could sense her relief. It was almost as great as his own. The last thing he wanted was a cold, calculated fuck. It would only highlight everything he'd lost.

12

It was Christmas Eve and Lucy wondered what on earth she was doing amongst all the other last-minute shoppers. But she couldn't bring herself to buy cheese from the supermarket – she wanted the living, breathing offerings to be had at the cheesemongers, the ones that smelled so much they had to be kept out in the scullery. Everyone always moaned about the stink of the Stilton and Pont l'Evêque, so she left it till the last minute.

At the cheese counter, she bumped into Lawrence.

'What are you and Kay doing for Christmas?'

'I'm at home. I've no idea what she's doing.'

Lawrence was tight-lipped and grim. Lucy wasn't sure what to say. Lawrence felt it was only polite to enlighten her.

'We've separated.'

He didn't elaborate and Lucy didn't expect him to. She always gave people time. She hoped that whatever had happened they could be reconciled. In the meantime, she couldn't bear to think of him on his own on Christmas Day.

'Listen – we're already nearly a dozen. One more won't make a difference. I've got a turkey the size of an ostrich. Please come and join us.'

People were notoriously unable to resist Lucy's invitations, even hardened cynics like Lawrence. Her warmth spilled over into your heart, somehow. He found himself accepting. Why should he spend Christmas Day on his own, anyway? Why should he be punished – it wasn't him that had been playing away. He didn't count the night with Kelly. He'd no longer considered himself married when that encounter took place.

Yes, Christmas lunch at the Liddiards could certainly be interesting. He was going to enjoy making Mickey squirm. He'd time it perfectly, so he'd be put right off his pudding. But he'd be discreet. The last thing he wanted was for Lucy to be hurt by all this. She was a lovely girl. She didn't deserve to be married to a shite like Liddiard.

On his way back to Barton Court, he dropped off a package at the Honeycote Arms for Kelly. It was a little amber heart on a silver chain she'd admired on their shopping trip – he'd managed to buy it while she was expertly assessing the various products at the make-up counters.

He drove away with hope in his heart, thinking of her face when she opened it the next morning. OK, so it might look as if he was trying to buy her, but he had to start somewhere. And it was only a trinket, a token.

An hour later, she'd phoned him on his mobile to thank him.

'You weren't supposed to open it till tomorrow, you naughty girl.'

'I've never been able to wait. It's beautiful. Thank you.'

'What are you doing tomorrow?'

'Staying with the family. It's going to be our last Christmas here.'

'Why? Where are you going?'

There was a little pause.

'I shouldn't tell you, but I don't see why I should keep it a secret. It can't make our situation any worse. The Liddiards are selling the Honeycote Arms. To pay off all their debts. They're in big trouble.'

Lawrence's knuckles whitened on his receiver as he flushed red with excitement.

'You should have told me this before.'

'Dad told me not to tell anyone.'

'Listen, you tell your dad not to worry. We might be able to sort something out. Tell him I'll be in touch after Christmas. But don't say a word to anyone else.'

Kelly put the phone down and felt a tingle of excitement in her veins. Meeting Lawrence had been a good thing. She was sure of that. He was the sort of guy that made things happen. Or, more to the point, stopped things from happening. She fingered the little amber heart at her neck and wondered whether to tell her father about the phone call she'd just had. Perhaps not – there'd be a little too much explaining to do. Her parents were quite broadminded – you had to be, running a pub – but she'd worked out that Lawrence must be more than twice her age.

Once she'd finished all her grocery shopping, Lucy still had a couple of presents to buy. She'd invited the Sherwyns for Christmas lunch and wanted to get them a little something each. And she hadn't got Mickey anything yet.

She slipped into James's gallery. It had been frantic for the past week, but was now quiet, as people didn't tend to panic-buy expensive paintings. Lucy felt herself relax in the gallery's elegant confines. The rich red of the walls contrasted with the pale oak beams and floorboards, choral music from King's College played quietly in the background and there was a delicious smell of mulled wine coming from somewhere.

James was delighted to see her.

'I'm in a panic. I haven't got Mickey a present yet. I haven't a clue, but I knew you would . . .' The irony was that Lucy had spent a long time searching for James's present before hitting on just the right gift. But she told herself that he was much harder to buy for than Mickey, who was easily pleased.

James, of course, found the perfect answer. A tiny little pen and ink drawing of a dog that looked just like Pokey. It was unsigned, therefore a reasonable price, and Lucy was delighted.

'You're a genius.' She tucked the carefully wrapped picture into one of her shopping bags.

'How are things with Mickey, anyway?' James asked. Casually, he hoped.

'Tons better. He seems much more relaxed. Thank God – I was starting to get worried.'

'Good.'

'By the way, what's Caroline doing tomorrow?'

James was surprised. Lucy rarely showed any interest in Caroline's whereabouts.

'Going to her parents.'

'I was going to say, do bring her to Honeycote if you want. For lunch. Or ask her up for a drink in the evening.'

James had to force himself to smile his thanks. He got the message. Lucy was telling him that she was all right. By inviting Caroline into the circle she was pushing him away, making sure he backed off. In other words, he was being dismissed. His services were no longer needed.

That evening, the little church at Honeycote was stuffed to the gills for midnight mass. The popularity of the vicar and the superlative choir always ensured a full turnout. The Liddiards, by dint of living at Honeycote House, always had the front pew. Ned, three rows back on the other side of the church, allowed himself a sidelong glance at Sophie. She looked just as he remembered her, not like the gilded angel from the other night. She was thinner than before, granted, but her hair was down and she was wearing no make-up. She was wearing a pale blue denim jacket and jeans. She looked nothing like the intimidating creature he'd fallen for. But Ned was amazed to find his heart was doing overtime nevertheless. He was in love with Sofa!

As he stared, she turned and looked straight into his eyes. He froze like a startled rabbit, not sure what to do. His heart melted as she smiled at him, not just a gesture of recognition, but a smile that seemed to come right from the heart. He beamed back as the organist pounded out the first few bars of 'Oh Come All Ye Faithful', then lifted his hand and tilted it to his mouth, to indicate a drink afterwards. Sophie nodded, and turned back to her hymn book.

Unable to wipe the grin off his face, Ned patted his pocket for the soft little package and, reassured by its presence, threw back his shoulders and sang joyfully.

As the congregation spilled out of the church into the crystal-clear night, wishing each other season's greetings and issuing invitations, Ned and Sophie slipped away. They sat on a tombstone away from the crowds, holding hands, laughing with nerves and excitement.

'I'm glad you're back to normal, Sofa. I was bricking it the other night. You looked so scary. I didn't dare speak to you.'

'I thought you were ignoring me.' Sophie looked at him shyly. 'I thought you fancied Mandy.'

'God no. I mean, she's a laugh and everything, but she's not really my type.' He smiled at her shyly. 'I've got you a present.'

He proffered the little package and Sophie opened it eagerly. Inside was a beautiful gossamer scarf, the colour and texture of fairies' wings, embroidered with tiny beads. Sophie was speechless – it was the prettiest thing she'd ever seen, and to think Ned had seen it and thought of her . . .

As Ned wrapped the scarf around her neck and, holding the ends, pulled her to him, Sophie smelled a waft of spicy vanilla. It was strangely familiar, but she thought perhaps the shop had wrapped the scarf in scented tissue paper. Anyway, she certainly didn't want to give it a second thought now. She closed her eyes as Ned took her in his arms and planted the gentlest, warmest kiss on her lips.

13

On Christmas morning, Lucy woke up at quarter to five, fifteen minutes before the alarm was due to go off. She switched off the alarm so as not to wake Mickey, pulled on some thick woollen socks and a jumper as the heating wasn't on yet, and tiptoed out of the bedroom.

In the kitchen, she surveyed the turkey thoughtfully and ran through a mental checklist of who was coming for lunch. Five Liddiards, James, Lawrence, the Sherwyns and the Walshes – it should be big enough. She scooped up liberal amounts of butter in her hands and massaged the skin with care, tucking herbs and lemon into the cavity, before covering it in a tent of foil and popping it into the Aga. She counted backwards carefully on her fingers, to make sure she'd calculated accurately for a two o'clock lunch.

Now the bit she liked best. She crept into the hallway and lifted the lid on a huge carved oak chest. Inside lay three fat, knobbly felt stockings, each one embroidered in chain stitch with its owner's initial. She pulled them out, enjoying their heavy weight, the mysterious lumps and bumps, and lugged them upstairs.

Patrick lay, beautiful, impassively arrogant as ever, one arm thrown carelessly above his head. Lucy wondered if she was soppy still giving him a stocking, and thought back fondly to the very first Christmas she'd spent at Honeycote. She'd stuffed Patrick's stocking full of traditional toys – a spinning top, a barrel of monkeys, a tin whistle, a wooden train, a bag of marbles – and had never been as gratified as when she'd seen his face as he opened it. His mother, apparently, had disapproved of Christmas, condemning it as commercial and materialistic, and as a concession the year before had allowed him one educational toy. Now, of course, the contents had changed, but Lucy couldn't bear to break with tradition, and liked to think that Patrick would be disappointed not to find his stocking at the bottom of his bed. He'd been harder than ever to buy for this year, and she worried that the gifts were rather boringly practical, though she'd been pleased with the torch shaped like a slim black credit card.

The girls had been easier. The hardest task was making sure that their presents were evenly distributed. In fact, Lucy had ended up getting them almost the same, blowing a fortune on body glitter and fake tattoos; knickers printed with the days of the week, an assortment of books and CDs and, of course, a calendar that never got turned past January.

Her deliveries over, she slipped back down to the chest, took out the presents she'd got for their guests and went to put them under the tree in the drawing room. The fireplace was festooned with greenery plundered from the garden, punctuated with ribbons of old-gold silk tied in fat bows. On the coffee table that usually held a jumble of magazines was an arrangement she'd thrown together, using baby pineapples, pomegranates and artichokes. On each windowsill was a huge vase of creamy roses tinged with coral.

The tree was a total contrast. Every decoration they'd had since the first tree she and Mickey had put up for Patrick was given a place. Every decoration any of the children had ever made was proudly reinstated each year. The result was a chaotic, over-the-top profusion that was so uncoordinated that it actually worked. There was no twee Shaker minimalism here. The whole point of Christmas tree decorations, thought Lucy, was that they had to be shiny and gaudy. The family usually had a competition to see who could find the most tasteless topping for the tree. Lucy had realized on Christmas Eve that no one had followed the tradition this year and had resurrected last year's – a sequinned Santa that sang over and over 'I Saw Mommy Kissing Santa Claus'. She thought it was rather indicative of the atmosphere in the house at the moment; everyone seemed distracted. She'd had to press-gang Sophie and Georgina into the preparations over the last couple of days, baking endless mince pies, threading the cards on to long strips of red ribbon and hanging them in the hall, polishing all the silver, black with unuse, so they could lay the table for Christmas lunch in the dining room. Lucy smiled as she remembered Sophie had been as high as a kite last night when they came back from drinks at the Walshes. She wondered if it was anything to do with the kiss she'd seen Ned give her daughter as they left. It seemed strange to think of Ned and Sophie romantically involved – Ned was almost like a second son to her. Perhaps that was why he'd blushed so furiously when Lucy had caught his eye and winked.

She placed the carefully wrapped packages under the

tree, then wondered if perhaps she should put James's somewhere safer. It was an antique goblet made of Murano glass, and fragile, so she put it on the mantelpiece out of harm's way. She knew James would love it – she knew his taste exactly. For a moment she considered their relationship. To some people it was no better than an affair, for they spent a lot of time together. In fact, she probably spent more time with James than she did with Mickey. The difference was, Mickey was totally aware of it. And anyway, she and James never had sex.

Lucy had never really considered sex with James although, deep down, she knew that if she gave off the right signals, he'd be willing. Not that he would ever make the first move; he was too much of a gentleman. But Lucy knew that James had never married because, if he did, their relationship would dwindle to nothing. Another woman would never put up with their friendship the way confident, unsuspecting Mickey did.

In many ways, she loved James, for he gave her the attention that Mickey often overlooked. Sometimes Lucy felt a little taken for granted and thought her reputation as a good sport wore a bit thin. She was extremely tolerant and good-natured when Mickey brought hordes of people back for food and drink after a day at the races. Or when Mickey enjoyed someone else's hospitality after one of these events and came back late and drunk. She didn't really mind, but then James was always on hand to make up for it, to pamper her with a lingering lunch in Cheltenham, or an open-air concert, or a wander round some National Trust garden. She'd need to put a gun to Mickey's head to endure any of those outings.

She wondered if James hadn't been there to fill this void

in her life, if her marriage would have been so successful so long. Did this mean she was exploiting James – what did he get out of it except the pleasure of her company? A lot, on reflection, thought Lucy. She looked after him well. He spent most of his spare time with her family, eating her food. Almost as if he were a brother. Which in a way he was, by marriage. Yes, that was it. James was just like a brother to her.

Reassured, Lucy decided to sneak back to bed for another hour before feeding the horses and starting on a mammoth potato-peeling session. She slid in beside Mickey, who'd been awake since she'd got up but was feigning sleep. He knew there were only a few hours to go before he had to tell Patrick about Monkey. As soon as the Sherwyns were here, the cat would be out of the bag. He was bitterly regretting what he'd considered to be such a smart move. But there was no going back on it. He'd spent the lot; the whole three grand. He consoled himself that at least he'd been responsible enough to pay off the worst of his debts. The ones that were in danger of getting him found out, anyway, like the petrol bill and the farrier. And the ones he couldn't manage without – namely the wine merchant.

Dammit – what was he worrying for? He'd paid for Monkey in the first place, hadn't he? He had every right to sell it. It wasn't as if Patrick even rode him any more – he'd outgrown the little horse years ago. He probably wouldn't mind at all.

Mickey started as he felt Lucy's warm hand creep under the waistband of his pyjamas. Oh God. He hoped and prayed that he wouldn't have a repeat performance of the other night with Kay; that the guilt and the stress and the drink weren't going to permanently take their toll. But no – he felt the familiar stiffening. Things were definitely on the up.

Mickey rolled over with a confident grin.

'Merry Christmas, darling.'

Over in Solihull, Mandy and Keith were exchanging presents and both secretly hoping that Sandra would neither embarrass nor insult them by phoning to wish them Merry Christmas. Mandy had bought him a pair of silver cufflinks in the shape of foxes' heads that he put on immediately. Then he gave her an envelope containing a voucher for half a dozen driving lessons, apologizing profusely for what he considered a very boring gift, and she protested, saying it was what she wanted.

She made them breakfast, scrambled eggs on granary toast, freshly squeezed orange juice and coffee. Keith finished his eggs appreciatively, then remembered something.

'I forgot – I got you something else.'

He disappeared out of the kitchen. Mandy started stacking the dishwasher. He came back in with an awkward-looking package wrapped in tartan paper. It felt like a belt. Puzzled, Mandy opened it.

It was a leather headcollar. She turned it over in her hands, mystified, till a little brass nameplate glinted up at her. She read the name engraved upon it. Monkey. She looked up at Keith, who was grinning from ear to ear.

'You're joking.'

'I'm not. He's yours. He's waiting for you at the Liddiards', so you'd better hurry up and get dressed.'

His daughter nearly knocked him flying as she enveloped him in a huge hug. Who was it who'd said it was better to give than to receive? They were bloody well right.

'You total sodding fucking arsehole.'

'Come on, Patrick. When's the last time you rode him, for God's sake? You're two stone too heavy—'

'That's my horse. You don't just go round selling other people's things. Certainly not without asking first.'

'I'm sorry. I honestly didn't think you'd mind.'

'Well, I do.'

He did. More than he would have thought. For an awful moment, Patrick thought he might cry.

'I want him back.'

'Sorry. No can do. I've spent the money.'

'On what? Not your wife, that's for sure. That wasn't three grand's worth of pyjamas.'

'Look, Patrick. There are things you don't understand—'

'Don't patronize me. There are things I understand perfectly, that I've been too polite to mention up until now. So don't give me that shit.'

Mickey gulped. This was even worse than he'd imagined. Patrick decided it was time to put the knife in. He was tired of pussyfooting round his father.

'The brewery's totally up the creek, isn't it?'

'Says who?'

'The world and his wife, as far as I can make out.'

'Idle gossip.'

'Kelly told me about the Honeycote Arms.'

Mickey rolled his eyes in exasperation. He'd made it clear to Ted it would be better for all of them if they kept the news quiet till the New Year. That's what you got for being honest and upfront with people. He needn't have told them what he was doing.

'We need some serious capital investment across the board. It's the only way.'

'We've always said we'd never get rid of any of the pubs.'

'In an ideal world. But that's not what we live in, is it? It's either sell the Honeycote Arms or get in some investor who'll stomp around in his jackboots telling us exactly how to run things. And the first thing he'd probably do is get rid of you, so if I were you I'd keep my mouth shut.'

Father and son glared at each other angrily.

'First you sell my horse. Then my birthright—'

'Don't be so melodramatic. It's a question of survival. Look, Patrick. You've had everything on a plate up till now. And I've never begrudged it for a single moment. So you could at least do me the courtesy of backing off. Things are tough enough without you behaving like a brat.'

Patrick bit his tongue. It was Christmas Day and he didn't want to spoil it. He turned on his heel and marched back into the house. Mickey was left in the courtyard and decided he'd better go and taste the wine he'd chosen for lunch. If it wasn't up to scratch there'd be time to chill down something else.

In the kitchen, Patrick was accosted by a flushed and slightly panic-stricken Sophie. She used his childhood nickname, which meant she wanted something.

'Patch. Would you absolutely, absolutely kill me if I gave your present to Ned?'

'I don't know. I don't know what it is yet.'

'I'll get you another one. In fact, I'll get you something even better in the sales. I've got to have something to give him.'

Patrick looked at Sophie and grinned.

'Is there something I should know?'

Sophie looked mortified. Patrick put her out of her misery.

'Of course he can have my present.'

'You won't tell him?'

'Course not. And, Soph – good on you. I always thought you'd be a perfect match.'

If it was possible, Sophie blushed even redder and ran upstairs to change the tag on the bottle of Ralph Lauren aftershave she'd bought him. Patrick was delighted. Ned was a decent bloke. He'd look after Sophie; he knew he would. And if he didn't, he'd have Patrick to answer to.

It had been a perfect, picture-book Christmas Day, thought Lucy. They'd had champagne and blinis with smoked salmon in the drawing room while everyone exchanged presents. Sophie had flitted about with a notepad and pen making a list of who'd got what, as everyone would get so drunk they'd have forgotten by the end of the day. She'd been wearing a silver scarf round her neck and kept exchanging little smiles with Ned that went unnoticed by nobody. Mickey was on good form, as he always was when hosting a houseful. Never happier than when filling people's glasses. The Walshes, as ever, were relieved to get away from the rigours of the farm. The Sherwyns mixed in well. Only Patrick had seemed tense, but had done his best to hide it – Lucy could only tell by the number of cigarettes he got through that something was bothering him. Trouble with Kelly, perhaps. James was delighted with his present. She knew that because he'd thanked her three times. Which was three more times than Mickey had – he'd admired the little picture she'd bought him for as long as was necessary to be polite, then tossed it to one side. She'd tried not to be hurt, then reasoned that Mickey had never been a great lover of art – as far as he was concerned, pictures were for covering up stains on the wall.

Things had only turned a little sour after lunch. Ned had persuaded the other youngsters to go for a walk. The adults were picking over the remnants of the cheese. Until now, no one had seen fit to mention Lawrence's plight, or question where Kay was, until Keith Sherwyn had looked at his watch and made a gloomy remark about not particularly wanting to go back to an empty house, although he supposed he ought. Lawrence had been drunk by then. Well, they all were, but he was clearly turning maudlin.

'Have you got any tips? It's something I'm going to have to get used to.'

He'd glared defiantly round the table.

'I suppose you're wondering where Kay has got to. I'll put you all out of your misery. I've no idea. All I know is she's not going to darken my door again.'

He'd taken a slurp of port and slammed the glass down. Lucy winced.

'She's only gone and got herself pregnant. Not mine, of course. So that's it. I've banished her. Mind you, no doubt she's found someone to sort it all out for her. Can't see Kay as a single mother, can you?'

He'd smirked around the table. There was a horrified silence. Mickey sloshed another good two inches of port into his glass and passed the decanter to his left with a trembling hand.

'More cheese, anyone?' murmured Lucy.

Sophie, Patrick, Mandy, Ned and Georgina walked off their lunch with an over-excited Pokey in tow. Mandy had been desperate to go and see Monkey again, perhaps even tack him up and go for a ride, but he'd lost a shoe and Lucy didn't think she'd be able to get the farrier until after the New Year. Mandy was consoled by the prospect of being in close proximity to Patrick. Sophie and Ned had taken the lead, tightly clutching mittened hands and stopping every now and then for an indiscreet snog that made Georgina gag with embarrassment.

Mandy fell into step beside Patrick.

'I'm really sorry about Monkey. Sophie told me he was yours. I didn't realize.'

Patrick nodded an indifferent acknowledgement of her apology.

'I'm not taking him straight away. Your dad said we could keep him at yours for a bit. We might be moving soon.'

'Really.'

Patrick was uninterested.

'Dad's going to sell his business. He wants to do something totally different. I think he'd like to move down here. So if we're nearby, you can visit Monkey whenever you like.'

Patrick looked at her.

'It's a big business, isn't it? He's going to make a few quid.'

'I don't think he cares how much he makes, as long as he gets rid of it.' She paused. 'But he'll get a few million, whatever.'

Patrick almost stopped dead in his tracks, but not

quite. He was a master at disguising his emotions. Instead he nodded politely.

'So what's he going to do instead?'

'I don't know. Anything, as long as it's got nothing to do with bathrooms. He wants to make a new start, now mum's left.'

Mandy sounded matter of fact, not self-pitying, so Patrick didn't feel the need to offer any sympathy on this front. Instead, he subtly changed tack.

'Listen, I'm really sorry about the other night.'

Mandy coloured furiously.

'I behaved appallingly. The thing is—' He ransacked his brain for a plausible platitude – 'I thought I was taking advantage of you. I thought you'd probably had too much to drink, like Sophie, and you'd regret it.'

'Oh no. I don't drink, really.'

Patrick stopped and turned her to face him. He tucked a strand of her long, shiny hair behind her ear, watching as she trembled under his touch, nervous as an unbroken foal.

He just had time to brush his lips against hers when Georgina stomped into view. He couldn't have paid her to make a more opportune appearance. The two sprang apart and resumed their walk.

'You're going home tonight, aren't you?'

'I think so.'

'What are you doing New Year's Eve?'

'I don't know.'

Patrick left a cruel gap in the conversation while he mulled the options over in his head. Honeycote House came into view. Patrick stopped and looked at it proudly. The thought of anyone else ever living there appalled him.

Yet he was strongly starting to suspect, from the snippets of information he'd picked up from his snoop round the brewery, from his conversation with Kelly and from the way his father was behaving, that it was not such a remote possibility. After all, people were turfed out of their ancestral seats all the time. But he couldn't just sit there and watch it happen, not like Mickey.

'If you're not doing anything, a mate of mine's having a party in Cheltenham. It should be a laugh.'

'Definitely. That would be great.'

'I'll call you nearer the time.'

'OK.'

Mandy smiled at him and her face lit up. She was really quite beautiful, realized Patrick.

The group stomped back into the hallway, kicking off wellies, dropping coats, scarves and gloves into a heap on the chest. Ned, overheated, took off the tie his mother had forced him into that morning and unbuttoned his collar. Sophie was looking at him in horror. With a strangled sob, she ran up the stairs.

'What is it?' Ned looked bewildered.

'You've got a sodding great lovebite on your neck,' Patrick told him.

Ned rushed to the nearest mirror and examined his neck anxiously. Bloody hell. Patrick was right. A big purply blotch reminded him of the moment Mayday had nipped him in a frenzy of passion two days earlier. Why the hell hadn't he noticed it? And how was he going to explain it away? He could hardly say he'd done it himself – it was anatomically impossible.

*

Sophie lay on her bed tearing at the gossamer scarf, which soon lay in shreds. She held it to her face, sobbing. The cloying scent it bore with it suddenly overpowered her as she remembered where she'd smelled it before. It was Mayday Perkins's perfume. The Horse and Groom always stank of it. Patrick's flying jacket sometimes stank of it, when they'd been out on a session together. And now Ned's present to her stank of it, because he'd been with her. She must have given him that lovebite. And not long ago, either.

Sophie couldn't believe it. She counted on her fingers. For nearly eighteen hours, ever since midnight mass, she'd been bursting with happiness, filled with a bubble of excitement that made her head, her heart, her every limb sing with joy. And now she'd been brought crashing cruelly down to earth.

By nine o'clock, everyone had gone. James had to see to his two Labradors who had been locked up all day. Lawrence had things to sort out at the garden centre, which was expecting its usual rush of Boxing Day visitors. The Walshes had to do whatever it was farmers had to do, as their livestock didn't recognize national holidays. Keith and Mandy took Sophie and Georgina back to Solihull – Keith had tickets booked for the pantomime in Birmingham on Boxing Day and invited the two girls along. Sophie had been only too glad to get away from everyone's curious stares at Honeycote and had cried all the way there. Mandy had been sweet, making sure the noise of the CD had covered her sobs so as not to embarrass her father, who anyway had Georgina jabbering away at him in the front seat.

In the kitchen, plates and bowls and glasses were stacked up on the table, surrounded by greasy serving bowls and cooking utensils. It was an unattractive proposition. Mickey, rigid with shock, offered to do the washing-up. It might take his mind off things for half an hour at least. But to his irritation, Lucy, fuelled by champagne and Pouilly-Fumé, wouldn't stop ranting on about poor Kay. She was scandalized, not by Kay's predicament, but by Lawrence's treatment of her.

'He can't just turf her out on to the street. Not if she's pregnant. Even if it's not his.'

'Course he can.'

'It's barbaric. I'm going to phone her. See if she's all right.'

'No!'

Lucy stared at Mickey, shocked by the aggression in his voice. She frowned, puzzled by his countenance. He was sweating profusely.

'Why not?'

'Because it's best not to get involved, that's all. Look, it's Christmas Day. Let Kay and Lawrence sort things out for themselves. I'm sure if she wants to talk she'll phone you.'

Lucy demurred. That was men for you. They never liked to get involved in other people's dramas. They didn't have a sense of solidarity like women. Lucy knew that if she was in Kay's position, heaven forbid, she'd appreciate a phone call. She'd feel a little bit better knowing somebody cared.

Over at Barton Court, Lawrence was lying on his bed, his head whirling, cursing himself. He usually liked to play his cards close to his chest, only today he'd drunk too much and said too much, he knew he had. But he couldn't bear Liddiard sitting there, so smug, with his perfect life, his perfect wife, his perfect family. All the things Lawrence knew he would never have. He'd wanted to piss all over Mickey's strawberry patch. Well, he'd certainly done that. The look on Mickey's face had been priceless. He'd almost dropped the port decanter. Lawrence had been a little ashamed by the look of genuine horror on Lucy's face – he hadn't wanted to spoil the party for her. So he'd made his apologies and left soon after his outburst. And here he was, all on his own, lying on his bed feeling like shit with only the thought that Mickey probably felt worse for consolation.

Lucy waited until Mickey had gone to check on the horses, then slipped into the little office off the kitchen and picked up the phone. She flipped through the address book till she found Kay's mobile number, then dialled. She was taken aback at how quickly it was answered and recoiled at the barrage that met her ears.

'Look, Mickey – haven't you got the message? I don't want to talk to you. Just forget I ever existed. You don't have to worry about me. Or the baby. So just fuck off out of my life, will you?'

The phone went dead. Lucy looked down at the handset and pressed the button that displayed the last five numbers to be dialled. Kay's. Kay's. Kay's. Kay's. Kay's.

14

Kay flicked her mobile phone on to voice mail and lay back weakly on her pillows. She'd spent all Christmas Day lying in her bed, the heavy curtains closing out all but a tiny chink of light. She knew the hotel staff were worried about her, but she didn't really care. They'd insisted on sending a tray up for lunch, but it had gone back barely touched.

She leaned over and poured herself another glass of wine. Damn, it was empty. She phoned room service and demanded another bottle to be sent up.

There was only one way out of her predicament. She'd read enough Catherine Cooksons to know that there was nothing that couldn't be solved by a skinful of gin and a hot bath. She didn't like gin, so Crozes-Hermitage would have to do.

When the duty manager knocked, she stumbled across the room, snatched the tray off him and slammed the door in his face before he could ask her to sign for it.

As Keith turned into his road, he looked fondly at the three sleeping girls. He was looking forward to taking them to the panto the next day. He hoped they didn't think they were too old for it. Anyway, there was a hunky

Australian soap star in it that they were all drooling over. He'd take them for cocktails afterwards. Non-alcoholic ones, of course, but he knew they'd enjoy it. And he certainly would. They were great company. Made him feel young again. And optimistic. Full of hope for the future. Things really were turning out for the best.

As he reached for the remote control that would open the security gates, Keith frowned to see a taxi parked on the road outside his drive. His heart sank as a frosted blonde with dark glasses emerged, waving gaily at them.

'Surprise! Merry Christmas!'

Oh God. Sandra. Bloody, bloody Sandra.

As Christmas Days went, reflected Patrick, this had been a weird one. There was nothing for it but to get totally out of it. He rolled a satisfyingly fat joint and lit up with defiance by the fire in the drawing room. As the pungent smoke entered his lungs, then his bloodstream, and started blurring the edges of his reality, Patrick started to relax and mull over the day's events.

Keith was seriously loaded. That was a given. And he was soon going to realize a major amount of cash, which, apparently, he wanted to spend. Another given was Mandy's infatuation with Patrick – of that he was totally confident. Seducing her was going to be like taking candy from a baby. Seducing Keith might be a little harder. He was clearly enchanted by the set-up at Honeycote, yet at the same time he was obviously a good businessman, someone who wouldn't invest in something out of sentimentality unless he thought it would give him a good return. But with the added attraction of his daughter being engaged to the son of the managing director – well, it would be a point of honour for Keith to get the brewery back on its feet.

Patrick was ruthless. If his plan meant wedding bells, then so be it. He could always get divorced. He wouldn't tell Mickey his idea just yet. Mickey wouldn't be able to cope with the calculation. That was why he was such a lousy businessman – he never had a plan. He just got swept along by the status quo.

No. He'd present it as a fait accompli. Patrick could see he was the only one capable of saving Honeycote Ales. But he was going to have to act fast.

He finished the joint with a sigh. At least it had taken his mind off his other problem. Kay. He'd been wondering all day what the hell Lawrence had been doing here on his own. Then Lucy, wide-eyed with scandal, had enlightened him. Kay was pregnant – with someone else's child . . .

Patrick decided he couldn't take that one on board just yet.

Later that evening, the chambermaid knocked on Kay's door to tidy up and turn her bed down. There was no answer, so she used her key to get in. The room was pitch dark, so she flipped on the light.

At first she thought Kay was dead. She was lying with her head over the side of the bed, limp as a rag doll. She was surrounded by empty glasses and bottles, and the smell of alcohol was overwhelming – a glass of red wine had fallen from her hand and stained the carpet. The girl backed out of the room and went running for help.

Keith was desperately trying to control his rage. Sandra swept back in with her matching luggage and a new fur-trimmed anorak as if nothing was amiss, and he wasn't going to confront her in front of the Liddiard girls, who looked a bit confused at her arrival. Mandy was mortified as her mother hugged her, probably for the first time in her life.

'Where have you *been*? I wanted to surprise you.' Sandra smiled round at them. She'd done that all right, thought Keith grimly.

'We went to lunch. With friends.'

Sandra raised her eyebrows, which had been plucked out and painted back in.

'How nice.' She smiled at Sophie and Georgina, who did a fantastic job of introducing themselves and being polite and chatty. Keith could see they were bewildered by what was going on, even though they were far too well brought up to show it.

He couldn't bear the palpable tension in the room. Mandy was excruciatingly embarrassed, but obviously felt guilty about it because you shouldn't feel like that about your own mother.

'Who'd like a drink? I certainly would,' Sandra chirruped gaily, clip-clopping over to the ice-maker and pumping several cubes into a gin glass.

'Actually, I think it's time the girls were in bed. It'll give us a chance for a chat.' He glared meaningfully at his wife, who pouted.

'I want to hear all about what you've been doing.'

Keith put his foot down and Mandy didn't need any encouragement. She fled upstairs with Sophie and Georgina, leaving just the two of them. Keith was stony-faced as he turned to his wife.

'I suppose you think I'm going to welcome you back with open arms?'

'Don't be angry with me. Not on Christmas Day.' Sandra batted her eyelashes at him coquettishly.

'You walk out without giving me the courtesy of any explanation, then expect to swan back in—'

Sandra put a placatory hand on his chest. Keith recoiled in distaste.

'I was wrong. I admit it. The thing is, darling, I just needed to give myself some space. It's not always easy being a woman in her . . . autumn years.' Sandra adored euphemisms. Her whole life was a euphemism. Everything utilitarian and ugly was covered up by something that only succeeded in drawing attention to it. 'We get these little panics. Little rushes of insecurity when we need to go and find ourselves. But now I have, now I've realized who the real me is.'

'Well, I'm very glad. Really I am—'

Sandra smiled benignly. For all his faults, Keith was a walkover when it came down to it.

'—because Mandy and I had a wonderful day today. The first Christmas I think I've ever really enjoyed. We were able to do exactly what we wanted. We didn't have anyone screaming a route march into our ear. We didn't have hordes of people we couldn't stand the sight of to entertain. It was . . . relaxing. Fun.'

Sandra wasn't sure the conversation was going quite the way she wanted it to, but she kept smiling all the same.

'Well, good. Because I did feel guilty.'

'Don't feel guilty, Sandra. Don't feel guilty at all. You've done us a favour. You've found out who you are.' Keith smiled grimly. 'And we've found out who we are.'

'What?'

'People in our own right. Who don't need you bossing us around, telling us who we are and what to do. What we've come to realize is, we're better off without you.'

Sandra's laugh started high and travelled down an octave, as she tried to control her panic.

'You don't mean that.'

'Oh yes I do. Basically, I want you out of here. But I'm prepared to give you a couple of weeks' grace while you find yourself somewhere. In the meantime, there are three perfectly good spare rooms upstairs. Pick whichever one you like. They've all got en suites.' He paused, then slipped the knife in. 'As good as anything you'd find in Benidorm.'

Sandra winced. It wasn't like Keith to be sarcastic. She didn't think it was worth retorting that she'd actually been in Puerto Banus and there was a world of difference. Shit – she'd got a lot of ground to make up. She didn't realize he'd minded her going off like that quite so much. Never mind, she'd give him a few days to calm down, then she'd start working on him. It shouldn't take long. She gave a tremulous sigh.

'If that's what you really want, sweetheart.'

'And don't waste your breath calling me sweetheart. It's not going to work.'

Keith's voice was harsh, and as he spoke he couldn't believe what he was saying. He'd never stood up to her before. And it wasn't as hard as he thought it would be. Basically because he didn't care if he never saw her again. He'd rediscovered his daughter, his lust for life, and that was enough for him. And there was no room for Sandra.

He watched her flounce out of the room. If you could flounce in a champagne velour jumpsuit cinched in with a tight gold lamé belt. With matching gold lamé sandals. Keith allowed a vision of Lucy Liddiard, with her understated grey cashmere sweater, to flash into his head and sighed.

The nurses in casualty were exasperated. Another bloody stomach pump. Why did people have to abuse themselves on Christmas Day? Why couldn't they hold off long enough to let other people enjoy a holiday? They had to admit, though, that this latest patient wasn't typical. She was very well dressed, and had come in on her own. She didn't have the rest of her drunken family standing round giving instructions.

When they'd finished they sent Kay up to a ward to sleep it off. Their only consolation was she would probably have the hangover from hell the next day.

Lucy arrived on James's doorstep looking like a traumatized heroine from a Victorian novel – pale, bedraggled and on the verge of collapse. As she fell into his arms, sobbing, James drew her inside and shut the door.

He couldn't get any sense out of her. She wouldn't tell him what was the matter. He just held her while she sobbed, then took her up to his best spare room, with its cherrywood sleigh bed and toile de Jouy curtains and crisp Egyptian cotton sheets that smelled of lavender water. He'd found her a couple of Mogadon that had been left behind years ago by a neurotic ex-girlfriend, and sat by her bed until she finally went to sleep.

As he made his way to his own bedroom, he smiled to himself. This was the moment he'd been waiting for for nearly twenty years.

15

Caroline leaped into her car and drove off down the pitted driveway of the livery yard as if the hounds of hell were after her. She reached the gates, then slowed to a halt, slumping over the steering wheel. Somehow she'd lost her momentum. The adrenalin that had caused her fit of fury had evaporated already. All the fight had gone out of her. She just wanted to curl up and go to sleep.

She was tired. Tired of working all the hours God sent and more, then going out to party. Tired of the discipline and willpower it took to keep her horse Demelza fit, keeping the determination to win alive, as if she had something to prove. She was nearly thirty and she was burning out. The truth was, she was getting too old for burning the candle at both ends. It was fine when you had youth on your side, but she obviously didn't any more.

Caroline looked back on the last two weeks and thought it wasn't surprising she was exhausted. She'd had to work twice as hard to meet her target for December, as half of it would be holiday. Then there were parties. Office parties. Other people's office parties. Boozy lunches with clients. And still up at five every morning to exercise Demelza. She was surviving on four hours sleep a night. No wonder she looked like one of the Addams family.

She craved sleep. She craved the opportunity to wake up in the morning with a clear head. She craved a meal that wasn't swimming in fat out of a foil carton or surrounded by a pile of chips. She dreaded to think what size she'd be if it weren't for the exercise. She had an awesome figure, she knew she did. She stood five foot nine in her stockinged feet, four feet of which were her legs, with a tiny waist and large, full breasts. She dressed to emphasize her good points and had a tendency towards severe, slightly sadomasochistic outfits – tight leather or suede trousers, spiky heels, skintight tops. With no make-up on she knew she looked featureless, with the non-existent eyebrows and lashes often suffered by redheads, but she'd perfected drawing these in. She was striking rather than beautiful, but she made sure she rarely went unnoticed. Now, she knew without looking in the mirror, she looked trashed. Her skin was pasty, with spots courtesy of an appalling diet and bags courtesy of too many late nights. Something had to change.

Until now, Caroline had always resisted commitment. She hated being looked after and found anyone else's attentions restricting and claustrophobic. From the moment she was tiny she'd been fiercely protective of her independence: even a mild query from her mother as to whether she needed a coat would evoke a defensive tongue-lashing. And now she was grown up, had long since left home, she still relished the fact that she had the freedom to do whatever she liked and never had to take anyone else into consideration. She didn't have to answer to anybody.

That's why James was perfect for her. He fitted in with her life; accepted it without demur if she changed plans at the last minute or stood him up. He understood her need for space totally and never seemed to want to get too close. But things were changing. She no longer felt the compulsion to keep him at arm's length, and it was slowly starting to dawn on her why people got married.

Caroline lifted her head up wearily from the steering wheel and lit a St Moritz. She was trying to cut down on her smoking, but she needed to calm down. The morning's confrontation had upset her more than she cared to admit. She'd totally lost it and had no one to blame but herself. She wanted to wipe the slate clean and start again, which was a first. Caroline never regretted anything. She was always right.

She'd gone to exercise Demelza that morning and had found the mare still in her box and waiting for the vet. There was an angry gash on her back leg, which Caroline could tell from a glance meant several hundred quid in the vet's pocket and at least a month's box rest; time and money she could ill afford. Furious, she'd confronted the nearest stable girl, who was still suffering from a Christmas hangover, to discover that Demelza had tripped over a water bucket and, becoming tangled in the wire handle, had panicked and backed into a barbed wire fence. Caroline's ensuing tantrum had been awesome. Accusations of negligence and carelessness rained upon the hapless groom, and were so vociferous that the yard owner had emerged from the warmth of his office to find the source of the profanities.

Ian had put Caroline right in no uncertain terms. She was six weeks behind with her livery, which denied her any right to abuse his staff. Not that she was entitled to treat any human being with such contempt, even if she'd been in credit. Caroline had raged back at him, and was taken aback when he replied with a single word:

'Off.'

'What?'

'Off my yard. I don't need clients like you, mouthing off and having tantrums. I've got a list of people waiting to keep their horses here, all with better manners than you.'

'Fine. I'll borrow a box and take her away now.'

'No, you won't.'

Caroline looked at him, puzzled.

'You can settle your bill first. Seven hundred and forty pounds, including worming and shoeing.'

'I'll write you a cheque.'

Caroline knew he wouldn't be able to bank it until the end of the week, by which time she'd have cancelled it.

'Cash only, I'm afraid. Until then I'm keeping the horse.'

For one of the few times in her life, Caroline had been speechless. She knew by the glint in his eye that Ian meant business. She wasn't about to back down either. Caroline had never tasted humble pie in her life. She turned on her heel and marched out of the yard.

Now, sitting in her Renault Mégane at the end of the drive, she drew hard on her cigarette and thought about what she'd done. She knew there was no way she could settle her bill. She'd been relying on Ian turning a blind eye to her late payments until well into the New Year. She'd already spent her Christmas bonus on presents and topping up her wardrobe. She sighed. Everything was catching up on her. Her looks, her health and her wallet were all suffering the effects of over-indulgence.

At the back of her mind, something else was troubling her too. As she turned on the engine resignedly, she allowed the thought headspace. She'd spent Christmas Day with her family: her dull, boring, ordinary family in their dull, boring, ordinary box on a dull, boring ordinary estate outside Evesham. Her two sisters were there, neither of whom had a shred of ambition or imagination, just one husband and two children apiece. Caroline had always scorned them for their narrow-mindedness, their passive acceptance of their lot, their willingness to conform. They were happy to sit in her parents' cramped dining room, round the table with its mismatched chairs, devouring overcooked sprouts and underdone potatoes washed down with below average wine. She shuddered at the memory – she'd even had to smoke outdoors, outside the sliding doors that led on to the patio, as one of her sisters was expecting again.

Nevertheless, she'd felt a twinge of jealousy at her sisters' bovine contentment. Their joy in their children was so genuine; she envied them their pleasure at her nieces' smiling faces as they ripped open their presents. They were obviously totally fulfilled and didn't spend their lives feeling as if they were on a treadmill in order to prove something. She must be going wrong somewhere . . .

It was time to take stock. Time to sit back and look at her life. She couldn't carry on the way she was. And anyway, in the back of her mind she knew she'd peaked. She'd got as high as she could at the newspaper. She'd started out five years ago doing telesales for the classified ad section and now she was the manager. To do any better for herself she'd have to move to a bigger paper in a bigger town. Or a city. Or, perish the thought, London. And she'd done as well as she was ever going to in her eventing without a better horse, which she couldn't afford. Her eyes misted over as she thought about poor Demelza, until unfamiliar tears were making their way down her cheeks. She brushed them away. Snivelling wasn't going to get her anywhere. Yes, it was definitely time for a plan of action. A change in lifestyle. Something drastic.

She needed a bit of security. Both literally and figuratively. She needed someone to share the responsibilities in life, the decisions, the bills – the ups and downs. Time to be mistress of her own house. Take things at a gentler pace. Even, God forbid, have babies eventually. She never thought she'd think it, but the prospect didn't seem as horrendous as usual.

Whatever happened, she knew she couldn't carry on juggling all her lives any more, being a split personality. She had her working life, where she was ruthless, a hard taskmistress because she had to be in order to produce the results that were expected. Then she had her eventing life, which involved hard work and self-sacrifice, exercising Demelza whatever the weather, but gave her an incredible high whenever she came away with a rosette or a cup. Even though she was only competing at an amateur level, she felt a sense of achievement that was hers and hers alone. Then she had her life with James, when she allowed herself to relax and be pampered. He was such a gentleman, so good at looking after her, she didn't know why she didn't spend more time in his company. She felt, with a sudden stab of guilt, that she took him for granted.

It was time to redress the balance. Put her career on the back burner. Maybe even give the riding a rest. It didn't necessarily mean she could never get on a horse again, but she didn't have to compete so hard and so often. She thought Demelza might like the break as well. She'd ridden her into the ground on more than one occasion, she knew it.

What she really needed to do was get her relationship with James on a firmer footing. Perhaps she'd suggest moving in with him; Caroline had always shied away from anything that smacked of commitment, but now the prospect seemed enticing. Her independence had somehow lost its allure. She'd lost her edge; she was going soft. But she didn't care. She had James to fall back on. She'd build herself a new life with him, one that they could both enjoy.

She was halfway down the bypass before she realized she'd left James's present behind. She'd meant to go home and shower and change before travelling down to see him, but events at the yard had precipitated things rather. Never mind. What did you get the man who had everything, anyway? With a wicked grin, Caroline thought of several things James would appreciate more than a hastily wrapped lambswool jumper.

Lucy woke from a deep, unnatural sleep at about half past nine, the clattering of hooves causing her to sit up in alarm. Had one of the horses escaped? She jumped out of bed and noticed her strange surroundings. Of course. She was in James's spare bedroom and the horses must have been the first arrivals heading for the Boxing Day meet in the market square. She flopped back down on the bed with a sigh, wishing she could return to a state of unconsciousness. She really didn't want to have to face the memories of the day before, but she knew she had to.

Mickey had been having an affair with Kay Oakley.

She asked herself why. Kay was certainly attractive, no one could deny that, but in a vampy, unnatural way that just didn't seem Mickey's style. She was always perfectly pleasant, more than willing to help whenever Lucy went to the garden centre to buy spring bulbs or roses, but there was a brittle air about her, something rather too business-like. She lacked warmth. Lucy wondered if perhaps it was because she'd never had children. Motherhood always mellowed people—

What on earth was she doing? Making excuses for the woman! Was she mad? Lucy knew she always gave people the benefit of the doubt. She wasn't entirely sure if that was a fault. Certainly the only person it had ever ended up hurting was herself, particularly on this occasion. She mustn't, mustn't, start making allowances for Kay.

She pondered the matter further. One thing was for sure, it wasn't because Mickey wasn't getting it at home. She calculated carefully, adding up their various bonks, which totalled a healthy average of five and a half a week. Unless they were guilt bonks . . . Mickey trying to cover up for his infidelity. It could explain why he always looked shattered.

Perhaps Kay was willing to do something in the bed-room stakes that she wasn't. Lucy tried to remember if Mickey had ever hinted at anything kinky, but thought not. After all, she wasn't hung up about where or when: outside, inside, morning, noon or night, she was always pretty willing. And she thought his preferences were fairly catholic. He was sensual, mildly adventurous, but not, she was pretty certain, an out and out pervert. Though perhaps he did harbour a desire for her to stomp round in nothing but her riding boots and whack his bottom with her crop, and he just hadn't liked to ask. Trouble was, Lucy couldn't really see Kay agreeing to that either, and knew that the reason for Mickey's infidelity was probably a little deeper rooted than mere sexual preference. But she didn't want to dig any deeper than the superficial, as that would have further-reaching implications upon their marriage.

She closed her eyes for a moment to assess how she felt. Apart from a dull, leaden feeling somewhere between her stomach and her heart, she felt nothing. She wasn't sure how she was supposed to feel. Nothing could have prepared her for this eventuality. If anyone had told her that she'd be confronting her husband's infidelity, she'd have laughed. Bad things just didn't happen to Lucy. Until now, she'd led a charmed life. She'd had an idyllic childhood, her courtship and marriage to Mickey had been a fairy tale and, apart from the morning sickness, bringing up the children had been free of any great drama—

Oh God! The girls. Lucy jolted up again with alarm before remembering that they were safely in Solihull with Keith and Mandy, and not due back again till tomorrow. She lay back on the pillow, temporarily relieved that she didn't have to confront them as yet. She wondered if she could put them off for yet another day while she gathered her wits. She could phone Keith, tell him she had a nasty stomach bug and didn't want to risk them catching it. She was sure he'd be happy to oblige: he'd been so grateful for their hospitality up till now. Lucy tucked the problem of Sophie and Georgina away for the time being. She couldn't begin to contemplate their reaction yet, how they would feel about this turn of events.

As she banished the prospect of revealing their father's extramarital activities to the back of her mind, there was a light tap on the door. Lucy sighed. She'd have to talk to James sooner or later. She couldn't really expect to turn up in the state she had and not give him an explanation. She hoped she'd be able to talk without breaking down again. She suspected that once she started to cry she'd never be able to stop. She cleared her throat to speak. Her voice came out slightly hoarse.

'Come in.'

James opened the door and peered round anxiously.

'I didn't wake you, did I?'

'No.'

He came in with a tray, bearing tea and brioches and apricot conserve.

'How are you feeling?'

'I'm not. I'm not feeling anything yet, thank God. I'm not allowing myself to.'

James sat down on the bed next to her, balancing the tray on the dressing table.

'Do you want to talk about it?'

'I suppose so. No point in pretending nothing's happened.'

James chose his words very, very carefully.

'So – he came clean, did he? I wondered when he would. Though I think he could have had better timing.'

He gave Lucy a wry smile. She blinked, confused.

'You mean you knew?'

'Yes. Graham Cowley put me in the picture. I know it's probably against the bank manager's Hippocratic oath, or whatever, but he was worried—'

'How on earth did Graham Cowley know?'

'He is your bank manager. And I am a shareholder, albeit a minor one. It's in my interests to know.'

Lucy looked utterly blank, as James well knew she might. He feigned puzzlement.

'Are we talking at cross purposes here?'

'I think we must be. What are you talking about?'

In at the deep end, thought James, as he dumped his brother in it right up to his neck. 'The brewery. It's in big trouble. As good as bust, unless Mickey pulls his finger out. Which apparently he's showing no signs of doing. He's out of his depth.'

James looked at Lucy, who looked shell-shocked.

'My God. You had no idea, did you?' James felt treacherous as he said it, but she had to know. It wouldn't be fair for her to be kept in the dark any longer. And he could gain the advantage if he was cunning.

Lucy put her head in her hands, her tortoiseshell locks falling over her face. James, for the millionth time in his life, just wanted to hold her. But he knew he had to stand firm until the time was right. Slowly, slowly, catchee monkey. He probed gently.

'So – if you knew nothing about the brewery . . . why are you here? What's happened?'

Lucy looked up at him. She was impossibly pale.

'Mickey's been screwing Kay Oakley.'

'Shit.' James assumed a suitably shocked expression, even though he'd been pretty certain of his brother's misdemeanours for some months now. 'Oh, Lucy.'

'I know.'

Lucy looked utterly wretched as he took her in his arms. But she didn't cry, just buried her head in his shoulder as he stroked her hair gently, soothing her as he would one of his dogs.

'I don't know why. And I don't know what to do. I wish I'd never found out.'

'No – it's better you know the truth. He can't go on living a lie, Lucy.'

Lucy choked back a sob. The thought that her marriage had been a lie sickened her to her stomach. She felt as if she'd jumped from a plane and had just realized her parachute wouldn't work. She was in emotional free fall, desperate to go back to the safety and security she'd once had, and living in terrible fear of what was to come, knowing that she couldn't possibly walk away unhurt. If only she hadn't picked up the phone. If only she'd listened to Mickey and kept out of Kay's business. She wondered how many other people knew. It was classic, wasn't it, the faithful wife being the last to know of her husband's infidelity? Was everyone in Honeycote watching her every move with bated breath, waiting for her to find out? It was like living in a soap opera. Only she didn't have a script, didn't know her lines, didn't know what to say next. She turned to James, slightly accusing.

'Did you know?'

'No. I promise you I didn't.'

James didn't feel he was lying, because he didn't actually have proof that it was Kay Mickey was screwing, even though he'd have put good money on it. But he wasn't going to make Lucy feel a bigger fool than she already did. He'd already neatly broken the news to her about the Liddiard finances – or lack of them. And his role wasn't to humiliate her. It was to bolster her up. Give her the support she needed, a shoulder to cry on that she would come to realize she couldn't live without. In other words, make up for her husband's shortcomings. Which shouldn't be difficult . . .

What he needed to do now was to inject some fighting spirit into her. Build up her strength so that she could fight her own battle. Make her angry. He knew Lucy rarely got angry. She was extraordinarily placid. Long-suffering, had she but known it. Which is how Mickey had got away with his behaviour for so many years. Other wives would have nagged him to death about his excessive drinking, his inability to take his muddy boots off, his habit of forgetting the social engagements that didn't matter to him. But Lucy just smiled fondly, or tutted in mild exasperation. Only now she was paying the price for her tolerance and James was damned if Mickey was going to get away with it again. Lucy deserved someone who appreciated her, not someone who abused her good nature. Not that Mickey didn't love her – James was certain he did – but with love like that, who needs it? He would put Lucy on a pedestal, respect her, appreciate her.

James stood up decisively.

'I'm going to run you a bath. Have a nice long soak. Then we can decide what to do about this mess.'

Lucy nodded dully. She looked at the devoré dress that James had hung carefully on a hanger the night before. He'd found it in a crumpled heap on the floor when he'd come to check on her. The dress had been perfect for Christmas Day, but now Lucy needed something warm to heat up the chill she felt deep inside her. She needed comfort clothing, not something that required poise and grace and elegance.

'I haven't got anything to wear. I can't put that back on.'

'I'll dig you something out.'

'I suppose I'll have to go back to Honeycote and get some clothes.' She sighed a deep sigh. She just wanted to hide. As long as she didn't have to confront Mickey, she could pretend nothing had really happened.

Ten minutes later, Lucy slid into a nearly scalding bath of Czech & Speake bubbles and tried to take in what James had just told her about Honeycote Ales. She felt consumed with guilt. No wonder Mickey had sought solace with another woman. Deep down Lucy had suspected something was wrong at the brewery for some time, but she'd buried it, hadn't asked any questions because she didn't really want to know. She didn't like nasty things, or anything difficult. She liked everything to run smoothly, look nice, for everyone to be happy, and she had been certain whatever the problem was it was just a glitch. They often had bad patches, but they always managed to struggle through them somehow. And anyway, she'd figured that if anything was irretrievably bad then Mickey would have told her . . .

But would he? He'd obviously wanted to keep the truth from her because he knew she couldn't deal with it. And the stress, the pressure, had driven him into another woman's arms. A woman like Kay, who was businesslike and realistic, would understand the implications of what he was going through and could probably offer him reassurance. Because she lived in the real world, unlike Lucy.

Lucy sank down under the bubbles, as if they might afford her some protection from the truth. Suddenly she felt horribly inadequate, responsible for the situation. If only she'd pressed a bit further when she'd asked Mickey if everything was all right, instead of accepting his platitudes so readily. She should have been supportive and offered solutions. She could even have offered to work at the brewery if that would have helped. Plenty of women helped out in their husband's businesses these days. Kay, for a start . . . God, who did she think she was, messing about playing horses and deliberately ignoring the tell-tale signs of economic hardship that were under her nose – the overdue accounts, the red bills she'd spotted lying around that had gone unpaid. She was superficial, shallow and selfish. As she turned on the hot tap to top up the water, hoping it would take away the chill that was creeping into her bones, Lucy concluded that Mickey's infidelity had been inevitable and she probably deserved everything she'd got.

Kay woke up on Boxing Day morning in a hospital ward bedecked with lurid tinsel – a half-hearted attempt to inject some festive cheer for the benefit of those inmates who were being kept in over Christmas. A nurse saw her eyes open and came to sit on her bed.

'How are you feeling?'

'Like death. What am I doing here?'

'You had your stomach pumped. You overdid it a bit yesterday.'

Kay sat up, then had to lie back down again as her head felt swimmy. She tried to take in the information. Did that mean she'd lost the baby?

'The baby . . . ?'

The nurse looked startled 'The baby?'

It was still there, then. If she'd had a miscarriage, they'd have noticed. She was in a hospital, for God's sake. She sighed.

'I'm pregnant.'

'How far gone are you?'

'Five months.'

The nurse frowned.

'I'd better get the consultant to come and have a word with you.' She looked at her watch. 'She'll be doing her rounds any minute. Do you want anything to drink?' She grinned conspiratorially. 'If I were you I'd have the hot chocolate. Everything else is undrinkable. And do you want anything to eat? You've missed breakfast, but I can do you some toast in the kitchen if you like.'

Kay agreed to cocoa and a couple of slices of toast, and was surprised to find she was ravenous. As she was finishing her meal, the consultant arrived, a weary young woman with heavy rings under her eyes who'd obviously been on duty far longer than was humanly acceptable. She sat on the side of Kay's bed and fixed her with a stern glare. Kay couldn't remember the last time anyone had done that.

'So, what have you been up to?'

Kay tried to defend herself.

'I didn't even know I was pregnant until a few days ago.'

The consultant did a double take that was straight out of a pantomime. Kay went on to explain.

'I thought I was infertile. My periods have always been all over the place, so when I didn't come on it never even occurred to me . . . I was going to have a termination. But apparently I can't. It's too late.'

'Well, getting blind drunk isn't going to help anyone. Least of all the baby. You should know better.'

'Have you got any idea what it's like? Thinking you'll never give birth, then finding out you're five months gone? When you never even wanted it in the first place?'

Kay could feel her voice rising with hysteria. Out of the corner of her eye she could see the other patients staring over at their conversation, intrigued. She supposed they must be bored. She couldn't blame them. Whatever happened, she had to get out of here as soon as possible.

'What about the father? What does he think?'

Kay knew this question was inevitable, but she hadn't realized it was going to hit so hard. She had to confront the issue. She hadn't really digested Lawrence's bombshell, which could only mean one thing. It had to be Mickey's baby.

No! It was her baby, and hers alone. That was the only way she was going to get through this. She was the one who was going to have to cope, so she didn't want anyone else to have any rights, any hold over her, any influence over the decisions she had to make. Kay knew that she was in for the duration now. She was going to have to have this child, whatever she decided to do afterwards. Suddenly, she was overcome by a feeling of panic.

'My God – it is going to be all right, isn't it?'

The consultant chose her words carefully.

'We don't have any firm evidence about binge-drinking on a foetus. But damage tends to be done in the early stages of development. It's not something I'd recommend you do again, but I suspect your baby will probably be all right.'

Kay felt tears of relief welling up in her eyes. The consultant softened.

'Would you like to see the baby? On a scan? It might reassure you.'

Kay looked down at the tin foil containing the last scrapings of butter and the chewy white crusts of her toast.

'Yes. I'd like that very much.'

On shaky legs, Kay followed the consultant through miles of corridor until they reached the antenatal unit. She was led into a room that was dark, womb-like. She couldn't believe how nervous she was.

Kay lay down on the bed. Her top was lifted up and a handful of clear jelly was rubbed on to her stomach, to allow the ultrasound to glide unhindered. The nurse sat down in front of a screen. Kay craned her neck and saw a murky grey swirl, like a ship's radar. As the nurse ran the ultrasound over her stomach, Kay waited, not sure what to expect, until the nurse smiled. She pointed out a flicker on the screen.

'There's the heart beat.'

The nurse went on to point out arms and legs and a perfect little spine. Kay was too overwhelmed to speak. A tiny little creature filled with life was growing inside her. She watched as it moved around almost in slow motion, independent of her, a being with its own needs and responses. The nurse was busy checking plot points, estimating the baby's size and age.

'I'd say you were about twenty-two weeks. And everything looks absolutely fine.'

The nurse looked at her. Tears were coursing down Kay's cheeks.

'It's all right – there's nothing to worry about.' She

patted her hand reassuringly. 'You've got a lovely healthy baby there. Everything's going to be fine.'

Denham House always left Caroline speechless with admiration. It was picture book, chocolate box – but luckily far enough off the main drag in Eldenbury to escape the rapturous gaze of all but the most energetic Americans. It was masculine in its proportions – square and solid, pleasingly symmetrical, with deep sash windows and ancient wisteria softening the already mellow edifice. No matter what time of day or what time of year, it always seemed to glow golden in the sunshine. James had pinned a tasteful, understated wreath to the front door in recognition of the festive season and two red silk ribbons around the trunks of the standard bay trees that stood either side of the entrance.

She pulled up, jumped out of the car and opened the large, black double gates that allowed her access to the courtyard at the side of the house. She parked and walked through the ivy-clad archway leading to the kitchen door. She didn't feel up to the grandeur of the hall, with its French chandelier and the priceless grandfather clock, the burnished walnut table and a vase always bursting with flowers that never seemed to wilt, but maintained a just-picked freshness until the day they were changed. The funny thing about James was he was so obsessive about detail, about everything looking perfect, that you could be tempted to think he was gay. But Caroline knew with a certainty he wasn't. If there was one thing that was positive about their relationship it was the sex.

She let herself into the kitchen and stopped short. There, at the table, sat Lucy Liddiard, wearing what looked suspiciously like one of James's shirts and some cotton long Johns tucked into a pair of thick socks. She looked delicate and fragile and irritatingly gorgeous. Caroline was immediately on her guard. Lucy always made her feel cumbersome, cheap and ginger.

'Merry Christmas,' said Caroline, in a tone that blatantly asked, 'What the fuck are you doing here?'

'Merry Christmas,' said Lucy, in a tone which gave absolutely nothing away. She was clutching a cup of tea. A proper cup, bone china, with a saucer. James didn't possess anything as commonplace as a mug. Caroline thought that as soon as she was in charge, that was the first thing that would be introduced.

'Is James here?'

Caroline's question incorporated a thousand others, but still Lucy shed no light on her presence.

'He's getting dressed.'

Caroline just managed to keep her temper under control. What the hell was going on? Lucy Liddiard was lolling about in James's kitchen, having brazenly raided his wardrobe, looking bedraggled and big-eyed and annoyingly vulnerable. She'd obviously just had a bath – the ends of her hair were still wet, and anyway, Caroline could smell the Czech & Speake James kept in his bathroom.

She hesitated, not too sure how to regain the advantage, and marched over to the Aga to put the kettle back on. She noticed with fury an untouched breakfast tray by the sink, with brioches and apricot conserve. James always had porridge or grilled bacon. What was going on? She turned to Lucy and smiled sweetly.

'I think it's coffee time, don't you? Did you have a nice Christmas?'

'Lovely, thanks.' Lucy's tone was dull, unconvincing. She obviously had no intention of explaining her presence. She was in another world. Caroline was wrong-footed. Notoriously confrontational, for once in her life she didn't feel she could go in with all guns blazing. Before she could decide on her next move, James entered, dressed down in a pair of faded jeans and a grey marl fisherman's sweater.

'Caroline.' It was a statement rather than a greeting. His voice wasn't exactly suffused with warmth. Nevertheless, Caroline went to give him a hug, to stamp her possession over him, but to her astonishment he put out a hand to stop her.

'You should have phoned. It's not a good time.'

Caroline's jaw dropped.

'Phoned? I didn't realize I needed to make an appointment.'

Flummoxed, she looked between James and Lucy. Lucy was gazing into space, still clutching her teacup. Caroline wondered if she was in some sort of post-coital reverie, if they'd been at it all night. If they had, neither of them looked in the least shamefaced. Feeling rather outnumbered, she put her hands on her hips.

'Does somebody want to tell me what's going on?'

James put a calming hand on her elbow and manoeuvred her out of the room. He spoke in a confidential undertone that Caroline found profoundly patronising.

'Lucy's having a bit of a crisis.'

'Well, so am I. I'm having a lot of a crisis. Demelza—'

James cut her off, uninterested.

'We need to talk.'

Speechless, Caroline followed him into his study. It smelled of beeswax and was piled high with papers and auction catalogues, back copies of *Country Life*. Something that could only be called a wireless cranked out Classic FM. James snapped it off and turned to face Caroline. She realized this was serious.

'I think we should give things a break.'

'Why?'

'Lucy's having a few problems. She's staying here for the time being, while she sorts things out. I think she needs some space.'

Caroline took in a sharp breath. If she'd had nails, they'd have been digging into her palms, but she'd bitten them to the quick on the journey down. She turned to James with an icy smile.

'I see. So Lucy Liddiard has a little tiff with her husband and you think you're in with a chance. Is that it?'

'Don't be ridiculous.'

'That's how it looks to me.'

'Caroline – she's family.'

Caroline just raised an eyebrow.

'So there's nothing going on but you don't want me here?'

'Look – maybe it's time we called it a day anyway. We weren't exactly heading for the altar, were we? Let's face it.'

Caroline couldn't believe the irony. Little did James know the plan she'd had in store for him.

'It's news to me. I thought we were quite happy! OK, so we don't live in each other's pockets. But isn't that what we both wanted . . . ?'

She trailed off. James was looking uncomfortable. Caroline knew he was weak and wouldn't be able to stand up to her. She just had to be persistent. Yet again she marvelled at how useful her sales training was in her everyday life. And anyway, she hadn't played her trump card yet. She smiled to herself as she walked over and grasped the brass of his belt buckle. She hooked her finger behind the leather and tugged. To her astonishment James grabbed her wrist and jerked her hand away.

'Just go, will you? Lucy needs me.'

Caroline didn't know whether to laugh or slap him round the face. She felt outraged. Ousted from her position by Lucy Liddiard? How bloody ironic could you get?

She'd known from the moment she set eyes on him that Mickey Liddiard could be tempted to play away from home. He was an easy target. True, he'd never tried it on with her, but she'd always put that down to fraternal loyalty. Given half the chance, she could have worked on Mickey, could have had him any day of the week. But she'd recognized that he was off limits; that it would have been ill-mannered to sleep with James's own brother when she didn't really want him. So out of deference to etiquette, she'd left him well alone.

But Lucy was obviously working from a different set of rules. That was the problem with these moneyed country types. They moved the bloody goalposts all the time. She was shamelessly sitting in James's kitchen, half dressed, and hadn't even looked mildly abashed.

Caroline was tempted to fly into one of her famous rages. That was one of the few advantages of having red hair – people were afraid of you when you got angry and tended to give in. She knew that was the case with James. He hated scenes and always backed down before she became too hysterical. But somehow, this time, she suspected this was not the way to play it. Getting angry would only highlight the difference between her and the ladylike paragon of virtue sitting in the kitchen, who undoubtedly never lost her cool. No, Caroline knew she had to retreat with dignity if she had any chance of winning the battle. Anyway, she needed time to think. James was obviously quite determined that his loyalties lay with Lucy, and she wasn't going to degrade herself by arguing with him about it. Better that she withdrew from the situation gracefully until she had a chance to think of a game plan.

'Fine. Merry fucking Christmas. Lucky I remembered to keep the receipt for your present.'

James hesitated. He'd wrapped an exquisite pair of Moroccan kelim slippers and a silk dressing gown for Caroline. He wondered if it would add insult to injury to give them to her, then decided yes, it probably would, as she stalked out of the study, through the hall and out of the front door without looking back. Never mind. He'd kept his receipt as well.

For the second time that day, Caroline leaped into her car in a towering fury and drove off at top speed. She grabbed for her packet of cigarettes and tried to shake one out. Empty. She knew there was no point in stopping at the newsagents. Already there was nowhere in Eldenbury to park – the square was filling up for the hunt with horseboxes and onlookers parking willy-nilly. She tooted impatiently at someone unloading a highly strung pony in the middle of the road and received a mouthful of abuse. Caroline put her foot down and roared past, not caring.

On automatic pilot, she pointed her car along the road that would eventually lead her back to the cramped one-bedroom starter home she'd reluctantly bought three years earlier, realizing that the rent she'd been paying was just dead money and she really should be getting on to the property ladder. It was totally soulless – she felt no inclination to inject any of her own personality into it – though in fact it was very revealing of her lifestyle. She thought of the tights and cotton wool balls littering her bedroom floor; the empty coffee cups and the CDs lying around without their cases. If she went home, she'd have to address all of that. A knot grew in her stomach as she thought how uninviting the prospect was; how much she'd been looking forward to spending a couple of days with James. Denham House was luxuriously indulgent: she'd been planning to lounge by the fire, reading a trashy novel and sipping champagne. Now she felt filled with gloom. She hadn't even left the heating on at her house. It would take hours to take the chill off.

The honeyed buildings either side of the road out of Eldenbury dwindled away and were replaced by drystone walls and trees. Caroline realized she was starving. There was a Little Chef a few miles further along the road. She'd stop and have a fry-up and two gallons of coffee. Bugger the spots. Hopefully it would be open on Boxing Day.

The thought cheered her and she put her foot down. As she passed the white sign whose black lettering pointed to Honeycote – 1½ miles – she wondered yet again what on earth had gone on in the Liddiard house the day before. James hadn't given her any details. He'd been irritatingly discreet.

Suddenly she slammed on her brakes. What was she thinking of, turning tail like that and fleeing obediently? She wasn't going to go without a fight. Surely she had a right to know what was going on? She turned the car round and retraced her journey, indicated right and swung into the lane that led to Honeycote House.

After Caroline had gone, James sat in his study for a few minutes to regain his composure. He needed a clear head and to be quite sure of his plan of campaign. Things were certainly in his favour, but the slightest error of judgement could tip the balance the other way. He looked through the lattice window out into his garden. The glass was so old that it gave a distorted view, but he always found the vision a pleasure, even now in the depths of winter when there was little flowering and frost still hovered in the shadiest corners, where the fingers of sunshine had not yet reached them. Two magnificent moss-covered urns stood either side of the path that dissected the lawn and led to an intricate knot garden he'd designed and grown himself from box seedlings. It had taken seven years to take proper shape, but the patience had paid off. It was his pride and joy.

The sight helped to calm him, bring him down, for he was as high as a kite. He felt like a dealer who had stumbled across a long-forgotten work of art in the corner of an auction room. He had to keep his find secret, play his cards close to his chest, feign disinterest until the moment of bidding when he had to hold his nerve until the prize was his, when at last he could take it home, dust it off and declare it as his own, in all its glory. For to him Lucy had always been a priceless treasure who had fallen by mishap into the wrong hands. And now it was only a matter of time before she could be claimed by her rightful owner, someone who would appreciate her beauty . . .

James thought of the years he had been waiting and

how, during all that time, everything he had bought, all the beautiful objects that he surrounded himself with, had been inspired by Lucy. Either because it reminded him of her, or because he knew it was something she would like. A graceful Lalique figure, arms stretching skywards. A sketch attributed to Augustus John. (James knew very well that he'd paid over the top for it; that the picture was more than likely a copy by some aspiring Blooms-bury wannabe – but he hadn't cared because the way the model's hair was pinned loosely on top of her head, the ends falling round her neck, reminded him so much of the neck he so wanted to kiss. He wanted to press his lips against that creamy skin and feel Lucy's pulse, her very life force . . .) A Limoges coffee set. An exquisite button-back Victorian nursing chair. An Aubusson rug whose soft, muted colours reminded him of a dress she'd been wearing . . . His entire house was a shrine to her. A temple. And at last she had come here to be worshipped and adored.

James knew there was still some dirty work to be done, and he was a little nervous. He'd kept his hands so clean up until now. Plus he felt slightly guilty. Mickey was his brother, after all. He was soon able to dispel his doubts, however. Surely it was his duty to rescue Lucy? And anyway, at the end of the day, it had to be her decision. If she didn't want him, she only had to say.

16

Caroline's car crunched over the gravel at Honeycote House. She thought the house looked unusually forbidding, then decided she was being fanciful. She tried the door knocker, giving it an assertive rap, but there was no reply. Somebody must be in, surely?

She tramped round the house looking for signs of life and found the back door ajar. It led into the scullery area, a glory hole that contained boots, boots and more boots, hats, collars, dog bowls, lead ropes, macs, binoculars, scarves, umbrellas, waxed jackets, picnic rugs and baskets – the whitewashed brick walls and the quarry tiles were barely visible amongst the family debris. Piled up by the back door were crates and crates of empty bottles. A huge wicker dog basket was abandoned, the food and drink bowls next to it disconcertingly empty. A stout oak door led down some steps to the wine cellars, another led to a cloakroom, and next to that was the door leading into the kitchen. She opened it tentatively and stepped inside.

The kitchen looked as though a bomb had hit it. No one had touched a thing since Christmas lunch the day before. The turkey was still out on the side, surrounded by a few neolithic stuffing balls. Stone-cold vegetables sat in their dishes, coated in congealed butter. Piles of unwashed crockery and grease-smeared glasses were stacked up by the sink. Wedges of cheese lay uncovered and drying. The smell of stale cooking, booze and unemptied ashtrays pervaded the air.

Yet despite the unpalatable squalor, Caroline could imagine the original splendour of the feast. Lucy was renowned for her hospitality, her ability to welcome the slightest acquaintance to her table and make them feel part of the family. Caroline felt a twinge of regret that she hadn't been there. You could always judge the success of a social occasion by the number of empty bottles, and there was a veritable battalion scattered around the room, waiting to join the rest in the crates outside.

Pokey was snoozing on the sofa, but slid to the ground and came to investigate the arrival of a relative stranger in her territory. She looked hungry, and Caroline tore a few strips off the unappetizing turkey to placate her. She walked through the kitchen, the metal tips of her spiked heels grating on the flagstones, and ventured out into the corridor that led to the hallway. The fairy lights on the Christmas tree were still blazing, seeking admiration in vain. Why hadn't anyone turned them off?

Caroline tiptoed into the drawing room and her heart leaped into her mouth. Mickey was stretched out on a large chenille sofa, and she thought for an awful moment that he was dead before detecting the slight rise and fall of his chest. She was relieved. She would have felt a moral obligation to attempt mouth to mouth resuscitation, and Mickey was not an inviting prospect, drunk, dishevelled and unshaven. She winced as she spotted an empty bottle of port by Mickey's elbow. It would have induced the worst sort of hangover, she knew from experience, and she mentally prescribed Paracetamol and strong, sweet tea, followed at a safe interval by copious amounts of toast and honey. She'd been in that state often enough to know that her remedy would alleviate all but the most vicious symptoms.

Before she woke Mickey, she looked around for any clues that might shed light on the mystery. A brass bucket by the fireplace was filled with wrapping paper that had been eagerly ripped off presents only twenty-four hours earlier, and some of these were still lying round the room. There was a pile that was obviously Lucy's: a pair of leather gloves trimmed with fur at the cuffs, a small suede-bound photo album, a tiny pair of heart-shaped silver earrings. They were just the sort of presents Caroline would have liked to receive. She thought with regret of the prosaic gifts her own family had bestowed on her. The latest Delia Smith from her mother, who wistfully hoped her daughter might start cooking one day as she'd never get a husband if she didn't. A CD rack from one of her sisters (actually, that would probably come in useful – but who wanted useful presents?) and a Body Shop gift basket from the other. Caroline wondered what James had bought her, but got the feeling that she was never going to find out. She'd had nothing that made her feel special, or wanted, or feminine, whereas Lucy's were all the sort of things she'd have loved, but would never buy for herself. For a moment she was tempted to chuck the whole lot on the fire, but managed to resist the urge.

She saw a glass on the mantelpiece, which she recognized as the Murano crystal James collected, and read the tag that had been tied to its stem: 'To James, all our love, Lucy xxx', it read, and Caroline noted with a wry smile that Mickey had added his signature, no doubt as instructed. But she knew it had been chosen by Lucy with James in mind, and felt sure when she'd written 'our love' she actually meant 'my'. Other gifts lay around the room, all no doubt perfectly chosen and perfectly wrapped and received with gasps of pleasure and delight. Honeycote always seemed to Caroline like something out of a magazine come to life; everything was always just right, somehow without trying. She pretended to scorn it, but deep down she knew she was jealous. Whatever she did always screamed 'high street'.

But now it looked as if the picture-book perfection was flawed. A light had gone out in the house. It wasn't just that the fire was lying dead, that there was a resounding silence, that no one had cleared up the mess. It was something deeper, and it made Caroline shiver. And it was the reason she'd found Lucy jumping into her shoes that morning. It was time to find out what was going on. She'd spent enough time snooping, trying to see if she could find any ammunition. Now she needed to bite the bullet.

She shook Mickey by the shoulder none too gently and he came to with a deeply unattractive snort, dispelling any fantasies she may ever have had about him. He looked confused when he saw her.

'Caroline? Have you come for lunch? James isn't here . . .'

'No, I know he isn't. Nobody is. And James is at Denham, with your wife.'

Caroline swallowed her impatience, as Mickey rubbed his head stupidly, not sure if he was dreaming.

'So what are you doing here?'

'I want to know what's going on. I came down to have

a nice cosy Boxing Day romp with my boyfriend and I got the old heave-ho. Not exactly what I wanted in my stocking.'

'Shit.'

'Total shit. He didn't even give me a present, just pushed me out of the door. Meanwhile your wife's sitting in his kitchen wearing his long johns. What's going on, Mickey?'

Mickey explained what had happened. That Lucy had found out about his affair with Kay and had gone running off to James. He, having no leg to stand on anyway, had just proceeded to get totally legless.

Caroline was incredulous.

'Kay Oakley!' What the hell did Mickey want to have an affair with her for? A person less like Lucy she couldn't imagine. Kay was harsh, a bit scary, even for Caroline, who wasn't intimidated by many people. Kay clearly worshipped money over everything, else why marry Lawrence, who was a cold and calculating fish and plug-ugly to boot. Furthermore, Caroline was pretty sure Kay didn't even have a sense of humour: she took herself and her position very seriously indeed. So what on earth was the attraction? 'For God's sake, Mickey. Kay Oakley? Why?'

Mickey looked at her dully. He was reminded of a joke he'd once heard.

'Why does a dog lick its balls?'

Caroline looked nonplussed. Mickey smiled wryly.

'Because it can.'

Caroline didn't think it could get any worse, until Mickey told her Kay was pregnant. He tried to reassure her that it was OK, that she was going to get rid of it, but like many women who suddenly become keenly aware of their body clocks, Caroline had become very judgemental and disapproving about abortions. Mickey thought she was being unrealistic – what century did she think she was living in? – and she snapped back at him.

'If you'd kept it zipped up, we wouldn't be having this debate, would we? And anyway, it's not Kay that's the problem, is it? It seems to me she's well out of the picture.'

'So what is the problem? Lawrence doesn't know it's mine.'

Privately, Caroline doubted if this was so. On the few occasions she'd met Lawrence, he'd struck her as all-seeing, prescient, with an almost Mafia-like calm and cunning that could prove deadly. She thought Mickey would be lucky not to find his entire stable yard decapitated and tucked up in his bed. But she didn't put voice to this observation, for there was a real threat only two miles up the road, and it was the only one she was interested in.

'Your brother. He's got her in his clutches now, hasn't he? He's got her imprisoned in that house of his. He could totally brainwash her in the next couple of hours, if he hasn't already.'

'Why would he want to do that?'

'For God's sake, Mickey. Get a grip. Don't tell me you've never noticed.'

'What?'

'That your brother is . . .' She searched for a word. 'Obsessed. That's the only word for it. He's obsessed with your wife.'

'James?' Mickey nearly fell off the sofa with shock.

'Do you honestly mean you haven't noticed the way he looks at her? When he thinks no one else is looking?'

269

Mickey looked utterly dumbfounded. It was obviously news to him.

'Do you go round with your eyes shut or something? Haven't you seen his body language?'

Mickey shook his head, baffled, and Caroline realized he didn't have a clue what she was on about. She supposed it was her sales training, as she'd been taught to observe people's behaviour in order to give herself the advantage whilst negotiating. It was a useful tool, and not just at work. She persevered with her theory.

'Believe me, Lucy's the only person your brother cares about. He certainly doesn't care about me. Not really. I know when he's screwing me he's thinking about her.'

Mickey winced.

'Don't worry. I haven't minded up till now. Because I've never considered Lucy a real threat. I've always thought she was out of James's reach. And anyway, I never wanted James to start paying me too much attention. Our relationship's always been about convenience. I cover up for his obsession . . .'

'And he pays your bills.'

Caroline glared at him.

'I earn enough to pay my own way, thank you.'

'Sorry, sorry.' Mickey wasn't tooled up for an argument, especially not with Caroline.

'And you're going to have to be nicer to me if you want me to help.'

'Help?'

'Help you get Lucy back. We're going to have to have a truce.'

'What do you mean?'

'You're not going to get her back sitting here feeling

sorry for yourself. Not while she's sitting in the lap of luxury at James's, being cosseted and pampered and adored. You've played right into his hands.'

'But Lucy's almost like a sister to him.'

'Don't be so bloody naive.'

'Do you think she's in love with him?' Mickey looked utterly horrified at the prospect. Caroline pondered this possibility.

'No. I don't. She loves you, Mickey. At least she did up till now.'

'I've fucked everything up, haven't I?'

'You've certainly made a good go of it. But if we play our cards right, we can sort it out.'

'Why do you care whether I get Lucy back? What's in it for you?'

'I want to marry James.'

Caroline couldn't believe what she'd said. The words had popped out before she had actually even thought them. She wished they hadn't when Mickey burst out laughing incredulously.

'You – get married? But you're Miss Independent. Miss Career Girl.'

'I can change, can't I?'

'What – just like that?'

'I've been doing a lot of thinking lately. I'm nearly thirty. I'm burning out. There's people younger and hungrier and fitter than me out there. I have to work harder than they do to prove myself, and frankly I'm knackered. I want a rest.'

'So what you need is a rich husband?'

'Why are you so cynical about me and James?'

'Come on, Caroline. You can't really pretend to me

he's the love of your life. The way you treat him—'

'James and I understand each other. And I don't mind living in Lucy's shadow. I'm always going to know I was second best, but I can live with that. Not many other women would, I can tell you.'

She fixed Mickey with a defiant glare.

'But I'm tired. I want to be looked after. And to have someone else to look after.' She paused for a moment. 'And I want . . . babies.'

There she went again. Voicing things; admitting them to someone else almost before she'd admitted it to herself.

Mickey eyed Caroline thoughtfully. Earth mother she was not. Caroline could read what he was thinking. She leaped in with a justifiable defence.

'Hormones are a terrible thing. I suppose otherwise, without them, the human race would have died out. Once they kick in, you know, there's nothing you can do about it.' She paused. 'I suppose that's why we're all here. It is the meaning of life.'

A tiny vision of his putative offspring crept into Mickey's head. He supposed Kay would have got rid of it by now. He sighed and put his head in his hands. Caroline misunderstood his despair.

'I'm sorry if you find the prospect of me as your sister-in-law so offensive—'

Mickey tried to protest, but Caroline was in full flow. A year of being marginalized by the Liddiards flooded out.

'You've never really liked me, have you? I've never been good enough for your brother, have I? I know what you all think. That all I'm interested in is James's money. But I work hard for my own money. I pay my own way. If James chooses to pamper me sometimes, that's his choice.

I certainly never ask for anything. I can't help it if he's well off. And that's not why I'm with him. I have got my pride, you know. I have got some self-respect.'

Mickey looked at Caroline and realized with alarm that her eyes were welling up. He panicked slightly – he hated it when women, any woman, cried, and the thought of Caroline in tears was most disconcerting. He patted her awkwardly on the hand, only to find her throwing herself on to his shoulder and dissolving into a torrent of tears. The stress of the morning had proved too much for her. She'd always prided herself on her strength, but it was all too much. The row at the yard, the confrontation with James, the realization that she was unhappy with her lot . . . Mickey tried his best to console her. Eventually her tears subsided and she managed a watery apology.

'I'm sorry. It's just been a crap day, that's all.'

She told him about Demelza. About the mess she'd got into because she was useless with money. About how she didn't have a clue what to do, and how she was furious with herself because it was her own stupid fault, for not budgeting and for carrying on regardless.

'You know, I could swallow my pride and ask James for the money. I know he'd bail me out. But I don't want to.'

Mickey smiled ruefully.

'Sounds like you and me are in the same boat.'

And he told her about the brewery. About the knife-edge it was on and how he didn't really have a clue what he was going to do about it. About how he'd even sold Patrick's horse to try and recoup some of his losses. And although his debts paled into insignificance next to the mess he'd made of his marriage, nevertheless it was a problem that wasn't going to go away.

*

Four miles away, Ned and Patrick were bowling down a tortuous lane in the Healey, wrapped up against the elements. They were on a Boxing Day treasure hunt for local classic car enthusiasts, organized by a formidable old bird called Agnes Porter-Wright, who hared round the lanes at top speed in a magnificent old Bentley with scant regard for her brakes. Patrick thought she was wonderful and wondered why there weren't more women like her these days – eccentric forces to be reckoned with. She had a vociferous boom that could be heard for three counties and dressed in fox fur and gardening trousers, with or without the family diamonds, depending on the time of day and the social occasion. The treasure hunt meant without, but she added a pair of motoring goggles for good measure.

Conditions on the hunt this year were glorious. The day was clear and bright, just warm enough to have dispelled the frost that could make driving on the more remote country lanes rather treacherous. It also meant those with convertibles could throw off their roofs with gay abandon and allow the wind to run free in their hair – those of them who still had it. The competitors were a motley crew, with Ned and Patrick being far and away the youngest, but that meant they enjoyed much attention. It was good clean fun, a chance to blow away the cobwebs after the over-indulgence of Christmas Day, and it had become something of a tradition between the two friends.

But Patrick was unable to enjoy the scene. He was livid with Ned. The stupid fool had missed three clues so far and they'd only gone five miles. At this rate they had no bloody hope whatsoever of bringing home the trophy. And Patrick was a competitive little beast. They'd won it for the past three years. It was a point of honour. OK, so the trophy was a rather unattractive lump of Cotswold stone stuck on a piece of wood, but that wasn't the point.

Patrick glanced over at Ned again. He wasn't looking at the clue sheet at all. He was gazing over the horizon lugubriously, looking faintly ridiculous in the leather Biggles hat he always insisted on wearing for the occasion, Patrick swore – the whole point of the treasure hunt was you had to keep your eyes peeled; never take your eye off the ball. You never knew where Agnes might have hidden the answer. He braked and swung the car round angrily, jerking Ned out of his reverie.

'What the hell are you doing?'

'Going back to the pub. There's no point. We're never going to win at this rate—'

'It's not the winning. It's the taking part.'

'Bollocks.'

He headed the car back to Eldenbury. Ned couldn't resist a dig.

'Nobody likes a bad loser.'

'I'm not going to be a loser at all. I'm not taking part if you're not going to pay attention.'

Ned sighed and shoved the clue sheet in the glove compartment. He wasn't in the mood to argue. He wasn't in the mood for anything. And actually, the pub sounded like a good idea. He was bloody freezing, despite his earflaps. Driving at speed meant the wind cut through you like a knife and Patrick, as ever, refused to put his roof up. Bloody poser.

*

An hour later, after they'd revealed their darkest, inner-most secrets and fears to each other, Mickey and Caroline found themselves forging an uneasy alliance. Their mutual wariness was put on hold and an element of trust sprang up. Mickey had to admit to himself, however, that he was rather disconcerted by the speed at which Caroline had regained her composure. One minute she'd been sobbing like a baby in his arms. Now here she was, brisk and busi-nesslike. He wasn't sure which side of her he preferred, especially as he was getting to the stage where a grim reality was starting to seep in through the remnants of his drunkenness, accompanied by a thumping headache. He knew from experience there was only one thing for it. Hair of the dog. He stood up, unsteady.

'Would you like a drink?'

Caroline smiled sweetly.

'Tea would be lovely.'

'I meant—'

'I know you did. But I want you to make a pot of tea and bring me a pad of paper and a pencil.'

'What?'

'We're going to make a plan.'

Mickey could see there was no point in arguing, so he did as she said, relaid and lit the fire, and was surprised to find that the tea was actually rather comforting. Caroline wasted no time in embarking on her agenda. He could see why she was a success at her job.

'Right. Tell me about your marketing strategy.'

Mickey looked a bit blank.

'I haven't really got one.'

'Don't be ridiculous. Of course you have. How do you sell your beer?'

'I supply my own pubs. I've got a captive audience. I don't need to market.'

'Well, it's obviously not working, is it? Or you wouldn't be practically bankrupt.'

'Overheads. Have you got any idea how much it costs to run a brewery?'

Caroline flapped her hand to indicate Mickey should shut up.

'We need to get your name out there. We need Honeycote Ales to be on every beer drinker's lips. It's good stuff, right?'

'Fantastic.'

'So you should let the world know it. For heaven's sake, Mickey – everything's about marketing these days. If you've got the right campaign behind you, you could piss in a bottle and make a success of it. But you've got an added advantage, because your product's good. It's a marketing dream. It's a slice of English country life; it never goes out of fashion. So you need a bit of hype. A celebrity chef who uses Honeycote Ale to cook his beef in beer. The bridegroom who demands it for his toast instead of champagne.' She paused for breath, but not for long. 'How many times have you been in the local paper? You should be in it every week, for one thing or another. And what about sponsorship? You should be sponsoring fences at the local point-to-point. Or the local rugby team. Anything to get your name out and about. It's just common sense.'

She stared at him curiously.

'Just out of interest, what have you been doing all this time?'

'Working bloody hard. That brewery's going round the clock sometimes, you know—'

'And you're there, are you? Shovelling all the hops or whatever – putting your back into it?'

'Sometimes, yes. I like to think I'm hands on.'

'Rubbish. You've been messing about. You've been handed a goose which should be laying golden eggs—'

'Actually, I've never considered money that important.'

Caroline laughed heartily.

'The only people who can afford to say that are ones who are stuffed to the gills with it. You've been born with a silver knife, fork and spoon in your mouth. And you'd better get real, Mickey. There'll be people queuing up to step into your shoes when you go belly up.'

She was telling him exactly what Cowley had said to him only days before. How could she be so well informed? Mickey felt a surge of resentment. How come everybody knew more about his own business than he did?

'How do you know so much about it? I mean, what gives you the right to criticize the way I run my business?'

'My job, that's what. OK, so I'm only in charge of advertising on the local paper. But it gives me a pretty good insight into what businesses work and why. I get all the gossip off the journalists – hot tips as to what leads to follow, who's doing well. It doesn't take long to build up a picture.'

Tight-lipped, Mickey stalked over to the window and looked out. If someone had told him he would be sitting down with Caroline Mason, drinking tea and drawing up a marketing plan for Honeycote Ales, he'd never have believed them. But at this stage of the game he had little choice. He had no other ally he could turn to.

By the end of the afternoon, he was pleasantly surprised to find himself coming round to what she was saying. Yes, she was abrasive and opinionated, wouldn't give an inch, but at least she was positive. And she got things done. She'd fetched her laptop from the car, and Mickey watched, fascinated, as she soon had an elaborate strategy typed up, with bullet points and graphs and targets. She printed it off on her portable printer and Mickey couldn't be anything other than impressed.

'Banks and investors love business plans. Even if your figures are totally unrealistic, they like to think you've thought it through. If nothing else, it will buy you some time with the bank.'

Mickey felt like retorting that he was forty-three years old, he'd been running his business for more than twenty years and he knew what a bloody business plan was. But when you compared their achievements, he'd managed to run a perfectly successful business into the ground, while Caroline had hit double bonus targets three months in a row. So he decided to shut up. And anyway, looking at the plan it was just the sort of thing that would send Cowley into ecstasies. He put it down on the coffee table with a smile.

'Well, after all that hard work, I think we deserve a drink, don't you?'

'No.'

Her tone was headmistressy. Mickey blinked in shock. 'What?'

'When's the last time you went without a drink?'

'I can't remember. But I could if I wanted to.'

'That's what they all say.'

Mickey frowned. What was she implying?

'You're never going to get Lucy back if you're as pissed as a fart when she turns up. What if she'd turned up instead of me this morning? You weren't a very attractive proposition, I can tell you. Snoring and dribbling all over the sofa—'

'Don't mince your words, Caroline. Say what you think.'

She smiled sweetly. 'I always do. And it's true. You can't carry on drowning your sorrows, Mickey. You need to sober up, get a grip, face up to your problems—'

Mickey sighed. He knew only too well she was right. He'd been on track for doing that, as well, until things had gone so wrong the day before.

'It's not that easy.'

'No. Of course it's not. Nothing worth doing ever is. But if you've got me breathing down your neck, you can do it. Face it, Mickey. You've got no choice. It's sink or swim.'

Caroline didn't like to admit that she herself could murder an enormous gin with not much tonic, but she had a point to prove. She had to set an example.

'If you're going to put that plan into action, you need a clear head. You don't want to be fuddled by booze. You might think it makes life easier in the short term, but it isn't doing you any favours. In fact, I'd go so far as to say you've got a problem.'

'What?'

Mickey was outraged. Caroline raised an arched eyebrow at his protestations.

'Well, if you haven't, it shouldn't be difficult to go without, should it?' she asked sweetly, and stood up. Mickey narrowed his eyes.

'OK, then. What next?'

'Have you seen the kitchen?'

Mickey grimaced.

'I'll start the washing-up. You go upstairs and make yourself look human. Have a shower and a shave, before anyone else sees you.'

Caroline started gathering up the tea things. Mickey was looking at her, open-mouthed. Nobody had ever spoken to him like that before. She looked down at him and grinned.

'Go on. I'll check you've done behind your ears when you come back down.'

As Mickey went upstairs, he found it was with a lighter heart than he'd had for the last twenty-four hours. Everything was going to be all right. He'd straighten out, sober up, show Lucy how much he'd changed. She'd forgive him, he was sure of it. Surely everyone was allowed one mistake?

In Eldenbury, Patrick managed to edge his car into a parking space that had just been vacated before anyone else spotted it. The market square was heaving. The meet had just been seen off in all its glory, leaving a throng of onlookers thirsty for yet more alcohol pouring into the Horse and Groom. It was an excellent hunting ground for talent: young girls wrapped up in fake furs and stripy hats, with their long legs and big boots, slugging back Bloody Marys and smoking. But this year neither Ned nor Patrick had a taste for it. They were both encumbered by their own problems, unable to enjoy the ritual that usually allowed them to be the centre of attention. Ned with his merry antics and Patrick with his to-die-for good looks made an irresistible combination.

But today Patrick's scowl marred his features, rendering him almost unnoticeable, and Ned felt less than merry. The two of them skulked on the outskirts of crowds of friends meeting up for the first time in ages. Patrick suddenly found it depressing how people had changed, gained weight and confidence, and didn't feel like exchanging small talk. Ned was oblivious, enmeshed in his gloom, his thick blond brows meeting in the middle. 'Might as well go and get totally trolleyed.'

They shuffled into the Horse and Groom and joined the queue at the bar. Mayday was behind the bar, valiantly pulling pints as if her life depended on it, and was puzzled when neither Patrick nor Ned would meet her eye. They were uncharacteristically truculent. She bit her lower lip and tossed back her hair, feeling hurt. She'd never asked anything of either of them. Why was she being ostracized?

Hugging their pints of Honeycote Christmas Ale, as rich and as satisfying as a three-course meal, Ned and Patrick squeezed themselves into a corner by the window to drown their respective sorrows. Ned was ahead of Patrick, as he'd been taking surreptitious nips from his hip-flask on the treasure hunt, to keep out both the cold and his conscience, so it wasn't long before he slipped into morose self-flagellation about his predicament.

Patrick was unsympathetic. As far as he was concerned, he'd made his own bed. Ned protested that sleeping with Mayday just didn't count, she was a rite of passage, fair game. Patrick just raised an eyebrow and suggested he tell that to Sophie. Ned sulked. Patrick clearly wasn't going to give an inch, or allow him any way out of his dilemma. He didn't care, because it wasn't his problem.

Patrick did care, very much, but was wrapped up in an even bigger dilemma that he couldn't voice to Ned. He had been deeply shocked by Lucy's revelation about Kay the night before. He was confident that whoever's baby Kay was carrying it wasn't his. If life had taught him one thing it was to always have safe sex. Patrick liked risks, but riding bareback wasn't one of them. On the other hand, he was pretty sure his father never gave safe sex a second thought from one day to the next. He'd be of the old school that considered contraception a woman's responsibility, if he considered it at all. Moreover, he knew Mickey never learned from his mistakes, and Patrick had been one of his biggest. Add to that the fact that Kay wasn't of the generation to carry a condom in her handbag and bingo – you could see how it had happened. Apparently Lawrence had been pretty confident it wasn't his, for whatever reason. Presumably they hadn't been having sex. So there it was, somewhere Patrick had a half-brother or sister that was destined for the incinerator, if it wasn't already there.

He couldn't help feeling sorry for Kay. He'd tried calling her that morning, but her phone was switched off. He'd have liked to have given her a bit of support, a kind word. She was a bit of a loner, was Kay – he knew instinctively she wouldn't be getting tea and sympathy from an old school friend. But he couldn't feel responsible for her predicament.

More pressing was his father's. Mickey must know the baby was his and must be feeling the pressure. As if he wasn't under enough already. If he could just steer his father through the next few weeks without him cracking . . .

Patrick went to the cigarette machine to replenish

his supply and found himself cornered by an indignant Mayday, hands on hips, tossing back her mane of hair defiantly.

'OK, so what's the matter with you two? Why are you blanking me? What have I done?'

Patrick put her straight in no uncertain terms.

'Why the hell did you give Ned a lovebite? You knew he was after Sophie . . .'

Mayday looked blank.

'Did I? I didn't realize . . .'

'Oh, come on—'

'I didn't do it on purpose! It must have been the heat of the moment. You know what I'm like.' Patrick rolled his eyes. He knew only too well. Mayday was stricken.

'Christ, I'm sorry. Why the hell didn't he wear a polo neck? What does he think they're for?'

'Why couldn't you have exercised some self-control for once, Mayday? I know you think that everything in trousers is fair game—'

Mayday chuckled, a deep throaty cigarette and whisky rumble that sounded like a Harley Davidson starting up.

'And you, of course, set an example to us all.' She smiled sweetly at Patrick. She didn't like being chastised. She never pretended to be anything other than pathologically promiscuous, so why should she be reprimanded? But Patrick persisted.

'At least I think about the possible consequences. Who might get hurt. Sophie was devastated.'

Mayday pouted defensively.

'Doesn't she know sleeping with me doesn't count?'

'Of course she doesn't. Sophie's an innocent. A romantic. She believes in love at first sight, happy ever after.'

'She'd better get real, then, hadn't she?'

Patrick didn't like to admit it, but Mayday had a point. There wasn't much hope for the likes of Sophie in this world. But he didn't want her to change. He didn't want her hardened and cynical – he wanted her notion of a fairy-tale romance to live on. And he truly believed that Ned, even though he could be an utter clot at times, was her Prince Charming. He was one of the few people on earth that Patrick respected and trusted, and considered worthy of his little sister. He wanted to make things right for them.

He looked at Mayday and was shocked to see that her eyes were glassy with unshed tears. He felt consumed with guilt all of a sudden – he'd been hard on her. She'd been in the line of fire and she couldn't really be held responsible for all his problems. Just the fifteen-stone one steadily getting pissed in the corner.

'Hey, listen . . .' He lifted his finger to catch a tear before it fell. He'd never thought of Mayday crying.

'I do have feelings, you know. I can't just be used and abused . . .'

Patrick enveloped her in a comforting hug. She'd always been a good friend to him. In fact, apart from Ned she was one of the few people he really trusted. But sometimes Mayday was her own worst enemy. She was the archetypal tart with a heart; she laid herself open to abuse. Was she someone else he was going to have to save from themselves?

He went through a mental checklist of his Herculean tasks. Winkle his way into Mandy's heart and get some dosh out of her dad for the brewery. Try to see if Kay was all right. Sort out Ned and Sophie. Placate Kelly – he still felt a prick of conscience when he thought about her. Save Mayday from herself. Christ, there wasn't going to be any time to relax and have fun.

He took a couple more pints back to their table. Ned downed his in one. It made him even more morose and Patrick was worried if they carried on he might start a fight. Ned wasn't aggressive, but he was clumsy and this sometimes landed him in trouble when spirits were high.

'Come on, Ned. Let's get you back home. You can go and sleep it off.'

Patrick thought it was time he got back home anyway. Boxing Day evening was usually open house at Honeycote House. Lucy cooked a huge ham and a side of spiced beef, which were laid out on the dining table surrounded by jewel-bright salads and pickles and chutneys. There was always a terrifying display of puddings, too, trifles and syllabubs and port wine jellies made in traditional moulds. People wandered in and out all evening, helping themselves until well into the early hours – friends, relatives, the vicar, the girls who helped muck out the horses. Patrick thought it was time he went back to help lay out the spread. He'd left the house very early that morning, before either Lucy or Mickey was up, and he had felt a pang of guilt at the sight of the washing-up from yesterday as he passed through the kitchen. Never mind, he'd make up for it by doing all the washing-up this evening, and making sure Lucy put her feet up. She deserved a bit of TLC – even if she didn't know it.

As soon as Mickey had gone upstairs, Caroline set to work. Every decanter in the dining room was emptied down the sink. She was sure some of it was outrageously expensive stuff, but she didn't care. This called for drastic measures. Then she gathered up every bottle she could find that hadn't been drunk, which wasn't many, and took them back down to the cellar. There was a huge iron key in the lock. She snapped it shut with a grim finality and tucked it in her bra. She checked the fridge. There were a few beers – she flipped the tops and emptied them too.

Her first task finished, she turned to the washing-up. She looked everywhere she could think of but she couldn't find a dishwasher. What was it with the Liddiards and their apparent fear of anything that made life easier? Even her parents, who hardly had a bean to rub together, had had a dishwasher since she could remember. There was nothing for it. Caroline, who never washed up if she could help it – only a coffee cup in the morning and a wine glass in the evening – braced herself, pulled on some rubber gloves and filled the sink with hot, soapy water.

When Patrick walked in at three o'clock, he was amazed to find Caroline in the kitchen, surrounded by piles of gleaming crockery and cutlery, with her arms up to their elbows in suds, about to start on the glasses. He eyed her suspiciously.

'What the fuck are you doing here?'

'Lovely to see you too, Patrick. Merry Christmas.'

Caroline held out her cheek for a kiss. Patrick ignored her. He'd never trusted Caroline an inch. 'Where's Lucy?'

Caroline threw him a tea towel.

'I'll wash. You dry.'

Patrick threw it back.

'Where's Dad?'

'Upstairs. Washing away his sins.'

'What?'

Caroline sighed. Patrick was going to have to find out sooner or later. And he might help with the damage limitation. She was worried about Sophie and Georgina, and how they would react to the situation. She was pretty sure Patrick would be useful when it came to pulling the wool over their eyes. If they could get this mess sorted out as quickly as possible, the ramifications would be minimal.

'Your dad's been having an affair. With Kay Oakley. Lucy's found out and gone running to James.'

'The stupid cow.'

'Who – Lucy?'

'No. Kay. How the hell did Lucy find out? Did Kay tell her?'

He'd bloody kill her if she had. He'd put his hands round her throat and choke the life out of her. But Caroline was shaking her head.

'One of the great clichés of modern life. Last number redial.'

Patrick groaned. He wished fervently he'd had nothing to drink, as it was stopping him from thinking clearly. All the plans he'd been neatly laying were out the window now. Caroline interrupted his train of thought.

'Look – if you're not going to help dry up, at least do something useful. Phone round all the people who are supposed to be coming tonight – fob them off. Tell them everyone's gone down with cholera or TB or something. The last thing we need is anyone else turning up and interfering.'

'Just out of interest, why are you?'

'What?'

'Interfering.'

'Believe it or not, I care about this family.'

She fixed him with a steely glare. Patrick was feeling particularly uncharitable, so he fired a shot that he knew he shouldn't.

'Well, you needn't think you're ever going to be part of it.'

Caroline took in a sharp breath. Patrick had hit her right below the belt, without realizing it. She turned on him, eyes blazing.

'What is this, some sort of conspiracy? What is so awful about the prospect of me marrying James? Your father seemed to find it absurd as well. He as good as accused me of only being after him for his money. I can assure you if that was the case I'd be after someone a lot older and a lot wealthier.' Caroline looked at him knowingly. 'You've never liked me, have you? Any of you. Is it because' – mock gasp of horror – 'my mother was a dinner lady?'

'I'd no idea your mother was a dinner lady. And if I had, it wouldn't make any difference. You're being paranoid.'

'I'm not.'

Caroline wanted Patrick to admit it – that his family didn't like her, that they didn't think she was good enough for James.

'Caroline – it's not your parents that make you not good enough for him. It's the way you treat him. You stand him up, you show him up. You get pissed in public and humiliate him—'

'Me?'

'James just isn't the sort of person who appreciates dancing on tables.'

No, Caroline thought to herself, he isn't. Because Lucy would never dream of dancing on a table. She'd never feel the need to draw attention to herself because she always had it, undivided, from everyone around her. Caroline sighed. Should she change who she was to please James? Actually, she didn't think she could. You couldn't go from being loud, extrovert and assertive to being gentle and unassuming. And there must have been something about her he'd liked in the first place. It had been over a year, after all. And actually, they never argued about anything.

Was she really that bad? Was she really as unattractive a proposition as Patrick was suggesting? She had a career, didn't she? If you wanted to talk about gold-diggers, then you only had to look at Kay Oakley. And come to think of it, what about Lucy? James had mentioned once that she had been Mickey's au pair or nanny or something.

She was aggrieved. Here she was trying to help Mickey out of the mire – he was obviously totally out of his depth and she'd been trying to get him to look at things objectively and apply a modicum of common sense to the whole mess. How dare Patrick swan in and judge her?

'OK – maybe I'm not top of the list when it comes to choosing eligible wives for your precious uncle. But let's put it another way, Patrick. Who would you rather have as your auntie? Me – or your stepmother?'

Patrick winced. He hated it whenever anyone referred to Lucy as his stepmother. It was too ugly a word.

'Because it's James she's gone running to. And he's welcomed her with open arms, I can tell you.'

Patrick snapped.

'Why don't you just shove off, Caroline? You're nothing to do with this family. You don't understand what's going on. Just get out.'

'How dare you? I'm only trying to help—'

'Why? What's in it for you?'

'I think you've misjudged me.'

Patrick gave a short, cynical laugh.

'Really?'

'You're an arrogant little shit.'

'Better than being a gold-digger.'

Caroline had never slapped a man round the face before – in her view it was a sign of defeat, a sign of verbal weakness – but she came pretty close. Instead, she took a deep breath, swallowed, smiled graciously and left.

For the third time that day, she jumped in her car seething with rage. She was furious with the Liddiards, all of them. Why didn't she just accept that they were a bunch of selfish, arrogant shits, and go out with someone normal?

Mickey came downstairs, washed and brushed and gleaming, to find Patrick in the kitchen poring over the business plan he and Caroline had spent so long agonizing over.

'Where's Caroline?'

'She had to go.' Patrick's tone was casual. He indicated the business plan. 'What's all this?'

'Some sort of business plan she made me bash out. Bloody good, actually.'

Patrick went to the fridge to look for a beer. There wasn't any. He frowned, and went to the cellar door for another tray of cans. The door was locked.

'Who's locked the door?'

'It must have been Caroline. She seems to think I drink too much.'

A further inspection revealed that all the decanters were empty. Mickey was silently impressed. This girl meant business. Patrick, however, was furious.

'Who does she think she is? I'll go out and get something.'

'No.'

'What?'

'She's right. If I can't do without a drink for twenty-four hours then I've obviously got a problem—'

'She said that?'

'Look, Patrick. If Lucy walks in here, I want a clear head, not to breathe fumes all over her.'

He couldn't quite meet Patrick's eye.

'I suppose she told you?'

'Yes.'

Neither father nor son knew quite what to say. Patrick couldn't bring himself to rebuke his own father, and certainly couldn't tell him the deal he'd done himself with Kay. He couldn't believe the cruel twist the cards had dealt, and how in a split second the whole deck had collapsed when it could so nearly have been all right.

'What are you going to do?'

Mickey sighed. 'I don't know. Talk to Lucy, I suppose. But Caroline says . . .'

He trailed off. He couldn't tell Patrick what Caroline had said, about his own brother worshipping his wife. Luckily, Patrick wasn't going to give him the chance to say anything.

'Who cares what Caroline says?'

Mickey sprang to her defence.

'You can think what you like about Caroline, but she's actually a good sort underneath it all. I wish she hadn't just gone like that. I wanted to say thanks.'

Patrick felt a bit sick. Perhaps he'd been too harsh on her. But she'd been her overbearing self, bossing him around, treating him like some little boy who didn't know the implications of what was happening around him. And he'd been tired and confused, overwhelmed by his responsibilities. He pushed her to the back of his mind. The last person he was going to worry about was Caroline.

17

Keith had thought he'd made it pretty clear to Sandra what her position was the night before. That she was to keep her head down and make herself scarce as soon as possible. Yet here she was again, the next morning, making her presence known when she'd been told quite clearly that she wasn't wanted. Any humbler person would have got the message, but here she was in the kitchen, letting rip as she realized there wasn't going to be room at the theatre for her. Keith remained impassive as she railed at him. He was bloody well not going to let her go to the pantomime, even if she had booked the tickets in the first place. As far as he was concerned, she'd given up her right to a seat the minute she'd walked out of the house. But she, of course, didn't see it that way.

'Look, Sandra, Mandy's invited Sophie and Georgina now, and that's the end of it. There's no room for anyone else.'

'But it was supposed to be a family outing.'

'Family.'

Keith tried the word as if it was totally new to him. He frowned.

'I wouldn't say we were a family, really, would you? We didn't have a family Christmas. We don't have family friends. We don't have family traditions. People with a sense of *family*' – he underlined the word with a heavy irony – 'don't go buggering off to Spain at the drop of a hat without a by your leave.'

Sandra looked deeply shocked. She'd thought that after a good night's sleep Keith would have calmed down, tried to see things from her point of view. After all, he'd never stood up to her before. All their married life he'd given in to her whims, anything for a quiet life. She'd always been in the driving seat and made all the decisions while he just made the money to pay for it all. She rallied.

'How long are these *friends* staying anyway?'

'As long as they like. Because Mandy's spent a lot of time enjoying their hospitality. And they very kindly asked us to spend Christmas with them, so I thought it was the least I could do to repay their generosity. And as I had a spare ticket for the panto – or at least thought I had—'

Sandra felt rising panic, but took in a deep breath – then realized she was being silly. She could use the time while they were out of the house very usefully indeed. She assumed a mask of understanding.

'Of course. I'm sorry. Off you all go.'

She'd waited till they were safely out of the drive before setting to work. Then she painstakingly searched the house from top to bottom for evidence of Keith's business interests. She wanted to know what he was actually worth, in case things really did get nasty. She spent a good hour and a half in the study, taking photocopies of various documents, until she had a neat file which she stored away in the box that contained the foot spa he'd bought her two Christmases before. She'd heard too many stories about sly husbands trying to disguise their assets – she wasn't going to give him half a chance. Satisfied that she'd done her homework, she was about to reward herself with a nice jangly gin and tonic when she spotted the answerphone. There was no flashing light indicating a fresh message: not surprisingly, as most people recognized the sanctity of family over the Christmas period. But she did wonder if there was anything worth listening to on it. A frosted talon hovered momentarily over the replay button before pressing it defiantly.

Keith came back from the pantomime full of resolve. He'd taken no notice of the plot at all, but had spent the entire two hours thinking about his life. He concluded that he needed to put things on an official footing, and told Sandra as such only ten minutes after walking through the door.

'I want a divorce.'

Sandra gripped the cut glass that held her gin. Her foot was jiggling up and down, her face rigid with bitterness.

'I'll take you for everything you've got.'

'I think not.'

She turned to face him triumphantly.

'I know you're selling the business. I'm entitled to half.'

She was pleased to see Keith looked shocked. Perfect. She wanted him to think she had her spies out; that every move he made would be known to her. In fact, she'd simply rewound all his answerphone messages and listened with particular interest to the one Roy had left a couple of days ago, saying he thought he'd found a buyer already.

Keith recovered himself and batted the ball back.

'If you know that, then you must know my other plans, too.'

She smiled tightly and nodded. From that Keith knew she was bluffing, as he hadn't mentioned a word to anyone else, so unless she was a mind-reader . . . He looked at her, saw how her maroon lipstick was bleeding into the little vertical lines that ran along her top lip. She glared back at him defiantly.

'So – what are you going to tell Mandy?'

'Me?'

'Absolutely. You're the one who wants a divorce, so you can tell her. And where are we going to live? You can't throw us out of here. We've got rights. This is the family home—'

'I think you'll find that as she's over eighteen those rights don't necessarily apply. And anyway, she'll probably live with me.'

Sandra flushed a dark puce.

'What have you been saying to her, you bastard?'

'Please, Sandra – we've got guests.'

'Oh yes. Your precious bloody Liddiards that you seem to worship so much all of a sudden. Your new best friends. Well, I'm telling you, Keith. You'll never be like them as long as you live.'

Keith looked at Sandra. She did sometimes have an uncanny knack of hitting you where it hurt. But, in fact, he was immune to her insults on this occasion. OK, he knew he'd never be like the Liddiards. That didn't mean he had to stoop as low as her. Her haranguing stiffened his resolve. If he was going to achieve anything in the next six months, it was to save Mandy from becoming a parody of her mother, taking on her values and her aspirations.

He didn't think it was too late. Mandy hadn't spent much time with her mother, after all. She hadn't been unduly influenced. You only had to look at them. Today Sandra was sporting a knitted ensemble in deep coral with batwing sleeves and the ubiquitous gold stilettos, highlighted hair blown dry into a rigid helmet. He could see a tidemark where her foundation ended, the foundation that showed up her facial hair rather than disguised her wrinkles.

Mandy, by contrast, was in cream jeans, a black polo neck and black suede boots, her hair caught loosely at her neck in a tortoiseshell clip. Arguably she had youth on her side where make-up was concerned, but even then she was able to resist the temptation of the young to slap it on with a trowel, and was content with a light brushing of mascara on her lashes and a slick of lip-gloss. Keith noticed that she had some colour in her cheeks from the time she'd spent outside at Honeycote. The sooner he could get her riding that little horse, the better. In fact, the sooner they moved to the countryside, the better. He wouldn't even sell The Cedars first. He'd buy somewhere cash—

Oh God. There he went again, buying his way in. But actually, did he really care? Yes, he had money, but was that such a fault? One thing was certain: if he couldn't use it to get what he wanted, then what was the point? The most important thing was that Sandra shouldn't get her hands on it. Keith had made sure that there was nothing of great importance lying around the house, just enough detail so that she wouldn't become suspicious if she went rifling through his filing cabinet.

His serious money was tucked away and totally untraceable, for he was a cunning investor. He'd got it all stashed away, quietly waiting for a window of opportunity to become apparent. Which he felt pretty sure it had.

Lawrence had woken up on Boxing Day feeling like hell. He'd hit the malt whisky in an attempt to reach the arms of Morpheus and was now regretting it deeply. Little memories of what had happened the day before were coming back to him in snatches and they made him squirm with embarrassment. The vision of Lucy's sympathetic face detracted from the pleasure of Mickey's shocked demeanour. Opening his mouth like that wasn't usually Lawrence's style at all. He blamed the excellent wine they'd been drinking. Wine of that quality slipped down so easily and loosened the tongue.

He spent the day at the garden centre. By the evening, he needed to get out. He didn't want to stay at home; the house felt like a mausoleum. What he needed was some company to take his mind off things.

He phoned Kelly and asked her out for dinner, but she was reluctant to leave her mother. Poor Eileen had been rushed off her feet. Even though the pub was closed on Christmas Day, all their relatives came to the Honeycote Arms for lunch, because of the space and the kitchen – twenty-seven of them altogether. Eileen insisted that she loved it, and that everyone did their bit, but it seemed unfair to Kelly that Eileen spent every night of the year rushing round serving people and didn't get the day off on Christmas Day, so she always tried to make it up to her on Boxing Day. She was going to give her a top-to-toe beauty treatment that evening, pamper her, take the aches and pains away. Lawrence felt a twinge of jealousy. He longed for one of Kelly's top-to-toe treatments, but today wasn't the time to ask. He persuaded her to come out for a quick drink instead, just two hours out of her day with her family, and she agreed. Despite her loyalty to her parents, she had to admit it was a strain keeping everyone's spirits up when they knew this was the last Christmas they'd be spending at the Honeycote Arms.

Lawrence took Kelly to the Lygon Arms in Broadway. There was no way anyone couldn't relax in its cosy, un-ashamed luxury. They sat down on a huge, squashy sofa in front of an enormous fire, which suffused the air with the sweet smell of woodsmoke. Kelly flopped back on the cushions with a sigh of contentment. Lawrence tried not to look at her chest, covered in pink fluffy angora. He focused instead on pouring her some champagne.

'So – come on, then, Kelly. Tell me your dreams.'

She told him about her goal. To have her own beauty salon. She'd only got six more months at college before she took her exams – and her tutors had told her she should fly through, as long as she concentrated on her theory. Lawrence privately vouched for her practical.

'But actually – that was before all this business with the pub. Now my dream is to help mum and dad get it back. Though I know that's impossible.'

She laughed, but Lawrence could see the sadness in her eyes and was yet again touched by her devotion to her parents. She patted him on the knee.

'So – come on then. Tell me yours.'

'Mine? Oh – nothing, really. I suppose I've achieved mine – the garden centre.'

He didn't want to tell her the truth. He would never tell anyone that all he dreamed of was a house filled with his children, sliding down banisters, sitting on rocking horses, a row of red wellies lined up by the back door. Little bodies hurling themselves at him as he came in from work, smothering him in hugs and kisses and patting his pockets for the treats he would always bring them. Exhausted children slumbering in their beds surrounded by teddies, dreaming their own dreams that he would do his damnedest to make come true . . .

He stopped himself. There was no point in having a dream that you knew could never come true. There had to be an element of attainability about a fantasy, some small chance that fed it and kept it alive.

But if he couldn't achieve his own fantasy, then he'd help Kelly achieve hers. Although it was beyond her wildest dreams, it was well within his powers. He'd fulfil his fantasies vicariously, through her.

He dropped her back home at half past seven. He supposed the easiest option would be to buy the pub off Honeycote Ales and keep Ted and Eileen on as managers. But somehow that seemed too pat an answer, plus it had the added disadvantage of giving Mickey Liddiard the cash he so badly needed. He wanted to ruin him, not help him out.

He sat in the car park and looked at the pub, wondering whether, if he didn't buy it, anyone else would. Ted and Eileen kept it ticking over, but that was about it. You couldn't just buy it and walk in; it certainly needed twenty odd grand throwing at it, if not more. The only reason anyone would really want it would be to convert into a house, though Lawrence knew from experience how reluctant local authorities were to grant permission to do this. Country pubs were becoming something of a rarity and the local council were usually desperate to keep villages alive.

As he sat there brooding, inspiration hit him with a flash. You might not get permission to convert any of the pubs into housing, but what about the brewery itself? It was bloody ripe for conversion, and what better man to do it than him? After all, wasn't that how he'd made his money in the first place, yuppyfying redundant buildings?

Lawrence felt a familiar tingle that meant he'd hit the jackpot in some way. He drove back home with a purpose. At the very least, this would take his mind off things.

The consultant came to talk to Kay again before she was finally discharged, to check her over and to see what she was going to do. She gave her a stern lecture. Whatever happened, Kay had to register properly with a GP, get some antenatal care and decide what sort of a birth she wanted. All Kay knew was she had to get out of the hospital. She'd had enough of the curious glances from the other patients, who were clearly all speculating on her condition. She wouldn't have been surprised if they were laying bets, and she couldn't blame them – anything to relieve the tedium of lying in that ghastly ward with those relentlessly cheerful carols blaring out.

Kay decided to go back to the hotel for a couple more days. Get some rest, get her head together. It was luxurious enough, and she was impressed to hear that the manager had phoned up twice to check on her welfare. She was sure she'd be well looked after while she contemplated her future, because the plans she'd made only four days ago were now obsolete. She certainly couldn't take on a job at the estate agent knowing she was due to give birth in just over three months – even if she could hide her condition under a well-cut jacket. And she'd have to phone the girl who owned the Coach House, tell her the deal was off, due to unforeseen circumstances. She wouldn't give her the details: the girl probably wouldn't believe her. She wasn't sure if she believed it herself.

She gathered her belongings together, thanked the consultant and the nurses, and strode out into the night air to find a taxi.

That evening, Caroline let herself into her house and immediately wished she'd gone somewhere – anywhere – else. The cold air jumped up and caught her in the back of the throat. She knew it would take at least an hour to warm up, even if she turned every heater up to full blast. She wondered about filling a hot water bottle, turning on the electric blanket and climbing into bed to mull over her predicament.

She thought of the optimism she'd woken with that morning. How she'd looked forward to a bracing ride to clear away the vestiges of Christmas over-indulgence, followed by a couple more days of indulgence with James, interspersed with a bit of merriment and high jinks at Honeycote House.

Now here she was, horseless, manless, moneyless, with nothing but a pretty clear message from most of the Liddiards that they thought she was a waste of space. Even though she'd been trying to help – albeit because she had a vested interest. But she was stung by their slurs, their intimations that she was only after James for his money, which couldn't be further from the truth. She admired him because he was everything she wasn't – controlled, patient, organized, tidy – and she was a great believer in opposites attracting. You couldn't live with someone who was your own mirror image. You'd end up boring each other to death. Perhaps that's what would happen to James and Lucy, if they ended up together. They'd suffocate each other with their understated bloody good taste.

OK. So the Liddiards had made it clear between them that she'd never be one of them. They'd slammed down the portcullis and pulled up the drawbridge. She'd got the message all right. She wasn't going to spend the rest of her life being patronized and looked down on.

It didn't do, did it, mixing with the wrong class? She should try someone ordinary, someone who knew how to have fun. She thought of Gerry, who'd started as a photographer on the paper three months ago and had hounded her from day one. He was cheeky, comical, with a wry sense of humour and absolutely no airs and graces. They'd have a laugh together.

She walked over to the phone and punched in his number. He'd given it to her often enough. He answered after three rings.

'Hello?'

'Gerry? It's Caroline.'

'Cazza! How are you doing?'

'Fine. I just wondered . . . that drink you're always going on about. Do you fancy it?'

There was a silence that Caroline could detect was embarrassed.

'Shit, Cazza. I'd have loved to. But . . . I'm going out with Gemma. You kept me hanging around too long, babe. I never thought I was in with a chance.'

Caroline put the phone down slowly, then picked up a

cup and threw it at the wall. It exploded with a satisfying smash, leaving a spattering of coffee in a four-foot radius. She tried a glass, with the same effect – red wine everywhere. Suddenly she found she couldn't stop. Everything within her reach was hurled at the wall, until she collapsed in a heap, crying despite herself. She'd sworn they wouldn't get to her. But what did she have? Fuck all.

Lawrence's hand was shaking with excitement as he sat at the kitchen table with a sheet of graph paper, trying to work out exactly how much living accommodation the brewery could offer.

He hadn't been able to remember the brewery's shape and size at first. A few square feet here and there would make a huge difference to the profit margins. He'd rummaged in the hallway until he found a pair of racing binoculars, then rushed out to his car. No. Too conspicuous. He went back inside and found the keys to the Fiesta that the garden centre staff borrowed sometimes. He could hardly bear the five minutes it took to reach Honeycote Ales. He found a vantage point and trained the binoculars on his prey, straining his eyes in the dark. Eventually he refreshed his memory as to its layout and greedily counted up the outbuildings, each one a potential unit yielding hard cash.

Now here he was, committing his plan to paper, and feeling an increasing sense of excitement. The time was right for a new challenge. The garden centre at Barton Court was running itself, having achieved its maximum potential. Expansion now would mean acquiring another branch and the thought of that bored Lawrence rigid. He hated doing the same thing twice.

He couldn't believe he hadn't thought of this before. He could already see the brochures. Glossy, exclusive, inviting . . . they'd be queuing up to view the show-home; buying apartments off plan. Bloody fantastic. Money up front. The whole enterprise would finance itself beautifully. And destroy the last generation of Liddiards. It would be on a par with pillaging and sacking.

Honeycote Grange. A huge pair of crested, gold-tipped, remote-control wrought-iron gates with an intercom and a video entryphone. Reproduction carriage lamps. Floodlit fountains with piddling cherubs. Lawrence knew that even he would never stoop that low, but it made him chuckle to think of it. That would be the ultimate humiliation for the Liddiards. New money pissing all over their heritage.

Lawrence had decided on exclusive apartments rather than houses. Because they would need security and maintenance and lots of little added luxuries that you could charge a fortune for. As well as a nice fat management fee. All the grounds could be landscaped and maintained by Barton Court – he could offload all his end-of-line garden statuary. He chuckled to himself. There was something in the saying 'To those that have . . .'

And to those that are in deep shit . . . Lawrence reached for the phone and dialled Cowley's home number. He didn't care if he was settling down to a nice relaxing Boxing Day supper of coronation turkey. This could mean mega bucks.

That night, at Denham House, both Lucy and James lay awake, but in separate rooms. Lucy had spent a lot of the day asleep, but James had insisted at about three o'clock that they should go out for a walk. He didn't think it was doing her any good to mope. The fresh air had, indeed, done her good, enough to get her head together to phone Keith Sherwyn and ask him to keep the girls for another day, which he'd said would be his pleasure – he'd take them to the sales.

But because she'd spent half the day asleep, she now couldn't. She knew that the next day she was going to have to confront Mickey. There was no point in putting it off. But she didn't know what to say. Worse than that, she didn't know what he was going to say. Her greatest fear was that he was going to tell her he didn't love her any more. Or, worse still, that he never had. She wondered how she could have gone for so long without noticing anything amiss. She went back over the last week, the last month, the last year, looking for signs of dissatisfaction, infidelity, and couldn't find any. Was it that she wasn't observant, or was he so cunning and clever that he'd managed to keep it hidden? She felt sick at the thought that the man she loved could have been so actively duplicitous. Had he and Kay spent their time making love and laughing at how easy she made it for them? Lucy tossed and turned as these images and worse tormented her and kept her from sleep.

Meanwhile, in the room next door, James congratulated himself on getting Lucy safely landed in his net, and wondered how long he should leave it before he made his next move. Was it best to close in while the wounds were fresh and raw, or was that too ungentlemanly for words?

At Honeycote House, Mickey lay alone in his marital bed, unable to take the cold chill off the sheets and watching the hands of the clock pass every hour. Every bone, every muscle, every nerve in his body was crying out for a drink to help him get to sleep, but he was determined to see the night through. By three o'clock in the morning he was ready to give in, but realized that there wasn't a drop to be had in the house, unless he took an axe and chopped the cellar door down. But he didn't want to have to explain that to anybody, so he screwed his eyes shut and counted sheep, which turned into fluffy barrels of beer, until eventually he dropped off into a troubled sleep just before dawn.

18

When Patrick came down to breakfast the next morning, he found Mickey surprisingly buoyant and optimistic. He made his son coffee, and Patrick pretended not to notice that his hands were shaking ever so slightly. There was a false heartiness about him that was disconcerting, but Patrick supposed it was better than him wallowing in self-pity. They didn't discuss Mickey's revelations of the day before. Instead, Mickey suggested that Patrick go and collect the girls from Keith and Mandy's, which suited Patrick's plans nicely. He didn't want to be around if there was going to be any sort of confrontation between Lucy and Mickey. He couldn't think of anything much more distasteful or unsettling. Patrick didn't like confrontation, unless he was in control. He certainly didn't like being on the periphery while anyone else washed their dirty linen. And he knew he would feel honour bound to intervene on Lucy's behalf, whatever happened, because at the end of the day his father was in the wrong. He'd always felt protective of Lucy, because he'd never forgotten how special and important she'd made him feel when he arrived at Honeycote all those years ago, and how she'd never made him feel marginalized even though Sophie and Georgina were her real daughters and he wasn't related to her in any way. But he really didn't want his loyalties put to the test, because he loved his father too. So Solihull was definitely a safer option. He took the keys to his father's Defender, even though it was the most uncomfortable ride known to man, as Lucy had the Volvo.

At about half ten, Mickey phoned James. He picked up the receiver and dialled before he could give himself time to think about it, and spoke heartily to his brother when he answered.

'James – is Lucy there? We need to speak.'

James was taken aback by his brother's lucidity. He thought he sounded surprisingly perky, and not at all drunk. He'd have put good money on him being plastered, even at that time in the morning. So wrong-footed was he that he went to get Lucy without demurring.

Lucy was wary.

'Hello?'

Mickey was deliberately upbeat.

'I just wanted you to know I've done the horses, so you needn't worry.' Actually, he'd rather enjoyed it. He thought he might do the mucking-out every morning. It helped clear your head and it was good exercise trundling barrows full of manure to the muck heap and back.

'I wasn't worried. I assumed you and Patrick could manage it between you.'

'Oh.' Mickey was a little put out that his gesture had been devalued so instantly.

'Anything else?'

'I thought we should . . . talk.'

There was a pause that could only be described as icy.

'I'll come over some time this morning. I've got to pick up some clothes anyway.'

Pick up some clothes? That didn't sound good. That sounded as if she wasn't planning on coming back in the near future. But Mickey told himself that once they'd spoken, once he'd reassured her and given her a demonstration of how he was going to mend his ways, then she'd mellow.

They said their polite, distant goodbyes, then Mickey charged around the house making sure everything was spick and span, even vacuuming up the needles under the Christmas tree. He carefully hung the picture Lucy had got him for Christmas in a prime spot in the drawing room, splashed on some aftershave, got out all the paraphernalia to make fresh coffee . . . He was pleased with his handiwork and even more pleased with the clearness of his head. Even when he didn't have a hangover, hadn't actually overdone it, he always felt slightly sluggish in the mornings.

Perhaps it was a good thing that all this had happened. He was meant to stand back and take an objective look at where his life was going. This was going to be the new regime. No drink, fresh air, exercise . . . and it wasn't even time for New Year resolutions yet.

Mickey felt his stomach lurch into his mouth as he heard a car coming up the drive. It couldn't be Lucy yet, could it? And anyway, Pokey was barking her head off, so it must be a stranger.

He looked out and suddenly his bullishness evaporated into thin air. Every fear and anxiety he'd had in the past couple of days came washing back over him. It was Cowley. And Mickey was pretty sure he hadn't popped by to drop in a belated Christmas card.

*

Graham Cowley hadn't liked Lawrence Oakley's attitude one little bit. There was a hidden assumption that when Lawrence said jump, you said 'How high?' And although Cowley liked to play the deferential bank manager, it was only when it suited him. He hadn't taken at all kindly to being phoned the night before and ordered to a meeting when he should have been relaxing at home. His wife had been very slitty-eyed about it, and rightly so. She'd made it quite clear that if he wasn't back in time for his pheasant casserole at lunchtime, he needn't bother at all.

They'd met in the Little Chef off the main Evesham Road. Cowley, who was always five minutes early for any appointment, had got there early so he could choose his spot and not give Lawrence the upper hand. And then Lawrence had swept in, put the cards on the table and told Cowley exactly how they were going to play them. He was presumptuous, to say the least. The truly galling thing was that of course his plan made total sense, on every level. But Cowley was going to admit that over his dead body.

He wondered how it was that Lawrence was so well informed about the state of Honeycote Ales, and then reasoned that you didn't need to be a rocket scientist to work it out and Lawrence was the type of businessman who saw opportunities before they presented themselves. He was like a vulture, pouncing on his victims before they even stopped breathing, pecking out their eyes before their blood had become cold.

Lawrence spread out a sketch of his plan for the brewery on the formica table. He'd worked on it all night, using the computer programme that the landscapers used in the garden centre. He'd put in all the features – the trees, the fountains, the rose beds – and it looked thoroughly professional. He was inordinately proud and thought he wouldn't mind living there himself. Excitedly, he outlined the project to Cowley, who was frowning.

'If it's planning permission you're worried about, don't be. The council will be falling over themselves to make that brewery residential. They don't like the traffic, you see. All those heavy delivery lorries thundering through Honeycote.'

'But it's a great source of employment locally.'

'Rubbish. They employ what – twenty max? And the project I'm talking about would employ that many easily in terms of maintenance. Plus it would bring the right calibre of resident into the village – people with money to spend. They'd rejuvenate the post office, the pub, attract other small businesses to the area . . .'

Suddenly, Cowley felt incredibly protective. In particular because the thought of losing Honeycote Ales was a travesty. It was local history; it was local economics, for God's sake. It had kept the village afloat for nearly a hundred and fifty years. OK, so he'd pulled Mickey in before Christmas, read him the riot act, painted him a pretty grim picture of what could happen if he didn't get his act together. And they hadn't been empty threats at all. But if he could stop Honeycote Ales being sacrificed in the name of progress, to the likes of Lawrence Oakley, then he damn well would. It was a matter of pride to him.

More to the point, Cowley didn't hold with Lawrence's description of the 'right calibre of resident'. It was bad enough that young people who had been born and bred in Honeycote had no hope of purchasing a house there, not when a simple three-bedroomed cottage would set you back the best part of a quarter of a million. Council houses were as rare as hen's teeth and most of them had been bought by their owners so they were out of the loop. Converting the brewery into luxury apartments would only drive the prices in the village ever higher, making it even more exclusive and out of reach, and Cowley didn't approve. He'd seen enough young men and women forced towards Evesham, towards starter homes on face-less estates that little resembled the rural idyll they'd been brought up in and were no longer allowed to be a part of.

There was a hiatus before Cowley could give his re-action, while the waitress brought coffee for them both. Cowley added cream and sugar and stirred deliberately slowly. He then took a sip, put his cup down carefully in its saucer and shook his head.

'It's out of the question. I consider it of utmost im-portance to both ourselves and the community to keep Honeycote Ales afloat at all costs.'

'Let's put it another way,' said Lawrence reasonably. 'How would the bank manage if Honeycote Ales went bankrupt and Barton Court moved its business else-where? You'd be up the proverbial creek without a paddle, wouldn't you?'

Cowley drew himself up with dignity.

'If that's a threat, then I think I'd better pretend to ignore it. Contrary to what you might think, our branch is not entirely dependent on the input of your business. And I wouldn't be a very good manager if I allowed my judgement of one client to be influenced by another.'

Lawrence gritted his teeth. He had to admit that he was rather flummoxed. Graham Cowley wasn't playing ball at all. They were talking about large sums of money here.

Millions, in fact. Which in a small branch like Eldenbury was make or break. He didn't have time to mess about, though, so he changed tack. In his experience, if threats didn't work in the first instance, bribery was always worth a go.

'Let's put it yet another way.' Lawrence paused for a moment, then leaned forward. 'What do you think of the new Jaguar?'

'Good morning, Mr Oakley.' Cowley put his coffee cup to one side, got up from his chair and left the room without shaking Lawrence's hand, which was the biggest insult he knew. Lawrence pushed his drawing away with impatience, managing to spill coffee all over it in the process, then snarled at the waitress when she dabbed at the mess ineffectually with a damp cloth. Frustrated, he scrunched the paper up into a ball and tossed it into the bin on his way out.

Cowley drove his sensible bank manager's car out of the car park. He laughed to himself as he looked back at the morning's conversation. Lawrence Oakley wasn't as clever as he thought he was. What on earth did he imagine people would think if they saw Graham Cowley driving around in a Jag? They'd know he was on the bung.

He thought he ought to have another word with Mickey, make sure he knew what people were saying about Honeycote Ales and reassure him that the bank really would be there to support him. The pep talk before Christmas had been a short, sharp shock designed to galvanize Mickey into action, shake him out of his complacency – Cowley had known Mickey long enough to know that would be the only tactic that would work. It was the sort of talk a headmaster gave to a promising but recalcitrant pupil in order to frighten him into doing well in his exams. He hadn't really meant any of his threats. Well, obviously if Mickey didn't pull his finger out, things could turn nasty, but he thought he'd seen the writing on the wall and was getting it together. Though judging by Lawrence's meeting today, word had already got out, which was a bad sign. Confidence was being lost.

He looked at his watch – there was just time for him to call in at Honeycote House and be home in time for his casserole, served with steaming mash and his wife's slow-cooked red cabbage.

When Sandra opened the door of The Cedars to Patrick Liddiard, she looked him up and down with glee. She welcomed him in effusively and he caught the whiff of gin fumes.

'They've gone to the sales. Never content, are they, women? They always want more.' She flashed him a conspiratorial smile containing several grand's worth of cosmetic dentistry.

'I thought I'd come and collect them. I suppose I should have phoned.' Patrick surveyed Sandra curiously, seeking any evidence of a genetic link between her and Mandy. She had a good figure for her age, he had to admit that – but somebody really should have had a quiet word. No one over twenty could carry off mock croc trousers if they didn't want to be laughed at.

'Never mind. You can come in and keep me company till they get back. I was starting to get a little bit bored. What's your poison? Gin and tonic?'

'I'll just have a beer. Thanks.'

Patrick followed Sandra tentatively into the house and watched in alarm as she poured herself a hefty top-up and got him a Bud.

'Fancy a nibble?'

There was so much innuendo in the query that Patrick felt suffused with relief when she popped open a can of Pringles and pushed them towards him. He wondered what time the girls had gone to the sales and prayed that they wouldn't stay out too long. Hopefully they wouldn't be in need of too much so soon after Christmas, but he knew James had given Sophie and Georgina spending money, for which they'd covered him in grateful hugs and kisses.

Half an hour later, while Sandra was regaling him with a detailed account of her weight for the past twenty years, he accepted a third beer. He was going to be over the limit, but he didn't have to drive back straight away. He flipped off the top and knocked it back.

'. . . the minute I go over eight and a half stone, that's it. Fruit juice and steamed vegetables until I'm back on target. There's absolutely no need to let yourself go just because you've reached a certain age.'

She smiled wolfishly at him and Patrick assumed he was supposed to say something.

'I can see you're in great shape.'

She positively glowed and rested a hand on his arm.

'You're a sweet boy.' She squeezed his biceps and raised her eyebrows appreciatively. 'I can see you are too.'

He looked down with distaste at her silvery-pink talons, imagining them embedded in his flesh. He tried not to shudder. Older women fascinated him, but there was a limit. He also tried to bury at the back of his mind the old adage about looking at the mother if you wanted to know how a girl would turn out . . .

Cowley had only stayed at Honeycote ten minutes. He didn't even really want a coffee, but Mickey insisted and rushed round finding sugar bowls and cream jugs like a cat on hot bricks. He just wanted Mickey to know that word was out; that someone had made an offer on the brewery. Mickey looked perturbed.

'Is it one of the big breweries? Why didn't they approach me direct?'

Cowley looked uncomfortable.

'It's not another brewery. It's a private purchaser – he wants to do a residential development.'

Mickey looked appalled.

'What – you mean apartments or something? One of those awful gated communities?'

'Yes.'

'Is it Tremletts?' Tremletts had a reputation in the area for buying up unmanageably large properties and converting them. Butler's pantries and boot rooms and libraries abounded – none of which ever saw a butler or a boot or a book.

'It's not Tremletts, no. It's a private individual, and he wants to remain anonymous. In fact, I'm breaching confidentiality by telling you this much, but I thought it was important you should know.'

'Well, you can tell him to forget it. Over my dead body.'

'That's my view entirely. But we can't get away from the fact that we've got a lot of hard work to do if we're going to be able to resist these hostile takeover bids.'

Mickey liked the way Cowley said 'we', as it implied some sort of spirit of co-operation between him and the bank, which marked a change of attitude. Cowley went on to underline the fact that the last thing he wanted was for Honeycote to go under, though he didn't want Mickey to gain a false sense of security from this admission. The forecast was grim, but not irredeemable. Now he'd fired a warning shot across the bow, it was time for the two of them to work more closely together. Mickey eagerly mentioned a marketing plan and made to fetch it, but Cowley waved it away.

'This is a bank holiday. Emphasis on the word bank. And my wife's waiting for me at home. It's more than my life's worth to be late.'

So they made an appointment for Mickey to come in the next week, once the bank was open again. They'd go through everything with a fine-tooth comb.

After he'd gone, Mickey considered what he'd been told. Someone wanted to develop the brewery. Actually, on reflection, it wasn't such a bad idea. He'd get a decent whack out of it, enough to cover his debts, he was sure. Perhaps he'd try to persuade Cowley to consider the offer. There was no point in trying to preserve Honeycote Ales out of sentiment – and Mickey suspected that deep down Cowley was a sentimental old fool. They could at least have a meeting with the developer, who'd have to sacrifice his anonymity—

Suddenly an icy cold trickle slid down his spine as he realized who the developer must be. The plan had Lawrence Oakley written all over it. Who else had the knowledge, the cash, the experience, the lack of conscience – not to mention the motive?

Which meant he must know about him and Kay. Mickey began to shake. This threw completely new light on the whole sorry mess. And just when he thought he was in control . . .

Kay slept the soundest sleep she'd had for days and woke up feeling thoroughly excited. Her entire world had been turned upside down, rugs had been pulled out, goalposts moved – yet she felt as if she was on the brink of her biggest adventure yet.

Before she got up, she lay still for a moment and concentrated. The nurse had told her that she should be able to feel the baby by now. For a while she felt nothing, and she panicked. Perhaps she'd pickled it in Crozes-Hermitage? Then suddenly she felt a flicker, a tiny little movement that could easily have been overlooked. It was followed by a barely perceptible sensation, like tiny little bubbles popping. That was it! That was her baby, shuffling around, trying to get comfy. Kay put her hands on her stomach protectively and the feeling went away. But she'd felt it, and the nurse had told her that in the next few weeks the movements would get stronger and stronger until they would be quite unmistakable.

Seeing her baby on the scan the day before had been an extraordinary moment. If anyone had told her of the happiness, the protectiveness, the utter fulfilment that would flood through her, she'd have laughed. But seeing it there on the screen in black and white had meant she could no longer deny what was happening to her. Of course, it wasn't going to be easy. Kay was no fool. She was on the brink of a huge test, emotionally, physically and practically. Single motherhood was no ball game; everyone knew that. But at least now she had something to hold on to, something that was hers and that no one could take away, something that was going to give her hope and a focus and, with any luck, great joy.

Because it was meant to be. Her baby was meant to be. Somebody up there had made sure that she got to this point, the point of no return. And she wasn't going to turn her back on it now. For heaven's sake, it was all she'd got. The only reason she had to live . . .

For the time being, however, she was in limbo, between the upheaval of the last couple of days and the decisions she knew she was going to have to make. But Kay was determined to enjoy the peace while she thought over her next move. All she had to consider was herself and the little being inside her – which was hardly any trouble at the moment. She marvelled at how well she felt, now she was rested, and realized she was starving.

She called up room service and enjoyed a delicious breakfast – home-made muesli with fresh chunks of apple and dates and full cream, mini Danish pastries and a huge cup of hot chocolate. Somehow she couldn't face either tea or coffee. As she set aside the tray she had to laugh at herself – she might not have put on too much weight so far, but if she continued devouring food at that rate she was going to run into serious problems. She'd eaten more calories in one meal than she usually consumed in a day – but she didn't care.

She flipped open her suitcase and regarded the few clothes she'd brought with her when she'd fled from Barton Court. Within minutes she concluded that absolutely none of her outfits were suitable or comfortable for a pregnant woman – they were all too streamlined, too harsh, too tailored, too fitted. Even her most casual clothes were sleek.

She decided she'd go to the sales. Bath was only fifteen miles away and had hundreds of shops that were bound to be brimming with suitable outfits. She had a new part to dress for, and she couldn't wait. She dug out the least severe of her clothes – a grey angora polo neck and a pair of bootcut black trousers from Joseph – and realized with delight she couldn't quite do the waist up. Thrilled with the novelty, she raided the hotel drawer until she found the mini sewing kit, and gave herself a bit of leeway with a safety pin. Then, scooping up her car keys and her credit cards, she set off on her mission.

Before Lucy went to see Mickey, James gave her a pep talk as she paced around the kitchen like a highly strung horse parading round the collecting ring. He soothed her, reassured her that he would always be there – he didn't add 'for you' as it sounded too cranky and American. Just before she left, she leaned against his chest for comfort, for support, for strength, and he squeezed her tight. To her it felt like reassurance, but he was in fact staking his claim. If he'd believed in voodoo he'd have made a wax doll of his brother and rammed every pin he could find into it.

And now he didn't want to speculate on events at Honeycote House, didn't want to torture himself imagining the various scenarios that might unfold, the worst of which was a cosy reconciliation. So he needed a task that was mindless, yet required absolute concentration. He lined all his shoes and boots up on the kitchen table, together with all the tins of polish he'd accumulated, then unearthed several of the neat strips of sheeting that Mrs Titcombe cut up whenever his bed linen was considered to be past its best. Then he began his ritual. Each shoe was inspected for need of repair, or new laces, then the appropriate polish was rubbed in. James spent the next hour and a half buffing, spitting and polishing until his face could be seen in every item of footwear he owned.

Lucy and Mickey faced each other across the drawing room, neither knowing how to start the confrontation. Did one begin with trivialities? Should he offer her a coffee? Or a kiss? She didn't look as if she wanted any sort of bodily contact. Her arms were crossed in front of her as she glared at him balefully. He'd seen other wives do that, when their husbands had lurched back home drunk and late for lunch, dinner, whatever. But it wasn't Lucy's style. Looking at her now, however, she might have been an expert, and spent a lifetime executing the piercing stare that was now making him writhe with discomfort.

'Well?'

Mickey didn't have a clue what to say. He'd never prepared himself for this eventuality and the awful reality of it shocked him. He was ashamed. Disgusted by his behaviour. He attempted a line of defence.

'It was one of those things.' How lame could you get? 'I don't expect you to understand.' He didn't add that he didn't really understand himself, as he wasn't sure whether that was a good thing or not. But for the life of him he couldn't think of anything that remotely resembled a defence. Short of saying that Kay was forcing him to have sex with her at gunpoint, there was no get-out clause.

'So – was she the first? Or the fifty-first?'

'Lucy . . .' Mickey had the gall to look hurt. He had a selective memory that allowed him to forget his previous indiscretions. He knew he was pretty safe where they were concerned. The barmaid in question had emigrated to Australia – he remembered a postcard arriving at the pub with a winsome koala that was pinned up for the benefit of the regulars. And the nurse had gone to seek her fame and fortune – or at least a better salary – in London. He was unlikely to get caught out, so as far as he was concerned they'd never happened.

'And how long? How long has it been going on?'

This was the killer. Mickey was gripped by a dilemma. If Lawrence knew, which he was pretty certain he did, was that because Kay had told him? And if so, what had she told him? How much detail had she gone into? And would Lawrence see fit to compare stories with Lucy? What would be better – to tell the truth so as not to be caught out at a later date? Or could he risk fudging it, passing it off as a one-off bonk with unfortunate consequences? And was a one-off any better than an on-going affair? It sounded more sordid, somehow. At least an affair had some depth to it . . . though the implications for Lucy weren't good. God, why was it that your penis always shouted louder than your brain?

Lucy just wanted him to say something. Anything. Even the tiniest, most pathetic attempt at self-defence, a hint of his motivation, would have been better than his blank, almost catatonic stare. She felt a sudden urge to slap him; Lucy, who was the world's most passive creature and never felt driven to any sort of physical retaliation, suddenly wanted to belt him across his self-satisfied chops. She let rip instead.

'For God's sake, Mickey. I've always given you the benefit of the doubt. I've sat there and smiled while you chatted other women up at the dinner table, turned a blind eye when you flirted. Because I never really thought you meant it. And in a way I was flattered that other women found you attractive. But I never thought you'd actually do anything. I always thought it was me you wanted.'

'It was!'

'You've got a funny way of showing it.' Lucy gave a bitter laugh; the sound was harsh and unfamiliar coming from her. 'I must be a total idiot – you've had me fooled all this time. You're nothing but a dirty old man, peering down women's cleavages and sticking your hand up their skirts. I bet they feel sorry for me, married to you with your wandering bloody hands—'

Mickey recoiled, the harsh words whipping at his heart like forty lashes. He was appalled that Lucy could think the things she was saying, let alone speak them. Could what she was saying be true? Was he a laughing stock, some sort of lech to be neatly dodged at cocktail parties? Was his image of himself as a charming flirt, a delectable rogue to be resisted if you could, some hideous distortion of the actual truth?

The truth, of course, was somewhere in between. Mickey was the archetypal ladies' man. Even the plainest woman blossomed under his attentions; he made them feel beautiful and desirable by the way he hung on their every word or at least gave that impression – he was adept at looking utterly absorbed while thinking about something else entirely. He took an interest, teased them, touched them – a light hand on the small of their back as he escorted them into dinner, a warm kiss goodbye that seemed full of promise. Yes, he was tactile, but he didn't bloody grope – he was quite sure he'd never stuck his hand up anyone's skirt in his life. Mickey sighed. He was desperate to defend his position, but how could he?

They quickly reached an impasse. Mickey's tongue was tied, which made him come across as surly, almost truculent, like a naughty child sulking because he'd been caught out. Which frustrated Lucy and made her over-react, invective pouring out because Mickey put up no barriers to stop her. Without the shield of alcohol, each accusation Lucy slung at him hit him like a cruel barb. And while there was a grain of truth in what she said, she didn't really think that of him – she would never have tolerated that kind of behaviour. But they were both feeling defensive and vulnerable, both terrified of what was going to happen, both keenly aware that how they reacted to the turn of events was going to have serious ramifications upon their future, and neither of them really knew what to think, feel or do.

Mickey leaned back against the fireplace, hooking his arm over the mantelpiece for support. Fuck Caroline – how dare she lock away all the last vestiges of booze? He felt himself starting to shake and knew she would mock him – DTs, she'd call it, but Mickey thought it was shock. Beads of sweat broke out on his forehead, yet he felt icy cold. He opened his mouth to speak, but didn't know what to say. He couldn't deny what he'd done. He couldn't excuse it either. What should he do? Beg, plead, grovel? Apologize? He supposed that would be a start.

'I'm sorry—'

Lucy looked at him witheringly.

'What for, Mickey? Why are you sorry, exactly? Because

you've been fucking someone else? Or because you got caught?'

He couldn't speak. Couldn't answer her. Suddenly he was terrified of his beautiful wife, who'd always been so gentle, who was never judgemental. He buried his head in his arms in despair, clinging on to the mantelpiece. Whatever he said would sound whinging, cringing.

Lucy looked at him in disgust. His silence spoke volumes. Obviously he didn't feel his actions were worth defending. Which must mean he didn't feel his marriage was worth saving. How could she have been taken in for so long? Mickey just wanted to have his cake and eat it. Selfish, self-indulgent bastard. It could only mean that he loved Kay; wanted her more than he wanted Lucy and Honeycote, and Sophie and Georgina and Patrick . . .

Lucy turned and ran out of the room, up the staircase and into their bedroom. The bed had been made up, obviously by Mickey, because the pillows weren't as she'd have them. Everything looked immaculate. There were no clothes littering the floor, no handfuls of loose change deposited here and there, no empty tea or coffee cups. But good housekeeping was hardly going to make up for the wrong he'd done her. If his untidiness had ever displeased her, she'd have done something about it long ago.

She flung open the wardrobe, pulled down a nubuck Gladstone bag and started throwing clothes in at random – the entire contents of her underwear drawer, a couple of nighties, jumpers, sweatshirts, jeans, socks – for some reason she packed lots of socks. She certainly wasn't going to need anything smart. Lucy didn't think she'd ever go out again. She grabbed her sheepskin-covered hot water bottle off the bed. She'd need that for comfort. She'd often hugged it to her when she had period pains and it was better than any teddy. She threw in the special hairbrush she needed to disentangle her curls, but didn't bother with any make-up or jewellery. Or toiletries – James's bathroom was better equipped than any hotel or pharmacy, and she'd already been given her own brand-new toothbrush, still in its cellophane wrapper. She added a couple of pairs of shoes, then snapped the bag shut.

Then she flew down the stairs again and out of the front door. Without saying goodbye. There was certainly nothing good about her departure and even 'bye' seemed superfluous. She threw the bag into the boot and was about to bang it shut when she remembered something and made her way back to the house.

'Pokey!' Lucy stood at the front door and called into the bowels of the house. She didn't have to call twice. Pokey shot out of the kitchen and skittered across the flagstones, then bounded after her mistress and leaped into the boot of her car without a backward glance.

Sophie had spent the day trailing round the shops after Georgina and Mandy, who, in an effort to cheer her up, had forced her into trying on millions of outfits at cut price. She was surprised to find she could now get into things she never thought she'd be able to wear, as she'd lost so much weight recently. She'd spent all of her waking hours up until Christmas resisting food, with some success. And here she was, looking at herself in a pair of snakeskin hipsters. Only a week ago she'd have been thrilled at the reflection that was staring back at her.

But what was the point?

She didn't go on to the others about how she was feeling.

There were girls at school who made an absolute meal of their affairs of the heart, banging on and on if they'd been chucked or two-timed or were suffering unrequited love. Sophie thought they were a pain – who wanted to hear ad nauseam what they were going through? She certainly didn't want to inflict her suffering on anyone else. She was more stoical, happy to suffer in silence. So she put on a brave face to the outside world even though inside she was gutted.

Mandy and Georgina were concerned. They sensed her unhappiness even though she chose not to voice it, but they didn't press her on the issue, which she appreciated. And the one good thing to come out of it was now she couldn't face food at all. She had no trouble resisting it whatsoever. And she was beginning to enjoy the gaping, griping emptiness inside her. It gave her a sense of achievement.

'Go on – buy them. They're less than half price.' Mandy was nudging her.

'Too tarty.' Sophie unzipped them hastily.

'Not if you wear them with clumpy boots and a big sweater. They're really cool.'

Sophie shook her head and put the trousers back on their hanger. She realized now why she was reluctant to buy them. They were just the sort of thing Mayday would wear. She wouldn't be seen dead in them.

Patrick was starting to panic when he finally heard the shoppers return. He saw Mandy blush pink with pleasure when she saw him and give him a shy smile, a little unsure. He'd returned it, pleased that he obviously still had some power over her. But now wasn't the time to pursue her.

His priority was to buttonhole Keith, who was looking rather grateful for a bit of male company. Patrick had studied Caroline's business plan carefully, while Mickey wasn't looking, so he felt fairly well-armed and confident that he could talk about Honeycote Ales with an assured manner. Make it look like an inviting prospect for a potential investor, dangle a few carrots . . .

There was a flurry of activity while everyone took off their coats and put away their bags, and Sandra went sulkily to make tea at Keith's light suggestion. Mandy and Patrick found themselves alone in the lounge. He walked over and gave her a kiss on the cheek – a non-committal gesture that indicated friendship but not necessarily intimacy.

'How are you?'

'Me? I'm fine. But I'm really worried about Sophie. She's devastated about Ned, you know. Even though she won't admit it.'

Patrick swore mentally, cursing his friend's weakness. He knew Sophie was putting a brave face on things, because she always did. And because she'd held on to him a fraction too long when he'd hugged her on arrival. He sighed.

'I can't turn back the clock, I'm afraid. Ned dunked his biscuit where he shouldn't have, end of story. I've bollocked him, I can tell you.'

'I just feel so sorry for her, and I don't know what to do. She's been so good about it. She hasn't said a word, but I know she's breaking her heart. She was crying last night in bed.'

She looked at Patrick, her eyes huge and round with sympathy. He felt a little stab of guilt, realizing he'd probably misjudged her. He'd thought she was fickle and shallow, but she seemed genuinely concerned for Sophie. Caring and considerate, not the superficial little strumpet he'd written her off as. He looked at Mandy with new eyes. Perhaps she was worth pursuing, regardless of the plot he'd hatched, using her as the bait to lure her father's wealth? She was certainly more his cup of tea than either Kay or Kelly. Suddenly the idea of a normal relationship, with no strings attached, where each person was on an equal footing, seemed very attractive to him. More than anything, he thought he might quite like some fun, and he felt sure he could have that with Mandy. He could take her riding (she'd got his bloody horse, after all), take her out in the Healey – she'd look good in that, with her hair streaming out behind her. And they had some unfinished business. Patrick remembered their encounter in the bathroom at Honeycote and how hard it had been for him to walk away . . .

He realized he was staring at her, and she was staring back, a little unnerved. But before he could do anything about it, the room suddenly filled. Georgina and Sophie brought the tea in and Sandra reappeared, having spent the past ten minutes redoing her make-up. She was ready for battle.

Keith was enjoying having a houseful of young people and insisted on ordering a huge Chinese meal for everyone. The Cedars seemed to have come to life, to have come out of its formaldehyde, which he would never have thought possible. There was music blaring and Mandy and Georgina were entertaining everyone, doing dance routines on the coffee table. Then Sandra had a bright idea and dug out her salsa CD – she'd been having classes at the gym before she disappeared off to Spain. Before Patrick could protest, he found himself in the middle of the lounge, embroiled in a demonstration.

Patrick got the hang of it straight away. One of his favourite films was the *Buena Vista Social Club*, and he had an instinctive feel for the rhythm. Unfortunately, Sandra didn't have any sense of timing whatsoever, nor had she attended enough classes to carry it off. Dancing with her was like pushing a vacuum cleaner round the room. When Sandra took advantage of a moment's break in the music to top up her drink, Patrick grabbed Mandy. The next track was fast and furious, but the two of them were naturals – twirling, thrusting, swaying their hips in time to the music in a display that was bordering on the erotic.

Everyone applauded wildly. Except Sandra, who had a face like a slapped arse. If there was one thing she couldn't stand, it was being upstaged by her daughter.

Patrick resigned himself to the fact that he wasn't going to get any business talked with Keith that evening, but it didn't matter. He was actually enjoying himself, having fun. Georgina managed to get Keith having a go at some simple dance steps, while Patrick danced with Sophie, who managed a smile. And when it came to eleven o'clock, and Patrick realized Sandra had been topping his drink up all night and he couldn't possibly drive, it made sense for him to stay over. As Keith said, what was the point of spare rooms if you didn't use them?

Kay sat on her hotel bed, sipping mineral water and gloating over the several bags of booty she'd emptied out upon it. She marvelled over the softness of the new colours she'd picked out for herself. Pale pink and powder blue were her new black. She didn't think she'd ever worn pink in her life. Anyone watching might have thought it was some sort of disguise. But no – Kay knew the truth. This was the new her! She'd shed her old skin like a snake, overnight, and was amazed at how comfortable she felt.

The strangest thing was, seeing that little being inside her had somehow reincarnated the umbilical cord that had once joined her to her own mother. She suddenly felt an uncontrollable urge to go running back home. She knew it was insanity, she knew they'd drive her mad, but she just wanted someone to hold her and love her unconditionally. Just as she was going to love her baby.

As she folded up her new purchases, snipped off the price tags and packed them away carefully, she apologized to the little blob with arms and legs she'd seen on the screen the day before, with the heartbeat that vacillated faster than a butterfly's wings.

'Sorry, sweetheart, you're going to have Slough on your birth certificate. But never mind – you'll survive. I did.' As she curled up into the freshly made bed, she didn't give any thought to the other space on the birth certificate. The one she would fill in with 'Father unknown'.

Patrick lay fast asleep, cocooned in peach splendour in one of the spare rooms at The Cedars, when something made him start awake. He'd been having the most extraordinary dream. Lucy was making breakfast in the kitchen at Honeycote, scrambled eggs just how he liked them, how she'd always cooked them for him ever since he was tiny. But when she brought his plate over to the table, he looked up and it was Mandy, not Lucy, smiling down at him. Patrick was puzzled. Dreams were weird; your mind played tricks on you . . .

Suddenly he heard the door close with a soft click and a figure crept into the room. It must be Mandy. Patrick was filled with a momentary and uncharacteristic panic. He wasn't ready for this. Yet here she was, and he had to admit the temptation was enormous. He took in a sharp breath as she pulled back the duvet and felt for his boxer shorts.

He had to stop her. He couldn't risk Keith catching them. That would spoil everything. Anyway, it was all moving too fast. He wanted to dictate the pace. If there was going to be anything between them, he didn't want hurried, secretive sex in her parents' house. As she began to massage him with unexpectedly experienced movements, he grabbed her wrist to stop her.

'Now come on – you know you like it.'

Patrick leaped out of bed with a yell. It wasn't Mandy at all. It was her bloody mother! He snapped on the light and Sandra, resplendent in bronze satin, blinked up at him drunkenly. She put a teasing finger to his lips, unsteady on her feet, and lurched against him. He grabbed her upper arms to stop her falling over.

'For God's sake – go back to your bedroom before someone hears.'

'No one's going to hear. I'll be very, very quiet. I promise.'

She smiled and lunged for his boxers again. Patrick dodged out of the way neatly and she fell straight against the mirrored wardrobe. She scrambled to her feet and tackled him again, till they both fell on the bed.

'Sandra!'

Keith stood in the doorway, furious.

'What the hell's going on?'

Sandra slid off the bed hastily. Patrick shut his eyes, hoping he'd wake up from this nightmare, and prayed his boxers were covering his modesty. Sandra was pointing a finger at him.

'It was his idea. He wouldn't leave me alone. Said he'd always wanted an older woman—'

Patrick opened his mouth to protest, but Keith got there first.

'You don't honestly expect me to believe that? Get back into your own room, Sandra. Some of us want some sleep.'

She was now sobbing quietly. Despite himself, Patrick felt a pang of pity as she was escorted from the room by her husband. But he felt even more sorry for Keith, who looked back at him with an expression of profound embarrassment and bewilderment. She was obviously a handful. Sooner he was rid of her the better.

Patrick pulled the duvet back up under his chin and concentrated on trying to get back to sleep. He was relieved it hadn't been Mandy coming to test his will-power. He wasn't sure he would have been able to resist and that would have left him in a position of weakness. The last thing he wanted was to compromise himself before he'd had a chance to speak to Keith. He began running through the business plan that Caroline had drawn up, but moments later he was asleep.

By the time Lucy got back to Denham House earlier that day, every single pair of James's shoes was gleaming and either in a cardboard box waiting to be taken to the cobbler for repair or back in place in his dressing room complete with shoe-trees. As he put away the brushes and polish carefully in the appointed cupboard, he heard her car outside. He walked over to the Aga to put the kettle on and waited for her to appear in the doorway.

Things had obviously gone badly. Very badly indeed. Which from James's point of view was good. Lucy was holding Pokey apologetically by the collar, desperately trying to be brave.

'Can she sleep in the garage or something? I couldn't leave her . . .'

'She can sleep in here with my two. I've got an old basket.'

Tears of gratitude sprang up in Lucy's eyes. James put the lid back down on the Aga. Bugger tea. He got out his two biggest balloons and his best Rémy. This was a brandy situation. Restorative for her and Dutch courage for him.

At six, James opened champagne, insisting that it was as good for consolation as it was for celebration. They curled up on the sofa. He didn't speak, or offer advice, or any judgement; just listened.

'I don't understand. Why? Twenty years, James . . .' She looked at him, bewildered. 'What am I supposed to do now? Is that it? Do I go? Or does he go? And what about the children – do we tell them? Or do I ignore the whole thing? Am I old-fashioned or stupid? Do I expect too much . . . ?'

Her head was obviously whirling with unanswered questions. He stroked her hair comfortingly. Eventually, her questions subsided and she became angry.

'I don't deserve this.'

'No.'

Lucy looked up in surprise. It was the first opinion

James had offered. Until then he'd been murmuring platitudes.

'You don't deserve it, Lucy. Not at all.'

He looked at her. It was now or never. He was never going to get the dice so loaded in his favour ever again. Unless he outlived his brother.

'I love you. You know that, don't you? I've always loved you.'

She nodded, wide-eyed. Gently, he wiped away the last of her tears with his thumb, then stroked her face. Gradually, the strokes turned to caresses which she didn't resist, giving him the courage to venture further and further until it was obvious that he was no longer offering comfort but pleasure. But she didn't pull away, seeming to take strength from his physical reassurance, melting into him and luxuriating under his attentions. He pulled her to him and kissed her. All along he said to himself that at the first sign of resistance he'd stop; that if there seemed to be any doubt, any frisson of fear, he'd do the gentlemanly thing. But she didn't resist. Not even when he unwrapped her like a precious parcel, touching her with reverence, raining kisses of adoration along her collarbone, on her neck, down her spine, until she shivered with delight. His hands traced the contours of her breasts, her hips, her stomach.

Suddenly, there they were, on his priceless Aubusson rug, in front of the fire he'd laid earlier. James had imagined this moment so many times, yet had never quite had the courage to picture such a perfect scene. He'd always assumed that the first time would be a disaster, but she pulled him to her as if she never wanted to let go, and there was a look in her eyes that he couldn't define, something almost savage, that he mistook for passion.

*

Later, with James asleep beside her, Lucy lay cocooned in a security blanket of alcohol and endorphins, allowing her thoughts to wander lazily back over the afternoon. She couldn't deny to herself that she'd been tempted to sleep with him before. She knew she held the cards, that he'd never do anything without taking her lead, and she'd never given it to him until now. But sometimes she'd caught him looking at her in a way that raised the hairs on the back of her neck. It was like standing on the edge of a cliff and feeling the urge to jump, though you knew you never would. But this time she had . . .

It had been so much easier, not to mention more pleasurable, to languish under James's attentions than face the pain inflicted by Mickey. She'd felt emotionally flayed alive after their confrontation at Honeycote. As if her heart had been ripped open, the wound left raw and bleeding. And when James kissed her, it had felt right. There was no sense of betrayal, or that this was in any way wrong. It was a salve to her wounds that she felt she deserved. Why should she suffer for someone else's wrongs?

She knew she should have stopped him before it went too far, but every inch of her wanted to succumb. She was desperate for their liaison to turn into a back-scratching, sweat-drenched frenzy. All she wanted was for him to screw the memory of Mickey out of her. She wanted an instant replacement; someone who would heal her wounds, stop her from grieving.

She knew it was selfish. And there was a moment she could have stopped him. He was on top of her. He held himself up on his arms, one either side of her, and gazed into her eyes.

'Is it all right?'

He was asking her permission. This was it: the point of no return. Lucy gave a mental shrug. She'd gone this far. She might as well go the whole way. You never knew: there might be fireworks, earthquakes, choirs of angels singing hallelujah . . . She smiled her assent.

As James edged his way into her slowly, she began rocking her hips back and forth, moving with him. Then the familiar waves of pleasure fused into a raging torrent that took her breath away, and the penny dropped. This must be why people had affairs – because the sex was so highly charged, so electric, so powered by the allure of the forbidden. Lucy almost laughed out loud at the realization that by being the perfect wife all these years she had been seriously missing out.

19

After Lucy had gone, Mickey sat shell-shocked in the kitchen for hours, not daring to move in case his feelings kicked in. He knew that he'd got no one to blame but himself. Here he was, alone and abandoned by everyone – even Pokey had slunk off to hide somewhere. He was surprised Lucy had left her here in his care. It was obvious she didn't think Mickey capable of so much as looking after a dog. Which he wasn't – he tried to remember the last time he'd fed her and couldn't.

Eventually he summoned up the energy to go out into the scullery to find a tin of food, and found the shelf empty. He rummaged about in a cupboard for some back-up supplies. Success – there was a sack of dried food, which he could mix with some gravy browning or something. He'd go to the Spar and get some tins later. Lifting out the sack, he spied a box of bottles. He pulled it towards him and inspected the contents. Six bottles of damson gin, 1998. Manna from heaven.

The cork came out with a satisfying squeak. The pale ruby liquid slid in a viscous stream into his glass. Thick, syrupy, bitter-sweet nectar trickled down Mickey's throat, his first drink for what seemed like months, though it was barely two days. It wasn't long before

Caroline's imaginary taunts were blocked out by its anaesthetizing effects. So what if he had no willpower? So what if he was weak? There was no point in trying to be strong. He'd lost his wife, to his own brother, and he was pretty likely to lose his livelihood. He'd lost all enthusiasm for the plans he and Caroline had drawn up together; couldn't face the prospect of entering into a spirit of co-operation with Cowley. He'd got no fight left in him because there was nothing worth fighting for. He couldn't pretend any longer. Better that everyone knew what a failure he was. In a way, Mickey thought, it would be best for everyone if he just set a match to the whole thing.

Ten seconds later he sat bolt upright. That wasn't such a bad idea. In fact, it was the best solution he'd come up with so far. A bloody insurance job – why hadn't he thought of it before?

Mickey rewarded himself with another two inches of damson gin while he thought through the implications. Surely torching the brewery was just a form of euthanasia? Hastening its inevitable demise; avoiding the agony of the death throes, the pain of making decisions that had been forced upon him. This way was quick and clean. The brewery would be gone; it would cost too much to build a replacement that was compliant with the twenty-first century. But Honeycote Ales could live on. The beer could be brewed under licence to the original recipe by one of the larger breweries; it was pretty commonplace in the industry. The tied houses could carry on. No one would know any different . . .

Except, of course, the twenty-odd people he employed. An image of them pricked at his conscience for a moment, but then he asked himself if, realistically, any of them would show him any loyalty if they were given a better offer. One or two ageing retainers, perhaps, but he could keep them on in some capacity somewhere to salve his conscience. But the others . . . Mickey was pretty sure most of them would find gainful employment elsewhere. He'd pull strings, dish out glowing references. And anyway, morale was plummeting. You could see that every day – uncertainty and dissatisfaction. They'd all probably be grateful for the chance to move on.

Trouble was, he wasn't entirely sure how to start a fire. One that wouldn't look suspicious, at any rate. They'd have forensic scientists crawling over the scene of the crime before you could say Bryant and May. How could he make it look like an accident? He supposed there were people you could pay to do that sort of thing for you, but this was Honeycote, not the East End of London. And Mickey thought that the less people knew about it the better. He didn't want to leave himself open to blackmail, after all. He wanted a stress-free life, a chance to start afresh with a clear(ish) conscience.

Mickey gave the practicalities of the task some careful thought over another inch of damson gin. He was pleased with his final solution. He'd force an entry into one of the downstairs storerooms. Leave a few cans of Diamond White and a few fag ends lying around. Perhaps some condoms for good measure – or perhaps not. He didn't fancy procuring those. But if he left traces of adolescent detritus in one of the storerooms, make it look as if they'd broken in for somewhere to den up and have a bit of a party, then a fire might be a logical conclusion. He'd go down to the bus shelter in the village, pick up some evidence. Then it would all look like a party that had got out of hand, the kids would have scarpered. And he'd have a nice fat cheque and a chance to start afresh without anyone knowing.

He went out to find the Defender, then remembered Patrick had it. Oh well – he'd have to borrow the Healey. He'd enjoyed driving it, on the one or two occasions that Patrick had let him get his hands on his precious motor car.

Mickey poked about in Patrick's bedroom until he found the keys in his flying jacket, then drove down into the village. He parked up behind the post office, then made his way as inconspicuously as he could down to the bus shelter. There were plenty of fag ends lying around. Even, miraculously, a single glove – he could leave that somewhere at the scene of the crime. He scooped the butts up into a carrier bag, then peered into the bin. He fished out a couple of pop cans, but could see no alcohol. He'd have to go further afield. He couldn't pull into one of his own pubs for fear of being recognized and remembered.

For someone who was totally sloshed he was covering his tracks remarkably well. Mickey slugged at the nearly empty bottle as he drove back up through the village towards the brewery. Then he realized the one weak spot in his plan. Matches. Fucking matches! He leaned over to the glove compartment and fished about, triumphantly laying his hands upon a stray lighter.

It was only when a lorry came thundering round the corner that Mickey noticed he was on the wrong side of the road and swerved.

*

The whirring of a helicopter overhead woke Lucy just before midnight. She sat up with a sudden start, her heart racing. For a moment she wasn't sure where she was, then reality started to filter its way into her brain. She was in bed with James. All of a sudden she felt filled with panic. What on earth had she done? For a moment she hoped that perhaps the whole thing had been a dream, but one look at James asleep beside her told her the truth. Anyway, the room smelled of her perfume and his cologne, rose and bergamot inextricably mingled with their combined sweat.

Lucy crept out of the bed and into the bathroom, where she surveyed her reflection in the mirror, thinking about what she'd done. Would she look any different to an outsider? Did she look like a wanton adulteress? She certainly felt like one – she could see exactly where the expression 'scarlet woman' came from. She was blushing with shame, red with guilt, her betrayal glowing like a beacon. She couldn't even look her own reflection in the eye. It made her feel sick. She gripped the porcelain of the sink, trying to keep the nausea down, but it was no good. She threw up brandy and champagne and bile; luminous, yellow bile that proved she was filled with poison.

She scrubbed and scrubbed at her teeth, and washed her face and hands. She thought about having a shower, but she didn't want to wake James. She put down the loo seat and sat with her head in her hands. It was throbbing, whether from the stress of the day or a surfeit of alcohol or a mixture of both she didn't know.

Post-coital triste wasn't the word for it. Lucy felt positively suicidal. Just for a moment, she'd enjoyed the luxury of being worshipped and pampered. It was pure indulgence, an utterly selfish revenge fuck, and the only person who was really going to suffer in the long term was James. She could see now just how easy it was to be unfaithful, in that moment of insecurity when you needed to be reassured. It was the ultimate displacement activity: after all, making love to James in front of a roaring log fire had been a far more inviting proposition than going over her confrontation with Mickey, analysing the implications and having to make some sort of decision about the next step. Yes, infidelity was certainly an enjoyable distraction. At the time, the emotions it awoke were more powerful and pleasurable than any other and over-rode anxieties. But screwing James really wasn't the answer to her problems. On the contrary, it had created yet another one.

Because she couldn't carry this charade on. She liked James. Loved him, even, as one did love members of one's family. And she was surprised at how much she'd enjoyed sex with him. But now, in the cold chill of the bathroom, she realized that she'd over-romanticized the success of their coupling. She should know that whatever James did, he always did it to perfection, whether it was decorating or cooking or making love.

For one moment, she toyed with the idea of stepping away from life at Honeycote and into James's life, for she knew without him saying it that he would welcome her. It would be like falling out of the frying pan into the feather bed. In her mind, James could provide everything she needed, practically. He was attractive, wealthy, a good friend, they had everything in common – almost more, in fact, than she had in common with Mickey. It was with James that Lucy pored over catalogues for the country house sales they both loved to frequent; it was James who often went with her to the concerts in Gloucester cathedral that brought a lump to her throat.

But she knew it was Mickey she belonged with. Mickey who was the flint that lit the spark inside her. For heaven's sake, she'd know that years ago, when she'd first met the two brothers. She'd made her choice then. She'd known she could have had either of them. But it was Mickey who excited her, whose unpredictability and unreliability made him more exasperating yet more lovable. And vulnerable. She was surprised when this occurred to her: that actually James wasn't vulnerable at all. He had a ruthless streak she'd seen him use in business that she felt sure he'd be capable of using in his personal life. And when she thought about it, he had. He was quite capable of culling girlfriends when they got too needy, too clingy, too close. She'd mopped up their tears on more than one occasion. This realization made her think of Caroline. He'd made it quite clear to her that she was expendable and hadn't done much to spare her feelings. The memory now made Lucy cringe. She'd been too wrapped up in her own problems at the time to care. But she could see now that James had been utterly ruthless.

Mickey wasn't ruthless. He was just weak.

How could she turn her back in a fit of pique on Mickey, on Honeycote, on her family and on the brewery just because of a single indiscretion? Especially when she hadn't even waited for an explanation for the wrong she'd been done. How could she possibly defend her actions, if she hadn't even allowed Mickey to defend his? She hadn't meant to be so savage with him. She couldn't get the image of his shell-shocked face as she'd left Honeycote out of her mind. She hadn't given him any chance to explain. No, she'd fled into the arms of the one man she knew loved her unconditionally, because she hadn't wanted the truth; she'd wanted to be protected. She was a coward, without the strength to face her demons.

She was an adult, she had responsibilities and whatever cards she had been dealt she had to play them, not just walk away. She could find the strength from somewhere, she was sure. There was too much to lose.

In the meantime, what should she tell James? She cursed herself. It would have been so much easier if she hadn't slept with him. Now she'd compromised herself. How best to let him down gently? And had she used him? Did she have to apologize for that, or was he to blame? Had he taken advantage of her vulnerability?

She was shivering now with the cold. She crept back across the carpet and slid under the warmth of the blankets. Next to her, James stirred in his sleep and opened his eyes. He smiled and reached out an arm to curl round her before falling back into a contented reverie. Lucy flinched at his touch; his arm was like lead, trapping her, pinning her down. James sat up.

'What is it?'

Lucy turned to face him, stricken.

'James—'

But before she could reveal her innermost thoughts, the shrill bell of the telephone on the bedside table cut through the moment. He didn't know which way to turn. Either way was bad news. He had a pretty good idea from the expression on her face what Lucy was going to say, so he picked up the phone decisively.

'James Liddiard.'

It was the hospital. Mickey Liddiard was in intensive care. He was about to go down to surgery. Did he have any idea how they could contact his wife?

20

James sped through the dark lanes of Gloucestershire then Oxfordshire with tight lips. Lucy sat miserable and dry-eyed beside him. He thanked God he hadn't had too much to drink – he'd deliberately held back on the champagne, pouring the lion's share down her throat. They didn't speak, except to confer on directions, just sat in surreal silence.

They arrived at the hospital and were ushered with haste through miles of corridor until they were shown into a waiting room. A consultant came in and spoke gently to Lucy as James held her hand. She couldn't take it all in, just key words that hit her in the gut – haemorrhage, blood clot, coma, unconscious, brain scan. They were all theoretical fears, but James had to admit to himself that it didn't sound good, even though the consultant kept reiterating that Mickey was in the best place. He'd been airlifted to hospital, apparently. The lorry driver he'd just missed before he crashed into the wall had recognized that this was a job for the air ambulance and had been pretty insistent on his mobile phone, which had certainly improved Mickey's chances. The bottom line was he had serious head injuries that needed checking out before they proceeded any further. The fact that his right leg was smashed to smithereens was secondary. He was going to have to undergo at least two operations.

Lucy was allowed to go and see her husband before he went down to theatre; they were getting ready for him now. James squeezed her hand as she was led away. She was warned that Mickey wasn't a pretty sight, probably unrecognizable.

James peered through the blinds into the room and saw Lucy at Mickey's bedside, her head bowed, holding his hand. Her lips moved silently. Her eyes were closed. Was she praying? He thought she probably was, and in that moment he realized he'd lost her. No matter what happened now, she'd slipped through his fingers. He'd possessed her for a few golden moments only, moments that he would treasure as long as he lived.

He stared at his brother's motionless figure, at the wires and drips and apparatus that were keeping him alive. There was one chance, he supposed ... But no matter how hard James tried, he couldn't quite bring himself to wish his brother dead.

As soon as the call came through from James outlining Mickey's predicament, Keith swung into action. Patrick had insisted on driving, but Keith wouldn't hear of it. He'd take them all over to the hospital in the Landcruiser. The girls were woken and stood, shocked and dazed, in the hallway, shivering even though the central heating never went off at The Cedars.

Sandra was hovering on the fringe of the action. The news was sobering by its very nature and she was horrified by what had happened, but not really sure what role she should take. It didn't help that she was being totally ignored. Until everyone was about to leave. Keith turned to her.

'I don't suppose I'll be back before tomorrow. I'll hang on until I know exactly what's going on. See what help I can be. I'll bring the girls back here if necessary.'

Sandra nodded, grateful that this new drama was going to take the heat away from the earlier incident.

'Shall I get some shopping in?'

Keith looked at her coldly.

'No. I think the best thing you can do is be gone by the time I get back.'

Sandra's mouth dropped open slackly. He could see every single white filling he'd paid for, to replace the myriad black ones. He jabbed the car keys in her direction to emphasize his seriousness.

'I mean it.'

The front door slammed shut and Sandra sank to her knees. Somehow she knew that Keith was deadly serious.

In the car, Keith had flicked the speakers to the back. A soothing Enya track was playing for the girls, who sat pale and anxious in their seats, unable to sleep but not wanting to talk either. Mandy had insisted on coming and Keith had relented: better that she gave Sophie and Georgina her support than found herself subjected to Sandra's hysterical ranting.

Keith looked at Patrick sideways. The shock, rather than ageing him, had taken years off him, and he looked like a young boy, white with the fear of the unknown. He was trying to look calm and in control, but Keith could see his jaw was clenched, and his fists. He felt a surge of almost paternal protectiveness. Patrick wasn't really much more than a child, in spite of the confident air he carried with him.

'Are you OK?'

Patrick nodded.

'I just want to get there. See Dad.' His voice trembled, ever so slightly. 'I can't believe it.'

'You know, if there is anything I can do to help . . .'

'You are helping. By driving us.'

Patrick smiled his thanks. Keith persisted.

'I meant with the brewery.' He paused. He had to be tactful. He didn't want to seem as if he was fishing for information; poking his nose in where it wasn't wanted. 'I get the feeling things are a bit . . .'

He trailed off, suddenly feeling that no matter how he put it he was intruding. After all, he was only working on instinct. None of the Liddiards had hinted there was anything amiss; but Keith was perceptive. And Mandy had told him she thought there might be money worries, out of concern for her friends.

Patrick sighed. This wasn't how it was supposed to happen. He'd wanted to be in control when he laid the bait down for Keith. But perhaps now was the time, otherwise events were going to take over and the golden window of opportunity would be lost. At least if the seeds were sown in Keith's mind, they could move forward quickly, for Patrick felt sure that speed was of the essence if the brewery was to be saved. Anyway, they had another thirty miles to go before they got to the hospital. It would take his mind off things. He didn't want to think about what had happened to Mickey, or indeed what might happen. Deep down he had a naive faith that his father was invincible, immortal, that he would walk away from the accident unharmed. He had to cling on to that belief, otherwise he was terribly afraid he might break down. And he had to be strong, for Lucy, for Sophie and Georgina, for himself.

'You're right. Dad's been worried sick for months.'

'What's the problem?'

'Cash flow, mainly. We want to move forward but we're being dragged under by our existing debts.'

'Many a good business has fallen at that fence.'

Patrick winced. He didn't need to hear that. He was going to have to strike a fine line, sound vaguely optimistic while at the same time subtly proffering the begging bowl.

'Thing is, we've got great plans, if only we could get ourselves out of the mire. It's extremely frustrating.'

Keith nodded in agreement.

'There must be hundreds of different directions you could take. I can see the potential.' He smiled self-deprecatingly. 'Even as a plumber.'

This was encouraging. It gave Patrick the courage to go on to describe the future of Honeycote Ales as he saw it. He'd memorized the bullet points on Caroline's outline, and he had to admit to himself it sounded convincing, an inviting investment project. Keith listened, interested. Patrick finished with a sigh.

'Trouble is, we haven't got any cash. The bank will lend, of course, but the rates are out of the question. It's that or sell a pub, which would be suicide. What's the point of having a brewery with no tied houses?'

'So you're looking for a . . . what do they call them these days? A business angel?'

'I suppose so. But it's got to be someone who

understands the way we do things. Not someone that will try and take over – stamp on everything we've done over the past hundred and fifty years. It needs to be someone sensitive, with creative flair, who appreciates it's a family business. We don't want anyone stepping on our toes.'

Patrick wanted to make that quite clear from the start. Keith seemed to take on board everything he was saying. He asked a few pertinent questions, which Patrick did his best to answer. He knew he was on dangerous ground, bullshitting like this, but Keith appeared to swallow his answers and be genuinely interested.

'So how much are you looking for? Two? Three?'

Patrick faltered. He didn't actually have a clue. Everything he'd said up to now was pure flannel – he'd been thinking on his feet. He didn't want to be pinned down to actual figures. He spoke carefully.

'I suppose we're looking at three. That's probably what we'd get if we sold one of our pubs.'

Keith frowned.

'Three hundred thousand?'

'Yes.'

'Oh. Right.' Keith was silent for a moment and Patrick panicked. Had he overestimated the depths of his coffers? Come across as too greedy? Keith smiled. 'Actually, I was thinking about millions. Two or three million. If you want to do the job properly, surely that's the sort of figure you'd be looking at?'

Patrick felt a bit sick. How bloody green could you get? Keith must be laughing his head off inwardly. If he could misjudge the amount needed that badly, Keith must know that everything else he'd been saying was utter nonsense. He'd screwed up big time.

They arrived at the hospital and parked in a cowed silence, the uncertainty of what they were to discover inside hanging over them. Keith ushered the Liddiards forwards through the door, with Mandy following anxiously behind. There was something comforting about Keith's presence, thought Patrick. He was a good bloke. Pity he'd messed up his pitch like that.

As they made their way through miles of luminously lit corridor, Keith thought about what Patrick had been saying. He didn't have much business experience, that much was obvious. But his ideas were spot on, and you couldn't get away from the fact that Honeycote Ales was oozing promise, given the right hand on the tiller. And Keith rather liked the idea of being a business angel. An image of himself as a fat little cherub hovering over the brewery giving divine guidance came into his head and he smiled.

One door closes as another door opens, he thought, as they arrived at the forbidding entrance of the Intensive Care Unit. Not that he wanted to step into anyone's grave. He hoped fervently that Mickey was all right. He thought he was a pretty decent bloke, even if he was a crap businessman.

By the time the girls were reunited with their mother, with many hugs and tears, the news was encouraging. The first operation had gone well. Whatever fears the surgeons might have had about internal bleeding were abated, and Mickey was critical but stable. They were happy enough with his progress to start rebuilding his leg, which was going to be a long and painstaking process. But the initial panic was over.

Lucy sent the girls home with James, with promises to ring if anything went wrong. After all, there was no point in them all crowding up the corridor, speculating and drinking disgusting coffee out of the machine. Mandy and Keith were going to stay on for a while with Patrick, then take him back to Solihull so he could collect the Defender and then go home.

Lucy looked a dreadful colour, almost green under the harsh fluorescent lighting. Her head was throbbing. Half of her longed for her bed, but the other half was too wired. Patrick went off for a cigarette, and she wished fervently that she smoked. If she'd ever come across a chain-smoking situation, then this was it.

Keith put a comforting hand on her shoulder.

'I know it's what everyone says, but if there's anything I can do—'

Lucy smiled at him gratefully.

'Thank you.'

Keith felt an urgent need to reassure her.

'He's going to be all right, you know.'

Lucy's chin wobbled. Keith thought it would probably be better if she let it all out. He braced himself for a flood of tears. But she seemed to recover herself. She turned to him with something that seemed like defiance.

'Actually, it would probably have been better for everyone if he'd died.'

Lucy screwed up her eyes, still fighting to hold back the tears, even though she wasn't sure exactly where to focus her looming grief: on Mickey's betrayal, her own shame at what she had done or the accident. She pressed her fists into her sockets for a moment to staunch the flow, then realized Keith was looking at her in utter bewilderment.

'Mickey's been having an affair. With Lawrence Oakley's wife.'

Keith thought back to Christmas Day lunch at Honeycote House and Lawrence's revelations. He was shocked. So Mickey was the culprit, was he? He hadn't met Mrs Oakley, but she must be something special for Mickey to jeopardize his marriage. Lucy gave him an ironic smile.

'So you're in good company. Our respective spouses have both done the dirty on us. What have we done to deserve it, do you think?'

Keith shrugged.

'I don't think you necessarily need to do anything to deserve it. I'm sure you didn't. And I don't suppose I did either. It's an occupational hazard once you get married.' He paused, then smiled ruefully. 'Sandra was there when I got home. I've told her not to be there when I get back. I've told her I want a divorce.'

Lucy started chewing the side of her finger. Her nerves were unravelling, fraying at the edges; she felt lightheaded. Almost as if she wasn't there. But she knew she was.

'How long do you think I should wait before I ask Mickey for one? Till he comes out of surgery? Or shall I give him a couple of days to recuperate?' She laughed – a trifle hysterically, but she thought she was entitled to be hysterical. Keith blinked.

'You don't want a divorce, surely?'

'Why not? He can screw who he likes then.'

Lucy knew she was overreacting, but she wanted reassurance and somehow she knew Keith would give it to her. He was a romantic deep down. And sure enough, Keith found himself virtually pleading with Lucy. It mattered to him that what the Liddiards had was kept intact. He didn't care about his own marriage, but he was determined that the perfection of life at Honeycote House, at Honeycote Ales, should be preserved. That way he could be sure it was attainable, that perhaps one day he could find the same perfection elsewhere. It was the Liddiards who'd given him hope, the courage to change his own life. One little flaw, one minor indiscretion on Mickey's part, wouldn't shatter his illusion.

'I'm not divorcing Sandra because she was unfaithful. In a funny way that doesn't matter to me. It happens all the time; people get tempted. I'm divorcing her because she never cared about us – me and her and Mandy – never thought about us as a family. She always put herself first. Mickey might have been unfaithful, but he cared – cares – about all of you. Anyone can see that. All of you sitting round that table on Christmas Day . . . you could feel the warmth. You don't know how envious I felt. I could never offer anyone that kind of hospitality, not in a million years.'

Lucy was about to open her mouth to protest, but Keith put his hand up to stop her. He was in full flow. What he was saying surprised even himself.

'I know what you're going to say. OK, so everything's been blown a bit off-course. But if you don't forgive him, think of what you'd be giving up. You don't know how lucky you are.'

Lucy's eyebrows shot up in the air. Lucky? Her philandering bastard of a husband had just driven into a brick wall, was on the operating table as they spoke, and she was supposed to be lucky? She'd be lucky if she wasn't organizing his funeral by the end of the day. She allowed her imagination to wander a bit further – Kay at the graveside, belly swollen with Mickey's love child, demanding its right to the inheritance. Oh yes, that was OK – she wouldn't get her hands on that because there wasn't anything to inherit. Only debts.

Oh God – what was she supposed to do about the brewery? They'd be starting up again in two days' time, having worked overtime up until Christmas to cover the demand. She supposed she'd have to go in and give them all a rousing speech. She imagined the workers lined up, caps in hand, waiting anxiously for news of the boss.

Lucy started as she realized Keith was still staring at her. She smiled distractedly. It was so sweet of him to care. To say such lovely things. But he obviously had a romantic view of their existence. He was saying something. What was it?

'Listen. I've said more than enough. But there's one more thing. I know things are a bit tough at the brewery at the moment—'

Understatement of the century.

'If you want any help. I mean, what I know about actual brewing you could probably write on the back of a postage stamp. But presumably that side of things runs itself. I do know about running a business, though . . .'

Which is more than I do, thought Lucy. Or James. Give him a painting to value or a piece of furniture to date and he was shit hot, but he'd never shown any interest in the brewery. And Patrick could hardly take over. Even though he was starting to sit up and take notice, he was far too young for the responsibility, and his father was gravely ill. There was only so much a young man could take on his shoulders. He couldn't be expected to make rational decisions under the circumstances.

Lucy smiled brightly at Keith. She was sure he was just being polite.

'Thank you. You're being very kind. You've already done enough . . .'

Keith put a reassuring arm round her. She was being so brave. He'd do anything to help, and gladly. He was more determined than ever to do everything he could to save the Liddiards' marriage, and their livelihood. It would give him the hope he needed, the courage to carry on and start a new life for himself. He had no incentive to pick up the pieces of his own marriage, but if he could help the Liddiards pick up theirs, who knew what he might find along the way?

Patrick was pacing up and down outside in a small courtyard where the nicotine dependent hung out – the concrete slabs were littered with defiant nub ends. He was berating himself while he chain-smoked. If only he'd had the balls to stay and confront his father that morning, had talked to him about his problems, instead of turning tail and fleeing to Solihull. They should have got everything out in the open, pulled together like a father and son. They could have made a plan, sorted things. Instead, his father was lying on the operating table. What if something went wrong and he died? He'd never forgive himself. He should have done more. Could easily have done so.

He felt a tap on his shoulder and turned to find Mandy looking at him anxiously. She was shocked by the distress on his face – a mask of pain that made him almost unrecognizable. She'd seen him slip away when he thought no one was looking.

'Are you OK?' She rolled her eyes as she said it. 'Sorry. Stupid question.'

'Fine. I just wanted a fag. I hate hospitals . . .' There was a catch in his throat. Patrick was horrified. He was going to break down, right in front of her. The harder he tried not to cry, the more he wanted to. Mandy didn't know what to do, whether to leave him in peace or not. But, she thought, if it was her, she'd want someone with her. So she put a hand on his arm, to tell him it was all right.

'Shit . . .' He was so angry with himself for losing control, but there was nothing he could do. A great tidal wave of terror rose up and engulfed him. Mandy held on to him as he sobbed great racking sobs of guilt and fear. Gone was the arrogant, almost cruel young man on whom she'd once wanted revenge. That seemed so long ago – now here she was holding a boy, a terrified, vulnerable boy. He clung to her fiercely.

'Shh – he's going to be fine. Your dad's going to be fine.'

Eventually his sobs subsided. Mandy continued to hold him, murmuring platitudes as a mother would to a child. And as she cradled him in her arms, Patrick felt a huge surge of warmth. He remembered the feeling dimly from his childhood, when Lucy had found him sobbing, worried that he was going to be sent away from Honeycote, and had scooped him up, consoled him. He'd got the same feeling of security then as he was getting from Mandy now. What he hadn't realized was that he was so vulnerable, that he needed someone to find strength from. He'd spent so much time recently trying to sort things out. He must have been mad to think he could do it all on his own, like some sort of superhero. That wasn't what it was all about. What he needed was someone to share things with. Someone to share the hopes, the dreams, the good times and the bad.

He clutched at her hand and as their fingers entwined he felt the courage flooding back into him. She bent to kiss his head, just to give him reassurance. But his face came up to meet hers, and their lips met through his tears.

When Mickey came round from his operations the next morning, he had difficulty sorting out fantasy from reality. He'd had some sort of crazy nightmare about going to burn down the brewery, and then a car crash. Thank God he was now awake. He'd have to do something about these persistent anxiety dreams. Perhaps get some sleeping tablets . . . He struggled to open his eyes; his lids seemed unnaturally heavy, but he finally managed it. There was a nurse at the bottom of his bed, wielding a chart.

It hadn't been a dream at all.

Mickey quickly shut his eyes again before the nurse could notice he was conscious. He dredged about in the sludge of his brain for a few more clues, not particularly liking anything he came across. Intermittent memories emerged: a confrontation with Lucy, though he couldn't remember the outcome. A meeting with Cowley, but again he couldn't quite recall the details. Though he was pretty sure it was bad news all round.

Mickey groaned inwardly. What a monumental balls-up. He wondered what sort of state he was in. He didn't feel as if he could move. Perhaps he was paralysed. Perhaps that was his punishment.

Fear and adrenalin were making his mind race. He tried desperately to assess his predicament. Who knew he was here, if anyone? Had he had any ID on him when he'd crashed? He supposed they'd be able to trace him from the car he was driving. With a sinking heart he remembered he'd been driving the Healey. Patrick's car. He hoped to God he hadn't smashed it up, though he supposed by his very presence in a hospital bed that he must have done. It was his son's pride and joy, and he'd taken it without asking. He was also pretty sure he wasn't insured to drive it. Patrick would be gutted.

Despite rising panic, Mickey tried to keep his breathing under control, so as not to attract attention. He didn't have long to decide what to do. All in all, his name was going to be mud with pretty much everyone. His wife, his son, his bank manager. Oh God – and Lawrence Oakley. He felt pretty certain Lawrence was on his tail for some reason. Was there anyone out there who wouldn't be baying for his blood?

His accident must have been pretty serious. He couldn't actually feel anything, so no doubt he was pumped up with painkillers, which didn't bode well. How long had he been here? What day was it? Had he been unconscious for minutes or months? It was spooky not knowing. He supposed he ought to notify his consciousness to the nurse, but he wanted the luxury of a few moments to get his thoughts together.

Even through the fug of the anaesthetic and the painkillers, a bright idea suddenly occurred to him. Perhaps he could pretend to have forgotten everything leading up to the accident. Could you prosecute somebody for something they couldn't remember? He thought it would be pretty pointless. He wondered how easy it would be to feign amnesia. How long could you keep it up, realistically?

He could give it a go for a while, then when everyone had forgotten his misdemeanours, when time the great healer had papered over the cracks, he could have total recall. Or perhaps not total – just enough to go back to being his old self with a convenient gap where his indiscretions lay.

No. That was exactly the sort of behaviour that had got him where he was now. Cowardly deception. Devious avoidance. A complete inability to face up to his sins. Mickey sighed heavily and the nurse looked up. She smiled brightly.

'Mr Liddiard.'

She hurried to his side with her chart.

'How are you feeling?'

Hunted. Persecuted. Terrified. Paranoid. Guilty. How long had she got?

'Fine,' he answered flatly. 'All things considered. How long have I been here?'

'I'll go and get your wife. I think she's down in the canteen. I'm sure she'll be glad to see you.'

Wouldn't bet on it, thought Mickey gloomily. A wave of wooziness came back over him and he wondered what time they brought round the drinks trolley.

When Lucy went to see Mickey, she didn't know how to behave. You couldn't berate someone who'd so narrowly escaped the jaws of death, but she felt disinclined to kiss him or even express her relief at his survival. He looked at her warily as she took her seat by him.

'How are you feeling?'

'I'm not. I'm too doped up to feel a thing.'

'Lucky you,' said Lucy drily, and Mickey flinched.

'Patrick's car . . . tell him I'm sorry.'

Lucy nodded. Mickey reached out a hand to touch her arm.

'I'm sorry,' he repeated.

She wasn't sure if he was reiterating his apology to Patrick or trying to apologize to her. She didn't really care. Sorry didn't change anything. It wasn't enough.

The consultant appeared. Mickey was going to have to stay in for observation for a while, because of his head injuries. As for his leg – that was going to be a very slow recovery. It had been pinned together in several places, and he was going to have to walk on crutches for weeks if not longer and undergo extensive physiotherapy. They should expect a difficult few months, especially as head injuries could mean character changes, depression. And the leg would be painful.

At the end of the litany, the consultant gave a rather rueful shrug.

'I suppose you should just think yourself lucky to be alive.'

Mickey sneaked a glance at Lucy, who offered a tight-lipped smile.

'Depends which way you look at it, really. Doesn't it?' she replied.

The consultant looked a little shocked at her tone, but Mickey wasn't. What did he expect? Of everything, it was going to be his marriage that was going to take longest to recuperate. How much care and attention was it going to need before it recovered? If indeed it did. Was it wrecked beyond repair – a write-off, like the Healey?

Patrick appeared tentatively in the doorway.

Lucy turned away as he went to embrace his father, something she hadn't been able to bring herself to do. It seemed unconditional love only thrived in your blood. Not in your heart.

Later that afternoon, Patrick stood in the village, solemnly watching a team from the nearby garage extricate what was left of his car from a brick wall and lift it on to a trailer. He shuddered as he saw the passenger side and thought of his father in there. The mechanics were impressed that he'd managed to smash the car up so thoroughly and still survive.

'Total write-off, mate.' They sympathized with the young man watching.

'Never mind. Insured, isn't it?'

Patrick shrugged. They missed the point. You couldn't just pick up the phone and order another one. It was unique. He'd spent months, years, lovingly restoring the vehicle, painstakingly tracking down the spare parts needed to set it off. You couldn't put a value on that.

He wanted to take Mickey by the arms and shake him till his teeth rattled. How could you love someone so much, yet totally resent them for fucking everything up? Yet again he thought of his father as a child; one of those winsome-looking brats who were repeatedly forgiven for smashing toys and spoiling games on account of their wide-eyed charm.

For what hadn't Mickey ruined? His marriage, the brewery, his son's own car ... Was it deliberate, some compulsion to annihilate everything near and dear to him, culminating in his own self-destruction – the one bit he hadn't actually managed to pull off? There were people like that. Patrick had known a boy at school. He'd had everything on a plate – wealth, good looks, brains – but he'd been drawn like a moth to a flame to drugs. His distraught parents had spent a fortune on rehab, but to no avail. Patrick had felt no pity for him when he'd finally overdosed and died.

Just as he felt no pity for his father now. Only a cold, silent fury that he was putting his family through all this pain and worry. As the Healey was winched on to the back of the truck, he turned to find his uncle standing there in his immaculate waxed jacket, its suede collar turned up to protect him from the cold.

'If you want a sub. To get another one—'

Patrick shook his head.

'If anyone should be paying, it's Dad.'

'The offer's there.' James smiled awkwardly. 'I know how hard you worked on it.'

Patrick smiled his thanks wanly. James put a hand on his shoulder. Patrick had always been a tough nut; he knew the boy would never admit to needing support, but he wanted his godson to know he was there if he needed him.

'If there's anything you want. Or need. You know I'm there. Whatever . . .'

He was sure Patrick would tell him he was fine. But to his surprise the boy turned to him.

'Have you ever fallen in love?'

'What?' James was startled.

'All of a sudden. When you least expected it. Hopelessly in love. So you can't think about anything else?'

James considered his reply cautiously. He wasn't sure where Patrick was coming from; what he knew, what he might be surmising or insinuating. He'd always been perceptive, and James had a guilty conscience. If he even had a sniff of what had gone on between him and Lucy . . .

But Patrick's query seemed to be genuine. He wasn't being facetious or provocative. He looked in pain, the pain James could remember only too well from all those years ago. And all the years since.

'Yes. Yes, I have.'

'What did you do? Did you tell her?'

'No. I didn't.' James couldn't look him in the eye. 'I didn't do anything and I've regretted it ever since.'

'Oh.' Patrick was intrigued, wondering which one of James's girlfriends it was. He'd never seemed particularly enamoured of any of them. Perhaps it was someone from long ago.

He was taken aback when his uncle took him by the arm and urged him fiercely: 'Whatever you do, Patrick, don't make the mistake I made. Don't let her go.'

Lucy eventually left the hospital in a taxi at about seven o'clock that evening having been reassured by the consultant that Mickey was out of danger, though not pain, which as far as she was concerned was just how she wanted it. She'd left him with a curt promise to return in the morning, and she could sense his relief before she'd even gone out of the door.

When she finally got home, she felt as if she had been away for days, although incredibly it had only been just over twenty-four hours since she and Mickey had confronted each other in the drawing room. The house stood stiffly to attention. It was immaculate on the surface. James and the girls had done their best to establish some order. It had given Sophie and Georgina something to do. But on closer inspection a multitude of sins had been hidden. Glasses and plates had been put away badly washed. Things had been put back in the wrong place. Lucy felt just the same. Calm and order on the outside but mayhem within.

It was wonderful to see the girls. They fell on her with hugs, and although she knew she should be reassuring them, she took strength from the fact that they were desperate to reassure her, running her a bath, bringing her pyjamas that they'd warmed on the Aga, making her boiled eggs with lots of toast. At one point she wondered how keen they'd be to fuss over her if they knew the truth, that she'd been screwing their uncle, but she banished the unsavoury thought from her mind. Thankfully James had made himself scarce, once he'd established that Lucy was happy to stay on her own at the house. He'd brought Pokey back, for protection. And Patrick was there, though at the moment he was brooding in his room. She could hear the moody, swirling sound of Radiohead coming through the floor: dark, gothic chords that matched his state of mind.

She thought Sophie looked pale. She'd barely touched her own egg.

'Are you OK, sweetheart?'

Sophie nodded rather unconvincingly. Georgina looked sharply between the two of them, opened her mouth as if to say something, then snapped it shut again. A tear sprang out and trickled down Sophie's cheek, plopping into her egg.

'Daddy *is* going to be all right, isn't he?'

'Of course he is, darling. You know he is. The consultant said he's badly injured, but he's out of danger. Honestly, there's nothing to worry about. We can go and see him in the morning.' That'll be something to look forward to, she added to herself. She smiled reassuringly at her daughters, thinking that what she really needed was some time on her own to think, without anyone breathing down her neck.

Later that evening, when Sophie and Georgina had gone to bed, Lucy and Patrick shared a bottle of wine. Each of them was secretly desperate to go to bed, to mull over their respective dilemmas, but there were serious issues to be discussed. Not least the brewery.

They debated Keith's offer to help. Lucy had thought he was just being kind, but when Patrick reiterated his offer, and pointed out the advantages, she realized that it was in fact a lifeline. She herself didn't have a clue what to do. The brewery had clearly reached crisis point, and Mickey obviously wasn't fit to make any decisions. Not that he had been before the accident, she thought bitterly.

For a moment, she wished she'd paid more attention to the business side of things over the years. Not that she envisaged herself taking over like some Danielle Steel heroine. She knew she hadn't been put on this earth to become Businesswoman of the Year. But at least if she had some clue as to the brewery's needs, she'd have a better idea of where to guide it.

She and Patrick went over the options.

'The thing is, Keith's seriously loaded. And he's interested. When are we going to get another chance to attract an investor? This is an ideal opportunity for him to get the measure of things.'

'That's what worries me. Who knows what else your father's shoved under the carpet?'

'What's the alternative? James isn't really interested in the brewery. He never has been. It's all he can do to turn up to the AGM.'

Lucy nodded. More than anything, she wanted to keep James away from the heart of the operation. The boundaries were too muddied as it was; she didn't want things any more complicated than they already were.

Perhaps an objective opinion, an unbiased figure at the helm, would be the best all round. And she was pretty sure that Keith could be trusted. He might just be the one to turn Honeycote Ales around. She and Patrick agreed they'd ask him to come on board, even if only temporarily, just to see them through this sticky patch.

Two days later, an emergency board meeting was held in Mickey's hospital room, much to the agitation of his consultant. Mickey felt like some ailing head of a Mafia clan, as Keith, Patrick, Cowley, Lucy and James sat round him on plastic chairs.

The idea was that Keith should take over as acting MD, with reference to Mickey at all times, and of course Cowley, who was a tiny bit anxious at the unconventional nature of the proceedings but whose gut told him that Keith was good news. He'd done some digging on the quiet; the bloke was as sound as a pound. Patrick was to be promoted to brewery manager, but was essentially at Keith's beck and call. James was on hand if necessary as a sounding board. In the meantime, Keith was to be given the books for the past five years, which he would no doubt go through with a fine-tooth comb, and it was agreed they would meet a month from now in order to discuss his possible investment.

They toasted the new alliance with polystyrene cups of tea from the canteen. It went without saying that Mickey wasn't allowed a sniff of alcohol, so no one was tactless enough to suggest champagne.

When they'd all gone, Mickey lay back on his pillow with a sigh of relief. He'd been in immense discomfort all the way through the meeting, and had done his best to concentrate, but it was clear to everyone present that he wasn't fit to make any sort of management decision for the moment. But he couldn't help feeling elated at the way things had turned out. He'd got away with it: escaped, if narrowly, death, bankruptcy and divorce, all in one fell swoop.

Yes, he'd definitely landed with his bum in the honey. And he'd learned by his mistakes. This time he was going to keep his nose to the grindstone, keep on the straight and narrow, keep his nose clean – every single cliché in the book.

He didn't dwell too long on just how boring it might be.

21

Keith Sherwyn didn't really believe in fate, kismet, any of those airy-fairy hippy theories. Life was what you made it and that was that. But he did think it was uncanny that he'd ended up at Honeycote Ales, for he had a strong feeling that they were made for each other, that this was where he belonged and that some unseen force had guided him here. Yet no matter how charming the brewery was, he could see that the writing was on the wall, that it was on the brink of disaster – and it was up to him to pull it back.

It didn't take him long to decide he was going to put his money in, because every day the brewery languished without investment it plummeted further beyond redemption. And Keith was a man of action, a man who trusted his own gut feelings, not to mention a man more than ready for a new challenge. The investment would have to go in phases: an initial injection with the ready cash he had available, followed by a more substantial dollop when the sale of his business went through. But a gentleman's agreement was made – because he knew that Mickey was, deep down, a gentleman, even though he'd lost the plot a bit – so that Keith could implement changes immediately and not have to worry about waiting for tedious legal i's to be dotted and t's to be crossed. He wanted to play with his new toy straight away.

So, for the first time in years, Keith found he was enjoying life.

His training as a plumber helped him assimilate the brewing process more quickly than he otherwise might. He struck up an immediate bond with Eric Giles, the general handyman-cum-engineer, whose initial wariness soon wore off as soon as he realized that Keith was as crazy about Honeycote Ales's industrial heritage as he was, and had no intention of whipping out some of the more antiquated workings and replacing them with sterile stainless steel efficiency. Eric stressed repeatedly that even a minor change could alter the perfection of the brew, as it was the original recipe which had been handed down by Mickey's great-grandfather and was kept under lock and key. Actually, it wasn't at all, it was in a plastic folder in the brewery office for all to see, but it made a nice legend.

Keith quickly came to the conclusion that nothing at the heart of the brewery was going to need touching. He was a firm believer in 'if it ain't broke, don't fix it'. It was what happened after the beer was brewed that was so wrong. There didn't seem to be any system in place for selling, marketing or promotion whatsoever. It was complacency that was the problem, an inbuilt arrogance that assumed that a perfect product meant profit. But implementing a marketing plan was going to be a long and complicated business. In the meantime, it was a question of patching up the damage that had already been done and boosting morale.

The first job he had to do was to go and reassure Ted and Eileen that their livelihood was safe. When Patrick had told him that Mickey was planning to sell the Honeycote Arms, Keith was horrified. In his opinion, that should be the last of the pubs to go – it bore the company name, for heaven's sake. It was an integral part of the brewery's history. It was there to be capitalized upon, exploited, made a flagship. It was decisions like this that were so wrong.

He'd phoned ahead to tell Ted and Eileen he was coming. He arrived to find them defensive, wary, and did his best to put them at their ease.

'I want to let you know that you're a valued part of the team. And that on no account is the pub going to be sold. On the contrary, we'll be investing in all of the pubs over the next two years. Substantially. We're going to be working on a complete refurbishment plan. A new corporate image, so that there's some continuity across the board – but allowing each pub to retain its own identity.'

'That's all very well,' said Ted. 'And I'm glad to hear it. But actually, Eileen and I have decided we've had enough. We reckon it was for the best. It's time we had a change – we've been here twenty years. We want to semi-retire. Run a B&B somewhere, so I can go fishing and Eileen can put her feet up.'

Keith was anxious to establish that there were no hard feelings and assured them that if they changed their minds it wouldn't be too late. And when he'd gone, Ted and Eileen agreed that you could tell he was a good sort, the sort you could trust. He wouldn't shaft you when you least expected it, not like Mickey Liddiard.

Three days after his accident, Mickey was in agony. He was up to his eyeballs in painkillers, but they did nothing for the icy disdain with which Lucy was treating him. He'd hoped being on the brink of death might elicit some sympathy from her, but as various of his skeletons insisted on falling out of the cupboard, so the nails were driven deeper into his coffin.

When she'd found out from Patrick and Keith about his plan to sell the Honeycote Arms, she'd been outraged. When she'd found out that he'd been three times over the limit when he'd smashed Patrick's car, and was likely to be banned from driving for two years, she was furious. And when he was off the critical list and had to be moved out of his private room on to a ward, she discovered he'd cashed in their private health insurance. As the nurses fussed round him, tucking in his blankets ready for him to be wheeled on to a general ward, she let rip.

'I give up, Mickey. I give up. What else am I going to find out? You're a liar!'

'I've never told you a lie, Lucy.'

'Let's not split hairs. You've hidden things from me. Deliberately concealed them. And that's not what marriage is about, in my book.'

'I'm sorry.'

'Not half as sorry as I am.'

'Please, Lucy.'

Mickey indicated the two nurses, who were exchanging scandalized glances over his head.

'I don't care who knows. I've already been made to look a fool ten times over.'

As the porter arrived to move him, Lucy gathered up her things and stalked out.

'Giving you GBH of the earhole, is she?' consoled the porter. Mickey shut his eyes.

'I deserve it.'

'She looked so pretty and nice, as well. Mind you, they're often the worst. My wife, she looks like a Rottweiler but her bark's worse than her bite.'

Mickey took little comfort from this and wondered miserably if things were ever going to be the same again. At least Sophie and Georgina still loved him. Mind you, they didn't know the half of it. But they'd been coming in as often as they could and took turns reading to him from the new Dick Francis he'd got for Christmas. Patrick was too wrapped up with Keith to visit very often, and Mickey didn't think he'd quite forgiven him for smashing up his car. He wondered if he could bribe the porter to nip out and get him a bottle of something to take the edge off his conscience, but then he remembered the consultant's warning. No booze. His liver was already looking rather sorry for itself and his body had enough to cope with. There was nothing left but prayer, and Mickey had always felt uncomfortable asking any favours from God, whom he suspected would want something in return that he couldn't give.

After her outburst, Lucy sat miserably in the car park, waiting to calm down before she drove home. She was so confused. She did feel betrayed and let down by Mickey, but deep in her heart she knew she'd done wrong as well. It was guilt as much as hurt that had made her overreact. Things had moved so fast she hadn't had time to reflect on what had happened between her and James. She'd made sure to keep him at arm's length over the last few days, but she was only putting off the day of reckoning. You couldn't really sleep with someone after twenty years of friendship and not discuss it with them. But Lucy didn't know what to say. She didn't know what to think. All day long her mind whirled, as she went through the motions of keeping the house and the family together. Thank God for mundane chores and horses that needing mucking-out. There was always something to do in order to put off facing up to reality.

Patrick spent the first few days after Mickey's accident high on a cocktail of anxiety and adrenalin. As soon as Keith was established in the driving seat, he breathed a sigh of relief, but realized he was going to have his work cut out for him. Keith wouldn't tolerate slackers, he could see that. Not that he wanted to slack. He couldn't wait to get his teeth into putting Honeycote Ales back on the map.

But until he'd seen Mandy and found out where he stood, he was in agony. After baring his very soul to her that night at the hospital, he felt naked and exposed. For the first time in his life, he really cared how someone felt about him. But he was too proud to go and ask. He couldn't bring himself to phone her. What would he say? He'd just have to wait until fate conspired to bring them together again, which he hoped wouldn't be long. He was working closely with her father, after all.

He didn't have long to wait. Mandy arrived at Honeycote House early one morning with Keith, who had some papers for Lucy to take to the hospital and sign. She wanted to see Monkey, who was still waiting for the farrier. Patrick jumped at the chance.

'He's in his stable. We can go and turn him out, if you like.'

'Great.'

They went out to the stables, where they changed Monkey's stable rug and Patrick watched as Mandy fussed over the little horse that had once belonged to him. They led him out to a paddock and watched as he trotted round in a circle, then lay down and luxuriated in a roll.

'I'd better go and muck him out.'

'It's OK. Mum's got a couple of girls from the village helping out while dad's in hospital.'

'No. I want to.'

She was determined, and Patrick admired her for it. She didn't mind getting her hands dirty. She was so unlike the little piece of Birmingham trash he'd mistaken her for. He watched as she shovelled manure into the barrow, which he duly trundled over to the muck heap. When he came back, she was shaking out a bale of fresh straw. He took a deep breath.

'Are you still free tomorrow night?'

Mandy looked at him, puzzled.

'New Year's Eve? My mate's party?' He remembered asking her on Christmas Day. When he hadn't really cared what her answer was, because he'd only been after her for her father's money. How things had changed.

'Oh yes. Um – I don't know. It depends if Dad's up to anything. I don't really want to leave him on his own . . .' She sounded reluctant and Patrick's stomach turned a somersault of disappointment. Then she seemed to think better of it. 'Actually, I'm sure he won't mind. New Year's Eve's not such a big deal for grown-ups, is it?'

'Great.' Patrick smiled, struggling to contain his jubilation as she smiled back at him. To his amazement, he couldn't find the bottle to kiss her. He'd never hesitated before, had always chosen his moment and pounced regardless with no fear of rejection. But suddenly he was rooted to the spot.

In the end, it was Mandy who leaned her pitchfork against the stable wall, curled her arm round his neck and pulled him to her. A little later they walked back into the kitchen, their eyes sparkling and their cheeks flushed . . .

Kay turned her car into Merton Drive, watching heads spin round in amazement. It wasn't the sort of place you saw a Porsche Boxster very often, being a safe, sensible, dull cul de sac filled with three- and four-bedroomed semis whose owners lacked both imagination and ambition. Kay thought it didn't look any different from the days when she'd lived there, apart from the odd conservatory that had been tacked on and the fact that the more adventurous had stained their larch-lap fences green rather than brown. She pulled into the drive of number twenty-seven and stopped. She knew the curtains over the road were twitching, even without looking.

She wondered if they were in. Her dad didn't like to open his shop in between Christmas and New Year. If people couldn't be bothered to buy their meat in advance and stick it in the freezer, that was their lookout. He deserved a holiday as much as the next person.

It had taken her a few days to pluck up the courage. She'd stayed on in Frome to build up her strength, emotional rather than physical, coming to terms with what was now her future. The days had been all right. She'd gone back to the hospital for advice, bought some books on giving birth, wandered round the shops familiarizing herself with all the bizarre paraphernalia that was going to be part of her life.

It was the nights that had got to her, the time when tiny little niggles become huge worries that then explode into panic. That was when the white-cold fear hit her, serrating her stomach. The compulsion to phone Lawrence had been overwhelming. She'd told herself he wasn't a monster, that surely he'd take pity, and more than once she'd grappled in the darkness for her mobile phone. Then she'd remembered his face when he'd shown her the letter and she'd put the phone back, curling up into a ball and waiting for sleep to take her through until daylight, when she could cope again.

She got out of the car and tried to walk up the path with an air of confidence to stop the neighbours speculating. But when her mother opened the door and a look of joy spread itself over her face on seeing her daughter, Kay's resolve collapsed.

'Mum . . .' She threw herself into her mother's arms. Sylvia held her, drew her gently inside and shut the door. Her father, Charlie, appeared, alarmed.

'Whatever's the matter? What's he done? I'll bloody kill him!'

Kay sobbed further. Her father's loyalty knew no bounds. Here he was, ready to protect her at all costs, when she'd barely acknowledged their presence over the past ten years.

'Ssh, Charlie. Leave her be. Go and put the kettle on.' Tea was Sylvia's solution to everything.

'But what's the matter?' Charlie wasn't going to be fobbed off.

'It's obvious, isn't it? She's pregnant. Aren't you, love?'

Kay nodded, still unable to speak through her tears, but knew from that moment on everything was going to be all right, as her parents welcomed her with open arms, never reproaching her for her neglect in recent years, the infrequent phone calls and even less frequent visits. Nor did they ask any probing questions. By the end of the evening, she was settled into what had been her old bedroom, with its pink candlewick bedspread, and was sitting down to her mum's Irish stew made with her dad's best end of lamb.

22

On New Year's Eve, the consultant said that Mickey could go home. He seemed to think he was doing him a favour, but Mickey quite liked the security of the public ward.

Lucy came to collect him. They drove home in relative silence. It was quite obvious to Mickey that he shouldn't expect banners and champagne and a welcome home cake. As they came up the drive, he cleared his throat and tried to sound conversational.

'Are we doing anything for New Year's Eve?'

Lucy glared at him.

'Strangely enough, Mickey, I haven't actually had time to organize anything. What with you nearly killing yourself and trying to stop the brewery going bankrupt.'

Mickey could have cried. It was so unlike Lucy to be sarcastic. What did he have to do to make it all right? He'd tried to say sorry, but she didn't want to talk. He held out some hope that once they were on home territory, things might get easier. Hospitals were hardly the place for a heart-to-heart; for conducting life-saving surgery on a twenty-year marriage.

But it was not the case. Far from it. Mickey was shocked when Lucy told him in no uncertain terms that she thought it was better for him to sleep in the sitting room.

He walked in, and saw the sofa bed pulled out and made up with proper sheets and blankets, and various of his belongings in place. It looked very cosy. And very permanent. Lucy didn't meet his eye.

'It'll save you walking up and down stairs. With your leg.'

They had a dismal New Year's Eve. Lucy produced a saucepan of limp pasta with a shop-bought sauce and ready-grated Parmesan. No salad. No wine. Patrick had gone out with Mandy and the girls had decided to stay over at some friends. Mickey felt a tiny bit hurt that they hadn't been there to welcome him home, until Lucy admitted she'd forgotten to tell them he was being let out. That's how important he was.

As he lay in his made-up bed and watched the countdown to midnight on the telly, Mickey thought he couldn't feel less significant. And the worst of it was, he deserved it.

In Merton Drive, Kay's brother Dan had brought round a bottle of Asti for his parents to see in the New Year. He was five years younger than Kay and had a gruelling job as a psychiatric nurse. He wasn't impressed to see his sister. He waited till his mother was out of the room before he laid into her with a sneer.

'So it's all gone tits up at the big house, has it? Come running home to mum, have you? You've got a nerve. You've cut her dead for the past ten years, with your bloody airs and graces and your posh car—'

Kay was gutted. Dan was articulating the sneaking

shame she'd felt in the back of her mind, but had managed to suppress. She couldn't even find the nerve to defend herself. He was right. How could she expect her mum and dad to drop everything and help her out?

Sylvia found Kay wiping away tears in the kitchen.

'Dan didn't mean it. He has a tough time. That wife of his doesn't lift a finger to help him; he works all the hours God sends and all she does is moan about what they haven't got.'

Kay was inconsolable.

'Look, love. Dan was annoyed because I was supposed to babysit for him tonight. I said I couldn't because you were here—'

'You should have, Mum. You didn't have to worry about me.'

'I babysit for him plenty of times. Don't you worry. Let her parents have the bother for once.'

Sylvia was very comforting, and Charlie, who was over-anxious to protect his daughter, said Dan deserved his ears boxed for speaking out of turn. As Kay lay in bed later, after sharing a tiny glass of Asti with them both at midnight, she thought of the vintage Dom Perignon she'd have had if she'd been with Lawrence and tried to convince herself she was happier where she was. Then she remembered she'd forgotten to cancel the dinner party she was supposed to have been hosting that evening and wasn't sure whether to laugh or cry.

Lawrence didn't know whether to laugh or cry either when he realized at six o'clock that he had ten dinner guests arriving at eight. Bloody Kay – she'd done it on purpose, he was sure. What the fuck was he supposed to do? It was too late to take them all out for dinner – anywhere decent was fully booked. He phoned Kelly, who calmed him down immediately. What he liked about her was she wasn't remotely fazed by his tantrums. And she was good in a crisis.

She turned up as good as gold an hour later with provisions provided by her mother's ample store cupboard, and Lawrence left her to it as she laid out a buffet while he showered and changed. His heart sank when he came down in his dinner jacket just as the doorbell rang. There on the dining table were battalions of scotch eggs and pork pies, vats of coleslaw and potato salad, and what Kelly had to identify as slices of cold black pudding. And pickled beetroot, for Christ's sake . . .

He got away with it. Just. His guests thought it was the height of ironic chic, and Lawrence played along. But he couldn't help thinking of the exquisite dinner Kay would have laid on. Even if she hadn't cooked it herself, it would have been faultless. Not that he could blame Kelly. She'd done her best, bless her. And at least they'd had vintage Dom Perignon to wash it all down.

At The Cedars, Keith was revelling in a bit of solitude. He'd worked his balls off at Honeycote for the past few days, and the last thing he wanted was a knees-up. He'd seen Mandy safely off for dinner with Patrick and now he was going to sit down with a plate of cheese and biscuits and a nice bottle of red wine, and go through all the details he'd been sent.

The estate agent hadn't even had a chance to get the particulars typed up properly before they'd had an offer on The Cedars. The buyers were in a position to proceed and so Keith accepted the offer; he wasn't even tempted to hang on for a better price, so eager was he to get shot of it. Then he'd phoned round all the estate agents in the Eldenbury area.

He knew what he wanted: an old, character property that he and Mandy could put their own stamp on, something not too large, but with a couple of acres so she could have Monkey at home. And it wasn't long before he thought he'd found the perfect place – a substantial cottage, in need of renovation, with a little paddock and a crumbling stable block and several outbuildings, one of which he felt sure would convert nicely into an office for him. It was in Kiplington, a little village about four miles away from Honeycote. It was ideal, and what was more the price didn't seem too bad as it needed quite a bit of work. They could do it up and sell it for quite a profit, he mused. Then he stopped – this wasn't supposed to be a moneymaking opportunity. This was a chance for a home, rather than a house, which was all The Cedars had ever been. He thought of Honeycote House. That was the feeling he wanted to create – a warm, inviting environment, which made you never want to leave. Though even Keith had noticed a frosty chill in the air of late . . .

When the phone rang at midnight, he picked up the receiver warily. It was Sandra, drunk and sobbing, wanting to start again. She was staying at a friend's and Keith imagined that she'd already outstayed her welcome. But he hardened his heart. There was no hope of a reconciliation; she'd be hearing from his solicitor . . . He felt a hint of remorse at that one. He'd got the best divorce lawyer in Birmingham, on the recommendation of a friend who'd been victim to the lawyer's ruthlessness and been taken to the cleaners by his wife.

Hanging up the phone, he wondered if he should have been less harsh. Lucy was a dignified example; she'd taken Mickey back. Was he a bad person because he couldn't find it in his heart to give Sandra a second chance?

Patrick and Mandy decided to skip his mate's party. They wanted nothing more than to be alone together, so they went out for a meal in Cheltenham and spent all evening gazing at each other over food that might as well have been sawdust for all the attention either of them paid it. They talked about everything. His dream was to take his next Healey, if he ever got one, on a rally across the Alps; hers was to become a good enough rider to start competing on Monkey in the summer. They both agreed they would help each other achieve their ambitions. Mandy offered to be his co-driver, even though she was a shocking map-reader. And Patrick offered to coach her on Monkey. After all, he knew all the tricks the little horse might pull; all his strengths and weaknesses.

Eventually the subject turned to Sophie. They'd both felt awful leaving her earlier that evening, but she'd in-sisted that she was fine. She and Georgina had gone for a sleepover with some other friends from school. Patrick was aware that what had happened between her and Ned at Christmas had been somewhat overlooked. It didn't help that she was so stoical and had never mentioned it to anyone. They'd all assumed she was tougher than she looked. But Mandy was worried about her.

'She looks terrible, Patrick. Don't you think?'

'Do you reckon she's anorexic?'

'I don't know. She's not eating enough to keep a bird alive, I know that.'

Patrick was furious. With himself and the rest of his family. They were all so wrapped up in themselves they'd forgotten about poor old Sophie and her misery. What was Lucy thinking about? She was her mother, for heaven's sake. She was the one who was supposed to be there for her when things went wrong. But Lucy had her own problems. She was exhausted from driving back and forth to the hospital to see Mickey, as well as running the house and looking after the horses.

There was only one cure for Sophie that he could think of. A fifteen-stone goon not a million miles from their own doorstep. He'd caused Sophie's problems in the first place. He could bloody well solve them. Patrick had enough faith in his friend to know he could do it. As the second hand on his watch raced towards midnight, he resolved to sort out his sister. She deserved to be as happy as he was. The bells rang out midnight and he reached out to stroke Mandy's cheek. She held his hand against her face. Just touching each other was enough; it was all they needed.

'Happy New Year,' said Patrick, and he hoped he spoke for all of them when he said it.

23

A couple of weeks later, after the girls had gone back to school, Patrick was biding his time until he found the perfect opportunity to implement his plan. It arrived one Saturday afternoon. Sophie had gone on from school to see a film with some friends in Cheltenham and Patrick had promised to pick her up. He got on the phone.

'Ned. Big favour time. There's no one to collect Sophie from the cinema. Mum's taken Dad to the hospital for physio and I've got to sort something out at the brewery. Can you get her for me?' May God strike him dead for lying, but he was pretty certain it would do the trick.

Ned opened the door of his Mini Cooper and groaned. He couldn't expect Sophie to travel in it – there was thick mud all over the floors, Jack Russell hairs all over the seats, fag ends spilling out of the ashtray, baler twine, hay, empty Mars Bar wrappers and, most shamefully of all, two blobs of chewing gum stuck to the dash. He attempted a perfunctory valeting, then gave up and compromised by pinching his mother's best picnic rug and spreading it over the passenger seat. He then gave the interior a thorough squirt with some air freshener and hoped for the best – it was nearly five and Sophie was due out at quarter to six.

He gunned off down the drive at top speed, swerving to avoid the potholes like some mad teenager let loose on the dodgems, until he came out on to the main road and turned left.

Patrick, the crafty sod, hadn't given him any time to think or say no, had just told him it was an emergency, Ned was so used to jumping when his friend said jump it was only now that he realized he and Sophie were going to come face to face for the first time since his dreadful faux pas and he didn't have a clue what he was going to say, or indeed how she was likely to react. All he knew was that he was being thrown in at the deep end and that he cared very, very much what the outcome was. He didn't want to blow it. He lit a fag to calm his nerves, then remembered that Sophie got car sick and chucked it out the window.

He arrived at the cinema and searched through the crowds for any sign of her. He didn't want her to think she'd been abandoned. She was just coming through the swing door and at first Ned didn't recognize her. She had on a pair of jeans and a bright pink cotton knit sweater that barely covered her midriff. Her skin seemed almost blue; her eyes were huge and hollow with dark rings underneath. She stopped dead when she saw Ned. He smiled as widely as his nerves would allow him.

'Patrick asked me to pick you up.'

'Oh.'

She looked like a startled woodland creature about to bound off into the undergrowth. Ned screwed up all his courage and walked towards her.

'Soph – I've been dying to speak to you for ages. There's so much I want to say – but I don't know what to say . . .' He faltered. Sophie said nothing, either to discourage or encourage him. But at least she hadn't run away, so he ploughed on.

'I need to explain about . . .' He couldn't quite bring himself to say lovebite, but he knew she knew what he meant. 'When I saw you at the dance you seemed so out of reach. I didn't think I had a hope in hell. I thought you'd grown out of me. And I was gutted. The bottom line is I got totally out of it and slept with Mayday. I should never have done it, I know that, but I'm a bloke. A stupid bloke at that. And I know everyone probably says it when they get caught out, but it didn't mean anything.'

Sophie looked as if she had half a mind to run away, but she didn't seem to have the strength. Ned walked over and gently took her bag off her. He put it on the floor and put his hands on her shoulders. She trembled at his touch. He pulled her to him – it was now or never. After all, he'd got nothing to lose.

'I've been a total plonker. All I can say is I'm sorry. And I want you to forgive me. Because . . .' Ned took in a huge breath. He'd never said this before to anyone in his life. 'I love you.'

There was a moment when she tensed, as if ready to take flight, but then she relaxed, fell against his chest in submission, capitulation, and wrapped her arms round his waist. She didn't need to say anything. Her actions spoke louder than any words of forgiveness.

Ned wrapped his huge arms round her and squeezed her tight. He could feel her ribs, her shoulder blades, through her sweater, as undernourished as an orphaned lamb who wouldn't feed and who Ned knew from experience would finally give up the fight for life and perish. He wasn't going to let her go the same way. He was going to build her up, get the roses back in her cheeks and the light back in her eyes.

They stood that way for some moments, Ned grinning his silly head off, bursting with love and pride. Sophie finally lifted her head from his shoulder and looked at him shyly. She was smiling too.

Ten minutes later, Ned swung into a pub car park.

He sat down and ordered sausage and mash for both of them. Sophie protested that she wanted a salad, but he put his foot down.

'You need to put some weight back on. You look dreadful. Like a bag of bones.'

Sophie was shocked. The only good thing that had happened lately was that she had got down to under nine stone and was practically a size ten.

'I'm serious,' Ned continued. 'It doesn't suit you. You look ill. I want the old Sophie back—'

'You mean the fat one—'

'You weren't fat. You were just right. Cuddly. Men like something to get hold of. At least I do. If I gave you a hug right now, you'd snap.'

Sophie stared at him with big eyes.

'Try it.'

'What?'

'Try it. Hug me. I won't snap, I promise.'

Ned didn't need any excuse. He scooped her up for the tenth time in half an hour and she nestled in to him. Ned had ignited a little warm glow inside her that was gradually thawing out the frozen feeling she'd had for the past few weeks, since Christmas Day, since her father's accident. She found she no longer craved the empty hollowness

393

she had been focusing on lately. Denying herself food had given her something to think about, had stopped her from brooding on her problems, and she'd revelled in her weight loss. But now she realized she was just starving hungry. She devoured her sausage and mash. And when the barmaid came to clear their plates and asked if they'd like dessert, she ordered bread and butter pudding.

Ned smothered it with cream when it arrived, and she protested out of habit. But she was laughing while he spooned it into her mouth, pretending to force-feed her like a reluctant child, and he knew things hadn't gone too far, that she hadn't toppled over the edge. He'd come to her rescue just in time.

James had popped into Budgens for some unsalted butter and a pot of Greek yoghurt when he saw Georgina filling up a trolley. He went to greet his niece.

'Georgie.'

'Hi, James.' She carried on filling up the trolley. She seemed subdued, not herself at all.

'Is everything OK?'

'No, it bloody isn't.'

James flinched. Georgina was known for being blunt, but she wasn't usually rude.

'What is it?'

To his horror, she burst into tears in the middle of the aisle. Noisy, childish sobs that drew attention to both of them.

'Georgie – for heaven's sake . . .'

'It's awful at home. Mum and Dad aren't speaking. It's horrible. Mum just makes bitchy remarks and Dad just sits there. And Mum can't even be bothered to do the shopping.

I got back from school at lunchtime and there was nothing to eat. I had to get Patrick to bring me here—'

She snivelled into his chest. James did his best to comfort her.

'Listen, Georgie. It's been a shock for everyone. I expect your dad's a bit depressed after his accident. And it's been a strain for your mum.'

'She doesn't care about Dad. I can tell.'

'Of course she does.'

'I'm going to ask if I can board. Then I won't have to sit there while they snipe at each other.'

James pressed his lips together. This wasn't how it was supposed to be. Georgina had her GCSEs in a few months' time. She needed love and support, not the breakdown of her family unit. He wiped her tears, helped her get her shopping together and pack it into the back of the Defender, then waited for Patrick to come back. He spoke to his nephew *sotto voce*.

'I gather things are pretty grim chez vous?'

Patrick shrugged.

'I'm out most of the time, to be honest. Or working. But it's not good, no.'

James said nothing, just patted Patrick on the shoulder as he got into the car.

James waited till Patrick had driven off, then phoned Honeycote on his mobile. Luckily for him Lucy answered.

'We need to speak. Now.'

'I'm about to cook supper.'

'No, you're not. I've just found Georgina in Budgens doing the bloody weekly shop, Lucy. Meet me at home in ten minutes.'

He hung up before Lucy could contradict. She stared at the receiver, her stomach churning. She'd deliberately avoided James since Mickey's accident. They'd come into contact with other people around, of course, but she hadn't come face to face with him to discuss what had gone on between them. She couldn't put it off any longer.

She had a feeling that whatever happened next, it was going to be a turning point. It filled her with a mixture of dread and relief. She knew things couldn't carry on the way they had been. She wasn't herself at all. She had no interest in anything; she could barely manage to get a meal on the table, and if it hadn't been for the children she wouldn't even have managed that. She just couldn't be bothered, and although she did next to nothing she felt tired all the time. And what was worst was that she was snappy, not just with Mickey, who deserved it, but with everyone, as if she had permanent PMT. And every time she heard herself snipe, she shrivelled up inside. She couldn't live with herself like this for the rest of her life, but she wasn't sure how to move on. She hurried out to her car, without telling Mickey where she was going.

James didn't even bother to offer Lucy a drink. He wanted to get straight on with what he had to say.

'For God's sake, Lucy. You've got to sort yourself out. Your whole family's being affected. Georgina was practically having a nervous breakdown in Budgens. She'll flunk her exams at this rate. You've got to snap out of it. There's no point in everyone wallowing in misery. Either make it up with Mickey and bloody well be happy. Or come and live with me.'

'You can't give me an ultimatum like that.'

'Of course I can.'

'It's none of your business.'

'Yes, it is. Because I love you, Lucy—'

Lucy put her hands up as if to fend him off.

'Please, James. I can't take emotional blackmail on top of everything else.'

'Hang on a minute. I haven't finished yet. I love you, but I also love Patrick and Sophie and Georgina. And, dare I say it, Mickey. But it's up to you, Lucy. You're the only one who can decide which way it's going to go. I know I'm forcing you into a corner, but there's too much at stake to sit there and watch while everyone's happiness goes down the plughole. You've got to make a decision.'

It was the most impassioned speech James had ever made in his life, and he had to hold his hands behind his back to stop them shaking. He looked at Lucy. She looked back at him defiantly.

'So it's you or Mickey? That's what you're saying?'

'I suppose so.'

Lucy contemplated going to live with James for a moment. She counted up the people it would affect if she did. Mickey, Sophie, Patrick, Georgina . . . And she didn't even know if she'd be happy with him. It would be a huge risk.

Whereas she thought she could be happy again with Mickey. She had been for twenty years, after all. She was just going to have to bite the bullet and forgive him. Move on. James was right. There was no point in everyone suffering. And she certainly couldn't go on with things the way they were. Life was dreary; a grinding emotional tedium that set her teeth on edge. The atmosphere in the house of late had been so oppressive that she couldn't even face guests; she couldn't be bothered to put on a brave face. She woke each day with a dull ache in her heart and went to bed at night desperate for sleep, her only escape. She didn't suppose it was any different for Mickey.

James clenched his fists while she turned things over in her mind, battling with himself to keep his distance. If he touched her, he'd be lost. Every inch of him wanted to sink to his knees in front of her and beg. Finally she turned to him with a sigh.

'I couldn't do it, James. I've got to stay.'

He sighed.

'Of course you have. I know that. But in that case, please make it up.'

Lucy moved towards him. He flinched inwardly: he didn't want physical contact with her. He didn't want her sympathy. So he said what he'd sworn to himself he wouldn't, just to keep her at arm's length. 'And don't forget – you're guilty too. You wouldn't have much of a leg to stand on if Mickey found out about us.'

Lucy looked at him sharply. Was that a threat? Would he ever tell his brother? She thought not; he'd have nothing to gain. But he certainly had a point.

James watched her go sadly. He couldn't deny that he'd had the tiniest pinprick of hope that she might chose him over her life at Honeycote. But he hadn't been surprised when she hadn't. Moreover, he was gracious enough to be able to hand her back to her family without protest; he wasn't so arrogant as to expect their happiness to be sacrificed for his sake. Yet again, he was doing the gentlemanly thing.

Lucy got back from her confrontation with James feeling utterly drained. As she walked back into the kitchen, Sophie flew into her arms, eyes shining.

'What is it?'

'It's Ned. We've made it up. He's taking me out clubbing tonight.' She looked at her mum anxiously. 'If that's OK? Patrick and Mandy are coming as well.'

'Of course it's OK, darling.'

Sophie was bubbling over with excitement and panic. 'What am I going to wear?'

Lucy spent the next half-hour going through Sophie's wardrobe with her, giggling and trying things on. She realized it was the first time she'd had fun this year; the first time she'd laughed. And as she saw the four of them off to Cheltenham, the girls looking incredibly glamorous and the boys each slightly anxious, but trying not to show it, she felt a pang of shame.

James was right. There was no point in her and Mickey spending the rest of their lives wallowing in misery. She allowed her imagination to wander as far as Sophie and Ned's wedding, she and Mickey sniping all the way to the church, undermining everything marriage stood for. Wedding vows might be a cliché, but they were true.

She walked into the sitting room. Mickey was in there watching some trashy Saturday evening game show. He looked up at her. He'd given up trying to smile at her lately; it only made her retreat further into herself. But to his astonishment she smiled at him. Very tentatively, and it didn't quite reach her eyes, but it was a start.

'We need to talk,' she said. 'We can't go on like this.' Tears sprang into her eyes. 'We need to . . .'

She could hardly get the words out.

'I don't want to live like this any more.'

Mickey swallowed. He wasn't sure what she was going

to say. Was she going to kick him out? Ask for a divorce? She'd got grounds. Unreasonable behaviour. Adultery. Take your pick.

'So what do you want?' His mouth was dry, but he thought he'd do the honourable thing for once. 'If you want a divorce—'

To his surprise, she looked at him horrified. An icy trickle ran down her spine. Perhaps that was what he wanted. Perhaps Mickey had been unhappy all this time. Perhaps it wasn't her choice at all, and he wanted out. She spoke in a whisper.

'Is that what you want?'

'My God, no!'

Mickey grabbed her.

'I want us back again. You and me. The way it used to be.'

He squeezed her so tight it hurt. For a moment she resisted, every muscle in her body rigid with tension. She'd spent so much time blocking him out lately that it went against the grain for her to capitulate. But as she felt the strength of his arms around her, and smelt his warm, familiar smell, she realized that all she wanted was to be held by him, for all the horrors of the past few weeks to recede and for the healing to begin. She relaxed, and as he hugged her to him even more tightly, she began to cry. She'd wept bitter tears on her own before now, but she hadn't been able to share them with him. The relief was enormous.

Eventually her tears subsided and she found she was able to snuggle into him.

'So – what do we do? Forget any of this ever happened?' Mickey knew he was being a tad optimistic.

'No. We can't do that.' She wiped her eyes. 'We can't forget it. Because that's the only way we can make sure it doesn't happen again.'

So they talked. And Mickey was surprised to find that what Lucy had found even more hurtful than his adultery was the fact he'd kept his problems a secret from her; that he hadn't been able to confide in her how desperate things had become. She told him that she'd felt a fool when the truth had come out, like some dippy little wife who couldn't be trusted. Mickey insisted that he'd just wanted to protect her, but Lucy insisted she didn't want to be protected. Perhaps if he'd been honest with her from the start, things might have turned out differently.

By the end of the evening, they had made a pact. From that day on, they would have no secrets from each other. And although both of them knew that it wouldn't be easy, that there would be sticky moments, at least they had a clean slate.

Most important of all, they both agreed, was that they had to trust each other. For what was a marriage without trust?

When Sophie, Patrick, Mandy and Ned came back at two in the morning after a tour of all the clubs in Cheltenham, they found Mickey and Lucy fast asleep on the sofa in front of the telly, which was still blaring. Lucy's head was on Mickey's shoulder and Pokey was at their feet. Sophie tucked a rug round the pair, and the four of them sneaked off to compare notes on their evening, none of them voicing the relief they felt that things were obviously going to be all right.

24

By mid February, there was a firm strategy in place at the brewery. A board meeting was held, where Patrick gave a very effective presentation outlining plans for each of the pubs. He'd produced a concise ream of graphs and pie charts illustrating sales targets, profit and loss margins, best and worst-case scenarios that made Cowley beam from ear to ear and which Mickey was surprised to find he understood.

Patrick was thriving under Keith's guidance. He'd taken up every challenge that was set him, and found that once he had started to look at ways of maximizing both efficiency and profit at the brewery, he was fired up with enthusiasm and full of inspiration. It was wonderful to be able to get his teeth into it at last. He couldn't blame his father for keeping him at arm's length all that time. He obviously hadn't wanted Patrick to get at the truth. But now it was all out in the open, Patrick let his imagination run riot, and found a mentor in Keith. Together they went to visit all of the tied houses, and it was up to Patrick to compile a report on each, summing up its strengths and weaknesses and suggesting what direction should be taken. At the same time, Patrick took it upon himself to visit rival pubs, and compiled a substantial document outlining the local competition, what worked, what didn't and why.

What Keith had found most astonishing was that there was no computer system in place at the brewery. It meant the company was ripe for pilfering. Patrick was shocked that he could even suggest it, but Keith told him not to be so naive. He wasn't pointing any fingers, but the place was probably haemorrhaging beer and spirits and soft drinks – all the wet goods that the brewery supplied to its tied houses. People had light fingers and if you offered it to them on a plate, they came to consider it a perk of the job. But a computer system and rigid stock control would soon put a stop to that. By the end of the meeting, they'd agreed to find quotes for the installation of a state-of-the-art computer system, which each of the tied houses was to be linked to.

Keith also felt strongly that the next step was to put a sales team in place, in order to increase their off-sales. Even if they boosted their tied trade by fifty per cent, which wouldn't come without considerable investment in the first place, they couldn't afford to ignore other sources of revenue. Sales and Marketing. That was what it was all about.

Mickey agreed. And he thought he knew just the person to mastermind the project. He told Keith about Caroline.

'She works as an ad manager for a local paper. But she's got her head screwed on, I can tell you.'

He showed Keith the marketing plan Caroline had drawn up. It seemed an eternity away. But the strategy held up. Keith smiled as he recognized several key points from Patrick's original pitch, but he didn't give anything away. Mickey persisted.

'She knows what the brewery's all about. She knows the area. She works bloody hard. James was always complaining that she had to work late.'

'Do you think she'll want to come and work for us?'

'I'll talk to her.'

Mickey was desperate to feel involved again. He'd been to visit the brewery a few times, but found himself exhausted. The consultants had warned him that his recovery would be slow and it was deeply frustrating. He wanted to put into practice all his resolutions, but the highlight of his day at the moment was trying to solve the conundrum on *Countdown*.

He knew Caroline was the right person for the job. He remembered her passion and enthusiasm the day she'd tried to help him out. If getting her on board was the only contribution he could make at the moment, he'd do everything in his power.

Caroline had gone back to Evesham to lick her wounds. Her treatment at the hands of the various Liddiards had shocked and subdued her. She kept her head down, worked hard, met her targets. And she grovelled to Ian, the owner of the yard where she kept Demelza. First, she apologized for her appalling behaviour on Boxing Day, then she offered to sell him Demelza. That way she could pay off her debts, both for her livery and her various credit cards, and have a bit left over. She was going to put it towards her Australia fund. She needed to get away, to travel. She was nearly thirty and she hadn't seen anything of the world. Perhaps life in another hemisphere would restore her faith in human nature.

So when she got a phone call from Mickey, she was

extremely wary. She listened as he outlined what he wanted from her: to put a marketing strategy in place and recruit a sales team.

'I know you're the girl for the job.'

Caroline snorted.

'After the way your brother and your son treated me? Why should I, Mickey? They treated me like shit.'

'This would be for me. Please, Caroline. I'm a prisoner in my own home. I need someone like you in there, batting for me. Someone I can trust.'

The old Liddiard charm and flattery oozed down the phone wire. By the end of the conversation, they'd reached a compromise. She was owed a couple of weeks' holiday, so she'd use that in the first instance just to test the water. She wasn't going to burn her bridges to come and work for Honeycote Ales. In return, she demanded two things. A hefty fee, which Mickey was going to have to finalize with Keith, but which would buy her a flight to Sydney. And an apology from Patrick. Both of which she got.

In certain quiet moments at the bank, Graham Cowley thought that God probably knew exactly what he'd been doing when he'd sent Mickey Liddiard crashing into that wall. It looked as if things really were going to turn out for the best at Honeycote Ales, and he was probably more pleased than anyone, as it had saved him from the thoroughly unpleasant task of calling in a loan. That was something he always hated doing, but he'd had a special place in his heart for the brewery and even though the Liddiards could be an ungrateful and arrogant bunch at times, they were also charming and eminently forgivable on both counts. It belonged in their hands.

The most pleasant surprise to him had been how well Patrick had turned out. He'd written him off as an overprivileged young oaf with more looks than brains, who was afraid of getting his hands dirty. But it showed just how wrong you could be. Cowley looked upon it as a lesson – it was never too late to learn in this business.

What surprised him even more, however, was that Lawrence Oakley hadn't retaliated after Cowley had rejected his plans out of hand. He wasn't the type to take no for an answer. At the very least Cowley had expected him to move his accounts elsewhere, but he hadn't. In fact, he'd been in to see Cowley on a couple of matters, asking him for advice. And he hadn't mentioned Honeycote Ales at all. Yet again it proved that you shouldn't make sweeping judgements.

The truth was, Lawrence had been chilled and chastened when he heard about Mickey's accident. For several days after his meeting with Cowley, he had prowled around the garden centre in a furious rage, making his employees' lives more miserable than ever. He'd worked out a plan to go over Cowley's head: he'd bloody well make sure that if he didn't lose his job over this one his chances of promotion would certainly be scuppered.

But somehow once he heard about the accident the edge went off his desire for revenge. What was the point of getting back at someone who to all intents and purposes was lying in hospital, who had nearly died? It would give him no satisfaction at all now to pull the rug out from under Mickey's feet. It would do nothing but make him look bad.

He wondered why that bothered him all of a sudden. Lawrence had never really cared what people thought of him, as long as they did what he wanted. Why was he getting a conscience at this stage in his life?

Deep down he knew it was because even if he did get revenge on Mickey, it wouldn't make him any happier. Because he suspected that Mickey wasn't really to blame. Lawrence could never escape from the fact that he had behaved appallingly towards Kay by hiding the truth from her about his infertility. Perhaps she had minded being childless more than she had admitted. Perhaps she'd had herself checked out on the quiet, just as he had, and discovered the fault must lie with Lawrence. Then, unable to confront him because the shutters were down, maybe she'd searched for a father elsewhere. And perhaps Mickey Liddiard had taken pity on her, had been happy to oblige . . .

He knew he was making allowances. He was pretty sure Kay had been with Mickey for the thrill. But it was only now, when the pang for fatherhood was so sharp, that he realized the injustice he had done his wife. They should have discussed it, found a way of getting round the problem together. There were miracles every day in the paper. And it wasn't as if he hadn't had the cash for the best treatment.

But he'd been a coward. And now it was too late.

So Lawrence threw himself into enjoying life with Kelly. Gradually they came out as an item. He tried not to play Professor Higgins to her Eliza Doolittle, but it was fun taking her to the best hotels and restaurants, teaching her about the good things in life, and she was a willing enough pupil. In return she made him laugh, kept him in touch with his younger side, stopped him taking himself too seriously. And, of course, showed him all the tricks she'd learned from *Cosmo*, which were proving pretty addictive.

But Lawrence couldn't deny that his relationship with Kelly was like gorging on a bar of chocolate – thoroughly enjoyable, but not particularly substantial. Besides, the prospect of taking the relationship any further was ridiculous. He certainly couldn't marry her. He was an empty vessel. He couldn't deprive another woman of the gift of motherhood.

Kay spent several weeks thinking and sleeping and putting on pounds courtesy of both her pregnancy and her mother's cooking, before deciding she couldn't stay under her parents' roof indefinitely. Despite the newfound cosy relationship she had with them, the clucking and the concern got too much at times, though it was becoming increasingly appreciated as her legs began to ache with the weight she was carrying.

She also knew that, although Lawrence had been generous, all things considered, a quarter of a million wasn't going to last long. She'd need to get a job. And she wanted it to be part-time. She wasn't going to abandon her baby from eight o'clock in the morning till six at night five days a week. She did her maths carefully. She'd give herself six months after the birth, to get back into shape and to get into some sort of routine, then she'd have to find herself work. By which time she would have familiarized herself with the local property market. She was fairly confident that she could walk back into being a negotiator – she'd been successful before and it wasn't a job where you necessarily needed youth on your side. Just a few well-chosen suits and an air of confidence.

In the meantime, she needed to find herself somewhere to live. She knew she had to make good her escape before the baby arrived, or she'd be sunk. She'd find somewhere within fifteen minutes' drive of her parents. That wasn't too close for comfort but close enough if she needed them. Or vice versa. Thus she began her search.

She found a tiny little house that was perfect. Ridiculously small for the price, but anything within spitting distance of the Thames was over the top. And it wasn't as if she needed much room. Two bedrooms. A kitchen. A living room. And a decent bathroom. She put in a cash offer, conditional upon exchanging within four weeks. It was pushing it, but she had the upper hand.

The moment she had the key she took her parents to see it. They couldn't understand why she wanted to move away, but they understood it was a fait accompli. Immediately her father set to work putting up shelves and Sylvia took her to a discount fabric warehouse to choose some soft furnishings. She'd run up some curtains for her in a trice.

Kay found it strangely enjoyable, shopping with her mother for nursery items. They settled on a soft creamy-yellow paint for the nursery walls. Kay found it hard to suppress a hysterical giggle when she found herself stencilling ducks and bunny rabbits around the room. Her dad found a remnant of soft cream carpet, which he put down, and built her a changing station out of MDF, so horrified was he by their price. Kay added some stencils to that as well, not believing that she was quite the same person. In fact, sometimes she could pretend she wasn't Mrs Kay Oakley at all. She didn't quite know who she was, but once her baby had arrived, she was sure she'd find out.

25

James had been to the brewery to sign yet another sheaf of the papers that were emanating from the reshuffle. He slipped out of the office and was about to go down the steps when he spied Caroline. She was just coming out of the Portakabin that had been put in place to hold the sales office while renovations were carried out in the old stable block. He halted momentarily in the doorway. He hadn't seen her since the day he'd booted her out of Denham House, though he knew she was working at the brewery. And doing very well, by all accounts. Mickey was hoping she would hand in her notice at the paper and come to work full time.

James watched her from afar. As her work was largely on the phone and the weather was still chilly, she was dressed in casual clothing. Tight jeans, a tight sweater and high boots: she dressed as ever to bring out her good points. Her curls were bound into a thick plait down her back, and she pushed her arms into a duckdown quilted jacket. He admired the swell of her breasts just before they disappeared under the zip and shivered at the memory of them on his bare chest. She tucked her chin into the collar and made her way over to the paddock, where Toby was waiting patiently for his nightly fuss.

James watched as she rubbed at the old horse's nose, fondling his ears roughly and scratching his poll. Toby butted back at her, loving the attention. He had little these days. She put her long arms round his neck and nuzzled him to her. James wondered if Caroline herself had any attention these days, and if so from whom. He didn't flatter himself enough to think that she had taken a vow of celibacy after his unceremonious dismissal.

He'd had time to think over the past few weeks. He and Lucy seemed to have an unspoken agreement that they avoided each other, that they never spoke about what had happened between them. She seemed to have taken what he'd said on board and he was relieved. He didn't want to feel responsible for bringing down an entire family. But now his life felt rather empty, because he no longer lived in hope. Before he had always had the hint of promise to spur him on.

He was resigned to the fact that he would never find another woman to love as fiercely and passionately, albeit secretly, as he did Lucy, and he was on a mission to fill the large hole she'd left in his heart. He'd spent quite a bit of time in London lately, trying to forget her. But the jaded blondes that were paraded in front of him by friends determined on matchmaking bored him rigid. They all seemed intent on finding out the extent of his bank balance, or shovelling up cocaine in the bathroom. They were deeply, deeply dull.

He didn't think he was asking for much. The only real prerequisite in any potential girlfriend was that she had to be so unlike Lucy he would never be reminded of what he was missing. And as he watched Caroline, he thought she couldn't be less like her. She was loud, extrovert, she couldn't cook to save her life and she was ambitious. The complete antithesis of the woman he loved. Add to that the fact that he actually quite liked her company, her spirit. She was perfect.

He'd got a bit of ground to make up first, though.

He walked up behind Caroline as she fed Toby a couple of Polos.

'You spoil him.'

She looked at him defiantly.

'Someone's got to.'

'I owe you an apology, Caroline. I behaved shabbily.'

Caroline couldn't help but smile. Only James could come up with an expression like 'shabbily'.

'You behaved like a total arse.' Caroline fed Toby another Polo.

'Will you come out to dinner? To show no hard feelings.'

Half of Caroline screamed no, she bloody well wouldn't – why should she let him get away with it? He'd treated her appallingly. He'd have to do better than that to earn her forgiveness. But the other half thought about the alternative – yet another night in front of the telly with a glass or three of Lambrusco, some dried-up old pitta bread and half a tub of hummus.

Later that evening they shared a table for two in the corner of the Knowing Pig, a local restaurant tipped for a Michelin star that served food fit for a seduction and wines to match. Caroline had gone home, showered, changed and chosen her outfit very carefully. She wore a double-breasted black velvet jacket with a barely visible zebra-skin skirt underneath and knee-length black patent boots with spiky, spiky heels. Men always looked at them and gulped.

She waited until they'd scraped up the last remnants of their crème brûlée before tackling the issue. She hoped the two bottles of wine they'd consumed would make James less likely to lie. *In vino veritas* . . .

'So – did you and Lucy . . . ?'

'Did me and Lucy what?'

Caroline rolled her eyes.

'Play dominoes. What do you think?'

James wasn't going to make it easy for her.

'What do *you* think?'

'I think you shagged the arse off each other.'

James smiled infuriatingly.

'Wrong.'

'You would say that, wouldn't you? I mean, you're trying to get back into my knickers, aren't you? So you're not going to admit getting into hers.'

Caroline leaned forward with a mischievous smile. James caught a glimpse of her cantilevered cleavage, encased in black lace. He swirled the last golden drops of pudding wine round in his glass.

'Caroline, the poor woman had just found out her husband had been unfaithful. She was devastated. The last thing on her mind was sex. Especially with her own brother-in-law. Honestly, your imagination runs wild.'

He smiled suggestively at her.

'You should put it to better use.'

Caroline drew herself up with dignity. She wasn't going to let him get away with it that easily.

'So why did you boot me out like that? On bloody Boxing Day, for God's sake.'

'I've always felt very protective of Lucy. Because I know exactly what my brother's like. I feel responsible for him in a way. Seeing what he'd done to her ripped me apart. I had to hold her hand through the whole thing. And I couldn't really expect you to understand.' James put a hand over Caroline's. She was about to snatch it away indignantly, but he pressed down on it urgently. He looked her in the eye. 'I made a big mistake. I'm sorry. Like you said, I was a total . . . shit. And I wouldn't blame you if you told me to take a running jump, but I'd like to start again.'

Caroline had forgotten quite how horny good food and good wine made her feel. And how utterly delicious and seductive James's bedroom was, with its flickering candles, its scented sheets, its hundreds of silk pillows and velvet cushions and the fur throw that he teased her was real wolf but she knew was fake, though it made her feel like Julie Christie in *Doctor Zhivago* just the same. And as James trickled Jo Malone body oil on to her breasts, she realized she'd been celibate since before Christmas. She didn't know if absence did make the heart grow fonder, but it definitely made the sex more explosive.

Afterwards, as they lay in an exhausted, tangled heap, she told him about selling Demelza and cried, because she missed her, and James began to understand that Caroline wasn't as tough as she pretended. He kissed away her tears and took her again, gently this time, and she cried again. And James realized that for the first time in years he'd made love to a woman without pretending it was Lucy.

Maybe, just maybe, he was cured.

*

Two weeks later, Caroline gave in her notice at the paper, came on board officially at Honeycote Ales, abandoned her cold and soulless starter home and moved into Denham House. One lazy Sunday morning James leaned over to her bedside table. She thought he was going to turn the radio on to listen to *The Archers* omnibus, but he was fiddling about in the drawer. Eventually he found what he was looking for.

A box. And inside the box, a ring. And in the ring, a socking great emerald that matched Caroline's eyes. Not so large as to be tasteless, of course. It was just right. Just like everything James chose. And it fitted her finger perfectly. He'd waited for her to say yes, before trying it on.

Bloody hell. She was going to be Mrs Liddiard. Mrs Caroline Liddiard, of Denham House, Eldenbury.

James asked everyone to brunch at Denham House a week later. He cooked a huge pile of pancakes with maple syrup and crispy bacon, served with champagne and cranberry juice.

After everyone had eaten their fill, he took his place by the fire and asked them all to charge their glasses. He had an announcement. He and Caroline were to be married at Honeycote Church in two months' time. Caroline stood next to him and blushed prettily. Everyone cheered and agreed that a wedding was just what was needed; it was something to look forward to. Sophie and Georgina were to be bridesmaids. Mickey was to be best man. And if Lucy looked a little pale when the announcement was made, no one mentioned it.

*

Back at home that afternoon, Sophie and Georgina offered to make tea while Lucy and Mickey went into the drawing room. There seemed to be a chill in the air, so Lucy laid a fire. Mickey leaned against the fireplace and chortled.

'Well, that was a turn up for the books, eh? Good old James. I didn't think he had it in him. I thought he was destined to be a bachelor for the rest of his life.'

Lucy didn't answer. She twisted up a strip of newspaper and stuffed it under some logs. Mickey rattled on.

'I'm sure they'll be happy. You know what they say, opposites attract. And Caroline's a good sort underneath. Heart of gold.'

Lucy faced the fireplace, clenching her fists and gritting her teeth. It took all her self-control not to rip the logs out of the fireplace and hurl them at him. If only he knew what she'd given up to be with him; what a sacrifice she'd made. Still, it had been her own choice, her decision made of her own free will.

They had their amnesty, their pact, but it hadn't been easy. Even though he was trying so desperately hard to be a good patient, Lucy knew Mickey got depressed, because of the pain and the slowness of his recovery and the frustration of not being able to do all the things he wanted. But he bore it all with a forced air of cheerfulness and optimism that she sometimes found wearing. They'd tried to make love, too, and that had been a disaster. It wasn't surprising, really, given the stress his body had suffered. Mickey, humiliated, had said give it time. Lucy had reassured him, kissed him and fallen asleep in his arms, but had to admit she'd been rather relieved.

Lucy lit a match. Her hand was shaking. She knew it

was now or never. She could turn to Mickey; tell him everything. Tell him what she'd sacrificed to stay with him. Tell him he'd destroyed all her trust and respect with his sordid affair. Tell him she could pick up the phone to James and he'd break off his engagement with Caroline on the spot just to be with her.

But of course she didn't. Her hand shook and she dropped the match on the hearth.

'Here – let me do it.' Mickey came over. Lucy turned away quickly, but not before he saw a tear on her cheek. She brushed it away and he said nothing, just busied himself lighting the fire. Sophie and Georgina burst in, carrying a tray of tea, laughing.

'Georgina says we'll have to wear turquoise polyester—'

'Or mauve. Probably mauve.'

Lucy turned to face them, fully composed. She smiled.

'Nonsense. I'm sure Caroline will let you choose what you want.'

'Do you think she's pregnant?' Georgina was gloriously blunt sometimes. 'Just think – we'll have cousins. Think of the money we could get for babysitting.'

'Don't be so mercenary. You should do it for nothing if they're relatives,' protested Sophie, who didn't have a calculating streak in her.

'You and Ned can. You can snog on the sofa then to your heart's content.'

Sophie thumped her sister good-naturedly. Lucy went to pour the tea. Patrick appeared and sat down near the fire with his dad. They started to chat idly about the brewery. Georgina got out a game of Jenga.

Lucy looked round the room and felt reassured. She'd been right to keep quiet. But as she passed round the cups, she thought it would all be so much easier to bear if only James hadn't looked so bloody happy.

She realized she was being an utter bitch. Behaving like a spoilt brat who wanted all the toys. She couldn't have her cake and eat it. And she did love Mickey, deep down. He was massaging her shoulders now, sensing her tension, and she didn't recoil at his touch. She put her hand on his and smiled up at him.

Running off with James would have been a gamble. Staying at Honeycote was a safe bet. It was hardly a bad option. And Lucy remembered what someone had told her once: that marriage wasn't supposed to be easy . . .

26

At Lilac Cottage, Sylvia had brought round the nursery curtains to hang. Sunlight streamed into the little room. It was an oasis of calm. Kay's old teddy bear lay in the Moses basket, while she sat in a wicker nursing chair by the window, surrounded by plump cushions. Barton Court and Lawrence and Honeycote and Mickey Liddiard could have been a million miles away.

Charlie and Sylvia stood in the doorway proudly. Kay seemed in a world of her own, smiling. Suddenly, she gave a gasp and clutched her stomach. Charlie rushed over, alarmed.

'What is it?'

Sylvia rolled her eyes.

'It's the baby. Very sensible. Waited till everything was ready. You go and get the car, Charlie. Have you got your bag?'

Kay nodded. This was it. Next time she stood in this bedroom, she'd have a baby in her arms. Her very own baby. Tears stung her eyes as she picked up her hospital bag.

As soon as Kay got to the hospital, the pains stopped. She wanted to go home again, but the nurses were worried about her blood pressure. She'd have to stay in. They sent a reluctant Sylvia home, promising to call if anything started. As soon as she'd gone, Kay told them under no circumstances did she want her mother around while she was giving birth. She'd ring her the minute it was all over, but not before. She could manage on her own. The midwife nodded knowingly, didn't bother wasting her breath to contradict. She knew from experience that Mrs Oakley would have her mother at her side in two minutes flat once she got going. She didn't bother to wonder about Mr Oakley. She'd seen too many strange combinations of parents and partners to think it out of the ordinary that there was no male present. In many ways it would make the birth a lot easier. Men either panicked or wanted to take control, while women stayed calm and empathized.

She settled Kay into a side room. There were plenty free that evening and she could see that Kay wasn't the type to benefit from chatting to the other expectant mothers, sharing horror stories about piles and swollen ankles, stretch marks and heartburn. She hooked her up to the foetal heart monitor, then a machine to measure her contractions.

Kay stared fixedly for two hours at the red line, which remained irritatingly constant. There were no significant peaks at all. The midwife had told her to ring the bell if the pattern changed, or if her waters broke, or if she had a 'show', whatever that was. She prodded at an unappetizing ham salad and tried to take in the fact that the odds were this time tomorrow she'd have a baby in her arms. A tiny little being for whom she was wholly responsible. She realized that for the first time in years she had butterflies – not adult nerves, but the sort you got when you were excited as a child, the night before your birthday or the summer holidays. She willed the machine to start showing some kind of action. Whatever happened, she wasn't staying here another night, baby or not. The plastic sheeting under the bed linen made her hot and sweaty, and the bed was too narrow to toss and turn. Someone down the corridor had evidently started their labour – the woman was lowing like a cow and Kay found it most disconcerting.

She asked the nurse for something to read and was brought a couple of dog-eared women's magazines, two years out of date, full of personal problems that made Kay's predicament look like a breeze. Eventually she nodded off, then woke with a start when the magazines crashed to the floor. She realized she'd been dreaming about Lawrence and wondered, just for a moment, what he was doing, before distracting herself with names. She had no idea what to call her baby and hoped that when she saw it something would come to her. Everything she'd thought of so far seemed too twee or too plain. She wanted something unique and special, but not something self-conscious or outlandish. She knew that what you called your child said a lot about your social standing. And of course the child was labelled for life. Her own name was borderline; she'd been tempted on more than one occasion to change it but hadn't been able to decide what to. And there was always the horrible possibility of someone from the past revealing the truth.

In the end the nurse gave her a sleeping tablet, as she'd need all the sleep she could get to save her strength for the next day. Kay reckoned it was probably a vitamin pill in disguise, a placebo to stop her ringing her bell every five minutes, but she did manage to sleep until five o'clock the next morning, when she lay in bed counting the seconds until the cornflake trolley came round. The graph was still boringly static.

At nine o'clock a cheery little consultant appeared and sent her down to delivery to have her waters broken. A midwife descended with a crochet hook and there was a wet puddle, but not a lot else. Singularly unimpressed, Kay just wanted to jump off the table, bed, trolley, whatever it was called, and do a runner. But she couldn't. One end of the lead from the monitor was shoved somewhere unspeakable and the other was hooked up to a machine that emitted reams of graphs which were undecipherable to Kay but evidently made interesting reading to whichever midwife deigned to come in and check up on her at irregular intervals.

Two hours of inactivity later, the consultant reappeared.

'We're going to have to put you on a drip. Get you moving.'

Thank God. Someone was actually going to do something at last. Kay watched with interest as a tube leading from a drip was inserted into the back of her hand. She shivered with excitement and the midwife patted her shoulder, thinking it was fear.

'Oxytocin. This'll get things started, no problem. Won't be long now.'

Never a truer word was spoken. Wham! Kay looked round for the train that had suddenly hit her in the back. She opened her mouth to speak, but found she had no breath. The very life force was being squeezed out of her by a band of metal. She was just starting to panic, when the pain went almost as quickly as it had come.

'What was that?'

'Well done. It was a contraction.'

'It can't have been. There's something wrong—'

The midwife chuckled.

'There'll be another one along in a minute. And they're going to get a lot stronger than that, my love. Remember your breathing.'

After that, the contractions came fast and furious. By the time Sylvia arrived, Kay was swearing like a trooper, livid with rage and fury and spitting with frustration at the midwife, who didn't bat an eyelid at the invectives hurled at her.

'Get me a fucking epidural! I don't care how much I have to pay.'

'It's far too late for that. You're nearly fully dilated. You won't be able to push.'

Two hours later, the pain had reached unbearable proportions. Kay was convinced she was going to die. She reached out wildly and grabbed her mother's hand, squeezing it. Sylvia gritted her teeth to block out the pain. She was finding it hard to cope with her daughter's distress. Kay was sobbing.

'For Christ's sake, get Lawrence on the phone. Get him here now!'

Lawrence would sort things out. He wouldn't let her suffer like this. He'd soon tell that sour-faced midwife what to do. He'd always been there for her; he'd always known what she wanted. They understood each other, Kay and Lawrence. They were meant for each other. Why the hell wasn't he here, just when she needed him most? She was going to die and he didn't realize.

'Are you sure?' Sylvia hesitated. Women said things they didn't mean when they were in the throes of giving birth.

'For God's sake, get him now! Before I bloody die . . .' Kay was becoming exhausted. At this rate, Lawrence would be here just in time for her funeral.

Sylvia nipped out of the delivery suite to use the payphone. She dialled Barton Court hastily. It was on divert to Lawrence's mobile. No answer, just his voice mail kicking in. She hesitated, wondering whether to leave a message and, if so, what, when the midwife popped her head round the door.

'Hurry up! The baby's crowning.'

Sylvia hung up and rushed back in, just in time to hear her daughter screaming blue murder. Four minutes later the midwife looked up with a beaming smile.

'It's a girl.'

Kay, who'd been convinced it was going to be a small horse, lay back with a sigh of relief. Sylvia wiped away a tear. The midwife proffered the bundle, smiling.

'What are you going to call her?'

'Flora.'

Sylvia questioned the wisdom of calling a child after a tub of marge, but thought that Kay would probably come to her senses the next day. It had been a long twelve hours.

The next morning Kay was in a mellow and dreamlike state. She sat with her baby snuggled up in the crook of her arm, a beatific smile on her face. Her mother almost didn't recognize her. She thought perhaps the nurses had administered her some sort of medication, some mind-altering drug. Kay was oblivious to the fact that her hair needed blow-drying. She'd managed a two-minute blast under the shower that morning while the paediatrician checked Flora over, but refused to be out of her daughter's reach any longer than was strictly necessary. Sylvia looked on in amazement as Kay put the baby to her breast without batting an eyelid, and the little doll suckled contentedly.

Sylvia had brought two cardigans and a hat that she'd been knitting in front of *Emmerdale* for the past couple of months. She was alarmed when Kay started crying with gratitude. She was sobbing and smiling simultaneously. Alarmed, Sylvia reached for the buzzer to call a nurse, but Kay shook her head.

'Do you want me to call Lawrence for you?'

Kay's face hardened.

'No.'

'But you were screaming the place down for him yesterday. Come on – it's the best time to bury the hatchet, when a baby's born.'

But as far as Kay was concerned, the matter was closed, and Sylvia was no further in on the secret. But one thing was certain. Yesterday's performance showed a chink in her armour. Kay could protest all she liked, but Sylvia knew her daughter still held a candle for Lawrence. If only she could get to the bottom of it . . . But it was unlikely, and for the time being the most important thing was Flora. Sylvia reached out for her granddaughter, rubbed her back to wind her and tried to decipher any family resemblance.

Nothing. At the moment, she just looked like a baby. A very pretty baby, but that was that.

27

The morning of James and Caroline's wedding, Lucy found Mickey standing in the stable yard in his suit, pale with nerves. He was alternately rehearsing his speech and feeling his pockets for the ring.

'I feel a bit of a hypocrite. I'm not exactly qualified to be a best man, am I?'

'Sssh,' said Lucy. She smoothed his lapels and fiddled with his cravat, until she was satisfied with his appearance. She didn't tell him that if anyone was a hypocrite, she was.

Lawrence slipped into his racing suit and was amazed at how loose the waistband had become since the last time he'd worn it. He knew he'd lost a bit of weight, but not that much. Since Kay had gone he'd lost interest in food, unless he was taking Kelly out, when he made the effort to feign an appetite out of politeness. Not that Kay had ever been a great cook, but she did a weekly Marks & Spencer shop that meant the fridge and freezer always used to be full of tempting nibbles and snacks. Now Lawrence filled up from the Spar shop attached to the garage on the main road, or the post office. Eating was a chore rather than a pleasure. He managed a piece of toast for breakfast, then grabbed some soup or a jacket potato from the garden centre café at lunch. He could sometimes be tempted into a piece of carrot cake or a brownie at teatime, if his manageress nagged him, but more often than not he fell into bed at night without bothering with supper.

He tied his tie with a flourish, found his racing binoculars, checked his wallet for cash and headed out for the car. He and Kelly were going to the races. Some friends had a box at Cheltenham and had asked them to join them for the afternoon. The invitation had come as a relief to Lawrence. He didn't want to be around Honeycote while the wedding of the year was taking place. Given another set of circumstances, he felt sure that he and Kay would be getting ready as guests, that they would have been asked to provide the wedding flowers . . .

Something else was bothering him. His mobile had rung yesterday, but he hadn't recognized the number, so he hadn't bothered answering. He hated unsolicited calls. But curiosity had got the better of him when he'd got home and he'd traced the code. Slough. It had been someone calling from Slough. And there was only one person he knew who had any connections with Slough whatsoever.

He tortured himself wondering if it was her, and if so what she wanted. Then he told himself to forget it, if it was that important she'd phone back . . .

As he approached the Honeycote Arms, something unusual caught his eye. A beautiful dark green Lagonda was pulled up on the car park. It was in concourse condition, the paintwork shining like glass, the leatherwork buffed and gleaming. A huge cream rosette was tied to the front, with two ribbons crossing the bonnet either side. It must be on its way to pick up Caroline, thought Lawrence, and felt a pang of envy at the optimism she and James would be feeling this morning. He watched as a young man with muscular forearms pulled up the bonnet by its brass handle, checking the oil and the water with care. He was in his early twenties, dressed in a chauffeur's uniform with shining boots, his dirty-blond hair slicked back behind his ears. He looked the embodiment of every woman's fantasy: servile yet arrogant. Lawrence envied him his youth, his strength, his beauty, then consoled himself by thinking he was probably gay. Who else would want to dress up like that on a Saturday morning?

He caught his breath as Kelly came out of the pub, carefully bearing a jug of water. She looked stunning in an ice pink chiffon dress and matching jacket. Her hair was tied back in a French plait; her sling-back heels were as high as ever. She looked the picture of prettiness. Lawrence looked forward with pleasure to showing her off.

She handed the jug to the young man, who teased her by threatening to tip the water all over her. Kelly threw up her hands in mock horror, laughing coquettishly. Lawrence's gut suddenly tightened as he watched the tableau. The two of them were perfectly contrasted. She was the picture of femininity; he of masculinity – Lawrence realized his previous diagnosis was way off the mark. And together they shared youth and beauty.

A lump rose to Lawrence's throat. He watched as the boy, man, whatever, filled up the water in the car engine, handed the jug back to Kelly and closed the bonnet. He almost couldn't watch as she carefully brushed back a lock of hair from his eyes with the tip of a manicured finger, always the perfectionist where appearance was concerned. The gesture was intimate, almost loving, certainly familiar.

The boy winked his thanks, jumped into the car and allowed a moment for Kelly to stand back before starting the engine and driving off. Kelly was left waving, a few stray curls escaping from her plait in the breeze, before she turned to walk back into the pub, unaware she was being watched.

Lawrence felt ill. Who was this young man? Clearly someone she knew well and had feelings for. He knew he should feel angry, protective, jealous. He knew he should chase after him with a blunderbuss. But all he felt was sadness, because he knew, whoever the boy was, that Kelly belonged with him. Or someone like him. Someone who could match her vitality. Not an old codger like him who was the wrong side of forty and old enough to be her father – a judgement he'd seen written across more than one face when he'd taken her out.

Kelly re-emerged from the pub, armed with her handbag and sunglasses – it was a bright and beautiful spring day. She opened the car door, beaming, and planted a kiss on his cheek. She seemed unabashed. He breathed in her scent as if for the last time. She nudged him with her elbow.

'Hey – guess what? Rick's driving the wedding car.'

Lawrence had to think fast for a moment. Rick? Of course! Kelly's brother, Rick, who worked at Crossways garage. He'd only seen him from a distance before, in his overalls and smothered in oil. He smiled weakly.

'I didn't recognize him.'

'Doesn't he scrub up well? It's his new Saturday job; thirty quid cash in hand per wedding.'

Strangely, Lawrence didn't feel any sense of relief at this innocent explanation, even though Rick was obviously no threat to him. The cruel fact still remained: he was too bloody old for her.

As Kelly scrambled into the front seat, he resolved to keep quiet for the time being. They might as well enjoy their last day out together – she'd been looking forward to the races all week. But after that it was time to bow out gracefully.

It had been fun while it lasted, but Lawrence didn't want to make a fool of himself any longer, and didn't want people to think badly of Kelly either. There was no doubt what people thought, especially when they clocked his car. That she was only after him for his money. She deserved someone who was on her wavelength; someone who knew what she was on about when she discussed Posh Spice's latest frock or some convoluted soap plot.

While Kelly fussed around, finding her handbag and touching up her lipstick, Lawrence wondered when would be the best moment to tell her. He didn't think she'd be upset. Especially when he revealed the consolation prize . . .

James and Caroline had decided on a small country wedding, to take place in the church at Honeycote and afterwards at Denham House. But by the time they added up their respective families, friends and business associates, the little church was filled with more than a hundred people eagerly awaiting the spectacle. As the familiar strains of the 'The Arrival of the Queen of Sheba' struck up, heads turned and necks were craned.

'Bloody hell,' muttered Mickey in admiration to his brother. James waited patiently until his bride arrived at his side before he appraised her.

Caroline looked stunning. It had taken hours of agonizing to choose her outfit, but she thought she'd got it right. It suited her personality, the occasion and the setting perfectly.

The dress itself was a simple sheath, in a deep cream duchesse satin that had a slightly gold tinge to it – not enough to be gaudy, but just enough to provide a shimmering depth. The pièce de résistance, over the top, was a frock coat in the same fabric, very fitted and tight at the waist, but with a skirt so long and full that it trailed behind her, leaving undulating pools of slithery satin shimmering in her wake. The cuffs and lapels had been hand-embroidered with tiny pearl beads. She wore cream kid boots with pointed toes and kitten heels; her hair was half piled on top of her head, secured with a tortoiseshell mantilla comb, with the rest coiled loosely in ringlets. In her hands, she held a hand-tied bouquet of Porcelina buff roses wittily mingled with hops. The church breathed a collective sigh of approval.

Behind her came Sophie and Georgina, in pale green silk with velvet wraps to keep off the chill April breeze, herding a little flock of Caroline's nieces, clad in Liberty lawn frocks and ballet slippers. Patrick and Ned, devilishly handsome in their morning suits, considered their duty as ushers done and slipped into their seats as the oak doors of the little church closed and the ceremony began.

Lucy was in the front row. She'd chosen a pale blue silk shift dress with a huge hat trimmed with ostrich feathers – simple but stunning; very Audrey Hepburn. She felt a surge of pride as she looked at her daughters, who both looked so grown up and so beautiful. And she felt a surge of pride at seeing Mickey standing tall next to his brother

432

– he'd been determined to get through the entire wedding without his walking stick. As she watched him search anxiously in his pocket for the little suede pouch that held the ring, she smiled to herself. He'd been so worried that everything should be right; nothing she said could reassure him, but she knew it was all going to be perfect.

James's voice rang out over the congregation as he began to repeat the vows. And as he slipped the ring on to Caroline's finger, Lucy thought back to the day Mickey had slid a ring on to her own. She looked down at her hand as if to check it was still there, though she knew it was. And as the bride and groom kissed, she wiped away a tear. It wasn't a tear of regret. She always cried at weddings.

Denham House had been transformed for the reception. Guests were ushered into the dining room, where French windows led out on to the terrace. The walled garden had been covered with a tarpaulin to give the effect of a marquee, with discreet heaters blasting out enough warmth to keep the chilly spring air at bay. The existing blooms were enhanced by pots and pots of spring flowers, so everywhere you turned there was a cluster of narcissi or grape hyacinths or crocuses or primroses. Tiny pinprick fairy lights were strung round hedges and bushes, and hundreds of candles flickered – great big waxy church candles perched on pillars, scented votives placed in glass containers along the walls and slender tapers stuck randomly into flower pots – so the whole garden twinkled like a fairy grotto. Long-stemmed cream roses, arum lilies and trailing ivy were tied on to tree trunks with big muslin bows, and the stone pathway that led to the knot garden had been scattered with rose petals.

Caroline and James had decided not to have a formal reception with a sit-down meal, preferring their guests to mingle and chatter, so the order of the day was substantial finger food, circulated by a battalion of pretty waitresses who were under strict instructions not to let anyone go hungry. James was a stickler for local produce, so on arrival guests were greeted with tiny white china cups filled with Evesham asparagus soup. Then followed Gloucester Old Spot sausages, lamb cutlets, venison carpaccio, tiny pork pies and Scotch quails' eggs, all locally procured . . . an endless array of canapes that were eagerly gobbled up. They were followed by miniature heart-shaped meringues, white chocolate profiteroles and tartes au citron. Everything was washed down with champagne – there was no point in messing about with anything else.

Caroline felt like a princess, as every girl deserves to on her wedding day, but she'd had no idea that you could really feel such happiness. As she moved from guest to guest, each one was touched by the joy that radiated from her. James stood by her, smiling, proud, protective, as they received each guest and their congratulations.

After the cake and the speeches, which left no one unmoved, Ned found a Whitney Houston CD in his car and slipped it into James's sound system. The speakers blasted the opening strains of 'I Will Always Love You' out through the French windows and on to the terrace. Drunken guests urged the bride and groom on to the impromptu dance floor. James, who would normally be horrified by such a public display, held out his hand to his bride. She glided into his arms and, resting her head on his shoulder, moved with him in a slow, languorous smooch, much to the delight of their audience.

Gradually other guests joined them on the dance floor. Ned, who was standing on a priceless stone urn conducting wildly, leaped off into the crowd to find Sophie, dragging her laughing and protesting into the arena. Patrick held out his hand to Mandy, who was feeling a little overwhelmed by the occasion. She slid her fingers into his and remembered the very first time she'd taken his hand, how she'd sworn to herself that one day she'd belong to him. And now she did, she found it incredible that it felt so right, that they were almost as one. She'd found hidden depths in Patrick that she'd never imagined and each revelation taught her something more about herself. Every day brought surprises. Life was exciting; a voyage of self-discovery that she didn't want to come to an end.

Mickey's leg was killing him, but it was a point of honour, a point of pride. He searched amongst the guests for Lucy. She was standing just inside the drawing room, looking out rather wistfully, Mickey thought, as if hoping for a partner. He insinuated himself into her eyeline and smiled an invitation.

For a moment he thought she hadn't seen him, as she seemed to look away over the top of his head to the bride and groom. But then she met his gaze with a smile, put down her glass and came to join him. He held her tight in his arms, his beautiful wife whose hair smelled of freesias, whose cheek was as soft as peach-skin against his, who made him forget the dreadful ache in his limbs as the music drew them together . . .

In the dining room, where he accepted yet another glass of champagne from a conscientious waitress, Keith Sherwyn watched the proceedings with an almost paternal smile. It didn't matter to him that he had no partner to glide across the mossy stones with. He wasn't ready for that just yet.

It was extraordinary to think that only a few months ago he'd been on a treadmill, striving to maintain an empire that was as spiritually stifling as it was financially rewarding. He shuddered to think that, if fate hadn't intervened, he might still be on that treadmill, dull, unfulfilled and taken for granted.

But now, the challenge of the brewery fulfilled him both creatively and as a businessman. He had a new home: he and Mandy were already making plans to renovate their cottage and in the meantime they were renting just outside Honeycote. And his daughter was clearly settled and content; the disruption between him and Sandra seemed to have done her no lasting harm. He thought Patrick was a perfect suitor for her. He let his imagination wander to another wedding in the future, where the Liddiard and Sherwyn interests were bound in holy matrimony – then chided himself. He didn't want to force a union; it was early days yet.

All in all it was a happy man that enjoyed the spectacle on the terrace. But deep inside there was a tiny flicker of hope that somewhere out there might be someone for him.

As dusk finally fell, James and Caroline began to work their way through their guests, saying their goodbyes. Patrick knew this was the time when every other guest would be distracted, wrapped up in the romance of the moment, wishing the happy couple well as they prepared to set off on their new life together. He grabbed Mandy's hand.

'Come on.'

She followed him, unquestioning. They slipped through the tunnel of the marquee into the house, out through the front door and on to the street. Patrick still revealed nothing, but led Mandy by the hand up the wide pavement, past the antique shops and estate agents and restaurants that made up Eldenbury. She followed him, wide-eyed and breathless with anticipation.

Finally, they reached the Horse and Groom. Patrick avoided the front entrance, as it was already thriving with drinkers and he didn't want an audience. He led Mandy round the side where a crooked wooden staircase led up to the first floor. He stopped outside an oak door. Mandy looked at him questioningly, but the smile dancing on her lips told him she knew the answer. Confident, Patrick clicked the latch softly and drew her inside.

Mandy's gasp of delight reassured him that Mayday had done him proud. She'd redeemed herself, following his instructions to the letter when, swept up by the romance of the occasion, he'd phoned her from James's house. The time had come: this was to be their moment, the moment they'd both been waiting for.

And Mayday, with her love of the dramatic and her sense of theatre, had dressed the room to create a fairytale setting. It was lit only by a huge candelabra and a fire burning softly in the grate. A lingering aroma hung in the air, not one of Mayday's usual heavy incense sticks, but something subtly exotic and sensual. Hidden speakers played smoky, sultry jazz that lingered on the consciousness without intruding. The bed was covered with scarlet velvet drapes; one single deep red rose placed on the pillows. A huge silver bucket held a bottle of champagne;

two heavy goblets awaited. Patrick couldn't help feeling they should have galloped up the high street on horses, thrown their mounts to the innkeeper, and that he should have carried her up the stairs, the highwayman and his lady . . .

Mandy looked round her in wonderment.

'It's beautiful,' she breathed.

'No,' said Patrick. 'You're beautiful.'

He pulled her into his arms. The time was right; the setting was right. He'd waited a long time, but it had to be perfect.

A parade of guests, many the worse for drink, shoes and hats discarded, staggered out into the street where the dark green Lagonda was waiting to whisk the married couple to the airport. Someone had bought sparklers, hundreds and hundreds of sparklers, and the guests formed an avenue, two lines facing each other, for James and Caroline to walk down amidst cheers and shouts of well-wishing.

Just down the road, on a patch of green, Keith had slipped away to tip someone the wink. It was his present to the bride and groom – he'd had no idea what to get them and he didn't want to be boring and choose something off the list, so he'd hit on a plan to make their departing moment a memorable one. He knew it was an ostentatious gesture, but he didn't care: so what if he was a flash Brummie with more money than taste? That's what he was and probably always would be, and he was proud of it. And anyway, everyone loved fireworks, didn't they?

He gave the pyrotechnician a discreet thumbs-up, just as James and Caroline were saying their final farewells, kissing Mickey and Lucy by the door of the waiting car.

As the first missile shot into the night sky, puzzled faces turned, alarmed by the noise. When it was joined by hundreds of other silver and gold stars that illuminated the whole street, the crowd applauded wildly. He'd been right – everyone loved fireworks. They brought a sense of magic to the occasion; made it a true celebration. Keith was gratified to see the guests' faces light up as they watched the spectacular display, which ended in the happy couple's initials entwined in a heart emblazoned across the sky for the whole of Gloucestershire and probably Worcestershire and Oxfordshire to see.

Sometimes it was right to be naff.

Mandy lay in Patrick's arms, laughing and crying at the same time, not sure if what she'd just experienced was real. Not that she could ever have imagined that in a million years. He muffled her cries with his lips, smiling and shushing her. She gazed at him, enraptured.

'I saw fireworks,' she said dreamily.

Patrick grinned at her.

'So did I.'

The two of them laughed, rolled into each other's arms and kissed each other back into a frenzy. This time Patrick entered her gently, controlling his movements and showing her how to move with him until they were making slow, languorous love, aware of each other this time and not just themselves.

As he lost himself inside her, it was then that Patrick realized he'd never actually made love to anyone before. He'd screwed, fucked, bonked, got his leg over and his end away, but this was the first time he'd tipped over the edge and fallen into someone's soul. It blew his mind.

As Lawrence drove the car back over the hill that led down to Honeycote, the sight of a thousand fireworks filled him with wonder. He pulled over to watch, then realized as a large 'C' entwined with a large 'J' exploded on to the horizon that it was James and Caroline's nuptial celebrations. Kelly was fast asleep beside him, and he thought about waking her, but the fireworks made him feel rather melancholy, reminding him of his own failed marriage vows.

The day had confirmed that the decision he was about to make was right. He'd seen the amused, arched eyebrows of the other wives as they mentally subtracted Kelly's age from his and gave each other knowing glances. He'd had envious digs in the ribs from his business associates, who made suggestive innuendos when none of the women were listening and made Lawrence feel like a dirty old man. Not only that, but he felt very protective of Kelly; the implications were that she was some sort of gold-digger, and he knew for a fact she was not.

He knew better than anyone that, despite appearances, Kelly was actually the sort of girl who'd like to spend her own money rather than anyone else's. She had aspirations and a work ethic, she wanted to be a success, own her own salon, buy her own Porsche. One day. Lawrence admired her deeply for that and, although he knew she was fiercely independent, he thought he could persuade her that a gentle leg up was not a cop out – especially when there were no strings attached.

As the last barrage of fireworks exploded into the night sky, Kelly stirred and woke. Lawrence put a gentle hand on her arm.

'Kelly?'
She looked at him wide-eyed with expectation.
'Yes?'
'We need to talk.'

28

Kelly was sad that her relationship with Lawrence was coming to an end. She was fond of him, but she was a realist. She knew he was too old for her and she wanted someone to fall in love with, not a sugar daddy.

His proposal, however, had filled her with excitement. He'd made it clear it would be a very businesslike arrangement. They would be partners in the business, he providing the premises, she the hard work and her expertise. The plan was to open the following autumn, which gave them time to find a suitable location and Kelly time to pass her exams; it would be no good her opening a beauty salon unqualified.

She'd decorate the salon in white, lilac and silver, soothing, calming colours, with wafting voile curtains and classical music in the background – that was classy. She could barely contain her excitement, though she knew it was going to be hard work. She'd have to do late-night openings, for women who worked. And Saturday would be her busiest day, of course. But Kelly had never been afraid of hard work. Her parents had taught her that. She'd helped out in the pub ever since she'd been able, though her parents had always stressed that she should follow her own career, not follow them into the trade.

She'd make sure she never forgot a client's name, or how they liked their coffee, or what their favourite colour nail varnish was. It was attention to detail that would keep people coming back. They liked to be pampered and they liked to be recognized. She wondered about a name. Perhaps her mum would help her choose. Eileen was so much happier, now that she and dad had decided to leave the Honeycote Arms. Things really were looking up.

Lawrence too was delighted with the project. It would give him something to think about besides the garden centre, although it was hardly a challenge on the scale of what he'd been planning to do at the brewery. But perhaps it was better to be motivated by altruism than revenge. He genuinely cared about Kelly and had an interest in her future. He could see that she was good at what she did, and didn't see the point of her wasting time being exploited at someone else's beauty salon when she could be reaping the profits for herself. He could keep an eye on things – though he suspected in a couple of years' time she'd be as sharp as the next one when it came to business. Eventually she could buy him out. He'd give her a favourable price. Or perhaps they could open another; start a small chain. As ever, Lawrence started thinking big, then laughed at himself. Lawrence Oakley, beauty salon magnate? No, he'd set Kelly up, get her up and running, then cut loose. After all, he'd got other, more important plans.

He wasn't sure how he was going to find Kay. She'd changed her mobile phone number; hadn't notified him of a landline. Well, he'd made it pretty clear that things had ended. He thought of hiring a private detective, but it seemed so tacky and sordid.

Then he thought about phoning her parents. He knew she wasn't close, but felt it unlikely that she'd sever all means of communication with them. She wouldn't deliberately hurt them.

When, a week later, Lawrence finally plucked up the courage to call Sylvia Porter, she sounded relieved.

'I don't know what's gone on between you, and I don't want to know.'

Not much you don't, thought Lawrence.

'All I know is that she needs you.'

'How do you know that?'

'She was screaming the place down for you in the delivery suite. You should have been there for her, you know. No matter what's gone on.'

There was a dumbfounded silence.

'Delivery suite?'

'I had to go in with her in the end. She insisted she could manage, but I know what it's like. No woman should have to give birth on her own.'

Lawrence gulped.

'She's . . . had the baby, then?'

'I'm only telling you because I don't think it's right, her bringing a baby up on her own. But for God's sake don't tell her I told you.'

'I won't. I promise.'

Sylvia gave him the address. Lawrence recognized the village. It wasn't a million miles from the house she'd sold him all those years ago. He memorized it instantly, thanked Sylvia hurriedly, then went out to his car before he could change his mind. Sylvia put her hands together and allowed herself a quick prayer. Her daughter was doing well, she was inordinately proud of her coping the way she did, but whichever way you looked at it, a baby needed a father and that was that.

Lilac Cottage was at the end of a row of little terraced houses, none of which, thankfully, had been blighted by the introduction of PVC windows or stone cladding. Lawrence stopped at the little gate and stared up the path to the smart navy pram that stood outside the front door. It was a proper Mary Poppins job, and must have taken up most of the hallway in what he could now see was the tiniest of dwellings. Typical Kay. Quality not quantity. He supposed she could have bought a more substantial modern house with the money he'd given her. But she'd been quite right to choose this; a much better investment. Lawrence felt a fleeting bolt of pride. She'd learned at the feet of a master all right.

He flicked back the latch and made his way up the path, coming to a halt by the pram. From inside, Kay watched him. She liked to put the baby outside for some fresh air each morning, but she always watched the pram like a hawk. He took a deep breath and shut his eyes for a moment, before bending down and looking in. Inside was an enchanting, doll-like creature, peaches and cream. He watched in wonder as the blankets rose and fell ever so slightly in time with her breath.

He looked up to see Kay standing in the doorway. He had to look twice, she'd changed so much. Motherhood had softened her once angular features. Her hair was longer, darker, and she'd twisted it up into a clip on top of her head. Loose strands fell onto her face, which was bare of make-up. Lawrence was surprised to see freckles. Even her clothes had changed. Gone was the aggressive power-dressing; the statement, the 'here I am' outfits. She wore a cream cable-knit sweater, sloppy enough to disguise the few extra pounds she was still carrying, over a long chambray skirt and espadrilles.

'What's her name?'

'Flora.'

Flora. The goddess of spring. Why had she chosen that name? His questioning eyes met hers and he was surprised to be met with a soft gaze, not a defiant stare. Kay smiled.

'Go on. Pick her up. She won't wake yet. She's out for the count.'

An assenting nod confirmed her invitation. Tentatively, Lawrence reached down and scooped up the soft pink bundle. He wasn't sure whether to pick up the preponderance of bedding that went with her, and hesitated.

'It's all right. She's tougher than she looks.'

As Lawrence drew the baby to his chest, a feeling of warmth enveloped him. And as Flora instinctively snuggled into his clasp, he wondered that it felt so right, so natural. He looked at Kay for reassurance and the warmth in her eyes, the pride, suddenly humbled him. It was this little bundle that was important and not whether she was his, or theirs, or Kay's. Pride, principle, ego – what did they matter?

He bent down to nuzzle the white blonde fuzz on her head. He tried to speak, but only a croak came out.

'She's beautiful.'

Just then the baby stirred, perhaps disturbed by the unfamiliar sounds and smells. But she didn't protest, just opened her eyes and gazed curiously upwards, one pink paw reaching out. And as he looked down at her,

Lawrence's heart did a huge somersault, for what he saw confirmed the wisdom of what he was about to do. The eyes he found himself staring at were a perfect match – not for his own, nor for Mickey's, but for Kay's. Twin green orbs, dark ringed, with their curiously russet centres. It was as if she was a clone of her mother, as if the reproductive process had been undergone without the help of another.

He cleared his throat of the huge lump that persisted.

'If you put this house on the market now, you'd get a good price. It's the right time of year to sell. Just bung up a few hanging baskets.'

'Oh, and where would I get those from?'

Her tone was teasing. Lawrence gave a self-deprecating grin.

'I'd give you a discount.'

The banter was light, disguising the deadly weight of the meaning underlying it. Flora waved her hand in the air, like a miniature referee, during what seemed to Lawrence like an interminable pause. Ignoring every sales trick he'd ever utilized, he made the next move, making himself vulnerable, probably for the first time in his life.

'Come back.'

It was more of a plea than a command, and Kay looked at him sharply. There was so much left unsaid, and they both knew it. They were equally guilty, equally innocent. Fear collected momentarily in the pit of her stomach and travelled up to her heart, until she felt it would burst. Could they really start again? They were both cynics, not romantics, but perhaps that would work in their favour.

Of course it could work. They had a focus now. Whereas before they'd been floundering in self-indulgence, unable to communicate because there was nothing to bond them except their empty success, which didn't seem to afford them any happiness.

Lawrence showed his cards, yet again, in a desperate attempt to close the deal.

'We'd better put her down for Cheltenham Ladies' College. We might already be too late.'

Kay heard the desperation underneath his flippancy. She pouted.

'Rubbish. Eldenbury High. I'm not letting her out of my sight now I've got her.'

Kay reached out and took Flora from his arms. Lawrence stood helpless, not sure how to take what she'd said. Was that the end of it? Was he being dismissed? Was she asserting her independence and throwing the offer back in his face?

Kay marched down the path and called back over her shoulder.

'Come on in. She needs a feed in a minute. She'll start squawking and then you'll know about it.' She grinned.

'You might change your mind.'

Minutes later, Lawrence held a furious red bundle that emitted ear-splitting shrieks as Kay desperately tried to cool down her bottle, and found himself laughing. The two of them, arch manipulators, putty in the hands of a tiny creature. Kay shook tiny droplets of milk on to her wrist and, satisfied that it wasn't going to cause further shrieking, handed the bottle to Lawrence.

'Come on. You're a new man, aren't you? You can do the nappy afterwards.'

Lawrence was amazed at Flora's tenacity as the six inches of milk fell to five, then four. Kay sat back and he looked at her.

'Well?'

'Who shall we put it on the market with?'

29

As she slid a huge pan of potatoes for roasting into the Aga oven, Lucy realized that she felt lighter-hearted than she had done for months. After all, she was preparing for what she loved best – friends and family round the table, mountains of food, gallons of wine . . . James and Caroline were due back from their honeymoon that afternoon. Mickey still wasn't up to driving long distances, so Patrick had offered to go and pick them up from the airport. They were coming back to Honeycote House for Sunday lunch to give everyone all the gory details about their fortnight in Tuscany. Everything was always a bit of an anticlimax after a wedding, so Lucy thought it was time for a get-together. Keith and Mandy were coming too; they'd become like extended family. And Ned. Though he'd always been around anyway, so he made no difference.

She looked around the kitchen, mentally working out her Sunday lunch timetable. Sunlight streamed in through the kitchen window, lifting the yellow walls to a golden glow. The air was filled with the rich smell of roasting pork, the juices melting into a bed of onions. Homemade apple sauce was cooking down in a pan. Carrots and spring greens were chopped, ready and waiting.

Lucy felt happy that everything was perfect and allowed herself to sit down for a moment to enjoy the peace. It felt like the old days again, warm, hospitable, welcoming. It was, thought Lucy, as if some sort of ghost had been laid. Which in a way perhaps it had.

She and Mickey had gone for a ride that morning, only at a walk, and a gentle one at that. Lucy had wanted to show Mickey the wonders she had worked on Phoenix, how the hours of patience she'd put in had turned the unpredictable animal into a perfect gentleman. As they had reached the brow of the hill that looked back down over Honeycote, allowing them a view of the house, the village and the brewery, they had gazed down in companionable silence.

As they both surveyed everything they could have lost, they each knew without speaking that life had gone beyond recrimination, beyond revenge. It was time to look forward. To enjoy everything they'd got. It had definitely been a turning point, as they each rode home with a lighter heart.

To anyone watching the Liddiards at lunch, they would have seemed like a normal, ordinary family sharing their experiences. No one could have guessed the turbulence they'd all been through to get to this point. But everyone understood their role, their boundaries, what could be said and what couldn't, what eye contact could be made and what should be avoided.

Mickey was just emerging from the cellar with a couple of well-chosen bottles of claret when Caroline came out of the loo that led off the scullery. He had to admit that she looked like a different woman. Sure, she had looked beautiful on her wedding day, but that had been with the help of various beauticians and hairdressers. Two weeks in the Tuscan spring sunshine had brought out a natural beauty: her skin was dusted with golden freckles, the whites of her eyes had lost the red veins of overwork and over-indulgence, and the copper flecks in her irises sparked.

Mickey went forward to greet her.

'Welcome back, Mrs Liddiard,' he teased.

'Thank you.'

She stood in front of him, smiling salaciously. Mickey could feel the warmth of the Siena sun radiating off her skin. He wanted to touch her, feel the warmth for himself through his fingertips. He leaned forward and brushed his lips against hers. They were full, luscious – honeymoon lips swollen with kissing. He imagined them devouring ripe figs on her wedding night. She took a step closer and he could feel her breasts against his chest. He held the kiss, savouring it, inhaling her scent of burnt honey and orange blossom; something delicious bought in Florence.

Suddenly, he felt a familiar surge of excitement. Relief flooded through him. He was getting an erection! Thank God! He'd been convinced he was never going to get another one in his life; that his real punishment was that he'd never be capable of sex again. The ultimate irony.

But no. Here it was. The hard evidence, so to speak. Mickey grinned in delight. He wanted to do a dance of triumph. He realized that Caroline was staring at him, bewildered but amused. He wanted to show off his achievement. But he supposed it wasn't really appropriate behaviour, and it might take some explaining if anyone walked in.

Their eyes met. Mickey stepped back reluctantly, willing his erection to dwindle. She looked at him, one eyebrow slightly raised, questioning his next move. He coughed, feeling he had to say something.

'I just wanted to say thank you.'

'What for?'

He could hardly say 'for giving me a raging hard on'. Even though he suspected she'd understand. She was a babe. James was a lucky chap.

'Saving me from myself.'

Caroline met his gaze, a small smile playing round her lips.

'It's a pleasure.'

Mickey turned and walked away, his slight limp still evident, despite the physio. He went back into the dining room. It was still alive with chatter; there was no hiatus as he took his place. No one had found his simultaneous absence with Caroline remotely suspicious, Lucy smiled and offered him another slice of banoffee pie. Mickey grinned and pushed his plate forward.

'I can resist anything except temptation.'

He met Caroline's gaze steadily as she took her seat opposite him. She raised her glass to him over the table with a wicked grin. Mickey turned pointedly and caressed Lucy's leg under the table. She looked at him, a little surprised. He'd been wary of real physical contact lately, being self-conscious about his lack of performance. Mickey smiled, satisfied that everything was still in full working order – it hadn't just been a fluke out there in the scullery. Though he supposed he still had to put it to the test. He couldn't wait until everyone had gone so he could take Lucy upstairs, check things out . . .

Caroline took a tiny sip of her red wine. She was glad Mickey hadn't made a pass at her. She wasn't quite sure what she'd have done if he had. But it hadn't come to that. He'd obviously learned his lesson.

She thought about her honeymoon. It had been an exquisite two weeks. James, of course, had been in seventh heaven, surrounded by so many treasures, and had bounded from church to gallery utterly enchanted with his surroundings. Caroline at first had found it boring – one painting looked much like the next to her – but slowly, under his expert tuition, she'd allowed herself to open up to new experiences and begun to appreciate a little of the treasures he was revelling in, even if deep down she had to admit she'd rather be shopping. But overall the warmth of the Tuscan sun and the rustic simplicity of the food and wine had been an assault on all her senses, and the intensity of their love-making had increased as the holiday went on. They'd been reluctant to leave their honeymoon suite on the last day, lingering in bed until the very last minute, so that they'd had barely any time to rush round Florence buying souvenirs.

And she suspected they'd brought back another souvenir, though she wasn't going to share that with anyone yet, just in case. But, she thought, if it was a girl, they could call her Siena.

Lucy had taken the pudding plates out to the kitchen and was in the pantry unwrapping the cheese from its waxed paper when she sensed a presence behind her. She turned to find James. He was smiling, tanned and handsome.

'I brought you a present.'

'You shouldn't have.'

Lucy wiped her hands on her apron and reached out to take a little package from him, wrapped up in white tissue paper and tied with a piece of ribbon stuck with blood red sealing wax.

It was a tiny, impressionistic sketch of a horse rearing, done in terracotta chalks and framed in a heavy, Venetian frame. Lucy knew it wasn't from a museum gift shop, that this was the real thing, and that it had probably cost more than the whole honeymoon put together. It was exquisite. She couldn't have chosen better herself.

'Thank you,' she breathed. 'But why?'

'You deserve it,' answered James simply. 'You've been through a lot.'

Lucy shrugged almost dismissively.

'We all have.'

'And it's just to remind you,' he went on, 'that I'll always be here for you.'

Lucy swallowed, not sure whether he meant that he'd always be a shoulder to cry on, or something more. She chose to interpret it as the former. It made life simpler, somehow.

'It's beautiful.' She leaned forward to kiss him her thanks. As his head came forward to meet hers, she caught the familiar scent of bergamot. She hadn't smelled it for over a fortnight.

Approaching footsteps made her turn. It was Patrick. For a fleeting moment, Lucy wondered if she should hide James's gift, cover it with the tissue it had been wrapped in, but surely she had no need to feel guilty.

'Look what James brought me back. From Tuscany.'

Patrick admired the little picture politely, but was more interested in where the cheese had got to. Lucy retrieved the rest of it from the shelf where it was breathing, safely out of Pokey's reach (she had a taste for Stilton) and handed the plate to Patrick. The two men went to rejoin the table. Before she followed them, Lucy tucked the picture into a kitchen drawer. She wasn't sure if James and Caroline had brought presents back for anyone else and she wasn't one to crow.

At the table, James cut himself a generous slice of Brie.

'By the way, there's a country house sale down near Bath on Tuesday. I thought I'd better start stocking up for the summer trade. Does anyone fancy joining me?'

Caroline shook her head.

'I'd love to, but there's piles to do at the brewery. I've got people coming for interviews, you name it . . .' Not to mention an appointment with the doctor.

'It promises to be a good one. These sales are getting few and far between these days.' James's tone was persuasive. Lucy looked at Mickey.

'Shall we go? We could do with a couple of new dining chairs. Especially as this family seems to keep getting bigger and bigger.'

Mickey shook his head.

'I've got a hectic week myself. Keith and I are hoping to finalize all the paperwork to do with the brewery this week. Why don't you go?'

Patrick chipped in.

'Yeah – you could see if there's anything we could use for the pubs. We've got big refurbishment plans. Stuffed moose heads, suits of armour – you know the sort of thing . . .'

Lucy grinned.

'I wouldn't be seen dead bidding for a moose head, thank you very much.' Lucy turned to James. 'But I'll come along for the ride, if you like.'

'I've got a copy of the catalogue. I'll drop it over tomorrow.'

It seemed it was agreed. Lucy hesitated, momentarily, not sure what everyone would think. No one seemed to bat an eyelid, however. To her, it was proof that the hideous events of the last few months were water under the bridge and she sat down with a sigh of relief. It was almost as if none of it had ever happened.

Mickey smiled to himself as he looked round the table at his family, talking and laughing, and marvelled at the way things had turned out. It could have been so different. Everything had teetered on the brink for a moment there: the brewery could have gone down the pan, his marriage could have collapsed . . . Christ, he'd nearly died, hadn't he? But somehow, miraculously, things had turned themselves round and everyone was happy.

He looked round at his family. Sophie was positively glowing. She'd lost that awful hollowness around the eyes and was putting a bit of weight back on, enough to make her look healthy again but not throw her into a panic about being fat. Patrick was relaxed, happy, confident – Mickey was proud of the maturity he'd shown over the past few weeks. Keith had praised him for his hard work, and he seemed to be thriving on the challenge. James and Caroline were basking in the aftermath of their honeymoon, quite obviously as happy as pigs in the proverbial. And Lucy – Mickey watched her as she handed round the Bath Olivers. She'd got back her old sparkle at last, thank goodness. He'd never have forgiven himself for extinguishing that. But she was herself again, laughing at something someone was saying, the strain of the last few months dissipating before his very eyes.

And Mickey himself was feeling better for the first time in weeks. The black glooms that had been descending upon him seemed to be getting fewer and fewer, he was in less pain and was actually managing without painkillers – just a couple to help him sleep at night. He felt hope rising in his chest, a green shoot as optimistic as the crocuses that were nudging up through the earth outside the window.

Mickey reached out and slid a bottle of Chablis towards him. He studied the familiar label, looked at the greeny-gold liquid in the bottle and imagined its flinty dryness, not to mention the welcome relief it would bring, the feeling that every responsibility was falling away from his shoulders. He wondered if anyone would notice if he sloshed a couple of inches into his glass – surely they were all too well-oiled to see or care? It would be the first drink he'd had for months. He tried to ignore the consultant's warning tones. He'd only have a taste, he argued to himself. He wasn't going to get drunk; merely propose a little toast. It was a celebration after all: everything was going to be all right . . .

He poured a good couple of inches into the glass nearest to him and tapped it with his fork to get everyone's attention. Chatter stopped and faces turned to him, surprised. He cleared his throat, slightly self-conscious. He wasn't usually given to displays of sentimentality.

'We're all back here together again and I just wanted to propose a toast. I wasn't sure who to, or what to – there are so many choices. James and Caroline, of course. But also to Keith, who has brought so many possibilities to the future of Honeycote Ales. Then there's Patrick, who's done so much to help me while I've been recuperating . . . the list goes ever on, so I thought I'd just make it a simple one.'

He put two fingers either side of the stem of the glass, as if to lift it, then slid it over towards Lucy. She took it from him, smiling her thanks, and he raised his tumbler of Malvern water in a toast.

'To everyone here round this table. To us.'

James caught Lucy's eye as she raised her glass. To her amazement, he gave her a conspiratorial wink. She looked away, sought Mickey's warm, proud gaze and smiled as she joined in the toast.

'To us.'

The Art of Stuffing a Stocking

I adore Christmas. Every moment of it, from the first glitter-encrusted window on the advent calendar prised open to reveal a sprig of holly or a robin, to the roaring of *Hark the Herald Angels* at Midnight Mass. And I'm a bit of a traditionalist. I don't want a shiny black artificial tree with synchronised disco lighting. I want a proper fir tree that smells of pine, even if it does drop its needles all over the carpet. I want the struggle of finding the nicest specimen in the field, dragging it home and fighting it into submission in the corner of the living room.

And as for lunch – it has to be turkey and stuffing and roast potatoes and sprouts and a proper round pudding that gets set alight. I don't want any fancy chef's take on the most important meal of the year – although I do want the best ingredients. Between Dickens and Delia, my Christmas is pretty much the same every year and I can't see it changing.

And my favourite part is the collation and stuffing of my boys' stockings. I've got three sons, the oldest older now than when I had him. When I once mildly suggested they were too old for stockings, there was outright horror. For them, it is the best part of the day, and even now we are all up by seven o'clock in the morning. (There is no

461

longer a pre-dawn thunder of little feet but I never have to wake them.)

We have developed a tradition of freshly squeezed orange juice, pots of coffee and a selection of warm pastries to accompany the grand unwrapping. And I still insist on the soundtrack of *The Snowman*, read by Bernard Cribbins – I'll have a quiet little weep while I'm plunging the cafetière as *Walking in the Air* soars out of the speakers. The boys roll their eyes, smiling, happy to indulge their mum.

Nothing is more evocative of Christmas than a fat stocking hanging by a fireplace or laid on the end of a bed. It was St Nicholas who inspired the tradition. He travelled around giving gifts to those in need. Hearing of a bereft widower who could not afford dowries for his three daughters, he flung some gold coins down the chimney. These promptly fell into the girls' stockings, hung up by the fireplace to dry. And now, in homage to the beloved poem, we carry on the tradition, hanging up our stockings with care on the night before Christmas in the hopes of St Nick's bounty.

Of course, a hefty old games-sock should suffice, plonked on the end of the bed with anticipation, but it's fun to go to town with bespoke stockings if you are of a crafty leaning. I am not, but my mother is, and has made everyone in the family gorgeous felt stockings embroidered with each person's initial. Of course there are myriad stockings available to buy too – trimmed with fur, beads, feathers, studded with sequins. I have seen a Highgrove stocking in red velvet and gold brocade; even one customised by Karl Lagerfeld. Like everything these days you can probably pay as much as you like, but it's nice to have something meaningful and home-made.

For some people, stockings aren't big enough and they resort to sacks: one year, when the presents were bigger than usual, I bought some potato sacks and sprayed their initials on with gold paint, but somehow, although the capacity was larger, they weren't as enticing as a dangling stocking.

I endeavour to keep the contents equal in value, which can be a challenge – but not as much as it was when the eldest was a teenager and the youngest a toddler. It's a useful time to top up with more luxurious versions of everyday items as a treat too.

My list of contents is boycentric, as I don't have daughters, but it can easily be adapted:

1. A satsuma in the toe – always! I forgot once, to roars of outrage. The satsuma is said to represent the balls of gold thrown down by St Nick.

2. Chocolate coins – a net bag full, or a single giant coin, all still readily available. There is nothing more satisfying then peeling back the foil to reveal slightly melted chocolate.

3. I've somehow managed to start a tradition of a pair of festive lounge bottoms, usually bedecked with reindeer or penguins or polar bears, which are worn religiously throughout the year and which must be supremely comfortable.

4. Socks. Always socks. Because no-one ever has enough socks, and there is no such thing as too many.

5. A book, a CD and a DVD. This is my nod to culture, as I buy them each something I think they will appreciate

but will also expand their horizons. Something they might not otherwise buy. Classic movies, like *The Godfather* or *The Italian Job*. Classic albums, like Joy Division or The Cure. And a book that will make them think or be useful. One year I got the drivers *How to Drive*, by The Stig. Sometimes I get them cookery books, to improve their culinary prowess. Or an inspirational biography. Sadly the internet is making these additions rather redundant, but I persevere.

6. Something silly, like drumstick pencils or novelty ice cube trays, which the shops are full of at this time of year but can be personalised to each child.

7. Something delicious to eat or drink – jelly beans or mojito mixes or sherbert flying saucers, or jars of mustard/chipotle sauce.

8. Gorgeous aftershave or shower gel.

9. A fiendish puzzle. Again, there are loads of these available around Christmas time, and they are perfect for when there is a slump in the day.

10. A useful age-appropriate tool or implement: a pen-knife, a corkscrew, a torch. Or a wallet, mobile phone case or key-ring.

Most of what I put in is practical or useful, with a luxurious edge, but the anticipation and the appreciation never wanes. I love watching their faces as they dig about, pulling out parcel after parcel. (The contents are carefully wrapped, by me, on Christmas Eve. I never do it in advance – that just seems too organised. I like to sit, surrounded by rustling paper, with a glass of champagne, the cellotape constantly elusive.)

And, of course, the dog has a stocking too – filled with

bags of treats and a smart new collar and a squeaky toy.

I can't imagine a time when I won't provide them with a stocking – though perhaps one day I will be doing it for their own children: sugar mice and packets of crayons and kaleidoscopes, eyes bright with excitement, little fingers fumbling to open the parcels while we all look on . . .

'Veronica Henry writes like a dream and I enjoyed
every minute of this brilliant novel'
Jill Mansell

A Country Life

**WANTED: Enthusiastic couple to breathe new life
into a traditional village pub.**

When Suzanna and Barney Blake take on the faded
Honeycote Arms in the heart of the Cotswolds, it's a fresh start
for both of them. But the Blakes aren't the only new arrivals in
the village looking for an escape.

Divorcee Ginny is hoping to reinvent herself after twenty years
of marriage. So how will her twin daughters – teenage girls
reeling from their parents' split – react to life in the sticks?

Damien sees Honeycote as the perfect hideaway – he's a single
dad with a lot of cash to flash. But before long rumours are
flying about how he earned it.

As Susannah and Barney pull their first pint on opening night,
they'll discover if escaping to the country will be their saving
grace or a recipe for trouble . . .

**Treat yourself to this charming, cheering story from
bestseller Veronica Henry. Available now!**

Originally published as *Making Hay*.

A Country Wedding

It was supposed to be a quiet country wedding. The village church, a marquee in the garden and a few carefully chosen guests. But no sooner have the invitations gone out than trouble arrives uninvited.

Bride-to-be Mandy is clashing with her mother who has very different ideas about what constitutes the perfect wedding. And despite his honourable intentions, the groom Patrick is getting cold feet . . . Then a ghost from the past turns up with a very unexpected guest indeed.

As the champagne goes on ice and the church bells ring out, it looks set to be a perfect day.

Everyone loves a wedding, don't they?

Don't miss this perfect comfort read, brimming with humour and heart, from bestseller Veronica Henry – order your copy today!

Originally published as *Just a Family Affair*.

Discover Your Next Read from
VERONICA HENRY

Home isn't always where the heart is . . .

Jamie Wilding's return home is not quite going to plan. A lot has changed in the picturesque Shropshire village of Upper Faviell since she left after the death of her mother. Her father is broke and behaving like a teenager. Her best friend's marriage is slowly falling apart. And the man she lost her heart to years ago is trying to buy her beloved family home.

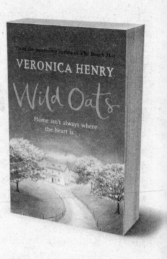

As Jamie attempts to fix the mess, she is forced to confront a long-standing family feud and the truth about her father, before she can finally listen to her own heart.

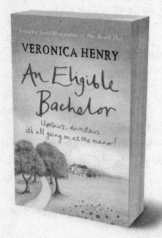

Upstairs, downstairs . . . it's all going on at the manor

When Guy wakes up with a terrible hang-over and a new fiancée, he tries not to panic. After all, Richenda is beautiful, famous, successful . . . what reason could he have for doubts?

As news of the engagement between the heir of Eversleigh Manor and the darling of prime-time television spreads through the village, Guy wonders if he's made a rash decision. Especially when he meets Honor, a new employee of the Manor who has a habit of getting under his skin. But Honor has her own troubles – a son who's missing, and an ex-boyfriend who has made an unexpected reappearance . . .

On Everdene Sands, a row of beach huts holds the secrets of the families who own them

'FOR SALE: a rare opportunity to purchase a beach hut on the spectacular Everdene Sands. "The Shack" has been in the family for fifty years, and was the first to be built on this renowned stretch of golden sand.'

Jane Milton doesn't want to sell her beloved beach hut, which has been the heart of so many family holidays and holds so many happy memories. But when her husband dies, leaving her with an overwhelming string of debts, she has no choice but to sell.

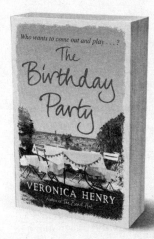

Secrets, rivalry, glamour – it's time for the party of the year . . .

Delilah has lived out her tempestuous marriage to hell-raiser Raf in the glare of the media spotlight. Now planning a milestone birthday, she has more on her mind than invitations.

Raf has been offered a part in a movie he can't refuse. But will he succumb to the temptations he's struggled to resist for the last ten years?

Delilah's three daughters are building careers of their own, only too aware that the press are waiting for them to slip up. For the Rafferty girls might look like angels, but they are only human.

It's the perfect recipe for a party like no other . . .

A short break can become the holiday of a lifetime

In a gorgeous quay-side hotel in Cornwall, the long weekend is just beginning . . .

Claire Marlowe owns 'The Townhouse by the Sea' with Luca, the hotel's charismatic chef. She ensures everything runs smoothly – until an unexpected arrival checks in and turns her whole world upside down.

And the rest of the guests arrive with their own baggage…

Here are affairs of the heart, secrets, lies and scandal– all wrapped up in one long, hot weekend.

A new life is just a ticket away

The Orient Express. Luxury. Mystery. Romance.

For one group of passengers settling in to their seats and taking their first sips of champagne, the journey from London to Venice is more than the trip of a lifetime.

A mysterious errand; a promise made to a dying friend; an unexpected proposal; a secret reaching back a lifetime. As the train sweeps on, revelations, confessions and assignations unfold against the most romantic and infamous setting in the world.

Return to Everdene Sands, setting for the *The Beach Hut*, and discover secrets, love, tragedy and dreams. It's going to be a summer to remember . . .

Summer appeared from nowhere that year in Everdene and for those lucky enough to own one of the beach huts, this was the summer of their dreams.

For Elodie, returning to Everdene means reawakening the memories of one summer fifty years ago. A summer when everything changed. But this summer is not all sunshine and surf – as secrets unfold, and some lives are changed for ever . . .

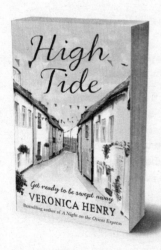

Pennfleet might be a small town, but there's never a dull moment in its narrow winding streets . . .

Kate has only planned a flying visit to clear out the family home after the death of her mother. When she finds an anonymous letter, she is drawn back into her own past.

Single dad Sam is juggling his deli and two lively teenagers, so romance is the last thing on his mind. Then Cupid fires an unexpected arrow – but what will his children think?

Nathan Fisher is happy with his lot, running picnic cruises up and down the river, but kissing the widow of the richest man in Pennfleet has disastrous consequences.

Vanessa knows what she has done is unseemly for a widow, but it's the most fun she's had for years. Must she always be on her best behaviour?

Everyone has a story . . . but will they get the happy ending they deserve?

Emilia has just returned to her idyllic Cotswold hometown to rescue the family business. Nightingale Books is a dream come true for book-lovers, but the best stories aren't just within the pages of the books she sells − Emilia's customers have their own tales to tell.

There's the lady of the manor who is hiding a secret close to her heart; the single dad looking for books to share with his son but who isn't quite what he seems; and the desperately shy chef trying to find the courage to talk to her crush . . .

And as for Emilia's story, can she keep the promise she made to her father and save Nightingale Books?

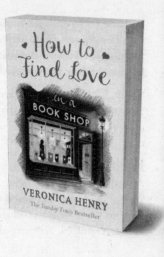

A gorgeous escapist read for anyone needing a hug in a book.

Hunter's Moon is the ultimate 'forever' house. Nestled by a river in the Peasebrook valley, it has been the Willoughbys' home for over fifty years, and now estate agent Belinda Baxter is determined to find the perfect family to live there. But the sale of the house unlocks decades of family secrets − and brings Belinda face to face with her own troubled past . . .

'A delight from start to finish' Jill Mansell

Pick up the next charming story by Veronica Henry today!